David Baldacci returns with the next blockbuster thriller in his #1 *New York Times* bestselling Memory Man series featuring detective Amos Decker—the man who can forget nothing.

THE FALLEN

Something sinister is going on in Baronville. The rust belt town has seen four bizarre murders in the space of two weeks. Cryptic clues left at the scenes—obscure bible verses, odd symbols—have the police stumped.

Amos Decker and his FBI colleague Alex Jamison are in Baronville visiting Alex's sister and her family. It's a bleak place: a former mill and mining town with a crumbling economy and rampant opioid addiction. Decker has only been there a few hours when he stumbles on a horrific double murder scene.

Then the next killing hits sickeningly close to home. And with the lives of people he cares about suddenly hanging in the balance, Decker begins to realize that the recent string of deaths may be only one small piece of a much larger scheme—with consequences that will reach far beyond Baronville.

Decker, with his singular talents, may be the only one who can crack this bizarre case. Only this time—when one mistake could cost him everything—Decker finds that his previously infallible memory may not be so trustworthy after all…

END GAME

THE FIX

"A compelling puzzler...Baldacci is a truly gifted storyteller, and this novel is a perfect "fix" for the thriller aficionado."
—Associated Press

"The set-up for THE FIX is one of the best this master of the thriller has ever come up with, and there is no letdown as Amos and his associates dig into an increasingly bizarre case...[Baldacci's] plotting is more masterful than ever, and THE FIX is nothing less than terrific from start to finish."
—*Connecticut News*

"Crackling with tension...Reads at a breakneck pace... Bestselling author David Baldacci delivers a thrill ride, as always. Big time. Pick up THE FIX, and you won't put it down until you reach the end. Guaranteed."
—*BookReporter.com*

"Cleverly perverse, full of surprises and touched throughout by the curious sense of congeniality."
—*Toronto Star*

"[Baldacci] continues to show why he is a master of mystery."
—*The Florida Times-Union*

NO MAN'S LAND

"Be prepared for an action-packed ride...Baldacci once again partners [John Puller] with Veronica Knox, making for a lethal and legendary combination. Anticipation intensifies on each page."
—*RT Book Reviews*

"This thriller, featuring U.S. Army criminal investigator John Puller, has a very plausible theme with a compelling and action-packed plot....[A] riveting and heart-wrenching story...NO MAN'S LAND is an edge-of-your-seat thriller. Readers will be hooked from page one."

—*Military Press*

"David Baldacci is one of America's favorite mystery writers, and he has earned that adulation fair and square. He is constantly turning out one readable and enjoyable adventure after another. His latest novel NO MAN'S LAND is his fourth John Puller story and it is a good one. It is fast reading from the start as the pages grab the readers' interest and off they go."
—*Huffington Post*

"[A novel of] dramatic depth and intensity...an unforgettable read...Action-packed and thought-provoking."
—Associated Press

"Bestseller Baldacci makes the implausible plausible in his riveting fourth thriller featuring U.S. Army criminal investigator John Puller...Baldacci maintains tension throughout and imbues his characters with enough humanity to make readers care what happens to them."

—*Publishers Weekly*

"This fast-paced ride will leave you guessing until the last page."

—*Virginia Living*

THE LAST MILE

"Entertaining and enlightening, *The Last Mile* is a rich novel that has much to offer...In the best Baldacci tradition, the action is fast and furious. But *The Last Mile* is more than a good action thriller. It sheds light on racism, a father-son relationship and capital punishment. Both Mars and Decker are substantive, solid characters....Utterly absorbing."

—Associated Press

"[Amos Decker is] one of the most unique protagonists seen in thriller fiction....David Baldacci has always been a top-notch thriller writer...[his] fertile imagination and intricate plotting abilities make each of his books a treat for thriller readers. *The Last Mile* is no exception."

—BookReporter.com

"The intricate details in Baldacci's explosive new novel engage until the final word. He's hit the pinnacle traveling the Deep South and exploring its traditions. Decker and his compatriots are characters to remember long after reading this impressive undertaking."   —*RT Book Reviews* (4 1/2 stars—Top Pick!)

"A compelling mystery with emotional resonance. Just when the story line heads to what seems an obvious conclusion, Baldacci veers off course with a surprising twist. The end result is another exciting read from a thriller master."

—*Library Journal* (Starred Review)

"Baldacci excels at developing interesting, three-dimensional protagonists...Baldacci fans will not be disappointed, and *The Last Mile* gives good reason to look forward to the next Amos Decker thriller."

—New York Journal of Books

THE GUILTY

"The story sings...Baldacci is a gifted storyteller, and he knows how to keep the pages turning."

—Associated Press

"Baldacci fans will not be disappointed. The action is slam-bang with his trademarked twist. Once past the climax, you'll find yourself flipping back and rereading to find the clues the author has sprinkled throughout."

—*Florida Times-Union*

"A fast-moving thriller that will force readers into that 'zone,' where you don't want to put the book down...Whether you are a diehard fan or a newcomer to his work, you will not be disappointed in *The Guilty*."

—*BookReporter*

"A first-class thriller...David Baldacci's four bestselling novels about government assassin Will Robie have straddled that line of edgy, high-concept suspense, augmented with a bit of the political thriller, and deep character studies. In *The Guilty*, Baldacci takes a different tack with a more personal, but just as thrilling tale about Will's past, giving compelling insight about how he became a man so willing to kill for his country."

—*Sun-Sentinel* (FL)

"David Baldacci has never been better than in *The Guilty*. His latest to feature conflicted assassin extraordinaire Will Robie takes the character—and series—to new heights...A stunning success from one of America's great literary talents."

—*Providence Sunday Journal*

"It's indisputable that Baldacci's handling of action just gets better and better...the action in small-town Texas will end up rivaling anything Robie has encountered in his long years of serving his government."

—NJ.com

"Another tremendous entry in the best-selling thrillermaster's increasingly impressive résumé...A multi-layered conspiracy tale that, despite the Grisham-esque backdrop of a legal mystery set in small-town Mississippi, quickly explodes into full-Baldacci thriller territory...It is the relationships that truly stand out. Among the most noteworthy is the rapport between Robie and Reel, with the professional and personal trust and respect that the two share for one another—having risked it all for each other several times before—feeling believable and compelling, not to mention being the source of a fair amount of witty banter. The tense dynamic between Robie and his father is palpable as well, and their shifting relationship—and how they both deal with the wounds of the past—is one of the book's highlights...A labyrinthine journey full of dead ends and surprising turns, with new reveals doled out at regular intervals as the story builds to its shocking conclusion, a spectacular double-twist climax that will leave even the most jaded thriller readers impressed."

—*The Strand Magazine*

MEMORY MAN

"It's big, bold and almost impossible to put down...Decker is one of the most unusual detectives any novelist has dreamed up...I called this novel a master class on the bestseller because of its fast-moving narrative, the originality of its hero and its irresistible plot....Highly entertaining."

— *Washington Post*

"David Baldacci has written another thriller that will have readers engaged from the first page....Baldacci is a master storyteller...*Memory Man* works because Amos Decker is an amazing character. Reading how Decker journeys from hitting rock bottom to finding ultimate redemption is nothing short of rewarding."

— Associated Press

"Perennial bestseller Baldacci unveils an offbeat hero with an unusual skill set and tragic past who takes on the evil mastermind behind a devastating school shooting.[Decker] proves a quirky, original antihero with a definite method to his madness...Readers will want to see Decker back on the printed page again and again."
— *Kirkus Reviews*

"[A] strong first in a new thriller series from bestseller Baldacci....Baldacci supplies a multitude of clever touches as his wounded bear of a detective takes on a most ingenious enemy."
— *Publishers Weekly*

THE ESCAPE

THE FALLEN

ALSO BY DAVID BALDACCI

MEMORY MAN SERIES
Memory Man
The Last Mile
The Fix
The Fallen

WILL ROBIE SERIES
The Innocent
The Hit
The Target
The Guilty
End Game

JOHN PULLER SERIES
Zero Day
The Forgotten
The Escape
No Man's Land

KING & MAXWELL SERIES
Split Second
Hour Game
Simple Genius
First Family
The Sixth Man
King and Maxwell

THE CAMEL CLUB SERIES
The Camel Club
The Collectors
Stone Cold
Divine Justice
Hell's Corner

THE SHAW SERIES
The Whole Truth
Deliver Us from Evil

STANDALONES
Absolute Power
Total Control
The Winner
The Simple Truth
Saving Faith
Wish You Well
Last Man Standing
The Christmas Train
True Blue
One Summer

SHORT STORIES
Waiting for Santa
No Time Left
Bullseye

DAVID BALDACCI

THE FALLEN

GRAND CENTRAL
PUBLISHING

NEW YORK   BOSTON

Copyright © 2018 by Columbus Rose, Ltd.

Cover design by Art Machine.
Cover copyright © 2018 by Hachette Book Group, Inc.

Grand Central Publishing

Hachette Book Group

1290 Avenue of the Americas, New York, NY 10104

grandcentralpublishing.com

twitter.com/grandcentralpub

First Edition: April 2018

Grand Central Publishing is a division of Hachette Book Group, Inc. The Grand Central Publishing name and logo is a trademark of Hachette Book Group, Inc.

The publisher is not responsible for websites (or their content) that are not owned by the publisher.

The Hachette Speakers Bureau provides a wide range of authors for speaking events. To find out more, go to www.hachettespeakersbureau.com or call (866) 376-6591.

Library of Congress Cataloging-in-Publication Data has been applied for.

ISBNs: 978-1-5387-6139-7 (hardcover), 978-1-5387-1366-2 (large print), 978-1-5387-6137-3 (ebook), 978-1-5387-6308-7 (signed edition), 978-1-5387-1373-0 (international)

Printed in the United States of America

LSC-C

10 9 8 7 6 5 4 3 2 1

To Cindi and John Harkes,
we're truly blessed to have you as friends

THE
FALLEN

CHAPTER

I

WHO KILLED YOU?

Or, who murdered *you?*

There was, after all, a distinct difference.

Amos Decker was standing on the rear deck of a house where he and his FBI colleague, Alex Jamison, were staying while visiting Jamison's sister. He used two fingers to neck-cradle his third bottle of beer of the evening while he contemplated these questions. He knew that most people never thought about these issues, because they had no reason to do so. Yet accurately answering the latter question dominated Decker's professional life, which was really the only life he had left.

He was also aware that the difference between the two queries was more complex than some might have believed.

For example, one could kill a person without legally committing murder.

There was accidental death: Your car inadvertently slams into another, with death as a result, or you drop a gun and it goes off and the bullet strikes a bystander. Someone was dead but it wasn't legally recognized as murder.

There was assisted suicide: A terminally ill person is suffering and wants to end it, and you help the person do so. The practice was legal in some places and unlawful in others. Again, someone was dead. Unlike the accidental death, the death *was* intentional, but it was not the same as murder, because it had been the choice of the deceased to end his life.

There was justifiable homicide, the best example of which was self-defense. There you intended to harm another, but the law said you had the right to defend yourself.

There *were* varying degrees of murder.

If you were negligent in causing that car accident or dropping your weapon, and someone died, you could be charged with involuntary manslaughter.

A spontaneous bludgeoning, resulting in death, could end with the perpetrator being charged with the more serious crime of voluntary manslaughter.

Second-degree murder, a close cousin to voluntary manslaughter, had the element of malice aforethought, and possibly recklessness, but not the additional one of premeditation, or *lying in wait*, as it was often called.

Decker sipped his beer as he went through the legal requirements of intentionally ending the life of another. The last one was the worst of all, in his estimation.

First-degree murder almost always required the specific elements of willfulness, premeditation, and *malice aforethought*. You wanted someone dead for your benefit and you laid out a plan in advance to make sure that death happened.

The harshest legal consequences of all were reserved for these heinous acts.

Going after these types of criminals was what Decker had done for almost his entire adult life.

He took another sip of beer.

I catch killers. It's really the only thing I'm good at.

He stared out at the night sky over northwestern Pennsylvania, near the Ohio border, in a place called Baronville. He heard it had once been a thriving mill and mining town, owing its very existence to the eponymous Baron family, which had dug the mines and built the mills. However, those engines of commerce were long since gone. What was left wasn't much. Yet people seemed to be getting by in a variety of ways, and with varying degrees of success. A similar pronouncement could be made about many places across America.

Inside the house, Alex Jamison was sharing a glass of white wine with her older sister, Amber, and talking to her precocious soon-to-be-six-year-old niece, Zoe. Decker and Jamison were here on vacation from solving crimes as part of a special task force at the FBI back in Washington. Decker had been reluctant to go with Jamison, but their boss, Special Agent Bogart, had insisted that he take some type of leave. And when Jamison had suggested that he accompany her on a visit to her sister, Decker couldn't think of a single other place to go.

So here I am.

He took another sip of his beer and studied his size fourteen feet.

When they had arrived here, introductions had been made, hugs given, pleasantries exchanged, bags put away, and Jamison had given out housewarming gifts to her sister and niece, because Amber and her family had only recently moved here. Dinner was prepared and eaten, but long before then Decker had run out of things to say and ideas of what would be socially acceptable to do. And that's when Jamison, who knew him perhaps better than anyone else, had discreetly suggested that he take his beer—and his awkwardness—outside, so the sisters could catch up in the way that women often did while no men were around.

The social awkwardness had not always been a part of him. The six-foot-five, three-hundred-pound–plus—well, maybe more than simply *plus*—Decker, a former professional football player, had once been outgoing, gregarious, a bit goofy even, fun-loving and always ready with a quip.

Then had come the vicious blindside hit to the head on the football field that had changed his life, and who he was, forever. The resulting brain trauma had almost killed him. And while he had survived, the blow had forced his brain to rewire itself to allow healing to occur. This process had left two distinct marks on him.

One was hyperthymesia, or perfect recall. Those possessing such a condition often could apply it only to autobiographical information, and often had below-average memory capacities in other aspects of their lives. But not Decker. It was as though someone had placed a camera with a limitless capacity to take pictures in his head. He was the *memory man*, unable to forget anything. Decker had found it a decidedly mixed blessing.

The second result of the hit was his developing synesthesia. He associated odd things, like death, with a color. In the case of death, it was a visceral electric blue that could raise the hairs on the back of Decker's neck and make him feel sick to his stomach.

Along with his brain change, his personality had been transformed. The gregarious fun-loving prankster had forever vanished, and in its place—

—Is me.

With his football career irreversibly over, he had gone on to become a cop and then a homicide detective in his hometown of Burlington, Ohio. He had been married to a wonderful woman named Cassandra, or Cassie as he always called her, and they had had a beautiful child named Molly.

Had.

It was all past tense, because he no longer had a wonderful wife or a beautiful child.

Who killed you?

Who murdered you?

Well, Decker had figured out who had taken his family from him. And the person had paid the ultimate price.

Yet it was nothing in comparison to the price that Decker had paid. That he would pay every minute until he drew his last breath.

"Aunt Alex says you can't forget anything."

Decker turned from these musings to the source of the query.

Zoe Mitchell, twin blonde ponytails, long-sleeved pink shirt with flowers on it, and white shorts showing off dimpled knees, stared curiously at him across the width of the wooden deck attached to the back of her house.

"My memory's pretty good, yeah," said Decker.

Zoe held up a sheet of paper. On it were about a dozen very long numbers. She passed it to him.

"Can you remember all these?" she asked hopefully.

Decker glanced at it and then handed the paper back to her.

"Does that mean you can't remember them?" said Zoe, the disappointment clear on her freckled face.

"No, it means that I already did."

He recited the numbers back to her, in the same order they appeared on the page, because that's what he saw in his head: the page of numbers.

She broke into a toothy grin. "That is so cool."

"You think so?" said Decker.

Her pale blue eyes widened at his remark. "Don't you?"

"Sometimes, yeah. It can be cool."

He leaned against the deck railing and sipped his beer while Zoe watched him.

"Aunt Alex says you catch bad people."

"We do it together. She's got good instincts."

Zoe looked puzzled by his response.

He explained, "She reads people really well. And she sees things that others don't."

"She's my favorite aunt."

"How many aunts do you have?"

She sighed. "A lot. None of them are as cool as Aunt Alex." Zoe brightened. "She came to visit because my birthday is almost here. I'm turning six."

"I know. She told me we're all going out to dinner for it."

Decker looked around awkwardly as Zoe continued to watch him.

"You're really, really big," she observed.

"Not the first time I've heard that."

"You won't let any of the bad people hurt Aunt Alex, will you?" she asked, her features and tone suddenly turning anxious.

Decker had been about to take a sip of beer. He slowly lowered the bottle. "No, I won't. I mean, I'll do my best never to let that happen," he added a bit lamely.

There was a low rumble of thunder in the distance.

"I guess a storm is coming," observed Decker quickly, looking for any way to change the subject.

He glanced at Zoe to find her innocent gaze still uncomfortably on him. He looked away as another guttural growl of thunder was heard.

Summer was over, but the thunderstorms often accompanying the segue into fall appeared to be bearing down on them.

"Definitely getting closer," said Decker, more to himself than to Zoe.

He looked at the rear yard of the house that backed up to Zoe's. It seemed an exact copy. Same footprint, same wooden deck off the back. Same patch of yard. Same type of maple smack in the middle of the wilting grass.

But there was one difference.

The lights in the other house were flickering now. On, then off. On, then off.

Decker looked to the sky. Despite the rumbles of thunder, there wasn't any lightning yet, at least that he could see. Also, the temperature had dropped some, and there was a low fog building that, along with the gathering clouds, obscured the sky even more.

A few moments later, he saw the reflection of red lights zip by overhead. He couldn't see the plane, but it was no doubt trying to make it in or out before the storm hit full force, he thought.

He glanced back at the house and watched the lights going on and off, almost like Morse code. It might be the humidity, he thought. Damp wiring could cause flickering.

He heard a noise somewhere. Then he heard it again. And another time. The same sound over and over. It was two distinct sounds, actually, one a solid thud and the other like something scraping against something.

Then a car started up. It had to be on the street that fronted the house he was looking at, he concluded. They'd be driving right into the gathering storm.

A few minutes passed and then came the initial lightning spear. It seemed to disappear right into the earth directly in front of him. It was followed by a much louder boom of thunder. The sky was growing increasingly black and ominous. The winds were pushing the system swiftly across the area.

"We better go inside," said Zoe nervously. "Mommy says that more people get hit by lightning than you think."

"Who lives in that house, Zoe?" Decker asked, pointing to the other house.

Zoe had her hand on the door leading back inside. She said, "I don't know."

Decker's gaze focused and then held on a sudden spark of light.

It was inside the other house, behind one of the windows. He didn't know if it was a light from inside simply reflecting off the glass, or whether the cause might be something more complicated, and potentially dangerous.

He set his beer down and hustled off the deck. But he needed to find out.

"Where are you going?" Zoe cried after him; her voice held a note of panic.

He called over his shoulder, "Go inside, Zoe, I just want to check on something."

Another crack of lightning was followed by such a deafening explosion of thunder that Zoe bolted inside, while Decker ran the other way.

Despite his bulk, Decker had been an elite athlete for many years. He grabbed the top of the fence separating the two properties, neatly swung over the barrier, and dropped inside the other yard.

He hustled across the grass toward the house. He could feel the temperature plummeting as the storm fully enveloped the area. The wind kicked up and buffeted him. He had grown up in the Midwest and was used to these dangerous weather systems that made the Ohio Valley their stomping grounds, conjuring up and then spinning off tornadoes like a cancer spawned mutant cells.

He knew the rain would be coming next, probably in sideways sheets.

He reached the house's pressure-treated deck and raced up the steps. He didn't look back at Amber's house, so he didn't see Alex Jamison come out and gaze quickly around for him.

He got to the window where he'd seen the reflection of light. He could now smell it, which confirmed his suspicions.

Electrical wiring had gotten mixed with liquid. He had investigated homicides involving arson, and the smell was unmistakable. There was a fire in there.

He put his face to the glass and peered inside. Electrical fires tended to move fast, usually behind walls where they could spread unseen until it was too late.

A moment later, he saw something that confirmed his worst fear: a flicker of flames and the rise of smoke.

Then he looked to the right as a spear of lightning lit up the whole area.

Decker froze at what he was seeing in the illumination provided by the lightning strike. A moment later, he broke free from his paralysis and ran to the back door. Without hesitating he hit it with his shoulder like he had many football blocking sleds. The flimsy door buckled under the massive impact and fell open.

The storm was screaming overhead now, so Decker couldn't hear Jamison calling to him. She had rushed off the deck and was running to the rear fence when Decker had crushed the door. The rain was falling hard now, whipped by the wind into a stinging frenzy, as the storm emptied millions of gallons of water over the western edge of the Keystone State. Jamison had run out of her shoes and was soaked before she was halfway to the fence.

A drenched Decker burst into the kitchen and turned right. He had his Beretta out and pointed in front of him. He now wished he hadn't had all that beer. He might need his fine motor skills to be better than they presently were.

He moved swiftly down the darkened hallway, bouncing off one wall. Something fell to the floor as he brushed against it.

It was a picture.

Decker cursed himself because he had just contaminated what was now a crime scene, an act he would have found unforgivable if someone else had done it. Yet it couldn't be helped. He didn't know what was going on here. What he had seen might just be the tip of the iceberg.

He cautiously poked first his gun and then his head around

the corner. He cleared the space with two long visual passes and straightened.

Decker now knew what had triggered first the spark and next the flames.

And the flickering lights.

Exposed electrical wires had indeed been commingled with liquid.

But it wasn't water.

It was blood.

2

D ECKER?"

Decker peered around the corner to see a soaked, shivering, and barefoot Jamison standing farther down the hall from where he'd just come.

"You got your gun?" he asked quietly. Wave after wave of electric blue light was pouring over him. He felt nauseous and dizzy.

Jamison shook her head.

He motioned her toward him.

She hurried forward, turned the corner, saw what Decker already had, and stopped dead.

"Good God!"

Decker nodded. It was a fitting expression for what they were both seeing.

After all, the man *was* hanging from the ceiling.

A rope had been inserted through a hook that had once held a chandelier that was now lying on the floor.

The noose had been placed around the man's neck.

Yet death by hanging did not typically cause blood loss.

Decker stared down at the wooden floor. The blood had pooled and then flowed toward the wall, where it had encountered the frayed electrical cord of a floor lamp and begun the electrical shorting process.

Before Jamison had appeared, Decker had used his foot to tap out the sparks after unplugging the cord. Part of a square of carpet and a dangling strip of wallpaper had caught on fire. He had used his wet jacket to beat out the flames on the wall, and had rolled up the carpet to smother the fire there. Then he'd stepped back so as not to further interfere with the crime scene. It was right then that Jamison had called out.

His gaze ran up and down the man's body, searching for a wound that might explain the copious amounts of blood.

He saw none. And he couldn't do a deeper probe now. That would have to await the police. But something else couldn't wait.

Giving voice to what he'd been thinking, Jamison whispered, "Do you think there's anyone else in the house?"

"That's what we need to find out. Do you have your phone?"

"No."

"Neither do I. And I didn't see one in here. Okay, I want you to go back to your sister's house and call the cops. I'll finish searching the place."

"Decker, you need to wait for the police. You have no backup."

"Someone may be hurt, or the killer may still be here."

"It's the latter possibility I'm worried about," hissed Jamison.

"I *am* a police officer," replied Decker. "I'm trained to do this, and I've got a gun. And the odds are very good that if the killer *is* still here, he's smaller than me. Now go."

Jamison slowly turned and then ran down the hall and back out into the rain.

Decker cleared the first floor. The house had a second story and, if it was a true copy of Jamison's sister's place, a basement. He moved back down the hall to the stairs leading up. He took the steps two at a time, feeling his thigh muscles tighten a bit with each upward lunge. While spending ten years in uniform before becoming a detective back in Ohio, he had gone into homes where people had died. There were procedures you followed to clear spaces as safely as possible, and all of them were grafted onto his brain. Still, it wasn't really like riding a bike, for one very compelling reason.

Bikes didn't shoot back at you.

There were two small bedrooms with closets upstairs and a Jack-and-Jill bathroom in between. Decker cleared all of them and found nothing. The place looked abandoned.

Maybe there was nothing to find except the hanging dead man

on the main floor. He slipped back downstairs and found the door to the basement.

There was a light switch at the top of the stairs, but Decker didn't move to turn it on. He didn't know if the electrical short had affected the lights in the rest of the house, but, right now, darkness was his friend. He tested each step before fully placing his weight on it. Still, there were some slight creaks and he winced with each one. He reached the bottom of the stairs without anyone trying to attack him.

He looked around. It was quite dark down here and he couldn't see very clearly, but the space appeared to be unfinished. There was the musty odor that one often associated with unfinished basements.

He cautiously moved forward and almost fell to the floor. Regaining his balance, he quickly retreated.

He had to risk a light now. He skittered back up the steps and flipped the switch. The lights came on. His gun pointed in front of him, he slowly came back down the stairs until he saw what he had tripped over.

The face looked up at him as the electric blue pulses once more started drumming against him.

It was a man, who looked to be in his late thirties. He had dark hair and pale skin, and was of a medium build. He appeared to be about five-ten, although it was hard to be accurate about that since he was lying on the floor.

All those observations flowed automatically through Decker's mind from his long career as a cop. And they were secondary to the single most important observation he was making.

The man was in a police uniform.

Decker knelt down next to him and checked for a pulse at his neck.

There was none, and the skin was very cold. He felt the limbs. They were stiff, indicating that rigor had begun. Decker's experience as a homicide detective caused him to automatically consider both the cause and the timing of the death.

He ran his gaze over the body, looking for wounds, but saw

none. He wasn't going to move the corpse. He had already compromised the crime scene enough.

He focused on the man's mouth. There was a bit of foaming there. That could be an indication of at least a couple of ways he could have died.

A fit.

Or poison.

Okay, cause of death is not obvious. What about timing?

He looked at the man's nostrils. Blowflies. Female. They'd already laid eggs, but the infestation was minimal. Blowflies could smell dead flesh from miles away and were a policeman's best friend, because with the biological death clock having commenced, the invasive insects would help determine the time of death.

But when Decker put all of these forensic elements together, mental alarms started sounding. Something was definitely not making sense.

If the limbs were stiff, that meant the deceased had been dead for a while. In fact, the body could be reversing the rigor and moving from the large muscle groups back to the small, which meant the person could have been dead quite a long time. And while that jibed with the coolness of the body, it most assuredly did not align with what else he was observing.

His thoughts were interrupted by the sound of sirens approaching.

He quickly retreated up the stairs, holstered his gun, stepped out onto the front porch, and waited.

A squad car pulled up to the house about fifteen seconds later.

While Decker had been inside, the storm had lessened somewhat, though lightning still crackled and thunder still boomed. At least it wasn't raining sideways anymore.

As the police officers exited their vehicle, Decker called out and held up his FBI creds. Both cops pulled their weapons and one trained his Maglite on Decker.

"Hands out where we can see them!" shouted one cop, who looked young and a little nervous.

Since Decker already had both hands up in the air where they could definitely be seen, he couldn't do anything more than say, "I'm a Fed. My partner called this in."

The cops advanced until they reached the stoop. The other cop, who looked to be in his forties, with a trim, graying mustache, holstered his gun, took the creds, and checked them. Then he illuminated Decker's face with his light.

"What's going on?" he asked.

"Two dead bodies inside. One hanging in the living room. One in the basement." Decker glanced at the man's uniform. "I don't know if he's a cop or not, but the guy in the basement is wearing the same type of uniform you are."

"What?" snapped the older cop.

"You say he's dead?" said the young cop, who was still pointing his gun.

Decker's gaze swiveled to him. "Yeah, he is. And could you aim your weapon somewhere other than at me?"

The young cop automatically looked to his partner, who nodded while handing back Decker's credentials.

"Show us," ordered the older cop.

At that moment, Jamison dashed around the corner.

The young cop swung his gun around and lined her up in his sights.

"No!" roared Decker. He leapt forward and hit the cop's arm just before he fired. The bullet sailed barely a foot above Jamison's head. She sprawled in the grass.

The younger cop stumbled back and pointed his sidearm at Decker's head.

"She's my partner," barked Decker. "She's the one who called you. Alex, are you okay?"

Jamison slowly rose and came toward them on jelly legs. She took a deep breath and nodded. "Yeah, I'm fine." But she looked like she might throw up.

The older cop gave his partner a piercing gaze, and asked to see Jamison's credentials. After reviewing them he handed them back and looked at his partner.

"You almost shot a Fed, Donny," he said severely. "And now

you're going to have a ton of paperwork to fill out while your butt is anchored to a desk job. And Internal Affairs will be all over you. Congratulations."

The younger cop holstered his weapon, scowled, and said nothing.

"Show us," the older cop said again.

"This way," replied Decker.

CHAPTER

3

I DON'T KNOW him," said the older cop, who on the way inside the house had told Decker and Jamison that he was Officer Will Curry. His partner shook his head too. They were looking down at the man in uniform lying on the floor of the basement. They had already seen the body upstairs, and neither of the officers had recognized him either.

Curry pointed to the man's chest. "No nameplate. We all wear one."

"Would you know him?" asked Decker. "I mean, is the police force that small around here?"

Curry thought about this for a few moments. "I don't know every person in uniform, but I do know a lot of them."

Decker said, "There's no pistol in his holster."

Curry nodded. "Yeah, I saw that. And there's no comm pack either. Look, I need to call this in. Homicide will be taking this over. Donny, we need to tape the perimeter. And don't let anybody near this place."

Donny left to do this while Curry pulled out his phone, walked over to a far corner of the basement, and made the call.

Decker knelt down and looked over the body.

Jamison gazed over his broad shoulder. "How did he die?" she asked.

"No obvious wounds. Just like the guy upstairs, although there's all that blood."

"Death by hanging is usually bloodless," said Jamison. "Unless something ruptured inside the guy and it came out somewhere."

"There was no blood on his clothes," replied Decker. "So, I don't see how that could be the case."

Curry came back over to them. "Okay, I'll need to get your statements, and you both need to get out of here. The detectives will have my head if they find you here."

They walked back upstairs and filed out the rear door. Curry noted the damage. "How'd that happen?"

"That would be me breaking into the house," said Decker. "I'll explain why."

The storm had mostly passed, the skies had cleared some, and a few stars could actually be seen overhead.

Curry pulled out his notepad. "Okay, let's hear it."

First Decker and then Jamison gave their accounts. As they finished they heard someone calling out to them.

"Alex, is everything okay?"

They all turned to see Amber and Zoe at the rear fence that separated the two properties.

"Go back inside, I'll be there in just a few minutes," Jamison called back. She turned to Curry as Amber and Zoe returned to their house.

"My sister Amber and her daughter, Zoe. We're visiting with them."

"So they live there?" said Curry.

"Yes."

"We'll need to talk to them. They might have seen something leading up to whatever happened to the two vics."

"Sure, that's fine," said Jamison.

"What is it that you two do at the FBI?" asked Curry.

"We track down people who hurt other people," said Decker. "Just like what happened in that house."

Curry seemed to sense where Decker was going with this. "This isn't a federal case."

"It's funny how things can appear to be one thing and then turn into something else," replied Decker. "So maybe we can help."

"Decker," said Jamison in an offended tone. "We're on vacation. We're here to get away from all that stuff."

"Maybe you are," said Decker. "But I had no reason to get away from 'all that stuff.'"

"Not my call," said Curry. "You can take it up with homicide."

"Fair enough," said Decker.

Curry closed his notebook. "But since you're here now, you got any thoughts on the matter?"

Decker glanced back at the house. "Hanging someone is personal. It's a control thing. It's a terrible way to die because that guy simply strangled to death, or maybe his vertebrae finally popped. Either way, it takes a while."

"And the blood?" asked Curry.

"Where did it come from? If he bled out somewhere else and the blood was collected and brought here and spread out on the floor, what was the point?"

"And the guy in the basement?" asked Curry.

"Is he a cop or not? If not, why was he in uniform? And again, how did he die? I didn't see an obvious wound, but there was some foam on the mouth, so it might be poison. And another thing. Who owns this house? Was it the two men? Or somebody else?"

Curry had reopened his notebook and was jotting things down. "Anything else?"

"Yeah. I think your ME might have a tricky time determining the time of death."

"Why's that?"

"Because what I saw tonight was pretty much forensically impossible."

CHAPTER

4

Amber had sent a reluctant Zoe off to bed and was now sitting with her sister and Decker in the living room of her home.

"Two men dead?" said Amber in a trembling voice. "Murdered? I can't believe it. In the house right behind us? My God!"

"The police will want to talk to you at some point," said her sister.

"Why?" asked Amber frantically. "We know nothing about it."

"Standard procedure," noted Decker in a calming voice. "Because of your proximity to the crime scene. Nothing to get anxious about. It's all routine."

"Have you called Frank yet?" asked Jamison, rubbing her sister's shoulder.

Frank Mitchell was Amber's husband.

"I tried to, but he's not answering his phone. When I called the office, they said he was in a meeting. With this new job, he's having to work ungodly hours."

"What does he do?" asked Decker.

"He's the assistant manager at a fulfillment center. They fill online orders for lots of different companies. That's why we moved here, because Frank got the job. He worked for the same company in Kentucky, but this is a step up for him. They employ a lot of people."

"Warehouses are the big job creators now," said Jamison knowingly. "I've been reading articles on it. It pays okay, above minimum wage, with benefits, but it's really physically hard work."

"Tell me about it," said Amber. "Frank worked as a picker at the one when we lived in Kentucky. It was nonstop movement. They scored him on how many packages he was able to process. Thank God Frank moved up into management. He's in his thirties, and in good shape, but the pace just wore him down, and he always had aches and pains."

Amber looked toward the back window, at the house where two people had been found dead. "I thought this was going to be a fresh start for us. But now here we are, next to a *murder* investigation."

Jamison said, "It could be something totally unconnected to the neighborhood. The two men in there might be from somewhere else."

Amber did not look convinced. "What am I supposed to tell Zoe? She's very sensitive and very observant. She's going to have a ton of questions."

"I can talk to her, if you like. Or Decker can."

Decker looked startled. "I think it's better if you speak to her, Alex," he said.

"But you were talking to her out on the deck."

"That's why I think it's better if you talk to her."

Jamison looked at her sister. "Amber, it's going to be okay."

"You don't understand."

"Don't understand what?" asked Decker.

"These aren't the only murders in Baronville recently. I saw it on TV."

"What other murders?" asked Decker quickly.

Amber was about to reply when someone knocked on the front door.

When she opened it, a man and a woman, both grim-faced, were standing on the front stoop.

The man was in his fifties, with a full head of gray hair. He was about five-eleven, his sloping chest running to a small potbelly that hung over his belt. The woman was petite and in her thirties, about five-three, with a wiry build, shoulder-length blonde hair, and pretty features. The man wore a rumpled suit. The collar of his white shirt had a small black stain and his tie was crooked. His teeth were uneven and darkened by nicotine. The woman had on a sleek black pantsuit with a pristine white blouse and two-inch chunky heels to bump up her height. And her teeth were a brilliant white.

They held out their badges and asked to come in.

"Detectives Marty Green and Donna Lassiter," said the man. "Do you live here?" he asked Amber.

She nodded. "I'm Amber Mitchell."

Green looked at Decker and Jamison. "Which means you two must have been first on the scene. We understand that you're also with the FBI? Mind if we see your IDs?"

Decker and Jamison held out their creds. Green gave them a perfunctory glance, but Lassiter scrutinized them.

Green said, "We've read your statements. Now we'd like to hear your story first-hand."

They all sat down in the living room. Lassiter said to Amber, "Ma'am, could I ask you to wait in the other room while we go over this with them? Thank you. We'll want to talk to you later, of course."

Amber quickly rose, glanced anxiously at her sister, and left.

The two homicide detectives settled their gazes on the pair.

Lassiter said, "Your IDs show you're not special agents."

"We're not," said Jamison. "We're civilians working for an FBI task force."

Green looked at Decker. "Civilians, huh? I've been a cop a long time and my nose tells me you're one too."

"Burlington, Ohio. Pounded a beat for ten and then a detective for about another decade before joining the Bureau."

Green cleared his throat and opened his notebook. "Okay, let's go over what happened tonight."

Decker spoke first and then Jamison.

Green methodically wrote it all down with pen and paper.

Decker noted that Lassiter used a small electronic notebook, her fingers flying efficiently over the keys.

When they'd finished telling their stories, Decker said, "Did you determine cause of death yet? Or ID them?"

Green started to say something, but Lassiter got there first. "Sorry, but it's our job to ask the questions, and yours to answer them."

Decker looked at Green. "Do I take that as a no on both counts?"

Green said, "We're working on it. There was a lot of blood, but no source that we could find."

"Yeah, I've been thinking about that. I didn't see any wounds on the guy hanging, but you'll need to check it against him, to see if it was his blood. They could have killed him, drained his blood, and strung him up."

Green grimaced. "That sounds like some kind of cult thing. Like a sacrifice."

"And if it's not the vic's blood?" said Lassiter.

"Then it might be somebody else's. And they might be in a database somewhere." He paused. "Or it might not be human blood."

Lassiter and Green looked stunned by this.

"What makes you think it's not human?" Green asked.

"I'm not saying I think that. I'm just saying that killing an animal and collecting its blood is less problematic than doing so with a human. Driving out here, we passed some farms with cows, goats, and pigs on them. I'm just saying it's a possibility. Now, the guy in the basement: Was he one of yours?"

Lassiter started to say something, but this time Green beat her to it. "No, he wasn't. But the uniform he had on *was* one of ours." He added, "The big question is, where did it come from? We're also tracking down the ownership of the house. Neither man had any ID on him."

During this exchange Lassiter was looking at her partner with unconcealed exasperation. She leaned over to Green, but in a voice both Decker and Jamison could clearly hear, she said, "Marty, we haven't ruled these two out as suspects."

Green glanced at her and his expression turned uncertain. He looked at Decker. "We'll need to check out your whereabouts during the time in question."

Decker nodded. "We only got into town tonight around six. We stopped for gas right before we arrived here and the credit card transaction record and the CCTV at the gas station will confirm that. After we had dinner, I came out on the back porch. It was dark by then. Alex's niece joined me a few minutes later. Alex was inside talking to her sister. Around eight-fifteen, I saw the spark and ran to the house and found the bodies. Alex called 911 a few minutes later. Your guys arrived shortly after that." He paused. "I checked the pulse of the guy downstairs just to make sure he was dead. I didn't have to do that with the guy hanging. The body in the basement was very cold even though it wasn't really all that cold down there. And the limbs were stiff. And he had blowflies in his nostrils and it looked like they had already laid eggs. But the infestation was minimal." He paused again and studied the pair for their reaction to this.

Green said, "If your alibis check out, then the time of death on both men might well eliminate you as suspects." He glanced sideways at his partner before continuing. "How many homicides have you handled, Agent Decker?"

"Hundreds," said Decker. "In Ohio and with the FBI. I'm technically on vacation, so if you want an extra pair of eyes, I'm available."

"Decker," admonished Jamison. "How is it a 'vacation' if you're going to work another case?"

"It's out of the question anyway," said Lassiter.

Decker kept his gaze on Green. "I was just offering because I understand that these aren't the only recent murders in town."

"Who told you that?" said Lassiter sharply.

"Is it true?" asked Decker.

Green glanced at Lassiter and nodded. "Unfortunately, it is true."

5

THUNK-THUNK.

The rear doors of the body wagon closed and off went the two unidentified corpses.

Decker and Jamison watched from the street as the vehicle passed by, followed by a patrol car.

Police tape fluttered in the breeze left over from the storm.

Detective Green walked over to them while Lassiter went back inside the house.

Green said, "We'll run their prints. Hopefully, that will turn up who they are."

"A lot of people aren't on databases," pointed out Jamison.

"But a lot of people are," countered Green.

Decker said, "So tell us about the other homicides."

Green unwrapped a stick of gum and started chewing, balling up the wrapper and sticking it in his pocket.

Decker watched him. "I had a partner back in Ohio who chewed gum all the time. She was trying to kick the smokes."

Green said, "I'm two years off the cancer sticks. But I've worn my teeth down to nothing."

"So, what other homicides?" Decker persisted.

"We got a lot of problems in this town. Businesses boarded up. Houses foreclosed on. Many with no jobs and no prospects of a job. Opioid addiction is through the roof."

"That's not just here," said Jamison. "It's all over."

Green continued. "When I was a kid the mines and mills were still operating. People had money. Dads worked, moms stayed home and raised the children. People went to church on Sunday. Downtown was alive and well. Then the mines and mills went belly-up and everything came tumbling down. Because it all depended on the mines and mills. They were the only reason there *was* a town."

"Baronville?" said Jamison. "My sister told me a little about it."

Green chewed his gum and nodded. "A long time ago, John Baron Sr. came to the area and discovered coal. He built the town because he needed workers for the mines. He made a fortune off that, and then opened coal and coke plants, then textile mills, and later a paper mill. And then he hit natural gas and made more money. My granddad told me old man Baron only had one setback in his whole life. His textile business soured and he was planning to sell it by the time he died. But other than that, the man never missed when it came to business. Baron built this huge mansion and lived like a king. But when he died things started going downhill. The businesses started tanking and were sold off. When the economy nosedived back in the seventies and then manufacturing went overseas, they all eventually went out of business. The music stopped and the good folks of Baronville were caught with no place to sit down. Been that way ever since."

Looking impatient, Decker said, "Are you going to tell us about the homicides or keep giving us a history lesson on Baronville?"

Green spit out his gum and stared directly at Decker.

"Four vics at two different crime scenes. Both happened in the span of two weeks, the last barely a week ago."

"Similarities? Patterns?" Decker wanted to know.

"Only in that each one was weird," replied Green, his lip curled in disgust.

"No leads?" asked Jamison.

"None worth following up on. And as you know, the more time goes by, the lower the odds of clearing a case."

"Tell me about them," said Decker.

At that moment Lassiter came out of the house and motioned to Green. "Marty, can you come and eyeball something?"

Green looked across the yard at her. "What is it?"

Lassiter glanced at Decker. "I don't want to say in front of *unauthorized* persons."

Green turned to him. "I'll be at the station house tomorrow morning. It's on Baron Boulevard. If you want to stop by."

"Baron again," noted Decker.

"You stay here long enough you'll be thoroughly sick of the name Baron," said Green.

"Are there any Barons left here?" asked Jamison.

"One," said Green. He trudged across the wet lawn toward Lassiter.

Jamison whirled on Decker. "I can't believe you're in the middle of another murder investigation. Back in D.C. you were an eyewitness to one. On Pennsylvania Avenue no less. Now here in the commonwealth of *Pennsylvania* you find two bodies."

"And since I'm here the least I can do is try to find who killed them."

"Don't you ever get tired of it?" asked Jamison wearily.

"It's what I do. If I didn't have this, I'd have nothing."

"Oh, if only more people could realize happiness through homicide," snapped Jamison.

"Alex, you're sounding punchy."

"I *am* punchy! But it doesn't look like they're going to let you work on the case. You heard Lassiter."

"And I also heard her partner. He wants help, even if she doesn't."

"But they may not let us work on the case," pointed out Jamison.

"If they've had multiple murders here they could use some help."

"You better not call Bogart and ask him to intervene on this."

Decker looked at her appraisingly. "But if *you* called him?"

"Oh, no, you're not putting me in the middle of this."

"Alex, there have been six *recent* unsolved murders in Baronville."

She flushed. "I know that!"

"And your sister and her family are living here. In fact, they were right next door to these latest murders."

Jamison's jaw dropped. "Decker, I can't believe you're playing the guilt card on me."

"People are dead, Alex."

"And the police can find out who did it."

"I'm not sure about that."

"Why?"

"Because Detectives Green and Lassiter apparently didn't catch a really big inconsistency in the crime scene. I gave them the chance to comment on it, but they didn't bite."

"What inconsistency?"

"Just trust me on that. I'm not sure they'll be up to the task, is all."

Jamison started to say something, but stopped and looked in the direction of the house where the two dead men had been found. Then she glanced at her sister's house.

She let out a long sigh. "Okay, okay," she said miserably.

"You don't have to do anything, Alex. Enjoy your vacation and your sister and her family and let me work the case."

Her face turned red. "Like I'm going to let you work this alone. I can't even believe you'd say that."

Now Decker looked uncertain. "It's...it's about Zoe."

"What about her?"

"She asked me to not let you get hurt by bad people."

"I appreciate that, Amos, I really do. But I'm a big girl, in case you hadn't noticed. I've trained at the FBI, so I'm in the best physical shape of my life. And I can handle a gun. And I'm ready to do my job."

Decker cracked a smile.

"What?" she demanded.

"I wish I could say I was in the best physical shape of my life."

"You were in the NFL. I doubt you'll ever be that fit again. But don't worry."

"What do you mean?"

Now it was her turn to smile. "*I'll* take care of *you*."

6

"THIS IS CRAZY," said Frank Mitchell.

He was sitting in his living room with Amber, Decker, and Jamison. It was after midnight and he had just arrived a few minutes earlier. He had finally called Amber back on the way home and been filled in about the murders.

Frank was about six-one, lean and muscular, with curly blond hair and long sideburns. He had on a white dress shirt open at the collar with a loosened tie around it and dark slacks. His socks drooped a bit and his black dress shoes were nicked at the toecaps.

Amber sat beside him, with Frank's arm protectively around her.

She said, "When I saw them talk about the other murders on TV, I was stunned. Things like that aren't supposed to happen in small towns like this. Now, I wish we'd never moved here."

Frank looked incredulously at his wife. "I got *transferred* here, Am. It's not like I had a choice."

"What can you tell us about these other murders?" asked Decker. "You mentioned you saw them on the TV?"

Amber shrugged. "I saw a report on the local news. I really didn't pay attention to the details, just that some people had been murdered and the police were investigating. And then I turned off the TV because Zoe came into the room."

Frank slid off his tie, tossed it on the coffee table, and rubbed his neck. He smiled ruefully. "I'm still not used to dressing up for work." He sat back. "Like I said, I could either take this job or keep working the line back in Kentucky." He glanced at Decker.

"I used to work retail before getting into fulfillment centers. But shopping malls are going down the tubes because everyone wants to buy online. I never finished my college degree. So here I am."

"Your mom got sick and you left school to help out at home, sweetie. And you're working hard and moving up in the company," added Amber encouragingly.

Frank smiled weakly and patted her arm. "Yeah, well, anyway, Baronville is it, at least for a while. The job pays almost double what I was making and the benefits are a lot better. And it's really cheap to live here. It's why they don't build many fulfillment centers in or around big cities. Land and everything else is too expensive."

"Well, areas like this can certainly use the jobs," pointed out Jamison.

"Problem is, we can't fill all our positions."

"Why not?" asked Jamison. "You'd think people would be banging down the door to get jobs there."

"They are. But they can't pass a drug test," said Frank. "We're starting to recruit from other parts of the state, and even across the border in Ohio."

Amber said, "We better get to bed. Frank's been working all day and I know he must be exhausted. Did you get some dinner, hon?"

"They ordered in pizza. I'm good." He glanced at Decker and Jamison and smiled shyly. "It's good to see you again, Alex. And it's nice to meet you, Amos. I sure wish your visit didn't have to have this awful thing connected to it."

Decker looked at him. "I know the police already talked to Amber. But did you ever see anyone in the house behind you?"

Frank thought about this. "No, not really. I moved here several months before Amber and Zoe, to get acclimated, learn my job, and set up the house and all. I leave early in the morning and get home pretty late at night. That's the way it'll be for a while. It's a big learning curve for me now that I'm in management. I've got to put in the extra time."

"You never saw anyone in the backyard there? Or at the window or back door?

Frank shook his head and glanced at Amber. She said, "I've never really even been out in the backyard. There's too much to do inside. Heck, I'm still unpacking moving boxes. That's the same thing I told the police."

"How did the people die?" asked Frank.

"The police aren't sure yet," said Decker.

"But you found the bodies," said Amber. "You must have some idea of how they died."

"I do. But it's not something I can share with you."

When Amber looked confused, her sister quickly said, "We might be assisting with the case. So we really can't talk about it."

"Assisting with the case! But I thought you were on vacation."

Jamison glanced sharply at Decker before answering her sister. "So did I. But apparently murder doesn't keep to a schedule. At least *my* schedule."

Amber involuntarily shivered. "My God. I still can't believe it. A murder right in our backyard, so to speak." She gazed at Decker. "I guess you must be used to this sort of thing."

Decker looked back at her. "You guessed wrong." He glanced at Jamison. "Up for a short ride?"

She stared at him dumbly but nodded resignedly.

* * *

Their vehicle was a rental, principally because Jamison's own car was a subcompact, which would have required Decker to bend his big body nearly in half to get in. And for such a long road trip, that was not a welcome prospect.

A Yukon had far more leg- and headroom.

"You said a *short* ride," said Jamison. "Gee, let me guess our destination."

"Just drive over to the next street, Alex."

"And may I ask why, since we've already been over there?"

"Just want to see something."

"We could just walk."

"It'll be easier in the truck."

As they pulled down the street Decker pointed at the sign posted at its entrance. "Dead end. No outlet."

"Well, *dead* end is an appropriate sign for this street tonight," noted Jamison.

The police were still there processing the scene and one of the officers glanced at them as they drove by. Before he could react, however, Jamison had driven past the house. She reached the end of the road, turned around, parked the SUV at the curb a half-dozen houses down from the crime scene, and cut the lights.

As they watched, Green and Lassiter appeared at the front door. In the illumination provided by the front porch light, the two detectives seemed to be in animated conversation.

"Is that what you wanted to see?" asked Jamison, yawning.

Decker shook his head. He wanted to see the street and the cars parked there. The homes here had no garages, only carports and street parking.

The only thing was, other than the cop cars and their SUV, there were no cars parked on the street, and none near the crime scene house. Decker looked at the houses up and down the street. None had lights on, but that might be due to the lateness of the hour.

"Most of these homes don't look lived in."

"Well, like we've been told, Baronville isn't exactly a hopping place."

"And that also means there won't be many eyes around that can help us with the comings and goings of the crime scene. They had to get the two men in there, either dead or alive. There's no attached garage on the house to pull into, so they would have been exposed at some point."

"Or the two guys could have walked in and been killed there."

Decker closed his eyes and thought about what he had seen and heard before the lights in the house had started going on and off because of the electrical short.

A plane going over.

A series of sounds: thuds and scrapes.

A car starting up.

The plane? Obviously, no connection.

The weird sounds? Maybe connected.

A car driving away after dumping the bodies there?

He closed his eyes more tightly. His perfect recall was best with visual things. But it was still far better than average with things of an auditory nature.

"What are you doing?" asked Jamison.

Decker scrunched up his face as her voice interrupted him while he was trying to precisely conjure the noises he'd heard.

"Decker, it's nearly one in the morning and I'm beat. We drove over six hours to get here. Well, *I* drove over six hours to get here."

Decker relaxed his features. "She's your sister. If we ever visit my sisters, I'll drive."

"Your two sisters live in California and Alaska, respectively. We're *not* driving to California or Alaska."

"Well, then I guess we won't be visiting them."

She sighed and sat back, fiddling with the turn signal on the steering column. "Why does this matter to you so much? I get that it's murder. And it's horrible. But you can't investigate every murder you run across."

"Why can't I?" he said brusquely.

She sputtered, "Because you just can't."

He shook his head. "We can agree to disagree."

A few moments of silence passed before she said, "You found who killed Cassie and Molly, Amos. They got what they deserved. But you can't solve every murder you come across. It's impossible. You'll just be setting yourself up to fail."

Decker said nothing in reply. He just stared out the window at the house where he had found the two dead men.

Finally, Jamison said, "Can we go back to my sister's house now? Or I'm just going to curl up in the back and go to sleep."

"We can go now."

She quickly drove off.

They were staying with the Mitchells in two guest bedrooms upstairs. Amber told them it had once been one large bedroom but they'd converted it into two. Although Zoe was nearly six years old, Amber and Frank wanted more children.

Jamison spoke briefly to her sister, who was still up waiting for them, and then said good night. She and Decker walked up the stairs and Jamison went to her room and Decker to his.

Later, he sat at the window and looked out onto the street. It looked a lot like his hometown in Ohio. Half alive and half dead. Maybe more dead than alive, actually.

He undressed and lay in bed staring at the ceiling.

In a way, perhaps in a significant way, Jamison had hit it right on the head.

I'm trying to catch Cassie and Molly's killer over and over again. And it will never end, because killers will always be out there. So this is my world and welcome to it.

7

DECKER HAD JUST finished putting on his shoes the next morning when his phone rang.

It was Detective Green.

"What's up?" asked Decker.

"The blood on the floor of the house?"

"Yeah?"

"You were right. It's not human."

"We'll meet you in half an hour."

* * *

Thirty-five minutes later Decker stared down at two metal tables on which lay the dead men from the house. Both had been autopsied. The Y-incision staples looked like the tracks of giant zippers across their chests.

A tired-looking Jamison was on his right, a crisp-eyed Detective Green on his left. The medical examiner was on the other side of the table. Detective Lassiter had not yet made an appearance.

"You're sure it's not human blood?" asked Decker.

The ME, a short, balding man with a paunch and a trim gray beard, nodded.

"Ran it last night, or early this morning more precisely, while I was doing these posts." He yawned. "Simple test. The specific reagent for human blood wasn't there. But it *is* blood. Probably some animal rather than synthetic. I'll do some more tests and see exactly what we're looking at."

Green said, "So somebody poured out a bunch of, I guess, animal blood under the guy hanging in the living room."

"And *did* he die by hanging?" asked Decker.

The ME nodded. "All signs point to that. Ligature mark on the neck, burst capillaries in the eyes."

"Petechial hemorrhaging in the sclera," said Decker absently.

This comment drew a sharp glance from Green.

With the ME's help Decker moved one of the bodies onto its side. He stared at the man's back. "This was the guy hanging?"

"That's right," said Green.

Decker laid the body back down and looked at the man's feet, ears, hands, and groin.

He frowned.

"What is it, Decker?" said Jamison.

Ignoring her question, Decker said, "His hands weren't bound. But no sign of defensive wounds. A guy getting hung is going to fight back. And he was a good-sized man and looked pretty fit."

The ME pointed to a spot on the back of the dead man's head. "Contusion here. Blunt force trauma. I think he was knocked out and then strung up. No need for restraints then."

"And this one?" asked Decker, as he looked over the second body, also turning it onto its side. "There was foam on his lips. Ordinarily, that could mean death by drowning. Or some type of poison."

"We're running toxicology tests on him," said the ME. "But there was no water in his lungs, so drowning is out for the cause of death. Could be a drug overdose. God knows we have enough of those around here. The cooler here holds twenty bodies. That used to be plenty. Never got filled up. Then the opioid crisis hit full force and the city had to buy a refrigerated trailer for excess capacity. We keep it out in the parking lot. And now it's always full too. I can't autopsy them all. Not enough time. If they come in with a needle sticking out of their arm, that's good enough for me on the cause of death."

Decker eyed the man incredulously for a moment, though the ME didn't seem to notice. Then Decker laid the body back down and said, "Doesn't account for the other guy hanging from the ceiling. Or the blood."

"No, it doesn't," agreed Green.

The door to the room opened and in walked Lassiter, dressed in the same clothes she had worn the previous night. It seemed that she had not been home.

Green said, "Donna, you should've gotten some shut-eye."

Lassiter wasn't looking at him. She was staring at Decker and Jamison.

"I thought we agreed that—"

Green turned to the ME. "So we probably got animal blood. What does that tell us?"

The ME shrugged. "I just find out how they died. You're the investigator." He looked at Decker. "I'm not a forensic pathologist. They're apparently in short supply and cost too much," he added with a grin. "And a town like this can't afford one. I'm just a local semi-retired doctor. Urologist. I do this job part-time. But the state prescribes a course you have to take. And there are continuing education courses you have to take."

"We might have to do better than that," said Decker, drawing a quick frown from the ME.

Decker turned to Green. "The blood, was it symbolic? A message? A ritual?"

"I don't think we can answer those questions yet," said Green.

Lassiter closed the door behind her and drew closer to the table, coming to stand right behind Decker. He didn't seem to notice her proximity.

"How about IDs on these guys?" he asked.

"We ran both their prints through AFIS," said Green. "No hits came back. I know AFIS isn't perfect, but if they're criminals they've never been arrested."

"Run them through other databases," said Decker. "They might be civilians who were getting background checks run for employment and things like that."

"We're doing that," said Lassiter.

Decker turned around to see her standing directly behind him.

Even though she was in heels, there was nearly a foot of height difference between them. He looked down at her and she looked up at him.

"Good," he said before turning back around to look at the bodies again. "I take it that neither of the men had any connection to the house? Didn't own it?"

"How do you know?" Lassiter blurted out.

"If they had, you probably would have identified them by now," said Decker. "But who *does* own the house?"

"The bank," answered Green. "It was in foreclosure. The previous owners defaulted on the loan and left town nearly a year ago. Place has been basically abandoned since then."

Decker said, "But the house had electricity, or else the blood wouldn't have fried the lamp cord and started a fire. Why would the power still be on after all that time?"

"Well, we have squatters around," said Green. "They crash in these abandoned houses for weeks or months, and they illegally tap into the electrical supply. And sometimes the banks rent the houses out to make some money while they're trying to sell them. They would need to have the juice on for that."

"Was that house rented out at any time?" asked Jamison.

"Still checking on that, but I don't think so."

Decker said, "The neighborhood looked pretty much empty. There were no cars parked on the street."

"Nothing unusual about that around here," said Green. "Baronville has lost about half its population. At our peak, when all the mines and mills and plants were cranking, we used to have almost double the people living here now. Nearly the size Erie is now. But no more."

Decker said, "The point is, there won't be many people able to help us with what happened at that house."

Green said, "There are only three houses on that street with people living in them. I spoke to one and Donna spoke to another, but they didn't see or hear anything. And prior to last night they had seen no activity at the house in question."

"Nothing?" said Decker.

"According to them, no," replied Green.

"Any reason to believe any of them might have been involved?" asked Jamison.

Lassiter answered. "Alice Martin is an elderly woman who's lived her whole life in Baronville. I actually know her because she was my Sunday school teacher. The second home is owned by an old man in a wheelchair named Fred Ross. The last house is the closest to the crime scene, but the man who lives there, Dan Bond, is blind. I spoke to Bond, and my partner talked to Mrs. Martin. I think we can safely rule out each of them as possible suspects."

Decker turned around to look at her again. "Why is that?"

Lassiter blinked. "Don't you think it's obvious?"

Decker glanced at Green. "There are some things about a murder investigation that are obvious. Ruling out someone as a suspect after one contact or an assumption is not one of them."

Decker could see Lassiter's face flush and her features turn ugly, but he plowed ahead.

He added, "So, Dan Bond and Alice Martin have been interviewed. Why haven't you talked to Fred Ross yet?"

Green said, "He wasn't home at the time. We're going to check with him, though."

"Any idea how one of your uniforms got on the dead guy?" asked Decker.

"None. All uniforms are accounted for, as far as we can tell."

"So maybe the source of the uniforms?" said Jamison.

"We're checking all that," interjected Lassiter, who looked like she was barely containing her anger. "We didn't just fall off a truck, you know."

Decker ignored this and pointed to a spot on the shoulder of the man found in the basement. "What's that?"

The ME said, "I noted that in my report. Maybe something was placed there and then removed."

"Any ideas?"

"Could be any number of things. Pain patch for one. Nicotine patch for another."

"Was he a smoker?" asked Jamison.

"His lungs showed some damage from smoking, yes. I'm esti-
mating that he wasn't yet forty, so if he had stopped smoking his
lungs most likely would have been able to regenerate."

"Guess it doesn't matter now," said Green.

The ME said, "The tox screens should show what was in it, if it
was a medication patch. If the drugs are still in the body, that is. If
the patch was taken off too long ago, the meds might have worked
through his system."

Decker eyed the man closely and said, "So, the big question:
Have you got a time-of-death determination yet?"

The ME said, "When I got to the house limbs were stiff on both,
so they were in rigor. I'd say they'd been dead about twenty hours
or so, or even far longer, since they might have actually been coming *out* of rigor at that point. I'll know better later."

"Did you take a core temp?"

The ME said in an annoyed tone, "Something went wrong with
my equipment. It was registering wacky numbers."

"Meaning really, really cold?"

The man looked surprised. "Yes, how did you know that?"

"So even without a core temp, twenty hours or even far longer
is your final verdict? You sure about that?"

The ME looked indignant that Decker seemed to be challenging
his conclusion. He said stiffly, "Yes, I am. Well, that they were
dead at least twenty hours. Why?"

"And are you sure the bodies weren't moved after they died?"

The ME shot a look at the corpses and then glanced back at
Decker.

"Yeah, I mean, I'm pretty sure, why?"

"I think you might want to take some additional forensics
classes beyond the minimum or maybe better yet, try another line
of work that doesn't involve performing postmortems."

The man said furiously, "What the hell is that supposed to mean?"

"I thought I was pretty clear." Decker turned to Green. "So, are
we good to go on this investigation? Working it together?"

Green looked at him curiously for a moment and said, "You
have to keep us looped in on *everything*. No exceptions."

"Agreed," said Decker quickly.

"From a practical point of view, how do you want to do this?" asked Green.

"There's a lot of ground to cover, so I say two and two," replied Decker. "That way we can each hit a crime scene."

Lassiter interjected, "Good, I'll go with you and your partner can go with Marty."

Jamison looked surprised by this. "Why? You have your team and we have ours."

"Because that way we'll be apprised and up to date on both sets of investigations," said Lassiter. "There won't have to be any long, drawn-out reports or multiple explanations. Saves everyone time and trouble."

"Works for me," said Decker distractedly, which drew a quick glare from Jamison.

* * *

As they were leaving the morgue, Jamison drew Lassiter aside.

"Just FYI, my partner is a little difficult to work with."

"Trust me, I'd spotted that myself," replied Lassiter.

"No, I'm not sure you have the full picture."

"Well, Marty's no peach to partner with either. But we're girls in guys' territory, right? We learn how to deal with it."

This unexpected comment drew a smile from Jamison. "I think that's the first thing you've said I agree with."

"Let's hope there's more in the future."

CHAPTER

8

CRIME SCENE NUMBER *Two.*

At least that was how Decker had designated it in his mind.

It had been an auto repair facility. An unexpected place for a murder. But then again, most everything about a murder was unexpected.

He and Lassiter climbed out of her car, a pale blue four-door Prius with limited legroom, at least for someone as tall as Decker. It was her personal ride. The department didn't have money in the budget for cars for their detectives, she'd told him on the drive over.

Decker said, "FYI, I saw at least six drug deals going down on the way here."

"Seven," replied Lassiter. "You might have missed the soccer mom with the little girl in the rear seat. Mom was getting her pop from the dude at the last traffic light before she dropped her kid off at daycare."

"And you drove right past?" said Decker.

"If I stopped every drug deal I saw, I wouldn't have the time to eat, sleep, or use the bathroom. I happen to know the woman. She won't take the pop now. She'll do it later, at home, when her hubby is there. He'll take care of her and the girl."

"What's the drug of choice around here?"

"Used to be OxyContin and then fentanyl. Now it's heroin even though fentanyl is far more potent."

"Must be impacting your crime rate."

"People burglarize their neighbor's house so they can sell the stuff for cash to service their addiction. Or a son embezzles his mom's bank account to do the same. Or a granny steals from her granddaughter's piggy bank. It's seriously demented stuff and happens every day."

"And heroin is popular because you get a gram of it for about fifty bucks and it'll last you a lot longer than fentanyl, or OxyContin, which runs about, what, eighty bucks a pill on the street?"

"Hell, you don't have to buy it on the street anymore. They'll deliver it right to your house, like pizza. Or they get it from pharmacies or the local Boy Scout troop leader. Or it comes down one of the drug pipelines around here. They crush and snort it, inject it. They even chew on fentanyl patches instead of putting them on their skin to get the pop."

"Maybe that mark on the dead guy was a fentanyl patch."

She nodded. "Could be. Our OD rate is up nearly seventy percent from last year. And the last ten cases we've investigated have been people over sixty-five. Some people call it 'Rust Belt Retirement.'"

"I left being a cop in Ohio before the opioid crisis really got going. But even back then we started calling it the zombie apocalypse."

"It's why we all carry Narcan with us."

"To resuscitate an OD?"

Lassiter nodded. "And the city enacted Good Samaritan laws, so you won't get in trouble if you report an overdose, even if you might be doing drugs as well. The woman we passed? Her husband keeps a Narcan kit at home. Rehab place in town started to give them out. Some say it's enabling. I say until we get this figured out, it's better to keep people alive. We got an army of addicts and a twenty-bed rehab center. Tell me how that makes sense. I think the town's just sick of it. They don't want to spend tax dollars they don't have on people they don't think give a damn. They hear methadone treatment center and think it's what meth addicts take to get their high and not the drug used to treat that addiction. They don't want 'these' people around them, not coming to grips with the fact that 'these' people are often members of their families. So some say let 'em die and good riddance."

"But not you?"

"It's hit pretty close to home with me, Decker. So, no, I don't say good riddance to a human being."

"Your family?" he asked.

"Not going there," she replied curtly.

As they reached the door of the repair facility, Decker said, "I take it since Mrs. Martin taught you in Sunday school that you grew up here?"

"I did. Though I went to college in Philly. Criminal justice degree at Temple. Then I came back here, joined the force, was a street cop for four years, passed my exams, became a sergeant, and then moved up to detective."

"Pretty fast-track for you."

"I worked my ass off for it."

"I'm sure you did, more than the guys had to."

"That's pretty astute of you, Decker."

"Did you shut the repair facility down after the crime, or did it close on its own?"

"The guy who ran it hit the state lottery for about six hundred thousand and got the hell out of here."

"You got a key?"

She pulled one from her pocket and unlocked the front door.

There was a small reception area, and beyond that, through a wall of glass interrupted by a door, Decker could see three service bays.

"Okay, take me through step by step."

"We got a call about a possible break-in. Uniforms responded. They found the bodies."

"Who called it in?"

"Anonymous. We tried to trace it but couldn't."

"That's unusual, because most people don't carry untraceable phones. Where did you find the bodies?"

She led him into the service bay area.

"Vic number one was found in the grease pit of this service bay." She pointed down in the hole.

"Cause of death?"

"A gunshot wound to the head sealed the deal."

"ID?"

"Michael Swanson. Black guy, early thirties. Low-level street dealer. Started his career right out of high school. He'd been arrested before on petty stuff. Did some short stints twice in the local lockup. But nothing too serious. Last address we had for him was an apartment on the outskirts of town. Very low-rent district."

"The second body?"

She led him over to a machine that was used to lift engine blocks out of vehicles.

"He was found wrapped in chains and hanging from this."

"Cause of death?"

"Same as Swanson. But he had a mark branded into his forehead."

"What sort of mark?"

"You ready for this?"

"I guess."

"It was a flame, but it was turned upside down."

"A torch, you mean? That's the symbol of the Greek god of death, Thanatos."

Lassiter's jaw slackened. "How did you know that?"

"I read a book once. With pictures. Who was he?"

"Bradley Costa. White, age thirty-five. He was a fairly recent transfer here. Worked at Baronville National Bank. A senior vice president."

"Pretty big title for a guy in his thirties."

"He came here from Wall Street and had a lot of experience. Those types don't show up here every day. He was described as a real go-getter."

"Any connection to Swanson?"

"Not that we can prove. He might have been a customer of Swanson's. Wouldn't be the first time a banker did drugs. And because of Costa's line of work, money laundering or some other financial shenanigans come to mind. But we couldn't get any traction on that angle either. And I don't think Swanson generated enough cash to need a money launderer."

"And yet both had their lives ended in this place," said Decker, looking around the space. "How did they get here?"

"We don't know. Costa didn't have any family that we know of, but his boss at the bank reported him missing. No one reported Swanson missing. I guess he moved in circles where he went missing a lot. Definitely out of the mainstream."

"The mainstream as it *used* to be," corrected Decker.

"Right."

"Any useful trace?"

"No prints. No spent cartridges. No tossed cigarette with DNA on it. Only blood belonged to the vics."

"And we're sure they were killed here?"

"Blood spatters say yes. And the ME said there was enough blood present to account for the shots and the bleed-outs to have occurred here."

"Was it the same ME I met today?"

"Yeah, Charlie Duncan. Why?"

Decker didn't answer.

She said, "And what did you mean that he should take some courses, or get out of the business of autopsies altogether? Do you think he was wrong on the time-of-death call?"

"I know that he missed two big inconsistencies." He turned to her. "But then you and your partner missed them too."

"Like what?" she said defensively.

"A body in a dank basement that's been dead longer than twenty hours and in full rigor is going to have a lot more than a few flies and a few unhatched eggs on it. Blowflies can locate a dead body and arrive within minutes of the death. The body hanging upstairs had no blowflies on it that I could see. The one in the basement only had a few. Each blowfly can lay over two hundred eggs, and those eggs hatch within eight to twenty-four hours into first-stage maggots. That's what I meant when I told the first officer on the scene that what I had observed was forensically impossible. A stiff corpse with only minimal insect infestation and not a single egg hatched? Your ME should have seen that right away. But he just focused on the rigor and not the entomology, lack of body decomp, and core temp factors. And he just assumed that his instrument was out of whack with the core temp instead of digging deeper to see why the body would be that cold, namely below ambient temperature. A competent ME has to look at the total package. Everything impacts everything else. Otherwise, you screw up and a bad guy gets to walk."

Lassiter looked taken aback by his comment. "O-kay," she said slowly. "I get where you're coming from. But the bodies were found inside. Wouldn't that have made a difference with the flies?"

"It can. But you'd be surprised at the places blowflies can get into. And here we had an empty house with an old basement probably filled with cracks and holes. Trust me, they would've gotten to it if the body had been there for twenty hours or longer."

"What was the *second* inconsistency?"

"Hypostasis, otherwise known as livor mortis. Once the heart stops pumping and the internal body decomposition commences, vessels get porous and the blood reacts solely to gravity and heads for the lowest spot. With a guy hanging that means he'll have blood collecting in his fingertips, earlobes, and feet. He might even have a death erection."

"What? A death erection?"

"Because when you die vertically, the blood also pools in the groin. Like a balloon filling up with water. Heart's no longer circulating, so there's no way for the blood to leave the spot once it gets there. In the morgue when I checked out the body of the guy hanging, the staining was on his back. That means he didn't die by being strung up and left there for twenty hours."

"Then he might have been killed elsewhere and brought to the house?"

Decker nodded. "Your ME didn't mention anything about the livor mortis inconsistency. He either didn't know about it or he just flat out screwed up."

"I'll have to go back and check with him."

"Good luck on that. So, why kill them here?"

"It was abandoned. It had grease pits. Equipment to hang someone."

"I was actually thinking about a broader question."

"What's that?"

"Why Baronville?"

9

Two people at a dining room table shotgunned to death.

That's what Green had just told Jamison.

Talk about a last meal.

They were in a house that seemed much like the residence where they had found the two dead men.

"Damnedest thing I'd ever seen," said Green as he chewed his gum. "Sitting right there, and bam. They both died instantly, the ME said. Close quarters with a shotgun usually has that effect."

"Did the vics live here?"

"Not as far as we know. No one lived here *legally*. The bank owned it too, like the other place."

"Any connection between the two people?"

Green consulted his official notebook. "None that we could run down. Different walks of life. No known ties."

"Tell me about them."

"Joyce Tanner was white and fifty-three years old. She worked at JC Penney before it closed. She was unemployed at the time of her death. She was divorced with no kids. Her ex left the area a long time ago. We're still trying to track him down, but there's no basis right now to believe he had anything to do with it. Toby Babbot was white and forty years old, on disability because of a work-related injury."

"Babbot have any family?"

"Never married, no kids that we could find."

"Were they from Baronville?"

"No. Babbot moved here from Pittsburgh about six years ago

and worked at a plant building air-conditioning units. Plant closed down. Then he did some miscellaneous work."

"And Tanner?"

"Her parents were killed in a car accident in Connecticut. She came here to live with her aunt and uncle about forty years ago. They raised her here and then they died too. Natural causes," he added.

"Any idea how the pair ended up here?"

"No. We canvassed the neighborhood after it happened. But you can see for yourself, there aren't that many folks around who could have seen something. So we got no leads at all."

"Were they eating dinner when it happened?"

"No. It was like they were made to sit in the chairs and then they were shot."

"Anything else about the deaths that was curious?" asked Jamison.

Green pointed to the wall that still bore the bloodstains from the homicide. "Their killer wrote something there with a Sharpie. We cut it out and collected it as evidence."

"What?"

"A Bible verse."

"Which one?"

"Not one of the well-known ones. I'm a good Methodist. Go to church every Sunday. And I still had to look it up."

Green glanced down at his notebook and flipped through some pages. "*Slaves, accept the authority of your masters, with all deference. For it is to your credit if being aware of God, you endure pain while suffering unjustly.*"

He closed his notebook and looked up at Jamison.

Jamison said promptly, "It's from the First Epistle of Peter, two-eighteen."

Green looked at her in surprise. "That's right. How did you know that?"

"My favorite uncle was a minister. I helped him teach Sunday school. He got me to read the Bible backward and forward. He was also a respected religious scholar and introduced me to a lot of writing and arguments on the subject."

"So, can you put on your religious scholar hat and give me some context on the verse?"

"Peter was imprisoned and beaten for his beliefs. So he might have been talking about keeping his own faith through that terrible experience. And there were a lot of slaves back then. It might have been a justification for keeping slaves and trying to tamp down any sign of insurrection. I mean, if God says it's okay?" She frowned. "Pretty diabolical, actually."

"Anything else?"

"Many religious scholars don't believe that Peter even wrote that epistle."

"Why?"

"Because the writing indicated an advanced knowledge of the Greek language and a scholarly background in philosophy that Peter simply didn't have. And widespread persecution of Christians didn't commence until long after Peter's death."

Green smiled. "Well, you're a fount of knowledge. Thanks."

However, Jamison frowned again. "But I don't see how that gets us any further along with the case unless you have any slave rings operating around here."

"It could be that it's a warning. Cross us and this will happen to you. But killing people who didn't even know each other and have no demonstrable connection? I don't get that. It could just be random, I guess."

Jamison mulled this over. "Look, Baronville isn't exactly a huge metropolis. Yet you have three separate crime scenes occurring very close together involving a pair of victims at each. Here there's a cryptic Bible verse written on the wall. Then there's animal blood at the crime scene we stumbled onto. What about the place where Decker and your partner are now?"

"A guy had a death mark on his forehead," said Green. "I guess that counts as weird."

"My point is, I can't believe that all these murders are not connected somehow. I really think we're dealing with one killer, or one set of killers, Detective."

Green sighed resignedly. "Great. Serial killings in Baronville.

The town is trying to get back on its feet and this crap is going to hit the national pipeline at some point and make it a lot harder for us to attract people here."

"You ever think about calling in reinforcements? State police?"

"Frankly, they've got their hands full. We're not the only town with problems. And state budgets have shrunk." He paused. "Decker sounds like he's good at this, though."

"He's the best I've ever seen. I think he's the best the FBI has ever seen."

"Well, then maybe we have a chance. Despite a few biting comments he's made, Decker seems easy enough to work with."

"Oh, just give it time," said Jamison, hiding a smile.

10

"Not hungry?"

Jamison stared across the table in the restaurant where she and Decker were eating dinner. They had each filled the other in on the respective crime scenes they had visited that day. And he had also told her that Lassiter was going to brief Green on Decker's doubts about the ME's time-of-death determination.

Decker, who had been picking at his meal, which had prompted Jamison's query, set down his knife and fork and picked up his glass of beer.

"Six murders," he said. "People with no clear connections. No obvious similarities, but maybe they're still all part of the same jigsaw puzzle."

"And we have to somehow make those pieces fit," said Jamison, who had put down her fork and knife too. She had chosen a glass of merlot over beer. She picked it up and took a sip.

"And if they don't?" he said.

She set her wine down and fiddled with her napkin. "But I told Green that I think these cases *have* to be connected. I mean, six weird murders in a place like this? What are the odds of them not being connected? Which means the two we found are tied to the other four."

"But we don't seem to be making much progress."

"Decker, we haven't even been working the case for a full day. It takes time. You know that better than anyone."

"We don't have that much time, Alex. We only have a week of vacation."

"Damn, I forgot about that."

"And something tells me this sucker is going to take longer than that."

"What do you want to do?"

"Work the case hard for now, but if we start bumping up against the end of our vacation we'll need to talk to Bogart and have him extend it, or let us work the case on behalf of the FBI."

Jamison frowned. "Somehow I don't think it's that simple, Decker."

"Well, it *should* be. Six people are dead who shouldn't be."

"I get that," she said nervously, as Decker's raised voice made several people at other tables look around at them. She added quickly, "So I told you what I learned at the house: the two victims, the Bible verse on the wall."

"Right," said Decker absently.

"What do you think about it?"

"I think it's a little much."

Jamison looked perplexed. "What does that mean?"

"I asked Lassiter a question and now I'll ask you. Why Baronville?"

"Why Baronville what?"

"Six unusual and inexplicable murders in this town. What's so special about this place that it garners that much unusual homicidal activity?"

"Even towns like this have their share of bizarre crimes."

"That's true, but there's something about this one that just seems off."

"But you *do* think they're connected?" she asked.

He nodded. "They're not copycats, though, because most of the critical details are different. I think we're looking at the same person or persons doing this."

"So was your perfect recall any use today?"

"I have nothing to remember that would be helpful."

"Really? Nothing?"

He said, "Actually, I heard a car drive away a few minutes before I saw the sparking from the electrical short."

Jamison sat straighter in her chair. "You told me that before, but did you *see* the car?"

"No. There was no clear sightline from where I was."

"Well, only three elderly people live on that street. So maybe they don't even drive. And there weren't any cars on the street when we drove over there. You think it could have been the killer leaving the house after dumping the bodies?"

"Could be. Blowflies can find a body very quickly."

Outside, it had started to rain and the temperature had dropped, bleeding off the earlier warmth of the day.

She said, "I told Green we'd come in tomorrow morning and share any ideas. How did you leave it with Lassiter?"

"I didn't leave it any way with her. She dropped me off at the house and that was that. Besides, I don't have any ideas."

"Some might come to you in the night."

"Doubtful."

"Hey, you're the one who wanted to work this case, Decker," barked Jamison. "So stop whining and start doing your job."

Decker glanced sharply at her, only to see that she was smiling at him.

He grinned sheepishly. "You're right. I'm being an idiot."

"Wow. I can count on one hand with fingers left over the number of times you've said that I was right."

"You're right more often than you think."

Her expression changed. "Zoe told me what you said. About my ability to read people and to see things others don't."

"Don't let it go to your head."

She smirked. "Thanks. Green said they'd have all the files ready for us to go over tomorrow."

Decker brightened at this comment. "Good. Maybe something will jump out."

They fell silent for a few moments.

"Talked to Melvin lately?" asked Jamison.

"No. He and Harper are traveling on vacation somewhere. The Mediterranean, I think. Why?"

"I know how close you and Melvin are. I guess you could have gone on vacation with them, but it might have been awkward with the three of you. Especially in the romantic Med."

Decker stared absently at his plate of food and didn't answer.

"FYI, there's a park near my sister's house with a jogging trail," noted Jamison.

He glanced up at her. "And why do I need to know that?"

"I know you've been working out, and you *have* dropped a lot of weight. Just want you to keep it up. You know, it's harder to get back in shape than it is to stay in shape."

"Thanks for enlightening me on that."

He glanced out the window onto the darkened street. A few cars rolled past. And there were a couple of pedestrians. Other than that, downtown Baronville was relatively quiet in the gathering storm. For now.

"What are you thinking about, Decker?"

He continued to stare out into the dark. "I'm wondering who's going to die next."

II

It had once been a mansion, perhaps beyond compare.

Now it was old, falling down, and possibly no longer salvageable.

It was from an era when money flowed freely, no income taxes were due, the world lived both more ostentatiously and more simply, and everyone knew his place. *Globalization* was not even a term, and information moved far more slowly, leading to a blissful ignorance among most.

Men were the breadwinners. They came home from work, spent time with their families, smoked their cigarettes, drank their beer, listened to the same radio programs and later TV shows as the rest of the country, went to bed, and got up to do it all over again, while women did the same on the home front.

John Baron looked out over what had once been the exquisitely landscaped rear grounds of his home, but was now merely dirt with weeds topping it.

He was a tall man, over six-three, with broad shoulders and a lean waist. He was physically strong and fit and always had been. However, at age fifty-three he could sense feebleness drifting into some of his muscle and stiffness into some of his joints.

His salt-and-pepper hair was long, and untouched by professional scissors.

His clothes were a hodgepodge of old things: a faded tuxedo jacket, a pair of dungarees, a white polo shirt, and an old leather belt to hold up the britches. On his feet were work boots. His weathered and handsome face was bristly with scruff.

He did not care about his appearance.

He lived alone. There was no one to impress.

His ancestral home was well over twenty-five thousand square feet, with more than half that again in outbuildings and other structures. It was far and away the largest home in the area, and maybe one of the biggest in the entire commonwealth of Pennsylvania. The estate had once covered hundreds of acres, set on the highest point in the eponymous town.

Fitting for the Barons to look down upon all others.

He had lived here since his birth. The only child of Benjamin and Dorothy Baron. The last married couple to reside here. Their son had never taken a wife.

John Baron had been a tremendous athlete, as well as smart and likable. His future seemed assured—enviable and inevitable.

Until his parents had died on the same night, victims of a horrible accident, or perhaps something else; the jury was still out on that. They left John, then only nineteen, as their sole heir. Though he knew his family was no longer fabulously wealthy, he had believed there was some money left.

Until the lawyer and accountant met with him and informed him that the assets left behind were outweighed by debt by a ratio of twenty to one. Now it was time to pay the piper, and the son would be the one to do it.

Thus, decades ago, Baron had sold off many of the remaining family assets and negotiated as skillfully as he could in a desperate battle to keep the house. However, the estate was buried under such a large mortgage that now most of his income simply went to pay the interest. Like his predecessors, he had also sold additional land around the estate. The hundreds of acres had been whittled down to a few dozen. The outbuildings were mostly in ruins. The mansion was a shabby wreck. When he died, without wife or children, he had no doubt that the bank would swoop in, sell it off, and down it would come, with something modern and fresh to take its place, if Baronville still existed by then.

Even the family cemetery, set far away from the house and surrounded by a six-foot brick wall, might well be dug up and moved.

He looked through the window of his study at land that as a boy he had run happily roamed over. He had a lot of stamina back then, but he could never sprint far enough to outrun the grounds of his home. It had been a both comforting and humbling feeling.

He looked over his shoulder at the walls of books. He had read them all and had managed to keep far more than he thought possible. The rarest volumes had long since been sold to pay bills. There was no point in keeping books if he didn't have a bookcase or a home in which to place them.

He rose, walked over to his desk, and sat down in the chair there. It creaked and groaned under his weight. Everything in this house creaked and groaned when touched.

I creak and groan simply by being alive.

By any measure it was a miserable existence. And one he would have to endure for the rest of his life.

He had had to come home from college to take care of affairs after his parents died. Then he had returned to school on his athletic scholarship, only to blow out his rotator. That was pretty much the death knell for a baseball pitcher. The next year his scholarship was revoked, and, having no funds to continue, he had left without a degree. Repeated attempts at starting a business had failed for want of capital. It seemed that those who had for so long lived under the boot of the Barons now thought it quite pleasing to turn off any aid whatsoever to the last of the family.

Even though other owners had run them for years, when the last mine and mill closed the ousted employees and indeed the entire town blamed only one person for their downfall. Though then only in his late twenties, John Baron had taken the full brunt of the town's displeasure. There was even a petition circulated to change the name of the town. It had failed, probably because the citizens wanted the name to remain so they could keep blaming the Baron family for their problems.

John Baron had become a pariah. He should have moved. Just walked away from the house and the town and this miserable excuse for a life. Yet he hadn't. He wasn't sure if it was stubbornness or lunacy or a potent mixture of both. Yet something in his head had prevented him from chucking it all and starting somewhere fresh. And things in your head could be very powerful, he had found.

Finally, he had sold enough property and paid down enough bills to allow himself to live here, not in any comfort, but just to exist, really. Any ambition to do more had faded along with the passage of years.

As he stared out into the nighttime he was thoroughly cognizant that he had royally screwed up what had commenced as a promising life.

And the town had faded right along with him.

Once-occupied homes and businesses sat empty. The mighty mills and mines his ancestor had erected were gone.

Baronville had come into existence as part of John Baron the First's dream for riches. Now the dream had become a nightmare. For all of them.

From his high perch, Baron would often watch the procession of funerals driving slowly to one of the cemeteries in town. The graveyards of the myriad churches had long since been filled. He knew fatal drug overdoses occurred far too frequently. With no hope, people were turning to needles and pills for something to make them forget how desperate their lives had become.

And yet he had also watched moving vans coming in, carrying with them new families with fresh hopes. He didn't know if they were just picking at a hollowed-out carcass. He didn't know if the town had a reasonable shot at a do-over.

But maybe it did.

Though it was fully beyond his control, he carried the demise of his family's creation as a personal failure. And he always would. And anyway, the town would never let him forget that he had indeed failed them.

He rose from behind his desk.

It was too early to go to bed. And he had somewhere he wanted to go. It was sort of a ritual of his, in fact.

He left the house by the kitchen door and entered the six-car garage that had held only one vehicle for the last three decades.

It was the old gardener's pale blue 1968 Suburban. Baron had had to let go all of the few remaining household staff after his parents' deaths, yet he had managed to hold on to the gardener, because there was a lot of property still to keep up. After the land was sold, however, that changed. The gardener, nearly ninety by then, had left his truck to Baron and gone to die in a nearby nursing home, having outlived his wife by several years.

It was fortunate that Baron had been an engineering student in college, with a mind that seemed to know intuitively how any type of mechanical apparatus worked. He had been coaxing life out of the Suburban all this time. Yet, after five decades, he wasn't sure how much life it had left.

Or how much I have left.

He climbed into the Suburban and drove out of the garage. The overhead doors no longer functioned, so he kept them open, with the key to the truck under the visor.

He wound his way down the hill, past the neighborhoods that had sprung up from Baron land and that held the best views in the city, other than his. At least the homes that were still occupied did.

He reached the main road and sped up.

He had money in his pocket. He intended to spend it.

The Mercury Bar was really the only place in town where he felt he could get some peace.

He pulled into a parking space on the street and got out.

He left the tuxedo jacket in the truck. He knew that he was an easy enough target around town without looking too eccentric.

He was a Baron. The last one.

And if his health remained intact, he had maybe thirty more years of this crap to endure. It was no wonder he needed a scotch and soda or two or three of them.

Yet tonight the current John Baron would get more than simply a drink.

12

Baron closed his eyes and inwardly groaned.

He reopened his eyes and kept his hands clasped around his cocktail. It was his—well, he couldn't remember how many he'd had. The previous ones had felt great going down, though.

This one was even better.

And then *they* had come along to spoil it.

"You that dude John Baron, ain't you?"

Baron looked over at the three young men who were standing next to his seat at the bar.

The young female bartender nervously wiped out a glass and watched the confrontation.

Baron lifted the glass to his lips, took a sip, and let the smooth scotch cut by soda work its way down his throat. He set the glass down and said, "I am. Is there an issue?"

The men were dressed in dirty jeans, T-shirts, and oversized sneakers with no laces, and two of them wore Pittsburgh Steelers caps.

The first man, the largest of the trio, grinned maliciously. "An issue? Man, we ain't got issues. But maybe you got some stuff hanging over you."

"Such as?"

"Your damn family screwing this whole town."

"And exactly how did they do that?"

"Closed the mines. Shut down the mills."

"After running them for decades and providing employment for much of the town? Probably for your parents. And grandparents.

And great-grandparents." He took another sip of his drink. "Thus I see no evidence that we *screwed* anybody."

"You ain't give me no job," said the man.

"I didn't know it was my job to give you a job," replied Baron.

The second man spoke up. "You live up in that big house on the hill. Think you're better'n we are."

"I can assure you that not only do I not think I'm better than anyone, I *know* that I'm not. As for the big house, looks can definitely be deceiving."

"My mom says you got old coins and jewels up there. She said you just pretend to be poor."

Baron turned to look at him. "*Pretend* to be poor? Who the hell would do that? Would you?" He looked at the other two men. "Or you?"

"Mom says you folks are inbred. Marry your sister and stuff. Screws up your mind. So maybe you *would* pretend to be poor."

"Well, I don't have a sister. And I'm not married. And I'm not pretending to be poor. So strike three and you're out."

"Don't think so," said the first man. He shoved Baron so hard he nearly toppled from his stool.

The bartender said, "Hey, don't make me call the cops. Leave him alone."

"You gonna let a girl fight your battles?" said the second man in a sneering tone.

"I'm warning you," said the bartender, her hand on her cell phone.

The man pushed Baron again. "You gonna do that? Hide behind a girl, asshole?"

Baron threw the rest of his drink in the man's face.

"No, I'm really not," he said, standing up and towering over them.

His face dripping with scotch and soda, the man swung his fist at Baron, who caught it and wrenched it up and then behind the man's back.

He gave him a hard push and sent him sprawling on the floor.

Baron blocked the blow from the second man and lashed out with his fist, catching him on the chin.

But the third man kidney-punched Baron from behind and he staggered and fell down against the bar.

The other two men jumped up and started punching and kicking him. There were other people in the bar, but none of them tried to stop the pounding Baron was taking.

Except one.

"FBI!"

Amos Decker had his weapon pointed at the men.

They all froze.

"Get away from him. Now!" barked Decker, who had just walked in to see this beating. After the men retreated, he glanced at Baron. "You okay?"

Baron, his lip bloody and his right eye puffy, struggled up and managed to stand while holding on to the bar, clutching at his side.

He rubbed his hand along his back and stretched. "No permanent damage, it seems," he said, though he did wince in pain.

"He threw his drink in my face," said the first man. "He started it."

The bartender said, "No he didn't. You jerks did."

Decker snapped, "And it's three on one and you guys are half his age?"

"You needn't detain them," said Baron.

"What?" said Decker.

Baron next looked at the bartender, who had started to punch in 911 on her phone. "You don't have to do that. These young men are obviously a bit intoxicated. I'm sure they meant no harm."

"I'm pretty sure they meant a lot of harm," countered Decker. "To you."

Baron held up his hand. "Nevertheless, it really won't do any good to have them arrested. And it might do far more bad."

"You sure?"

"Quite sure, thank you."

Decker glared at the men. "You so much as think about touching this guy, your asses are mine. Do you understand?"

The largest of them glared at Decker as he wiped scotch from his eyes. "Whatever."

Decker holstered his gun, marched forward, grabbed him by his shirt, and slammed him up against the wall. "No, not 'whatever.' *Do you understand*?"

"I understand, I understand, okay? Shit!"

Decker let him go and pushed him toward the exit. "Now clear out!"

The three men slowly left, each of them looking back at Decker and Baron before the last one slammed the door behind him.

Decker looked at Baron. "What was that all about?"

"Didn't you hear?"

"No, I apparently came in too late."

"Well, the gist of it was that the town is going to hell and it's my fault."

"Okay," said Decker slowly.

"It's not the first time I've heard it, and it's doubtful it will be the last."

"So people here hold grudges, I take it?"

"People here hold many things. Can I buy you a drink as a way of thanks?"

Decker sat down at the bar and Baron resumed his seat.

He put out a hand. "Formal introductions. I'm John Baron the Fourth."

Decker shook his hand. "Amos Decker. I take it the town is named after your family?"

"You would be correct in that, yes. It used to be a good thing, actually. A point of pride. It no longer is, I'm afraid. Well, I suppose you saw that for yourself."

The bartender said, "Whatever you want, it's on the house, John. And here, take this." She handed him a plastic baggie of ice, which he placed against the bruise on his face.

"Very kind of you, Cindi," said Baron, smiling at her. He ordered a fresh scotch and soda. Decker asked for a beer.

"Here on business?" asked Baron.

"Vacation."

Baron looked bemused. "You actually came here for...pleasure?"

"My partner has family here. She's visiting. I tagged along. We're staying with them."

Baron took a sip of his drink. "And where is your partner now?"

"Back at the house. I wasn't ready to go to sleep."

"And are you enjoying our little paradise?"

"Can't say that I am, actually. Maybe it has to do with a bunch of murders."

Baron nodded thoughtfully. "I heard about that. Sounded pretty awful. But hard times lead to bad things."

"That's your explanation?"

"I don't have an explanation. I'm just slowly becoming drunk and jabbering away."

"Do you do that often?"

"I don't have much else to do. I come here for about an hour once a week, and then I go home and never leave until I come back here, except to run a short errand or two. And I really have no obligations or responsibilities to get in the way of that little routine."

"Lucky you."

"Maybe not so lucky, actually. So, when you came in you called out, 'FBI.' Are you a special agent or was that just hyperbole?"

"I'm just a regular cop, but I work with the Bureau."

"Where are you from?"

"Burlington, Ohio. Rust Belt town like this one."

"Indeed. And have you been reading into the town's history and my family's culpability in its demise?"

"A little."

"It's partly true, you know. The town was created because my ancestor, after whom I'm named, discovered a particularly rich vein of coal. Much of it went to Pittsburgh for the blast furnaces in the steel mills. That was why he built coal and coke plants too. And after that he built textile mills. And then he discovered natural gas. He also ran many other businesses and actually owned much of Baronville. In fact, most of the town was in his employ back then. A regular Energizer Bunny of an entrepreneur, with far more luck and capitalistic drive than his family has experienced since."

"I heard about all the businesses he built. But I hadn't heard about the steel component."

Baron nodded. "The coke used in making steel is derived from coal after it undergoes a distillation process. And back then coal was abundant and relatively cheap. Steel magnates flourished, and so did those who supplied their enterprises. In that regard John Baron Sr. was following a tried-and-true formula. He was a ruthless man, so I understand. He crushed unions, paid off corrupt politicians, polluted rivers and the air and the ground. He paid his workers as little as he possibly could and treated people in general as badly as he could. He made an immense fortune and his descendants sponged off that accomplishment."

"But then it all came tumbling down?"

"It almost always comes tumbling down. America, in general, doesn't like economic dynasties. Families like the Rockefellers are the exception rather than the rule. We each pull ourselves up by our own bootstraps. Or at least that's how the theory is supposed to work. I guess there are enough people on the Forbes List who inherited their money to lay waste to that supposition."

"But your family still had money?"

"Some. At least for a time."

"Did you know any of the people murdered?"

Baron looked over at him with a curious expression. "That's quite an abrupt segue. Why do you ask?"

"I'm a cop. I ask questions in the hope of solving crimes."

"Who were the victims again?"

Decker told him. "The last two have not been identified yet."

"I can't say that I know any of them."

However, Decker noticed the man's hesitation.

"You sure about that?"

Baron held up his drink. "I'm hardly ever sure of anything. Especially in the Mercury Bar."

Decker glanced at the bartender, who was listening intently to their conversation while pretending to wipe down the bar. She was quite beautiful, with shoulder-length blonde hair and a tall, lean figure outfitted in black jeans and a sleeveless blouse revealing wiry tanned arms.

Decker looked back at Baron. "You really come here once a week?"

"There's hardly any other place to go." He glanced at the bartender. "And I prefer the company here."

The woman smiled at this, caught Decker staring at her, and quickly turned her attention to putting dirty glasses into a dishwasher behind the bar.

"Can I get your address?"

"Why?" asked Baron.

"I may want to talk to you again."

"Why?"

"I already told you. I'm a cop trying to solve a crime."

"Well, then look to the highest spot in town and you will see the biggest, ugliest home. FYI, the doorbell does not work and I don't get up early."

Baron drained his glass and inclined his head at the bartender and slid some cash across to pay for the drinks. "Thank you, Cindi. See you next time." He patted Decker on the shoulder. "And thank you, Mr. Decker, for saving my ass."

He walked unsteadily away.

"Hey, are you okay to drive?" Decker called after him.

Baron turned, gave a low bow, and held up a hand. "I am absolutely not okay to drive, but I will make a valiant attempt regardless, considering the odds are very good that whatever I might hit will have my family's name engraved upon it, which will lessen my legal liability."

Decker watched him go for a few moments and then turned back to the bartender.

Only she was gone too.

13

FILES. AND MORE files.

Paper bones with very little meat.

Decker dropped the last of them on a pile in the middle of the desk, sat back, and breathed in the stale air that seemed to permeate Baronville's police headquarters on Baron Boulevard. Right next door was Baronville City Hall.

Jamison sat across from him taking notes. Decker, with his perfect memory, never needed to do that. He idly watched her pen gliding over the paper. The door opened a moment later and Detective Green came in.

"Any luck?" he asked as he popped a stick of gum into his mouth.

Jamison finished the sentence she was writing and looked up.

Decker closed his eyes. "Joyce Tanner and Toby Babbot were unemployed. Michael Swanson was a drug dealer. Bradley Costa was an SVP at a bank. And they all lived alone. No family. Tanner had been married but subsequently got divorced."

Green closed the door behind him. "Yeah, well, that we already knew."

Decker opened his eyes. "What was Babbot's disability?" He glanced at Green, who was taking a seat across from him.

"The file just said he was disabled," pointed out Jamison. "It didn't say how or why."

"Is that relevant?" asked Green.

"Everything is relevant until you can show it's not," said Decker.

"I'll check." Green leaned back in his chair. "So, nothing really jumped out at you?" he asked.

Before either Decker or Jamison could answer, the door opened again and Lassiter came in. She was dressed in a beige jacket and knee-length skirt with chunky heels. Her hair was loose around her shoulders.

"So, have I missed anything at the powwow?" she asked, taking a seat next to Green.

"Not much," said her partner. "Just a follow-up question that may or may not be 'relevant.'"

Decker stared at the opposite wall. "I met John Baron last night."

Jamison looked surprised by this but kept silent.

Decker continued, "Some young punks were roughing him up. I intervened. But he declined to press charges. Any idea why?"

"Guilt, maybe," replied Green.

"About what?" asked Jamison.

"It's complicated," said Lassiter.

"I've got lots of time," replied Decker. "I'm technically on vacation." He clasped his hands in front of him and studied her with an expectant expression.

Lassiter looked uncomfortably at Green and said, "Okay, the Baron family basically exploited this place and then sold out to companies that eventually shuttered everything. They lived in great luxury high up on the hill, while the rest of the town suffered and slowly died. And we're still dying."

"Did the present John Baron have anything to do with that?" asked Decker.

Lassiter shook her head. "No. He was in college when his parents died. But he's lived up there ever since."

"So why blame him?" asked Jamison.

"He's a *Baron*," interjected Green.

"So guilt by association?" said Jamison.

"I'm not saying it's right or fair, I'm just saying that's how it is," replied Green. "I've personally got nothing against the guy. He never hurt me or anyone I cared about."

"Lucky you," said Lassiter.

Jamison looked at her. "Did he hurt someone you cared about?"

Lassiter put up a hand. "It has nothing to do with anything."

Green added with a glance at Decker, "And to paraphrase you, I don't see how this little trip into the sordid history of Baronville is helping us solve six murders."

Decker said, "I asked Baron if he knew any of the vics and he said he didn't."

"Well, other than maybe the banker, I wouldn't imagine he would," observed Lassiter. "A street-level drug dealer doesn't exactly run in the same circles as a Baron."

Decker said, "Even though you claim he moves in different 'circles,' maybe he *does* know Swanson or one of the others."

"So you didn't believe his answer?" asked Green sharply.

"I don't believe anyone, *initially*," replied Decker.

"Okay, but do you have any *helpful* thoughts?" Green indicated the pile of files.

"We need to run through all the vics again, because I believe they have to be connected," said Decker.

"We already did that," protested Green.

"Fresh eyes," countered Decker. "We'll need the keys to all their places."

"But we haven't even identified the last two," pointed out Lassiter.

"But you have the other four."

Green said in a disappointed tone, "I guess it was wishful thinking, but I thought you Feds would swoop in and solve this sucker overnight."

"Did your partner fill you in on your ME's time-of-death and other related screw-ups?" asked Decker.

Green looked a bit sheepish. "Yeah, she did. Blowflies and livor mortis. That was a good catch, actually. We're looking at it all again."

"Great, while you're doing that, let me throw you *another* bone so you feel like we're *swooping* onto something."

"What bone?" asked Lassiter.

"Ask your ME to check to see if the 'nonhuman' blood found at the crime scene is *pig's* blood. I think he can probably do that without screwing it up."

"Pig's blood?" exclaimed Green. "Why in the world would you think that?"

"You watch any old cop shows?"

"What, you mean *Law & Order*?" asked Green.

"Farther back than that."

"What does that have to do with anything?" asked Lassiter.

"It might have everything to do with it," replied Decker.

CHAPTER

14

Pig's blood?" said Jamison as they drove down the street.

"Just a shot in the dark. Let's see how it plays out."

"You didn't tell me you met with John Baron last night."

"Well, now you know."

"What was he like?"

"Tall, lean, thick graying hair, in his fifties. Good-looking guy. Elegant, like a movie star or model. And erudite, with a formal way of speaking. But he's handy with a quip. And even though the punks were a lot younger than he was, it looks like he tagged a couple of them before they got the upper hand. So the guy can fight."

"He was really attacked at the bar?"

"Three idiots who apparently have a grudge against the Barons."

"Well, if Lassiter is any indication, the whole town seems to hold a grudge. Do you really think their surname is *Baron*? That seems coincidental."

"I really haven't looked into that, nor do I care," replied Decker.

"Do you actually believe Baron's involved in the murders?"

"I have no idea. But when I asked him if he knew any of the vics, I didn't believe his answer."

"Why?"

"My gut."

"Well, your gut has proven pretty accurate."

"Good thing, since I have such a big one."

"Pretty fast with a quip yourself. So where to?"

"Joyce Tanner's place. We'll take them one at a time."

* * *

Joyce Tanner's "place" was a basement apartment in a rickety wooden building that looked as though a strong gust of wind might bring it down.

Green had provided Decker with a key.

"Surprised Green and Lassiter didn't insist on coming," observed Jamison as they gazed around the small front room.

"As Green not so subtly intimated, I think they're disappointed we haven't already solved it. I don't think they want to waste any more time with us. And Lassiter didn't even want us involved in the first place."

"That may have changed. I seemed to connect with her. But, boy, she really doesn't like the Baron family."

"Based on what I saw last night, I doubt you'd find many here that do like the past or present Barons. There were about twenty people in the bar last night and not one of them did anything to help the guy. Didn't even take out their phones to call the cops." He paused. "Except for the bartender. She seemed to like him. And he definitely liked her."

"Place looks pretty tidy," noted Jamison, gazing around.

"They've already dusted for prints, so no need for latex gloves. Let's get to it."

* * *

"Not much here," opined Jamison after they finished searching. "I wonder what will happen to her personal belongings?"

"Green said she has a distant cousin in Kentucky coming in."

"A bit after the fact."

"Apparently it's her only family. She and her ex divorced a long time ago and he left the area. They had no kids."

He sat on the bed and looked around. What Decker liked more

than anything else was to use his prodigious memory to spot inconsistencies. It was almost like placing a template over some fresh material. If something, no matter how seemingly insignificant, didn't match, he would be able to spot it.

Yet somehow that method had failed him here.

But other assets he possessed had not. Like common sense.

"Green said she'd been living here for about a year," he noted.

"Right."

"The file also said she got laid off from JC Penney six months ago and had been unemployed ever since."

"Right again."

"So how did she pay her rent and other expenses? Her unemployment check couldn't cover all of it. And if she had a bunch of money in savings, I doubt she'd be living in a place like this. And the file said her retail job offered no severance."

"And she had a car. So there was gas, insurance, and expenses like that," added Jamison. "You think someone was helping her?"

"Well, I don't know that someone *wasn't* helping her. And this looks like the sort of place that if your rent check was late, your ass is out on the street. Trust me, I've lived in places like that."

"So have I."

"Let's check out her ride," Decker said.

The vehicle, a twelve-year-old gray Nissan, was parked on the street.

Decker used a key that Green had given him to open the car door.

"She was a smoker," said Jamison, as she waved her hand in front of her face in an attempt to dispel the stench. "You could probably get lung cancer just by sitting in here for a few days."

Decker had squeezed his big body into the driver's seat of the compact car and was looking around.

Jamison noted a pair of fuzzy dice hanging from the rearview mirror.

"Think she was into gambling?"

"Lots of people have fuzzy dice who never rolled a pair for real," said Decker.

"I was just kidding."

"From what Green and Lassiter could find out, the last time anyone saw her was three days before her death."

"A lot can happen in three days."

"I also wonder how she was paying her credit card bill."

Jamison said, "So again perhaps a secret source of money? Maybe it's tied to her murder. Drugs? That would connect her to Swanson at least."

They climbed out of the car and Decker walked around it. He stopped and knelt next to the rear passenger tire. He used the car key to dig something out of the tread. He finally freed the object and held it up.

"A nail," said Jamison.

"More precisely, it's a framing nail, that they use in a powered nail gun."

"She could have picked that up anywhere at any time."

"Don't think so. Look at the tire."

With the nail removed, it was already deflating. They could hear air escaping.

"It's not rusted or anything. And if it had been there a while and she had driven on it, the nail would have worked itself through the surface of the tread and the tire would have started leaking and then gone flat. And this tire looks newer than the others. The inspection sticker on the windshield shows that she had it inspected this month. I bet the tire didn't pass inspection and she had to replace it with this one."

"Okay, but she still could have picked up the nail anywhere, like the parking lot of a hardware store."

"Possibly, but these nails are set in a strip carrier, sort of like an ammo belt on a machine gun. They don't just fall out."

Jamison took a picture of the tire and nail with her phone. "Anything else?"

"Tanner's car is here, so that means she got to the house where her body was found another way, unless whoever killed her drove it back here."

"Maybe she went in her killer's car?"

"Or did she go separately? Maybe with Toby Babbot?"

"Decker, the police can show no connection between those two."

"You're wrong, they have one very strong connection."

"What's that?"

"They died together."

CHAPTER

15

BEFORE HE WAS murdered, Toby Babbot didn't live in a house or an apartment. He resided in an old dented mobile home trailer a few miles outside of town. The road in was part gravel and part dirt, and the small plot of yellowed grass surrounding the trailer was encircled by trees.

Jamison pulled their SUV to a stop in front of the trailer and they got out.

Decker immediately pulled his gun. "Someone's inside," he whispered to Jamison, who also drew her weapon.

Decker had glimpsed a shadow pass in front of one of the trailer's windows.

"Do you think there's a back door?" asked Jamison as they approached.

The next moment they heard someone running away from the rear of the trailer.

"I guess that answers that," said Decker as he raced toward the dwelling, Jamison hard on his heels.

They reached the corner of the structure and stopped for a few moments, scanning the area behind it.

"There!" barked Jamison, pointing toward the right side of the thick woods.

She and Decker reached the tree line and plunged ahead. Though Decker was big and bulky and not in the best of shape, he maneuvered around the trees with a surprising nimbleness. Only he had lost sight of the person and stopped so abruptly that Jamison ran into him.

Gasping, Decker looked around. The sounds of the person running seemed to echo from all directions.

"Where did he go?" said Jamison.

Decker shook his head. "Lost him."

They heard a car door slam shut and an engine roar to life.

Decker once again sprinted forward, yet he broke free of the trees only in time to see twin taillights disappearing down another gravel road.

Jamison joined him a few moments later. They were both bent over sucking in air.

Regaining her breath, Jamison said, "I will never pull your chain again about not being in shape."

Decker straightened and muttered, "Well, I wasn't fast enough to catch the person. I couldn't even see if it was a man or a woman. And I got zip on the vehicle, not even a letter on the license plate." He kicked a rusty old can lying on the ground.

"Decker, we did all we could."

"Let's at least see if we can find out what they were looking for," he grumbled, stalking off toward the trailer.

They went in through the rear door.

"No forced entry here. And the front door didn't look damaged either."

"So it was either open or the person had a key," reasoned Jamison.

Inside, the place didn't look like it had been searched. Yet there was stuff everywhere, neatly stacked on tables, chairs, counters, and the floor.

"Pack rat," said Decker knowingly. "But when you don't have a lot, you don't throw anything away."

"Green said they got no prints from here other than Babbot's."

"So no visitors, unless they wore gloves."

"Well, the place just had a visitor," Jamison pointed out.

When they were finished searching, Decker leaned against the wall in the tiny kitchen. "No grab bars or special toilet in the bath. No wheelchair access. But a bunch of empty bottles for prescription painkillers. So what was his disability?"

"Green said he was going to check."

"If it were obvious he wouldn't have to check. And where's the guy's car?"

Jamison looked out the front window. "Maybe he didn't have one."

"He did at some point. There are wheel ruts in the dirt. He probably parked in the same spot every time. And there are old empty cans of Valvoline motor oil behind the trailer."

"Maybe Babbot drove his car to the house where his body was found."

"If he did, that should have been in the file. Since it wasn't I'm assuming that's not what happened."

Decker went back over to a table built into the wall halfway between the kitchen and the front room.

There was a large pad of graph paper on it.

He sat down at the table and looked at the pad. "I wonder what this is for?"

Jamison joined him and stared down at the paper.

"I used something like that when I would do my math homework in high school, but my pad was a lot smaller."

Decker bent down and looked more closely at the top sheet. "There are impressions on it."

"You mean from whatever was written on the sheet above it?"

Decker nodded. "I think so."

He carefully tore off the sheet and handed it to Jamison, who slid it into a plastic evidence pouch she had brought from the SUV and then placed it into her bag.

Decker picked up some magazines from a table and flipped through them. He did the same with some books on a small shelf. "Babbot had an interesting mix of reading tastes," he said. "From porn to mechanical to guns to history to conspiracy theories."

"Sounds just like a lot of America," said Jamison impishly.

Decker next picked up an empty prescription bottle from the kitchen counter. "And unfortunately, this is a lot of America." He eyed the label. "This was Percocet. But there were other empty bottles for Vicodin, OxyContin, Tylox, and Demerol. All potent stuff."

"And all addictive. Overmedicating. It's one reason we have an opioid crisis."

"Dr. Freedman," he said, reading off the prescription label. "That was the name on the other bottles."

"Then Freedman might know about the disability," replied Jamison.

Decker looked around. "I wonder how long Babbot lived here? He was on disability. It doesn't exactly pay enough to allow you to live in luxury. And if he had to move recently because his bills were adding up, we could at least have a shot at talking to a neighbor. They might be able to tell us something helpful about Babbot. Green will probably have that information."

He looked out the rear window at the trees and grumbled, "Here all we have are squirrels and deer."

"What was that?" said Jamison suddenly.

Decker looked at her. "What?"

"Thought I heard something. At the front of the trailer."

They went over to the front window and looked out. It was very dark now.

"I don't see anything," said Decker.

"Might have been an animal."

He sniffed the air. "You smell that?"

Jamison took a whiff. "Smoke?"

"Fire," said Decker.

They ran to the front door. Decker grabbed the knob and turned it. But the door didn't budge.

They looked at each other.

"The noise I heard?" said Jamison.

Decker ran to the back door and tried to open it.

"Both doors are jammed," he called out.

There was a whoosh and one end of the trailer erupted in flames. They burst from the floor and quickly ignited the walls and ceiling.

"Oh my God!" screamed Jamison. "Decker!"

Decker was looking around as the flames crept closer.

Books and magazines were bursting into flames. The air was thick with smoke. Jamison started coughing violently. They backed away from the approaching fire but there was no way out.

Before they'd come inside, Decker had glimpsed a propane tank attached to the back side of the trailer about halfway along the frame. Once the flames hit that, the whole thing was going to go up.

The smoke was so heavy now he could barely see Jamison. The windows were far too small to crawl through, but he used a chair to smash one open anyway, leaned his head out, and gulped in some fresh air.

He pulled his gun and shot out the front door lock. He tried the door. It still wouldn't budge.

"Alex, get on my back."

"What?" gasped Jamison.

"Piggyback. Now!"

She jumped onto his back and locked her legs around his waist.

"Keep your head down," he bellowed.

He backed up, got a running start, and smashed right into the door.

It buckled and partially gave way. He put his shoulder down, set his legs into a squat and erupted forward again. The door came off its hinges and fell into the yard.

The next moment Decker was stumbling to their Yukon with Jamison still clinging to his back.

Decker looked behind him. The flames had reached the front door—or where the door had been. That was about the midpoint of the trailer.

That meant they had maybe a few seconds.

Breathing heavily now, he carried Jamison behind the SUV. Then he dropped to his knees, and Jamison hopped off him.

"Get under the truck, Alex, now!" he gasped.

He helped push her under the Yukon until just her feet were exposed. Decker was too big to fit under the vehicle. He covered her feet with his body.

The next instant, the flames reached the propane tank.

The resulting explosion lifted the trailer entirely off its cin-derblock foundation, pieces of it flying in all directions. Objects came down and hit the big Yukon, which had been buffeted by the concussive force of the detonation. Decker heard the windshield crack. Something punched into the vehicle's roof.

Jamison screamed.

Decker could not seem to catch his breath. His chest was tight-ening. It felt like a huge weight dead center of his broad chest.

Shit! Am I having a heart attack? Now?

The next instant something dropped from the sky and struck him in the head.

Everything went black for Amos Decker.

CHAPTER

16

It was a new color.

Yellow.

Blue meant death in his synesthetic brain.

So what the hell did yellow mean?

Heaven?

Am I dead?

He couldn't seem to open his eyes, so maybe he was.

Yet the fact that his eyes weren't open and he could still see the color yellow meant that he was viewing it in his head. Was that evidence of conscious thought and thus life?

Or was it his *afterlife*?

He felt something. A poke, a prod. It seemed distant and distinct from him.

His ears hurt. But he could sense something there too.

He was vaguely aware of a loud sound. Like a cannon going off.

He could feel nothing else about himself. Just the sound. And the color yellow.

And the poke and the prod.

The sensation in his ears continued. Growing in intensity.

Something hit his face. Lightly, then harder.

He tried to open his eyes, but the only thing he seemed able to manage was to scrunch up his forehead.

The next blow on his face did the trick.

With a monumental effort, he managed to blink.

At first all he saw was darkness.

Then he glimpsed something in the middle of that darkness. It was hairy and close to him; he could smell its breath.

Then his eyes closed again. He seemed to sink into the ground.

He remembered now. They had been out in the woods.

The trailer.

The trailer had exploded.

Then Decker stopped thinking. His chest stopped rising.

He had a moment's sensation of the hairy creature's breaths coming closer.

An animal. An animal come to feast on him.

He dropped into unconsciousness. He dropped into something maybe more than that.

Right before everything went black again he felt his mouth being prodded open. And then something hit him right below his chest.

Black.

He had no idea how much time had passed.

He felt himself jerk up and then fall to the side. He vomited and lay there moaning for a few seconds.

He felt something on his arm and pushed it away violently. Then Decker got to his knees and tried to scramble away.

He thought of the hairy creature. The pokes and prods. The breath. The blow to his chest. He was scared. Terrified. Was it a bear?

"Amos!"

At the sound of her voice Decker stopped scrambling, turned, and dropped to his butt, panting.

Jamison was on her haunches a few feet away. She looked dirty and disheveled, but unhurt. Yet there was such a look of terror in her features that Decker could only gape.

"A-Alex, are you okay?"

She rose on unsteady feet. "Me? You...stopped breathing. I had to perform CPR."

Decker touched his lips and then his sternum.

CPR?

That had been Jamison breathing and pounding life back into him.

"That was you? I just saw…hair. I thought it was an animal. A big, hairy animal."

Jamison frowned and pushed her thick hair out of her face. "Well, that's the first time I've been equated with a big, hairy animal." Her features softened. "Are you feeling okay now?"

Decker took a deep breath and rubbed the back of his head. When he took his hand away, it was bloody. "I felt something hit me back there. I guess it did some damage."

"Oh no," exclaimed Jamison. She took out her phone, engaged the flashlight feature, and examined the back of his head. "It's cut, a deep gash. You need medical attention."

She pulled some tissues from her bag and pressed them against the wound. "Here, hold that there."

Decker did so. "I thought I'd had a heart attack, but I don't think that's possible. I'd be out for the count."

He slowly rose to his feet and looked around. The trailer was gone. Their Yukon was heavily damaged.

"You saved my life," he said.

"Well, you certainly saved mine." She pointed at where the trailer had been. "That would have been our crematorium."

He nodded and took a series of long, deep breaths. "It must have been all that smoke in my lungs. And then running."

"With me on your back. And then your head wound. It must have been debris from the explosion that hit you. I wish you could have fit under the car."

"Even when I was thinner I really never could have fit under even an SUV."

"We need to call an ambulance."

"We need to call somebody if we want to get back to town." He looked at the two front tires of the Yukon. They were flat and the wheels were pushed in. "And the fire department needs to come out here and douse those flames before the forest catches on fire."

Jamison pulled out her phone and called Green, succinctly explaining to him what had happened. The detective promised a response ASAP.

She put the phone away and looked back at the trailer. "Somebody really wanted us dead."

"That's actually a good thing."

"What do you mean?" she said, looking horrified by his words.

"It means we're making somebody nervous. Which means we're heading in the right direction. Which *is* a good thing."

"It wouldn't be so good if we were dead!" snapped Jamison.

"Do you have the graph paper?"

"What?"

The graph paper from the house?"

"My God, Decker, we were nearly killed. And you apparently *did* die. And all you can think about is the case?"

When he didn't say anything, she sighed, pulled out the graph paper from the evidence pouch in her bag, and handed it to him.

With the tissues stuck to his head, Decker laid the paper on the ground and used the flashlight feature on his cell phone to go over it. He held the light an inch from the paper and still had to squint to make things out.

"See anything?" she asked.

"Just impressions from the pencil or pen he used to draw something on the sheet above this one. It looks to be pretty large. It covers most of the sheet. I'll take a better look at it when we have some decent light."

He clicked off the phone light, handed the paper back to Jamison, rose, and leaned against the truck bumper.

Jamison said, "Do you think whoever it was we chased came back and tried to kill us?"

"I don't know. Could be, but that would have been a risk."

"So maybe somebody else? Do you think we were followed?"

Decker looked back at the dirt and gravel road. "It would have been hard for anyone to follow us here without us seeing them."

She looked back at the trailer. "Good thing we went over that before it disappeared. Though we didn't find anything, really."

"We found some things."

"Like what?"

He suddenly clutched his head and groaned.

"Decker, what is it?" asked Jamison anxiously.

"Just the mother of all headaches."

A few minutes later two police cars, an ambulance, and two fire engines showed up.

The firemen dealt with the trailer, dousing it and the surrounding area with water. Two EMTs checked out Jamison and Decker. She had some bumps and bruises and some smoke inhalation. They treated her and gave her oxygen. They did the same with Decker, but after examining his head wound and testing his cognitive responses, they insisted that he go to the hospital for an X-ray and other tests.

"I don't have a concussion," said Decker. "At least not a bad one."

Jamison admonished, "Decker, you stopped breathing. So you're *going* to the hospital. I'll ride with you in the ambulance."

As they drove off, Decker lay back on the gurney with a bloody bandage wrapped around his head. Jamison had wiped her dirty face and tried to get some stains off her clothes with a clean wet cloth that one of the EMTs had given her.

"I'm going to have to get some new clothes. When packing for this trip, I didn't account for being nearly drowned in a monsoon and then almost blown up." She leaned back against the interior wall of the ambulance and closed her eyes while Decker stared at her from the gurney.

Decker said quietly, "So, Alex, are you enjoying it?"

She opened her eyes and gave him a bewildered look. "Enjoying *what*?"

"Your vacation."

17

Green said, "He had a metal plate put in his head from an industrial accident."

Decker was in the process of being discharged from the hospital. Despite his protests to the contrary, he *had* suffered a concussion. They had determined that his heart had stopped due to a combination of the blow to the head and smoke inhalation. In lieu of sutures they had glued his scalp back together, and consequently his hair stuck up like a cockatoo's feathers. He also had on dark glasses because of the concussion.

"I feel like I have a metal plate in *my* head," groused Decker.

Green was walking beside the wheelchair taking Decker to a new rental truck Jamison had arranged. She was behind the wheelchair pushing Decker along.

"So Toby Babbot's disability was brain-related?" asked Jamison.

"Appears to be. His employment history had been spotty since then. A few menial jobs. Living on unemployment. When that ran out he got on partial disability. But it didn't pay much."

"And where did he live before he moved to the trailer?" asked Decker.

"He shared a house with a woman, Betsy O'Connor. Strictly platonic, at least that's what she claimed when I talked to her last week."

"What was the connection?" asked Jamison.

"They knew each other. Both fell on hard times. They couldn't afford the place separately, but they could together. It actually happens a lot here."

"So why did he move out?" asked Decker.

"Couldn't keep a job, and while O'Connor worked a number of jobs, her salary alone couldn't cover the rent and utilities. They lost the house and had to split up. She lives in an apartment on the east side of town with two other roommates. And Babbot apparently found that abandoned trailer in the woods and moved in there. Not sure if he lived anywhere else in between residing with O'Connor and then at the trailer."

"Did he have a car?"

"He did. But he lost it to the bank."

"So how'd he get around?" asked Jamison.

"I don't know."

"How do you think he got to the house where he was found dead with Joyce Tanner?" asked Jamison.

"Maybe his killer took him there."

As they reached the new rental, Decker stood up, though he was still a bit shaky. Green put a supportive arm around him.

"You sure you're okay? Maybe you should spend the night in the hospital."

"I'm good. I'm actually hungry. I'll be fine after I eat."

"I can recommend a place over on Baron Square. The Little Eatery. Good food and not pricey. Not that we really have pricey here."

"Baron Square, huh?" said Jamison. "You just can't get away from the name, can you?"

"I'd have to move," said Green, smiling. "Oh, and I had our arson guy check out the trailer. Don't know what was used to lock you both in, that's long since gone. But he found remnants of something like a Molotov cocktail and a pile of dry wood under the trailer that showed evidence of being the point of origin of the fire. Even with all the rain we had, that wood would have gone up in an instant. And that trailer was really old. Doubt it would pass fire code these days."

Jamison drove them to her sister's house, where they cleaned up and regrouped downstairs about thirty minutes later. Even though it was nearly nine, Frank Mitchell was still at work and Amber and

Zoe were at a school event. Jamison had not told her sister what had happened to them. She checked her watch. "It's getting late. I hope they're still serving."

As they headed to the truck, she noted that he had taken his glasses off. "The doctor said for you to keep the glasses on."

"He also told me to sit in a dark room in complete quiet. I've had concussions before, Alex. This one is no big deal."

"Okay," she said, not looking convinced. They drove along in silence for a few minutes. "Decker, with all the years you played football, do you ever worry about...?"

"What, CTE, dementia?"

"Well, yeah."

"Every game I played I came out of it feeling like I'd been in a car accident. Every play helmets would smack together. It is what it is. I can't do anything about what might be coming for me."

"Pretty fatalistic attitude."

"Pretty *realistic* attitude. But the good thing is I barely played in the pros, so maybe there's hope for me. NFL players hit a lot harder than college players do."

"I hope you're right. We need that brain of yours to find bad guys."

"We need to put together a list of people to talk to. Dr. Freedman and Betsy O'Connor, and anyone connected to Joyce Tanner. And we need to find out what Tanner was living on. We also need to visit Bradley Costa's workplace and home. And then we need to check out where Michael Swanson called home."

"Look, while I know that we both believe all these murders are connected, we really have no evidence that they are."

He eyed her appraisingly. "Even if they aren't connected, should we stop investigating?"

Jamison looked taken aback. "No, of course not. I'm just saying—"

"I'm just *saying* that if there is one murderer or more than one murderer working together or separately, they still deserve to be held accountable for their crimes. Because I don't know any other way to approach it."

Jamison sighed and nodded. "I get the logic. But it's a long list of people. Could take a while. Longer than a week," she pointed out.

"Could be. You should call Bogart and tell him we might need to extend."

"No, *you* can call him. This was your idea. I just wanted to come here and visit my sister and my niece, not get involved in another murder investigation."

Decker didn't say anything.

"We were almost killed tonight," added Jamison.

"Yeah, I know. I was there, Alex."

"Whoever did it might try again, if we keep going on this."

"I told you I could do it. That you could just hang with your family."

"And I wouldn't sleep a wink if I wasn't doing it with you."

"So where does that leave us?"

"I guess it leaves us investigating a bunch of either separate or connected murders. Together."

Decker turned to her.

"I'm going to do all I can to keep you safe, Alex."

"I know. You promised Zoe."

"No, you're my partner. We have each other's backs. Remember? You told me that before."

"I remember, Amos. And you've already saved my life a bunch of times. But I have to rely on myself as well as you. And the same for you."

"No argument there."

* * *

The Little Eatery was still open and they ate their meal in a half-full dining room, where they continually caught people stealing glances at them.

"Word apparently travels fast in Baronville," noted Jamison.

"Word travels fast in every small town," replied Decker, swallowing the last piece of his steak. "We have a dead guy with a metal plate in his head living on disability in a trailer in the woods that just got blown up. We have Joyce Tanner, unemployed from JC Penney, living on who knows what."

"And four more dead."

Decker looked down at his phone, which had just buzzed. He frowned and put down his fork.

"What is it?" asked Jamison. "Someone else dead?"

"No. It's a text from Green answering my question."

"Which one?"

"Whether it was pig's blood."

"Was it?"

"Yes."

"So what does that mean, since you never bothered to tell me?" she said, clearly irritated.

Decker didn't answer. He punched in a phone number and stared at the ceiling while it rang. Then the person answered.

"Detective Green, this is Decker. I just got your text."

"Right, pig's blood it is. What made you think of it?"

"It was a long shot and I wish I had been wrong. This means we need to check another database for the two dead men in that house."

"We checked all the criminal and civilian databases we have access to."

"I don't think they're civilians or criminals."

"Then what do you think they are?"

"Cops."

CHAPTER

18

W HY COPS?" ASKED Jamison as they were driving to police headquarters.

"You're too young to know it, but in the sixties and seventies
'pig' was a commonly used derogatory term for police. That's why
I mentioned the old cop shows on TV. So the vic in the policeman
uniform coupled with the pig's blood starts to make some sense.
And that might mean we're talking killers from a certain generation."

"Maybe not," countered Jamison. "The term's obviously made
a comeback. It's being used by other groups now."

"Okay, but we have to find out first if the two dead men we
found *were* cops. I could be totally off base with my theory."

"God, this is like a horror show."

"I never ran into a murder that had any positive elements,
Alex."

Decker looked out the window. "If they are cops, you have
to wonder where they're from. They would've been identified by
now if they were local."

"From another state, then?"

"Why would they be here? I'm assuming they were performing
in some professional capacity. Local cops almost never cross state
lines."

He stopped speaking and stared off once more.

"Wait a minute, Decker, are you thinking what I think you are?"

"They could be *Feds*, Alex."

* * *

Green and Lassiter were waiting for them at the station.

"We've run the prints through databases we have access to," said Green. "But it's limited. And we got zero hits."

Decker said, "I can get them run by the FBI. Just get me a set of the digital prints." He looked at Jamison. "I guess I'm going to have that talk with Bogart after all."

"Lucky you," replied Jamison.

Decker called Bogart from the privacy of an empty office at the police station.

To FBI special agent Bogart's credit, he didn't scream or even interrupt as Decker laid out what had happened.

"Can you send me the prints now?" asked Bogart.

"Soon as I hang up with you."

"If they are Feds this is going to turn into a shit storm, Decker."

"It pretty much already is."

Decker and Jamison waited at Green and Lassiter's desks, which were situated next to each other in the open room of the detectives' section of the station. There was one other plainclothesman working at another desk.

Thirty minutes passed and then Decker's phone buzzed. He and Jamison stepped into the empty office to answer it.

It was Bogart.

Decker put it on speaker so that Jamison could hear.

"We ran the prints through our own employee database and got nothing. Then we provided the prints through our liaison office to sister agencies."

"And did they get a hit?"

"No. We heard back from all of them except one."

"Which one?"

"DEA."

"Okay, did you contact them when they didn't get back to you?"

"We did and found out that a DEA special ops team is going to be arriving in Baronville in about two hours."

"So the dead guys *were* with them?" asked Jamison.

"That's the thing—they'll neither confirm nor deny that."

"But if they're sending a team?"

"That could mean a lot of different things. But I've got a buddy over in the D.C. office at DEA. I talked to him before I called you. He said this has gone right up to the DEA director's office. Look, I can jump on an agency plane and be up there in about two hours."

"No, you have enough on your plate."

"And you two *are* supposed to be on vacation."

"I was wondering when you were going to get to that," said Decker.

"I tried to talk him out of it," chimed in Jamison. "But you know Decker can't resist a good murder."

"Seriously, there is something going on here that I don't like," said Bogart.

"There are a lot of things going on here that I don't like, principally a bunch of murdered people. And me and Alex almost ending up roasted."

"I'm going to monitor the situation from here. When the DEA show up they're going to want to talk to you."

"I just don't know how much I have to tell them. It's pretty early yet."

"The point is the DEA will play things close to the vest."

"Just like all our alphabet agency friends," noted Jamison. "Remember the DIA? Talk about zipped lips."

Bogart said, "And if the dead men are two of theirs, they're going to want to take the lead. There might be a turf battle."

Decker said, "I'm just here to find the truth. Somebody else can play the politics."

"Which is why I'm asking *you*, Alex, to play the counterfoil to the DEA. They're going to come in like a tank brigade. They're going to run right over the locals for sure. Just don't let them do that to you. You have the right to be there. You were asked to join the investigation. They can't force you out."

"I'll do my best," she said.

"And if the dynamics on this shift, I can inject the Bureau

into the situation. And we can go toe-to-toe with anybody. Good luck."

Decker put his phone away and looked at Jamison.

He grumbled, "Turf battles and office politics. I hate that crap."

She smiled and said, "So, Decker, are you enjoying *your* vacation yet?"

CHAPTER

19

THE EIGHT-PERSON DEA team blew in with the intensity of a Cat Four hurricane.

It was led by Special Agent Kate Kemper. She introduced herself to Decker and the others with a handshake like a grip of iron and a face set in granite. She was in her midforties, average height, but wiry, with dirty blonde hair and the determined features of a person who had faced many obstacles in life and had overcome them all.

"I need to see the bodies," she said firmly.

Green nodded. "They're in the morgue. Are they yours?"

"Let me see the bodies and then we'll talk. To the extent I can."

Green frowned at this, but nodded. "Let's go for a ride."

The DEA team followed Green, Lassiter, Decker, and Jamison over to the morgue.

Inside, the drawers were opened and the metal beds rolled out.

The sheets were lifted and Kemper stared down at the first man, and then the second.

Decker watched her closely while she did this.

"Thank you," she said to the ME. "We will be taking possession of the remains." She turned to Green. "And we will be taking over this investigation."

Green said, "You can work it and I can't stop you. But you can't stop us from working on it."

Kemper took out her phone. "I sure as hell can. With one call."

Green looked ready to protest when Jamison intervened.

"Look, this is going to be a long, complicated investigation with many moving parts. It seems to me that the better path is to marshal all of the assets that we have to tackle this sucker." She looked at Kemper. "The DEA can ride point. But the FBI is already engaged and we want to see this through. Baronville has been the scene of six murders now, and to cut the local cops out of investigating the crimes seems like it could turn into a field day for the media. That's not going to help anyone except a network's TV ratings. And that would distract us from finding out who killed these people."

Everyone looked at Kemper to see her reaction to this.

At first it looked like she might be put off by Jamison's words. But then she nodded. "Ground rules: All investigations flow through me. Leads, clues, interview notes, results. DEA is the central clearinghouse."

Decker said, "I believe that all six of the murders are connected. If they are, that means your two guys had to be involved in all of that in some way."

"I don't see how that could be possible," retorted Kemper.

"I think I might," said Decker.

"How?" she shot back.

"First, I need to know how long they had been undercover."

"Who the hell told you they were undercover?" Kemper snapped.

"No one told me."

Jamison said, "Then, Decker, how did you know?"

He looked around at the array of DEA agents. "The FBI makes inquiries about possibly two dead agents. All sister agencies give the FBI a negative response except for yours," he said, indicating Kemper. "Not only did you not respond, the inquiry went right up to the top at DEA and a special team is dispatched almost immediately."

"But the undercover part?" asked Kemper. "They could just be agents."

"Two agents in the normal course of business go missing, you'd know right away. But two *undercover* cops won't be checking in regularly. They go missing, you wouldn't necessarily know unless they missed a check-in with their agency point of contact."

"And how do you know so much about undercover operations?" asked Kemper suspiciously.

"Believe it or not, back when I was a cop in Ohio, I worked undercover. My naturally scruffy appearance seemed to fit right in. And I'm a big guy. Most people bought the fact that I was an enforcer looking for work. And I wouldn't check in for days because the bad guys keep a close watch over you. It's not like you can run off and text the cops every five minutes. You go undercover, you live the role. You're freewheeling. You have to build your cred. You have to breathe with the scum. So what were they doing?"

"No one in this room is cleared to know that other than me and my team," said Kemper sharply.

"Makes it pretty difficult to work together, then," noted Decker.

"I said I was the clearinghouse, not that we would be working the investigation *together*."

Decker looked at Green. "Okay, I guess we just investigate the other four murders, which are not officially part of DEA's pissing contest, but are squarely within your jurisdiction. Then if we find out there's overlap, we can call in the FBI to come and run point. We solve the whole case and DEA looks like the chumps they are."

"You are way out of line, mister!" barked Kemper.

Decker eyeballed her. "No, what's out of line is we've wasted so much time over absolutely nothing but bullshit because your agency's ego is apparently more important to you than finding out who murdered two of your guys. If this is how you run your investigation, knock yourself out. But it's not how I run mine. So, speaking on behalf of the FBI at least, screw this, and we'll see you around."

He walked out of the room.

Kemper watched him go and then eyed Jamison. "It that your position too?"

"He's my partner, so, yeah, it is. And you know what else? He happens to be right."

She walked out. A moment later Green followed, along with Lassiter.

CHAPTER

20

Decker lay in his bed at the Mitchells' house rubbing his glued-together scalp.

It was late, and he was tired and his head was throbbing.

He hadn't been entirely honest with Jamison. It was true he had taken many hits as a football player. And he'd suffered a number of concussions over the course of his football career. But this injury felt different. It felt *deeper*. More *invasive*.

The X-ray had shown that whatever had hit him had not penetrated his skull. There was no crack, no fracture, yet he still felt *weird*, and not just because his brain had bounced off the inside of his skull, which was basically the definition of a concussion. He just wasn't sure why he felt so different.

Sleep would not come, so at around three in the morning, he showered, dressed, and went downstairs.

On the kitchen counter, he saw a slip of paper. He picked it up. It was the sheet of numbers that Zoe had shown him to see if he could remember them.

On a whim, he decided to put the matter to a test. He set the paper down.

He dialed the page up in his head and went down the columns. Everything was going fine until he got near the end. Then something in his head skipped, like a DVD with a scratch on its surface.

I can't see the last two numbers.

In a semi-daze, he walked out the back door and sat down in a wicker chair on the rear deck. It was fortunate that where he was sitting was partially covered by an overhang, because a fine rain was falling. Although it wouldn't really have mattered to Decker. He had certainly sat out in the rain before. And even *slept* in the rain when he'd been temporarily homeless back in Ohio.

He rubbed his temples. His perfect recall had been with him so long that he often took it for granted. There were elements of it that he also hated, like not being able to let time erode the horrific memories of his family's having been murdered. But still, he had come to count on his remarkable gift to help him solve crimes. And if it was now becoming fallible?

He closed his eyes and brought the page of numbers back up. This time he could see the last two numbers, but not three in the middle. They were fuzzed over, like someone had smudged the ink in which they'd been written.

Well, that's great.

He stared across at the house that had been the genesis of the current investigation. If he hadn't been standing out here having a beer and looking around, he and Jamison would never have been involved in any of this.

Who murdered you?

Decker wanted to know the answer to that question more than any other.

"Are you okay, Mr. Amos?"

Decker turned to see Zoe Mitchell standing in the doorway of the house in her pink PJs. She was holding a neon green blanket and her thumb hovered near her mouth. She looked anxious.

"I'm fine, Zoe."

"Aunt Alex said you hurt your head."

"It was nothing. Just a bump. You can't sleep?"

She walked out and sat cross-legged on the deck next to him, her blanket held tightly to her chest. "Sometimes I just wake up. Then I go get some milk, but Mom forgot to get it today." She stopped talking and stuck her thumb in her mouth.

When Decker looked down at her, he was suddenly seeing another little girl: his daughter, Molly.

"Does your blanket have a name?" he asked quietly.

Zoe shook her head.

"My daughter had a blanket too. She named it Hermione. You know, from *Harry Potter*? Hermione Granger."

"My mom won't read the books to me or let me see the movies yet. She says I'm not old enough."

"Well, when you are old enough you'll love them."

"What's your daughter's name?"

"Molly."

"Is she older than me?"

Decker looked away, a sudden catch in his throat. It had been stupid to bring up Molly.

He nodded. "About six years older than you."

"How come she didn't come here with you?"

Yeah, a really bad idea.

"She had—school."

"Oh. So, her mom is with her?"

"Yes, they're both together, that's right."

Zoe gazed over at the house where the two men had been found.

"Are you and Aunt Alex doing stuff with what happened over there?"

"We're helping the police look into it."

Zoe put her thumb back in her mouth and sucked on it, her eyes wide and her brow furrowed. "Mommy said people *died* in that house," she mumbled.

"Look, Zoe, you don't have to think about any of that, okay? It has nothing to do with you or your family."

"Aunt Alex *is* my family. And you said you were helping the police."

This caught Decker off guard. "Right. I know that. I mean…" His voice trailed off as Zoe looked up at him hopelessly.

"You…you should go back to bed, Zoe. It's really late."

"Why aren't *you* in bed?"

"Sometimes you have so much going on inside your head, you just can't sleep."

"This helps me," Zoe said, holding out her blanket for Decker to take.

He smiled at this kind gesture by the little girl. He touched the blanket and said, "Thanks, but I think you and your blanket need to stay together. It's just better that way."

Zoe cuddled with her blanket, stood, and walked back to the door.

She turned and said, "I hope you don't get hurt any more, Mr. Amos."

Decker looked at her. "I'll try not to."

After she went back inside, Decker stared again at the house behind them. He closed his eyes and let his memories unspool like film across his mind.

His eyes popped open.

And for good reason.

Normally, his memories came back to him just as he had seen them. He had always considered the process *pristine*. Just like when Zoe had shown him the sheet of numbers and he had memorized them.

But now, like the problem in trying to see the numbers, the memories were erratic and disjointed, as though frames were jumbled together and running out of order through his mind. It was disconcerting, annoying, and Decker eventually put it down to his head injury.

The *weird* head injury.

He settled back in his chair and made his meandering way through the frames of their first night in Baronville. What he had seen. What he had heard.

The car driving away.

The plane flying over.

The spark of light in the window.

The grisly discoveries.

Then, out of order, the two noises he had heard. Thud and scrape.

Decker didn't like not knowing something. Yet not knowing something was part of being an investigator. He often didn't know anything right up until he knew *everything*.

He suddenly wanted to take a walk.

He went back inside and quietly searched for an umbrella to protect him against the rain. Ordinarily he wouldn't have cared about getting a little wet, but he had to take into account his head wound.

He opened the closet door off the front entrance.

Inside there was an umbrella leaning against the wall.

And there was something else.

It was a roll of architectural blueprints leaning next to a cheap battered briefcase.

At first, Decker figured they might be for the house, but it was a big sheaf for such a modest residence.

Curious, he unrolled the plans and laid them out on the foyer floor. He took out his cell phone and used the flashlight feature to look over the top page.

It was a large building, laid out in grids.

Decker noted the writing at the top.

It was the fulfillment center where Frank Mitchell worked.

That made sense. He was in management there. The facility was relatively new.

He rolled the plans back up and put them away.

He stepped outside, put up the umbrella, and started to walk down the street. He reached the end, turned the corner, and walked over to the next block.

He wanted to see something.

The Murder House, as he now termed it.

There were lights on in the house and a police cruiser was parked in front.

Behind the cruiser were parked two black SUVs. As he watched, an officer in a yellow slicker got out. A guy in a DEA windbreaker climbed out of one of the SUVs and joined the cop on the property patrol.

Kemper was clearly relying on the locals for nothing.

Decker ran his gaze over the house, the plot of land, the few parked cars on the street, and all the dark houses up and down it.

He looked up at the sky where the plane had flown over.

Then he looked down the street again.

That was odd. He checked his watch.

Three-forty.

There were lights on in one of the houses about six doors down and on the opposite side of the street.

He headed in that direction.

CHAPTER

21

"You're up late, young fella. Or else up early."

As Decker approached the house with the light on, he saw an old man sitting on the covered porch in his wheelchair. He also noted the wooden ramp leading up to the porch.

The wood-shingled house was small and in disrepair. The sole tree out front was full of dead leaves. The small lawn had gone to weeds. Everything had a wasted look to it, as though it were all just waiting to die.

Parked in the carport next to the house was an old passenger van.

Decker stopped in front of the house. "So are you."

The man was wrinkled and sunken in the wheelchair. His head was bald and covered with brown splotches from sun damage. He wore wire-rimmed spectacles. He shrugged. "Get to my age, what's time matter?" He tugged his sweater more tightly around him and shivered slightly. Though it was humid with the rain, he had a blanket over his legs.

The man must have noticed that Decker was looking at the blanket.

"Summer, winter, hell, it don't matter. Still get the chills. Docs say it's a circulation problem. I say it's my pipes getting clogged with living too long. See, that's a reason to not be around too many years. Everything falls apart."

"So you live here?"

"What's it look like?"

"You're Fred Ross?"

"Who wants to know?" Ross snapped.

"Me. I'm Amos Decker."

"Amos? Haven't heard that name in a long time. Reminds me of that show, *Amos 'n Andy*? Long time ago. Hell, everything's a long time ago. Goes with being old. I'm eighty-five. Most days I feel like I'm a hundred and eighty-five. Some days I wake up and wonder who the hell I am. How'd that old man get in my body? It ain't no fun."

Decker drew closer to the porch. The rain had ceased, so he lowered his umbrella. "Were you here two nights ago, Mr. Ross?"

Lassiter had said that Ross had probably not been home, but Decker wanted to hear this for himself.

Ross looked down the street. "You mean when whatever happened there happened?"

"Yeah."

"You a cop?"

"Yeah."

"Saw them go in earlier," Ross said, pointing down the street. "Looked like Feds to me."

"How do you know that?"

"I watch TV."

"So, were you here that night?"

Ross shook his head. "Hospital. Had a breathing problem. I'm okay now. I get lots of breathing problems. Folks at the emergency room know me on a first-name basis. Ain't nothing to be proud of, I can tell you that. If you're old and rich, that's one thing. But old and poor, I don't recommend it, Amos."

"I'm sorry to hear that. Have the police been by to see you?"

"No. I just got back today, see. Or yesterday now, I guess."

"You live alone?"

Ross nodded. "The missus died, oh, nearly twenty years ago now. Smoking. Don't never smoke, Amos, 'less you want to die in godawful agony."

"You ever see anybody around that house, Mr. Ross? Anybody at all? Even if they seemed innocuous. Or anything that seemed odd, out of place?"

His gaze boring into Decker, Ross said, "Eyes ain't too good, so I don't see much at all no more."

"I see you're wearing glasses. And you said you saw the 'Feds' at the house."

Ross took his glasses off and wiped them on his sweater. "Most houses on this street are empty. Baronville, mostly empty too." He put the specs back on.

"But a new fulfillment center is here."

Ross shrugged. "Ain't enough jobs to bring the town back. And don't pay what the old jobs paid. Hell, nothing pays like the old jobs did. I never went to college, never had the chance, but I had me a good-paying job. Now, if you don't know computers, you're screwed." He held up his hands. "Nobody builds nothing no more. Just typing crap on a keyboard. That's all folks do now. Typing. I mean, hell, what kinda job is that?"

"Did you work at the mines or the mills?"

"Coal, paper mill, and then the textile mill. At the mills, I fixed the machines. Did some of that at the coke plant too. When you come into this town back then, you could smell the stench. The coal, and the crap we used to make the paper. I heard the Barons used to call it the smell of money. Screw them. Now the Mexicans and Orientals do all that for pennies a day. Before long they'll have damn robots doing it. Then the Chinamen and Mexies will be out of a job too." He cackled. "Used to be a railroad line that ran right through the middle of town to take the coal and coke to the Pittsburgh steel mills and also to other parts of the country to keep the lights on. Yeah, I was a miner, but I got outta that early. Paid good but, hell, who wants black lung, right? What my missus died of, really, and she never stepped foot in a mine. Didn't want that crap inside me. No sir."

"Did you know the Baron family?"

"Assholes, all of 'em."

Ross spat on the porch.

"Why's that?"

"Created this place and then let it go to hell, that's why. That man sits in that big house on the hill and looks down on all of us. Son of a bitch!"

"John Baron, you mean?"

"Asshole."

"But you earned a good living, right? You said you did."

"Well, I worked for it. Nobody ever gave me a damn thing. Worked my hands to the bone. Sure, I made money, but they made a helluva lot more."

"Do you have any family?"

"One son who never comes to see the man what brought him into this world. Screw him."

Decker eyed the wheelchair. "What happened to you?"

Behind the glass lenses Ross's eyes seemed to shrink to the size of black pellets. "What happened to me? Hell, life happened to me, all you need to know."

"Okay. Did you ever see anyone around that house?"

"You say you're a cop? How do I know that? I'm old, so I'm skeptical of everything and everybody."

Decker approached him and held out his creds.

"FBI, huh?" said Ross, his small eyes gazing from puckered sockets over the identification card. He looked down the street. "Feds all over the place. Why's that? Two dead bodies in that house, the TV said. Why's that federal stuff, I wonder?"

"Lots of stuff is federal stuff," replied Decker.

"Too much," snapped Ross with another dollop of spit delivered to his porch. "Government is into every damn thing we do. I'm sick of it."

"So you're into every person for themselves?"

"I'm into keeping the government outta my business. And I'm into the government stop taking sides of folks that don't need no help. Look at me, I got nothing. You don't see me crying about it. You don't see me asking for handouts because I got some problem, or because I feel like somebody didn't give me a fair shot. Hell, nothing about life is fair. You don't like it, go back to where you come from, is what I say, and don't let the American flag hit you on the ass on your way out."

"Interesting philosophy," noted Decker.

"Hell, I don't know nothing about philosophy. I just see the world with my own two eyes. For what it really is."

"And what is the world, really?"

"Not nearly as good as it used to be for people like me."

Decker decided to shift the discussion. "So, you maybe saw people around that house, you said?"

"I forget now."

"Mr. Ross, if you know something you really need to tell me."

"Why's that, I wonder? 'Cause you're a Fed? That supposed to be some magic word or something?"

"No, I'm a cop trying to find out the truth."

Ross grinned maliciously. "That's what they say on TV too. I didn't believe it then, don't believe it now."

"If you saw something and don't tell us, the people who killed those men might come to the same realization. That you might have seen something. You could be in danger."

In answer, Ross lifted the blanket covering his withered legs to reveal a sawed-off shotgun. He lifted the muzzle in Decker's general direction.

"Had this baby a long time. Remington double ought Magnum load. Locked and loaded. Anybody comes after me, *they're* in danger. Including Feds. And I don't fire no warning shots. Never saw the need."

Decker took a step back. "Just so you know, threatening a federal officer is a crime. And if you fire that kind of load with a shortened barrel it'll knock you and your wheelchair right through a wall with the recoil and dislodge any fillings you might have. And your chances for a second shot are nil because you'll probably have a concussion."

"Who gives a damn about a concussion if whatever I'm firing at looks like a piece of Swiss cheese?"

"And I'm pretty sure sawed-off shotguns are illegal in Pennsylvania. I could arrest you for possessing one."

The old man leaned forward. "Maybe you'll learn this, Amos, while you're here, and maybe you won't."

"What's that?"

"There ain't nothing really illegal in Baronville."

CHAPTER

22

Decker!"

Decker had just passed by the Murder House when the person called out.

It was Kate Kemper. She was standing in the front doorway.

Decker stopped and turned to look at her.

"What are you doing here?" she asked, coming toward him.

"Just out for a walk," he said.

She checked her watch. "And your walk just happens to take you past here at four o'clock in the morning?"

She came to stand in front of him, while he looked over her shoulder at the house.

"Just itching to get back inside there, aren't you?" she said.

He focused on her. "Wouldn't you be too, if you were me?"

She looked at his sticking-up hair. "I meant to ask you about your hairdo when we first met, but I figured maybe it was just the way you wore it."

"I had a head injury."

"How'd you get that?"

"An exploding trailer."

She gaped. "What? How did that happen?"

"We were checking out a mobile home trailer when someone decided to turn it into an oven with me and my partner inside. We got out before we got barbecued, but the thing went boom when the propane tank ignited, and part of the boom hit me in the head."

"Do you know who did it?"

"Not yet. But I'm working on it. I take it personally when someone tries to kill me."

"I would too." She studied him. "I checked you out since our last meeting. The Bureau speaks incredibly highly of you."

"Uh-huh. Find anything interesting inside?"

She cocked her head. "Not into flattery?"

"I never really saw its value."

"Okay," she said, looking at him appraisingly. "I guess the answer to your question depends on how you define 'interesting.'"

"How would you define it?"

"How about forensically? The ME got back to us with some more information. Care to hear it?"

"I didn't think you wanted us involved."

"I just said things had to run through me."

"I'm listening."

"The man in the basement overdosed on carfentanil. It's an anesthetic used for large animals, like elephants. It's about the strongest commercial opiate out there. The Russians use it as a weapon of *assassination*."

"That would account for the foam on his lips."

Kemper smiled strangely at this, but continued, "The guy you found hanging died by strangulation."

"But it couldn't be from the hanging."

Kemper hiked her eyebrows. "So you knew that already?"

Decker nodded. "And I hope you're not relying on the local ME, because he also royally screwed up the time of death. I know more about forensics than he does."

Kemper looked at him curiously. "How do you know he screwed up the TOD?"

"He completely missed obvious red flags in the evidence. And by your look, you know that to be the case. So tell me what else you found."

"How do you know I found out anything else?"

"Because you strike me as someone who likes to do things her way, and not rely on the locals to spoon-feed you information."

She smiled. "I'm beginning to see another side of you, Decker."

"I've got a lot of them. So what did you learn?"

"You're right. I brought in my own medical examiner. She looked over the bodies and the test results and came to certain conclusions that were not exactly in line with the local ME's results. But let me hear your analysis of the TOD first."

"Rigor starts about two hours after death, beginning in the small muscles, face, neck, and moves outward to the larger muscle groups in the body's extremities. The process then reverses itself. Full rigor is typically reached around twelve to eighteen hours after death. The body can remain stiff for a similar time range. Then rigor begins to reverse and completely resolves itself after anywhere from thirty-six to forty-eight hours, depending on certain factors, including environmental, and the body eventually becomes flaccid." He paused before continuing. "Now, let's apply that here. Vics dead twenty hours or longer in an abandoned house and one of them in a moldy basement? They'd be covered in insects and eggs, along with the beginnings of body decomp. And the limbs of the guy in the basement didn't feel stiff in the way that people in rigor usually do. They were off somehow, at least to my touch. And they were way too cold for the ambient temp of that place. The ME should have seen that from his core temp test, but he just assumed his thermometer was broken."

Kemper was nodding the whole time he was talking. "Now let me tell you what my person thinks. She thinks the vics *were* killed around the time the local ME thought, but under a very different scenario." She stopped and studied him. "Care to think how that's possible, taking into account what you know?"

He looked at the house again and said slowly, as though thinking out loud, "The only thing that would explain the facts is if they were killed somewhere else twenty hours or more before they were discovered by me, and kept in extremely cold conditions in an enclosed container, like a freezer, so the bodies wouldn't commence undergoing rigor and the insects couldn't get to them. Once the bodies were taken out of that enclosed environment the process of rigor would begin. And that would also account for why the local ME's body temp gauge was throwing off wacky numbers, and also the peculiar stiffness of the limbs. It wouldn't be due to the chemical reaction of dead muscles in rigor, but a frozen body thawing out. And the blowflies detect dead bodies based on things like scents from the corpse's release of fluid and gases. If the bodies were frozen, that might have inhibited those scents from being released. And if the bodies were only there for a short while, the insect infestation wouldn't have been all that much, which matches the facts of the crime scene." He paused. "But if that was the case there wouldn't have been foam on the guy's lips. It would have long since disappeared."

"Not if they placed a concocted residue there when they laid the body out, because they knew the tox tests would show the drugs in his system and that the foaming would probably be present if he'd just been left there right after he died."

"Does your ME think the bodies were moved after death?"

"She *knows* at least one of them was. The livor mortis staining showed that."

"The guy hanging, right?" Decker nodded. "I saw that the staining was on his back. No way that could have happened if he'd been strung up and left there."

"Exactly what my ME said," noted Kemper. "And there were actually *two* sets of ligature marks. The local ME either missed that or just didn't note or understand the difference. The marks made by the rope were clearly done postmortem."

"So whoever did this was sweating the details and maybe hoping for a less than crackerjack medical examiner doing the posts. And they almost got their wish. How'd your person figure the freezer scenario?"

"It was really the only way to explain the forensic inconsistencies. And there was evidence of an abrasion on the shoulder of one of the vics."

"We saw that. They were speculating it might have been from a medical patch of some kind."

"My ME believes it was a freezer burn on the skin from where it was left exposed. She said she was pretty certain it occurred postmortem. But she made a point of telling me that her TOD was a guess, really, because if the bodies were placed in a freezer right after death and then put in that house, that precludes making an accurate calculation for the time of death."

"So whoever did this wanted to make sure that we would not be able to show precisely when the guys really died."

"And by doing that they take away a key tool of any homicide investigation."

"Alibis or a lack thereof become pretty much meaningless," said Decker thoughtfully.

"Exactly."

"The bodies had to be transported here at some point, relatively close to the time that I discovered them. There was no deep freezer in that house, so the bodies were kept on ice somewhere else before being brought here."

"You said you heard a car?"

"I did. I also heard a noise."

"What kind of noise?"

"It was more like a series of sounds. Scraping and clunks."

"Nothing else?"

"A plane flying over. Other than that, nothing. So how does someone carry two corpses into that house and no one sees a thing?"

"Well, I understand there aren't many people left in this neighborhood."

"But the killers couldn't be sure a car wouldn't drive down the street. Or someone wouldn't look out their window. I mean, it only takes one pair of eyes." He fell silent for a moment. "Now, do you want to tell me what your men were doing here? And why they were undercover? If they were hanging out with a bad crowd, I think we can narrow our list of suspects, especially in a place like this."

She pursed her lips and stared at him. "This goes no farther."

"No farther," repeated Decker.

"Will Beatty and Doug Smith, they were the two dead men in that house. Beatty was in the basement. Smith was the one hanging."

"And they worked undercover for the DEA?"

"Yes and no," was her surprising reply.

"How exactly is that possible?" asked Decker.

"They *did* work undercover for us. And then they went rogue."

"How do you know they went rogue? Maybe their cover just got blown."

"We entertained that possibility until something happened to disabuse us of that notion."

"What was that?"

"They were working with a guy named Randy Haas."

"Was he DEA too?"

"No. He was a bad guy who we had on a short leash feeding us info. He was working with Beatty and Smith. If he screwed us, he was going to prison for life."

"What happened with Haas?"

"He was given a fatal dose of morphine. But with his dying breath, he pointed the finger at Beatty and Smith as his killers."

"Did he say why?"

"No. Just that it was them."

"Why would they kill him?"

"Don't know."

"And you believe Haas's statement?"

"Dying declaration. What reason would he have to lie? And on top of that we'd been unable to get hold of Beatty or Smith."

"Whoever killed Beatty and Smith *knew* they were cops. They dressed one as a cop and poured pig's blood around the other one."

"But the fact is, they'd gone over to the dark side."

"Well, some folks just aren't very forgiving," said Decker. "Especially those already on the dark side."

23

AFTER ONLY THREE hours of sleep, Decker went downstairs to find Zoe finishing her breakfast in the kitchen before going to school.

He poured himself a cup of coffee and accepted a toasted bagel from Amber, who was rushing around the kitchen packing Zoe's lunch and also handling the laundry in a small room adjacent to it. Frank, he was told, had already left for work.

Decker wearily sat down across from Zoe and drank his coffee and munched on his bagel while she spooned cereal into her mouth.

When he looked over at her, he found the little girl staring at him.

"You went out last night," she said. "I saw you from my window."

"I couldn't sleep, like I told you. But why were you still up? I thought you went back to bed?"

Zoe shrugged and tapped her spoon against her bowl.

"Zoe, hurry up," said her mother from the laundry room. "We have to leave in five minutes and you still need to brush your teeth and comb your hair. And do you have your book bag, young lady? And your flute?"

Zoe rolled her eyes and took another mouthful of cereal, her gaze still on Decker. "Have you found the bad people yet?" she asked.

"Not yet, no. Still working on it."

"Your hair looks funny."

"It usually does."

"No, I mean it's all stuck up in the middle."

"I, uh, accidentally got some glue there."

Zoe perked up at this. "I put glue in my hair one time. But it wasn't an accident. Mom was really mad. She had to use scissors to cut it out. Want me to cut it out for you?" She lowered her voice. "Mom doesn't really like me to use scissors when she's not around, but we don't have to tell her."

"Thanks, but I think I'll just let it grow out."

Zoe returned to her cereal, clearly disappointed.

Amber burst into the kitchen. "Okay, are you ready?" she asked her daughter.

"I still have to brush my teeth and hair. And I couldn't find my flute."

"I know today's your birthday, but get going, young lady."

Zoe held up her half-empty bowl. "But, Mom," she began.

"Oh, no, you're not pulling that again. You can finish it in the car. Now, go! And don't come downstairs without your flute. I saw it on your dresser last night."

Zoe slowly rose, and weakly waved goodbye to Decker.

"Happy Birthday, Zoe," said Decker.

After she left the room, Amber took a few deep breaths. "Kids."

"Yeah," said Decker.

"I've never had a son but they can't be harder than girls."

"I never had a son," said Decker. "Just a daughter."

Amber stiffened and slowly sat down across from Decker.

She said nervously, "Alex told me about…"

"Yeah," said Decker.

"I'm so sorry."

"Yeah," said Decker.

When he said nothing else, Amber rose and said awkwardly, "I…um, I have to get Zoe to school."

"Yeah," said Decker, staring down at the table.

* * *

A few minutes later, Jamison joined him and poured herself a cup of coffee.

"I saw Agent Kemper last night, or early this morning, depending on how you look at it," he said.

She sat down openmouthed across from him.

"Where?"

"At the house where we found the dead guys."

"What were you doing over there?"

"Couldn't sleep. Took a walk past the Murder House. Met Fred Ross, the neighbor who Green and Lassiter haven't spoken with yet. He's a hard-ass prick with a sawed-off shotgun under his blanket. Thought he was going to shoot me."

"Jesus, Decker, can't you just go to sleep like the rest of us?"

"He said he wasn't home at the time. But he said something else."

"What?"

"He said he'd come to realize that nothing is really illegal in Baronville."

She frowned. "What did he mean by that?"

"I don't know. After I left him I was walking back here when Kemper came out of the Murder House."

"Did she cop an attitude?"

"No, she seemed to have mellowed out, actually. She told me something about the two dead men. They *were* DEA agents. Will Beatty and Doug Smith. Beatty was the one in the basement. Undercover, like I thought. Only she said they had gone rogue."

"Gone rogue? What does that mean?"

"They allegedly killed a bad guy they were working with. Man named Randy Haas. And it looks like Beatty and Smith were killed earlier and put on ice to screw with the TOD calculation. Kemper brought in her own medical examiner because she didn't trust the local one."

"Well, neither did you. I guess this proves you right."

"Beatty died from a massive drug overdose of a super powerful opiate, obviously forced into him. Smith was strangled, but not by the rope."

"So they were brought to that house already dead?"

"Appears so."

"Why go to all that trouble?"

"No idea."

"That was a big risk bringing two dead guys to that house. Someone might have seen something."

"I know. That part is inexplicable."

"So Beatty and Smith had gone bad, then?"

"That's what Kemper thinks."

"And you? What do you think?"

"I don't know enough to think anything, really. I'm still collecting information."

"So what do we do?"

"We keep digging. Next up is Bradley Costa, the banker. We're going to his place of business first. And then his house. After that, we check out Michael Swanson. And then I want to go and talk to John Baron the Fourth."

"Baron? Why?"

"Like I said before, I think he was lying about knowing some of the victims. Anyone who lies about something like that, I want to get to know him better."

"From what you said, he seems like an interesting person."

"He *is* an interesting person. But that doesn't mean he's not involved in this." He added thoughtfully, "I wonder why he stays in a town that hates his guts?"

"Maybe he's a sucker for punishment."

"Or maybe there's another reason."

Decker reached over and snagged the page of numbers off the counter and held it up.

"What's that?" she asked.

Decker explained about Zoe testing his memory.

"I think Zoe is really intrigued by you."

"Not the point. I looked at the page again, after my concussion, and I couldn't remember the last two numbers. Then I looked at it again and I could remember the last two numbers, but not some of the figures in the middle."

"You think it's connected to your head injury?"

"I don't know. It's possible. Maybe probable."

He looked so glum that Jamison said, "Decker, your having a phenomenal memory is awesome. But it's not the only thing that makes you great at what you do. You've been a cop for over twenty years. You see stuff. You figure stuff out, like no one else I've ever seen. And you don't give up."

"Maybe."

"There's no maybe about it."

"Thanks, Alex. I appreciate that."

"Wow, maybe that concussion had some *positive* results."

"What do you mean by that?"

She sighed. "Never mind." Jamison looked up at him, fingering her coffee cup. "Is Kemper really okay with us working this?"

"I think so. But even if she weren't I'd still be doing it."

"You never worry about the politics or optics of a situation, do you?"

"When it comes to murder, I never saw a reason to," replied Decker.

CHAPTER

24

Decker looked around and frowned. He didn't like banks. Not since they had foreclosed on both his house and his car back in Burlington, leaving him with no roof over his head and no wheels under his butt.

Bradley Costa's office at Baronville National Bank was spacious and filled with mementos from local events. The bank had sponsored everything from high school debate squads to Little League baseball teams, as well as the local Kiwanis and VFW branches.

The key to the city lay on his desk. There were no family photos because Costa had been single with no kids. They learned he had been born in New York, in Queens, gone to college at Syracuse, gotten his MBA at NYU, and worked on Wall Street before moving to Baronville.

Jamison studied the pictures on the wall. "Photo ops with the governor, the mayor, the town council, the police chief. And over there the local historical society, the ladies' garden club, and the Daughters of the American Revolution. He was definitely a schmoozer."

Decker's gaze swept around the room.

It was neat, organized, efficient. And at the center of it was a man who'd been shot to death in an auto repair facility with a local drug dealer with whom he'd apparently had no connection.

They had spoken to people at the bank who'd worked with Costa. He had been uniformly described as friendly, hardworking, and scrupulously honest. They could give no reason for his murder, and none of them thought he could have had any connection to Michael Swanson.

"You think maybe Costa had a secret life no one else knew about?" Jamison asked.

Decker picked up a photo from the dead banker's desk. It was of Costa and a young woman.

"I know her," he said.

"From where?"

"She was the bartender at the Mercury Bar. Her name is Cindi. She and John Baron are friends."

Jamison glanced at the photo. "Costa was a good-looking guy. And this Cindi is really beautiful. Maybe they were dating?"

"Let's find out," said Decker.

Jamison went and got Costa's secretary, Emily Hayes, and they asked her about the picture.

Hayes said, "I think that was taken at a local business gathering Brad organized. He made a point of holding as many of those as possible. Baronville has some pockets of success and wealth, and Brad was good at tapping into that. He had cocktail parties and events at his home, that sort of thing. We've never had anyone here who really did that. He was a real go-getter. He had the energy that we truly needed. He'll be sorely missed."

From her look and tone Decker wondered if the fiftyish Hayes might have had a thing for the young and charismatic banker.

"So you know the woman?" he asked.

"Oh yes, that's Cindi Riley. She owns the Mercury Bar."

"She owns it?" said Decker with mild surprise. "She seems a little young to own a bar."

"Well, her father owned it before her. She's a good businesswoman, though, in her own right."

"Were Costa and Ms. Riley dating?"

"Not that I know of, no."

"Okay, but this was the only picture on Costa's desk. I'm assuming he had his picture taken with lots of businesspeople."

Hayes looked perplexed. "I don't know what to tell you. As far as I know, Brad kept his personal life separate from work. And I wasn't privy to him dating anyone."

"How about John Baron?" asked Decker.

The woman frowned. "What about him?"

"Was he a client of the bank's?"

"He used to have an account here, yes."

"Did he know Costa?"

"If he did, I was unaware of it." She stopped and her features turned thoughtful. "Now that I think about it, I believe the bank *does* hold the mortgage on the Baron property. But I don't know the details of that."

"Would Costa have handled that transaction?"

"It's certainly possible, but I don't know for sure. I don't have the authority to look into client accounts and disclose them to anyone."

"Okay, do you *know* Baron personally?" asked Decker.

Hayes pursed her lips. "No, I do not."

"You sound a bit hostile," said Jamison.

Hayes gave her a piercing stare. "My grandfather died in one of the Baron mines. And my mother did backbreaking work at the textile plant for years. Then she showed up one day for her shift and there was a sign on the door saying that it was closed. Permanently. No warning. And there was supposed to be a pension plan. But that was gone too. She died soon after, probably from all the stress."

"But hadn't the Barons long since sold out by then?" asked Decker.

She folded her arms over her chest and looked at him crossly. "And do you really think the Barons would've treated their workers any differently if they'd still been in charge?"

Decker said, "What else can you tell us about Costa? Did he come in to work the day he went missing?"

"Yes. He worked all day. Mr. Beecher, our president, called the police when Brad didn't show up for work the next day and we couldn't reach him."

"But nothing seemed out of the ordinary at work that day?"

"Not that I'm aware of. He seemed fine. The police asked me that too, but I told them the same thing."

"And after work, did he have plans that night?"

"Not that I'm aware of, but then again, he wouldn't have told me."

"Did Costa have any problems with anyone here?" asked Decker. "Or maybe with one of his clients?"

"Not that I'm aware of."

"You keep saying that a lot," said Decker. "*Would* you be aware of it?"

She bristled a bit but said, "I'm his secretary, so I probably would. He got along fine with everyone here. In fact, everyone liked him. He was a very happy person. As far as clients, the bank has had to call in some loans and foreclose on some properties, certainly. But people here pay their bills if they can. If they can't and they have to lose their homes or their cars, they understand that. A contract is a contract."

"Very fair-minded of them," said Decker, whose tone betrayed that he did not actually believe this.

"Will you be going to Mr. Costa's residence next?" Hayes asked.

"Why?" said Decker.

"You might want to water the flowers, is all."

"So you've been there?" said Decker.

"I assisted with some of his business get-togethers," she said primly.

After they left the building, Jamison said, "Well, she was tight-lipped, but maybe she doesn't know anything either."

"Or maybe she was just lying," replied Decker.

CHAPTER

25

W ELL, THE FLOWERS *do* need watering," observed Jamison.

They were standing in the middle of Costa's loft in downtown Baronville.

It was open and airy, with exposed brick walls, and decorated with a flair that might have come from the combination of a deep wallet and professional design assistance.

"It's nice," said Jamison as she looked around the space. "No expense spared, I'd say. There was a plaque downstairs that said this was one of the old textile mills. At least the Baron family left something to the townspeople."

"Well, Costa won't be enjoying it anymore," noted Decker.

He glanced at a shelf built into one wall. On it were various framed photos.

He went over and studied them one by one.

"Look at this."

Jamison joined him.

He was pointing to a photo of a Little League baseball team holding a banner.

"So what? We saw from his office that the bank sponsored baseball teams."

"Right, but look at the coach."

Jamison ran her eye over the tall, lean man smiling back in the picture.

"Good-looking guy. Who is he?"

"John Baron."

"What? You're kidding."

He looked at the date engraved on the frame. "This was taken a year ago. So Baron coached a team sponsored by the bank but doesn't know Costa, one of the bigwigs there?"

"Well, I guess that's possible. I mean, you don't have to meet the coach to sponsor a team. You just have to write a check."

"But this is the only business-related photo here," said Decker. "The rest are of mountains and rivers and the sights of the area. Costa might have been an amateur photographer. But why only this one photo here? The other Little League team pics are in his office."

"I don't know."

He walked over to the window and pointed. "That must be John Baron's place up there on the hill."

Jamison joined him at the window. "Wow, even from here you can tell it's huge."

"And apparently falling apart."

"Well, I can only imagine the upkeep. It must cost a fortune just to heat the place."

"I don't think Baron has a fortune, not anymore."

"He might only live in a portion of it."

"It wasn't cheap to furnish *this* space," said Decker, turning his attention back to the apartment.

"I guess Costa's job paid relatively well. And I would imagine the cost of living here is pretty low. And he probably saved some bucks from his time in New York."

"Granted, but why here?"

"What?"

"He worked on Wall Street. Why come to Baronville and work in a bank? Last time I looked, they had banks on Wall Street. This is like the exact opposite of what the guy was used to."

"Some people want change," replied Jamison.

"That much change? You come to a dying town? With what expectations?"

"That you'll have an opportunity and things will turn around. Like his secretary said, he was happy, he was generating business. He had this place."

"And he ends up dead from a gunshot, hanging from a chain in an auto repair facility with a brand on his forehead. Some opportunity."

"Decker, he couldn't have *known* that would happen," pointed out Jamison.

Decker didn't answer her. He just kept looking around.

Jamison said, "Green told us that Joyce Tanner was laid off from JC Penney. Nothing suspicious there. Five other people were laid off at the same time. And then the store ended up closing. No ties to Costa, at least that we can see. And none to Babbot. We haven't checked into Michael Swanson yet. Maybe they were all buying drugs from him."

"We didn't find any drug paraphernalia at Babbot's place. And none was found here or at Joyce Tanner's apartment. And no one we talked to mentioned that they had seen signs of illicit drug use by Costa, Tanner, or Babbot."

"But drugs might still be involved somehow. Babbot was on heavy painkillers. And the *DEA* is here, after all."

Decker tapped his finger against the wall of glass overlooking the city.

"Maybe they have no connection to each other," he said.

"Meaning their deaths were random?"

"Not necessarily."

"Well, if they don't have a connection to each other, then by default, doesn't that mean their deaths *were* random?"

"Not if the four of them all had a connection to *another* person, but not to each other. The spider in the web, the hub of the wheel. *That* person might be the common denominator."

Jamison sat down in a chair and mulled this over.

"But who could that person be?"

"Well, if I knew that I'd be able to solve the case," said Decker. "Let's go."

Jamison jumped up. "Where?"

"Michael Swanson's last digs."

* * *

The last known address for Swanson, given to them by Detective Green, was a motel in an area of Baronville that was about as rundown as either Decker or Jamison had seen so far.

"Looks like where I used to live," said Decker as he stared around the small room with a communal bath down the hall. They had been told by the manager of the motel that Swanson had left there two months ago. There was no forwarding address.

They went back to the manager's office after looking over the empty room. "Did the police come by?" asked Jamison.

The manager, a grizzled, reedy man in his fifties, nodded. "And I told them the same thing I told you. Mike left here about eight weeks ago. Haven't seen him since."

"Well, you won't see him again, since he's dead," noted Decker.

"Hell, everybody knew Mike sold drugs. You live in that world, you die in that world."

"What else can you tell us about him?" asked Jamison.

"He was actually a nice guy. Not too much in the upstairs, if you catch my drift. But he helped out around here. Assisted some of the other residents. But for the drug stuff, he would have been okay. I'm actually sorry he's dead."

"So you let him stay here even though he was into drugs?" asked Jamison.

The man shrugged. "Hell, lady, if that were the case, I wouldn't be able to rent to about half the people in Baronville, including my own mother, and she's in her late seventies."

"Anybody ever visit him here?" asked Decker.

"Not really. I don't think he had many friends."

"Did you see him shortly before he went missing?"

"Truth is, I hadn't seen Mike since he left here."

"Did he have any enemies?" asked Jamison.

"Not so's I know. But he sold drugs, so he might have."

"Did he have a car?"

"No. But he had a bike. He took it with him when he left."

"Do you know what it looked like?" asked Decker.

"Yeah, it had two wheels."

They walked out of the place not knowing much more than when they'd walked in.

Jamison leaned against the side of their truck and said, "Well, this case is moving about as fast as a bike *without* two wheels."

Decker looked over her shoulder. "You really can see it from just about everywhere in Baronville. Must be a sore point for the locals."

Jamison looked at where he was indicating.

"John Baron's ancestral estate?"

"And our next stop." Decker checked his watch. "He should be up by now."

26

DECREPIT.

That was the word that came to mind as Decker studied the outside of the Baron mansion.

He had pounded twice on the battered double front doors and had heard nothing in return.

Jamison said, "Maybe he's not home."

"It's a big house. Maybe he has to walk a long way to answer the door. And he told me he's usually here."

A few moments later they indeed heard footsteps approaching.

The door swung open and John Baron the Fourth looked back at them.

Decker noted that he was wearing the same clothes as the other night. His hair was just as disheveled and his eyes were full of sleep.

"Did we wake you?" Decker asked, giving him a long look, since it was late in the afternoon.

Baron smiled and stretched out his long frame.

"Actually, you did. I was up before, of course. Rolled out of bed right around noon as usual. This was just a refresher nap before I go to bed tonight."

He glanced at a wide-eyed Jamison. "And who do we have here?" he said.

"We have here, Alex Jamison," said Jamison. "I'm Decker's partner."

"Lucky you, Decker," said Baron. "Now, to what do I owe the pleasure of your visit?"

"We're investigating the murders," said Decker.

"So you told me."

"We'd like to ask you some questions."

The smile remained at full wattage. "And why's that?"

"Just routine."

"Right. That's what they say when they have no grounds to ask questions but want to come in anyway. Well, I would be delighted, but only if the charming Alex here gets to ask questions too."

He backed away and waved them in.

They stepped through and he closed the door behind them.

Jamison immediately shivered, because there was a chilly draft in the hall.

Baron noted this and said, "I don't turn the heat on officially until January. So we have some months to go until warmth returns. Oil-fired furnace. Beastly expensive. And one must live within one's means."

He led them down the hall. As they passed open doorways on both sides of the grand passage they glimpsed rooms of immense size with decorations and furnishings from many decades ago. The atmosphere in each was one of decay.

"Quite a place," said Jamison.

"Actually the craftsmanship was abysmal and the materials were the cheapest available."

"Why is that?" asked Decker.

"Because Baron the First was loath to part with a dime. I think his role model was Ebenezer Scrooge. But he wanted a symbol of his wealth on display for all the town to see. And this was the result."

"And the workers? They weren't any good?"

"Oh, I heard they were excellent. But they hated their employer and so they did crappy work. At least that's the family gossip."

He pointed through an open doorway. "The gun room."

He led them inside a space about twenty feet square. On three walls were rows and rows of gun racks, but they only contained a few long guns: one antique over-and-under shotgun, three hunting rifles, and an elegant-looking flintlock. In glass cabinets in the center of the room were a few sets of pistols, blunderbusses, old bullets, and assorted hunting accessories.

"Baron the First fancied himself lord of the fiefdom, and he liked to look the part."

"Did he hunt?" asked Decker.

"Only for money. And he didn't use a gun. Just a knife to stab people in the back."

Jamison raised her eyebrows at this remark. "There were obviously a lot more guns in here at one time," she observed.

"There was a lot more of *everything* here at one time. As for the guns, I sell them off occasionally to help pay the expenses on this place. But as you can clearly see, I'm running out of assets. Now, on to my little inner sanctum."

Baron ushered them down the hall and into what looked to be a large study straight out of an early-twentieth-century period piece. There was an enormous partner's desk set near the rear wall. Resting on it was an old computer, which still looked out of place with all the other antiquated trappings. Bookcases, low tables stacked with books and papers, an ancient freestanding metal globe, and a leather couch that sagged nearly to the floor were set around the room. Against one wall was a heavily carved credenza upon which sat a line of half-empty bottles of alcohol with cut crystal glasses set in front of them. There were two other upholstered chairs in the room across from the desk, which Baron waved them into as he settled himself down behind his desk and moved some stacks of papers and books out of the way.

Decker's chair creaked ominously with his weight, but it held. Behind Baron were dark green drapes that were heavily stained.

Decker eyed the boxy computer. "So, what is it that you do for a living?"

"How do you know I don't live off an immense fortune left to me?" asked Baron, but his grin showed that the question was not serious. He pointed to the computer. "I actually do research for a number of professors at Penn State and U Penn. It doesn't pay all that well, but I can do it from here and it provides some income."

"What sort of research?" asked Jamison.

"Mostly history. I like looking into the past. Allows me to forget my present circumstances and leaves me no time to dwell on my possible future prospects, or, more accurately, the lack thereof."

"Have you researched your own family history?" asked Decker.

"Just what's been passed down from generation to generation. It's nothing you haven't seen with other friendly neighborhood robber barons."

"Speaking of Barons," said Jamison. "I was wondering if that was really the family name, or if it was chosen by John Baron the First."

"As far as I know it's our real name, though I would put nothing past my ancestor in pretty much any department."

He put his hands behind his head, sat back, placed his long feet on the desk, and said, "Okay, I'm ready for your *routine* questioning."

Jamison took out her recorder.

When Decker didn't do likewise, Baron said, "Does your partner docket everything for you?"

"No, I have a pretty good memory."

"I'm sure that comes in incredibly handy."

"Yeah, it can."

"So, the routine questions?"

"I asked you before if you knew any of the victims."

"I vaguely remember that."

"And do you vaguely remember telling me you didn't?"

"Possibly."

"Either you do or you don't, Mr. Baron," interjected Jamison.

He looked at her and smiled disarmingly. "My dear Alex, normally I would answer such a question without hesitation, but at the time it was asked by your colleague here, I had imbibed quite a bit of alcohol. In other words, I was drunk. I should have walked home. As it was, I nearly drove my truck into the river. But may I say your query was exceptionally well phrased and spot-on with its content?"

Jamison looked taken aback. "Oh, okay."

Baron turned back to Decker. "Now that I'm reasonably sober, shall we try again?"

Decker once more told him the names, leaving out the now identified DEA agents.

"Well, I've lived in Baronville really my whole life, other than a truncated stint in college. I suppose if these people lived here their whole lives I could have met them, or run into them, or known them in some way without actually remembering precise details."

"Joyce Tanner lived here for over forty years. She was about your age. Swanson lived here his whole life but he was in his thirties. Costa and Babbot were more recent arrivals."

"I can't say that any of them ring a bell."

"We found a photo of you and a Little League team. The kids were holding a championship banner. It was dated from last year."

Baron smiled. "That's because we won the state championship last year."

"Congratulations. The bank sponsored your team. Costa was an SVP there. He had the photo in his home."

"Did he? I wonder why?" Baron turned to Jamison. "I played baseball in college, on scholarship. I was actually drafted by the Braves my freshman year."

"Impressive," Jamison said.

"I was a pitcher. Had a good, live arm. And I could hit too. Good wheels."

"So what happened?"

Baron once more smiled disarmingly. "It's otherwise known as life." He looked at Decker. "I coached the Little League teams here for about ten years. But my last was the year we won the championship."

"Why your last year? They don't like winning here?"

"People said I was too controversial. Translation: I was too Baron for them."

"So why did they allow you to coach for a decade?" asked Decker. "Were you less Baron back then?"

"I'm not sure. You'd have to take that up with the good people of the town. It might be because they got to order me around and scream at me if we did poorly. So, to play that theory out to its logical conclusion, maybe they were pissed off that I coached a state championship team and that's why when I showed up for the season's spring training this year I was politely told that my services would no longer be required."

"Who told you that?"

"I don't remember the gentleman's name. Just that his tone was...gleeful."

"Why do you stay, Mr. Baron?" asked Decker. "Why stay and take all this crap every day?"

Baron took his feet off his desk and sat forward. Though his look was more serious, there was amusement still in his light blue eyes. "It may sound a bit masochistic, but I've come to enjoy the duel. And if I leave, that means they've won. And besides, where else would I go?"

"Hell of a way to live your life."

"Isn't it, though? Still, it is my humble life after all."

"So you still say you don't know Bradley Costa?"

"Can't say that I do. I just coached the kids. The bank paid for the uniforms, baseballs, and juice boxes." He abruptly stood. "I'd show you around the house, but you might need a tetanus booster first. How about I take you both on a tour of the grounds? They're not nearly as grand as they used to be, but it might provide a diversion from life in Baronville for about a half hour. And there is a lovely if rather ghoulish walk to the family crypt."

Before they could answer he simply walked from the room.

Jamison looked over at Decker. "Wow, just walking out like that. Who does that remind you of?"

He looked at her. "Who?"

Her only response was an exaggerated eye roll.

27

Baron had slipped an arm through Jamison's as they took a winding paved road down to the family burial ground.

"It's an old-fashioned concept now, of course," remarked Baron. "Burying ourselves on our property. But back then it was the thing to do. That's why there's a paved road like this, because the funeral procession would drive down to it. I even have a spot ready and waiting for me when my time is up. I hope the funds will be there to actually allow me to be interred."

Jamison said, "Do you *want* to be buried here?"

"I don't want to die at all, but it's not up to me, is it?"

There was a brick wall over six feet high set around the site, surrounded by thick trees, which threw everything into gloomy relief.

"Yes, it is very oppressive here," said Baron, perhaps reacting to Jamison's subdued expression.

He took a key from his pocket and opened a rusty wrought iron gate, the only entrance to the burial ground.

He pointed to an inscription written on a brass plate bolted to the wall next to the gate.

"That's Latin?" said Jamison.

"Very good, Alex," said Baron.

"What does it say?" asked Decker.

"Something like, 'Screw unto others as you would have them screw unto you,'" replied Baron.

"It does not say that," Jamison said with a laugh.

"Well, perhaps just in spirit. The loose translation is something like, 'Here lie the mighty Barons for all time. Peons take notice.'"

Jamison laughed again.

He led them inside the spacious grounds. Most of the graves were marked by an elaborate piece of marble or granite with the name of the dead on them. The stones were all neatly arranged and perfectly straight and upright. Someone clearly had been taking care of them. In the very center of the site was a large marble mausoleum badly stained by the elements.

Baron led them over to it and patted the rusted wrought iron door that was the entrance to the structure. All around the door the marble was stained with patina from the metal leaching onto the stone. The exterior walls were covered in dirt and grime and streaks of white mixed with rust stains and clumps of fungus.

"In here lies our founder and benefactor, the aforementioned John Quarles Baron the First," he announced. "He along with his wife, Abigail, and their children reside in there. Along with other family members who died after them."

"It must be spacious inside," noted Decker.

"It represents another bone of contention with those *living* in Baronville that the Baron dead here are housed better than they are."

Decker noted that on one side the mausoleum had sunk a few inches into the ground. "Structural problems?" he asked.

"I think we can blame it on his being cheap, even with his final resting place."

"It's pretty grimy," observed Jamison.

"I come down here from time to time to take care of the grounds and the other grave markers. But I don't bother with this one. You can't power wash this thing or use acid. It would just damage it or cause the marble to disintegrate. And I'm not scrubbing it by hand. I wouldn't do that even if I had loved Baron the First, which I don't."

He held up another key. "Would you like to see inside?"

Jamison immediately drew back, but Decker said, "Sure."

Baron unlocked the door and pushed it open. He led the way inside.

Decker followed and Jamison reluctantly brought up the rear.

On either side of the space were crypts set in long shelves on the walls. In the very center was a large granite crypt stained with age and moisture. Baron led them up to it.

"My ancestor, if not in the flesh, at least in the bone. He of course had to take center stage."

Decker and Jamison gazed down at the last resting place of John Baron the First.

"Impressive," said Decker. "Is everyone in here a Baron?"

Baron shrugged. "I haven't actually been in here since I was a little boy and my grandmother died. That's her spot over there," he added, pointing to a crypt along the left side of the wall. "I remember that this was the creepiest place I'd ever been in, and could barely wait to get out."

Decker continued to look around the space. The smell of mildew was fierce in here. Two of the walls were blackened with what looked like mold or fungus. Another wall had heavy smears of white, which mirrored those on the outside. The ceiling was blotched and stained with water damage.

He moved forward and bumped his leg against one crypt that jutted out into the main space.

Rubbing his thigh, he looked down at the etched name on the marble.

Abigail Baron.

Baron noted what Decker was looking at and said, "The man obviously wanted his eternal life all to himself, with even his wife shunted off to the side." He looked around. "It's full now, so no more admissions are possible. My spot is outside."

"I can see why you wanted to get out of here when you were little," said Jamison, slowly looking around. "I mean, it's all about…death."

Baron led them back outside and locked the door.

Jamison stepped off to one side of the mausoleum and inspected what looked to be the newest graves on the grounds, though from the dates on the tombstones they were over thirty years old.

"Are these your parents?" she asked.

Baron slowly turned from the mausoleum and looked at the twin tombstones.

"My father, Benjamin, and my mother, Dorothy. Dearly departed, as they say."

Decker walked over and read the information on the grave markers. "They were only in their forties. And they died on the same day. What happened?"

"Not really sure," said Baron as he joined them.

Decker and Jamison stared at him. "What do you mean?" Decker asked. "You should know how they died."

"There are certain people who believe they died in an accident. And there are certain people who believe they committed suicide."

"Which one do you believe?" asked Jamison.

"Neither."

"So how do you think they died?" she said.

He looked directly at her. "I think they were murdered."

"Those are three *very* different possibilities," said a clearly surprised Jamison.

"Yes, they are."

"Why do you think they were murdered?" asked Decker.

"Let's take a walk. There's a large pond on the grounds. And while their blooming period is long over, the foliage of the rhododendrons is still quite lovely," he added in a somber tone.

Baron led them down a well-worn path through stands of trees. Farther down he turned right.

"The grounds used to encompass the land all the way to the bottom where you reach the road heading into town," he explained. "But the property was sold off over the years. There's not much left, but what is, I think, are the prettiest parts."

He led them out of the woods and past a long column of rhododendrons to a large pond whose surface was half covered with vegetation. The ground sloped down toward it on all sides.

"I would come here as a child," said Baron, gazing at the water as they neared the edge. "We could never swim in it. You see the plant growth? The vines reach all the way to the bottom. You can easily become entangled. Indeed, one of my ancestors nearly drowned in there. Ever since then we would only come down to admire it. Or take a little rowboat across to the other side. It's quite deep in the center. And it used to have fish stocked, but that was a long time ago."

"And your parents?" prompted Jamison.

"My parents died in there," he said simply.

"But you just said no one went swimming in there."

"They weren't swimming. They were in their car."

Decker said, "How did a car get here?"

"Back then there was a road leading from the house to here. A long time ago my great-grandfather had it put in. That was when money was more plentiful. They would drive their cars here and picnic. They'd spend the whole day here, I was told. When I was a child, I remember my father bringing me and my mother down here, though we never had the luxury of an all-day picnic. But it was still very nice. Some of my happiest times here were with my parents."

He sat down cross-legged on the grass. Decker and Jamison remained standing.

"Now I come here sometimes just to think. And look at the water. And drink," Baron added. "I was in college at the time, just beginning my second year, when I got a call from the police. They had found my parents in their car at the bottom of the pond. They were quite dead, of course."

"My God," said Jamison.

Baron looked up at her. "I doubt God had anything to do with it." He glanced back at the water.

"What did the police say at the time?" asked Decker.

"They were convinced it was either an accident or, more likely, some sort of suicide pact. Even back then we were paupers, though I didn't know it. My parents were feeling the strain of keeping up the Baron image without the financial resources to do so. You see the house the way it is now. Back then it was better and we could still afford help both in the house and with the grounds, but it was difficult. My father was a good man. He could see the handwriting on the wall. He went to college and law school. He made a good living as an attorney, but it wasn't nearly enough to maintain all that the Barons had accumulated. My mother brought some money to the marriage, but it wasn't enough either."

"So why not sell the house and grounds and move?" asked Jamison.

"Even back then the house was crushed under a mortgage, which really made it unmarketable. And there were tax bills and other debts, all of which accumulated interest. It seemed like the harder my father worked to pay them off, the faster the debts grew. He kept going, but he ended up robbing Peter to pay Paul. I know they were thrilled when I received a baseball scholarship to college."

"He could have declared bankruptcy," suggested Decker.

"To him it was a matter of honor. He was not going to walk away from it."

"So he might have felt desperate," observed Jamison.

Baron abruptly stood. "Not desperate enough to kill himself. And even if he had come to that decision, he certainly would never have suggested that my mother join him in the hereafter." He paused. "I would like to think that the subject of their only child might have come into any such decision-making process, and that my parents would not have wanted to leave me all alone."

"Could it have been an accident, then?" said Jamison.

"I don't see how. You couldn't accidentally drive your car into the pond. It had to have been deliberate."

"But you think it was deliberate *murder*?" said Decker. "Did your parents have enemies?"

"They had enemies simply by being Barons."

"What did the police conclude?"

"I'm not sure they ever officially concluded anything. They did tell me that they suspected my parents had died either accidentally, or intentionally by their own hand. But no suicide note could be found."

Decker nodded. "Could they have been incapacitated first and then placed in the car? With the slope, all someone would have to do was put the car in neutral and it would roll right into the water."

"I asked the police that."

"And what did they say?"

"That it was still an ongoing investigation and they couldn't provide those details."

"And when the investigation no longer was ongoing?" asked Jamison.

"Apparently it still is, because the police never released a definitive finding one way or another. And they still won't answer any of my questions."

"You still ask?" said Jamison.

"About once or twice a year. I used to write letters or make phone calls. Now I do it by email directly to the police commissioner."

"And does the commissioner answer you?"

"With language that would be inappropriate to use in front of a lady," replied Baron, with a glance at Jamison. "And now, unless you have anything further, I really need to get back to that nap." He abruptly walked off.

Jamison turned to Decker, who was still staring at the pond.

"Now that is one complicated man," she said. "Shooting one-liners one second and then telling us his parents were murdered the next."

Decker glanced back in the direction of Baron, who was just disappearing into the woods.

"Decker? Did you hear me?"

He nodded.

"Do you think his parents could have been murdered?"

"I'm in no position to say one way or another. And that's not why we're here. We have six *recent* murders to investigate." He turned back to look at the pond.

"But you *are* curious, aren't you? I can tell."

Decker turned and walked past her.

"Wait a minute, where are you going?"

"While Baron is 'napping,' I want to look around."

28

DECKER, WE CAN'T just barge into the man's house while he's here. We don't have a warrant."

She was hustling after Decker and caught up to him after he cleared the tree line and the mansion and other buildings came into view once more.

"I just want to look around the grounds and maybe in some of the outbuildings."

"We still need a warrant to do that."

"Do we?"

"You damn well know we do."

Ignoring this, he kept walking until he reached the garage, which was not attached to the house but was separated by a lumpy brick courtyard. The garage had six bays, and all six were wide open, allowing them to see clearly inside.

"Just the one Suburban," observed Decker. "Looks pretty old."

The truck sat a bit crooked in the bay closest to the house.

"I don't see anything that jumps out," said Jamison.

Decker stepped into the garage and examined one of the walls.

"Look at this, Alex."

She drew up next to him and looked at the hole in the wall.

"It's a hole, so what?"

Decker pointed around. "There're holes over there and over there. And I noticed some in the house when we were passing down the hall. And they were in his study too."

Jamison's face screwed up. "That's weird. Do you think he has rats? And they opened the walls to check for that? Or mold?"

"That might be it. I would imagine a place like this is overrun with vermin and mold."

"Great, and we've been breathing it all this time."

"Well, he's been breathing it all his life." Decker glanced over her shoulder. "Maybe we'll have better luck with that building over there." He headed off to a structure set about a hundred yards away.

Jamison hurried after him, glancing back at the house to see if perhaps Baron was watching them.

Decker reached the building.

It had stone walls, a tin roof, and a thick wooden door, with a pair of windows bracketing the front portal.

"What do you think this is?" asked Jamison.

"One way to find out."

Decker opened the door and stepped inside.

Jamison scooted in after him, looking uncomfortable at this illegal intrusion.

Inside were shelves with clay pots, an old copper sink, stacks of wooden boxes with faded writing on the sides, and hooks on the wall from which a variety of gardening tools and instruments hung. On the countertops were old seed packets and long, shallow wooden boxes with metal mesh over them. Next to that were some old leather-bound journals.

Jamison opened one and looked down at the spidery writing that included plant references, weather, soil conditions, and lists of supplies and materials.

"It's a potting shed," she concluded. "I haven't seen one of them since, well, I never have except on HGTV. Some of the entries in this journal are dated eighty years ago."

"They probably had a full-time outdoor staff way back when. Maybe a flower and kitchen garden."

Decker tried the tap and water came out.

"Really smells in here," said Jamison. "And look, there are holes in the wall here too. I bet there are whole colonies of critters living inside there."

Decker opened some drawers. "And you have rotting soil and

mulch and maybe decaying plants, plus mold and mildew collected over the decades. Not a nice mixture, but—"

He stopped talking when he opened what looked to be a closet door and peered inside.

"Check this out."

Inside the space was a pillow, a thin rolled-up mattress, a blanket, and a small duffel.

Jamison peered over his shoulder. "Do you think someone was staying here?"

"Maybe." Decker pulled out the duffel, set it on the counter, and opened it. Inside were a couple of threadbare shirts, a dirty pair of men's dungarees, sneakers, and a rolled-up canvas fanny pack.

When Decker unrolled it, Jamison said, "Damn."

They looked down at a trio of syringes, three needles with corks on the tips, a few vials of liquid, a spoon, a crack pipe, a length of elasticized rubber, some plastic baggies containing white powder, a Bic lighter, four joints, and a clasp knife.

"Basically, your classic druggie's survival pack," said Decker.

"You think this belongs to Baron?"

Decker held up the pants to his legs.

"Baron is about two inches shorter than me. These pants are for a guy under six feet, so no, I don't think so."

"Some squatter, then?"

"That's more likely."

"Do you think Baron knows about it?"

Decker stared out the window at the main house. "I don't know. There's a direct sightline from here to there. Unless whoever it was came and went at night."

"Well, they probably would if they were here illegally."

"But why pick this place when we've been told that there are lots of empty *homes* in Baronville where people squat? Why come all the way up here to a crappy old potting shed? It's not like you could come and go so easily. And if the guy is squatting, it's not like he can drive a car right up here and not expect to be seen. He can get water from the tap, but I don't see any food around. How does he eat? And there's no bathroom here."

Jamison said, "So maybe Baron *does* know about it. Maybe he feeds him and lets him use the facilities in the house."

"So he's feeding a druggie and allowing the guy to stay in the old potting shed. Why?"

"Baron is sort of down and out too. Maybe he feels sorry for the guy."

Decker shook his head. "I could better understand that if Baron were rolling in dough, which he's not. And apparently everybody in town hates him."

"Maybe this guy isn't from Baronville."

"If so, how did he come to be here? You wouldn't look at this place from a distance and be able to see that it was run-down. And how could he know only one person lived here? Or that there were outbuildings where he could stay?"

"He might have talked to some people in Baronville and learned all that."

"I wonder where this guy is now?" He looked at the drugs and the accompanying paraphernalia. "And why leave this here? Most druggies I ran into when I was a cop would never leave their stash behind."

He picked up one of the plastic baggies. "Nickel bag of coke. About a gram's worth. These vials are probably heroin. Three to four bucks a pop in a metro area. Maybe more in a place like this. The elastic band is used to pulse the vein for the injection site. The lighter and the spoon are to make crack from the cocaine. Water and a pinch of baking soda. You stir off the residue, then you smoke the liquid coke in the pipe." He looked closely at the three syringes. "Never seen three needles for one druggie, though."

"Maybe he's trying to avoid infections."

"You mostly get that if you're sharing needles with someone else."

After a thorough search they turned up a few more items: a bottle of antiseptic wipes, two cell phones, a list of phone numbers written out on paper. And, cleverly hidden behind a cut-out panel under the sink where the pipes went into the wall, they found the pot of gold.

Or drugs, rather.

Fifty baggies of powdered coke, twenty vials of liquid heroin, and ten rocks of crack, along with a roll of cash rubber-banded together, and a loaded Sig Sauer nine-millimeter with the serial numbers filed off.

"Decker, this guy's not a user. He's a dealer."

Decker didn't answer because he was staring at something on the floor.

Jamison looked at the spot. "It's a narrow line in the dust," she said. "Like something was dragged over it."

Decker got down on his knees to examine the mark more closely.

He stood and looked at Jamison. "What do you want to bet the person staying here won't be coming back?"

"What do you mean?"

"That mark isn't from something being dragged over the floor. It's from a *bike* tire. I think we just found Michael Swanson's final place of residence."

CHAPTER

29

THEY HAD TAKEN photos of what they had discovered in the potting shed and then put everything back. Since they had no warrant, anything they found would not be admissible in court if it ever came to that.

They drove off and wound their way back down the hill to Baronville.

"Do we tell Green and Lassiter what we found?" asked Jamison as she steered the vehicle.

Decker shook his head. "No, they'd be pissed about what we did, and there's no need to fight that battle right now. And we have no idea if that stuff really belongs to Swanson. It's just a hunch. But his old landlord did say he rode a bike."

"Long ride up here and back."

"Hey, if it's the only wheels you have?"

"So where does that lead us?"

"To the possibility that John Baron is lying to us. He says he didn't know Costa; I'm convinced he did."

"Come on, Decker, lots of businesses sponsor Little League teams. You can't expect a bank bigwig to know all the coaches."

"Granted. But I wouldn't expect a *bigwig* to keep a photo of the team at his house either. And it's not like Baronville National Bank is Goldman Sachs or Citibank. Everybody probably knows everybody else. And if that stuff does or did belong to Swanson, then that means that Baron possibly knew *two* of the four victims. And Costa's secretary said the bank holds the mortgage on this place. For all we know, Costa is the point of contact for Baron."

"We could ask for alibis from him."

Decker shook his head. "I don't want to go there with him, not yet. He's cagey. And he apparently is alone a lot of the time, so what sort of alibi could he reasonably provide for two sets of murders?"

Jamison glanced at the truck's clock. "Oh no, we're going to be late."

Decker glanced at her. "For what?"

"Zoe's birthday dinner."

"Do we have to go?"

She looked at him, dumbstruck. "*I'm* the one who's taking them to dinner, Decker. It's at the nicest restaurant in town. You knew about this. It's one of the reasons we're visiting them now. To celebrate Zoe's sixth birthday. I have her presents in the back of the truck at least, so we don't have to go back to the house."

"But we're in the middle of an investigation."

"And we've been working on it all day. And we have to eat. So we're going to the dinner."

"But—"

"No buts, Decker. We're going!"

"Alex—"

Jamison made a slashing motion with her free hand. "Not another word. She's my niece and I love her more than anything."

Decker sighed and slumped back against his seat.

* * *

The restaurant was half full. When Jamison had said this was the best restaurant in Baronville, Decker hadn't known what to expect. But it was comfortably furnished and sparkling clean. The wait staff wore white shirts and black bow ties, the napkins were linen, and the menu had some dishes Decker had never heard of but that sounded tantalizing.

Amber and Zoe were in dresses, and even Decker could tell that

Amber had taken time with her makeup and her and her daughter's hair. This was apparently a big deal. Decker's mind took him back to his own daughter's birthdays. They *were* big deals.

He glanced at Jamison, who gazed adoringly at her niece.

"Did you have a good day at school, Zoe?" she asked.

"It was okay."

Amber said, "It's always tough starting in a new school. But you'll make friends, Zoe. You always do."

"Yeah," said Zoe, staring dejectedly at the tabletop.

Decker studied her. There was something in his head he wanted to say, but for some reason he couldn't make it come out. Then it occurred to him that he had superimposed his dead daughter's face over Zoe's. He looked away, rubbing at his temples.

Okay, Decker, that is definitely not healthy.

"Where's Frank?" asked Jamison.

Her sister made a face. "Work. Something came up. He should be here soon, though."

"Sounds like a tough job," said Decker.

"Well, at least it's a good-paying job," said Amber. "And one that's not backbreaking. Even though we already did some renovations on it, once Frank gets established here, we're thinking about selling our current house and buying a larger place. There are some beautiful old homes here sitting empty. They just need some TLC."

Zoe looked at her mother in a betrayed fashion. "Does that mean we'll have to move again?"

Amber looked nervous. "It won't be for a while, sweetie."

Despite this assurance, Zoe slumped back in her seat looking sad.

Noting this, Jamison said, "How about you open your presents now, Zoe?" She pulled two boxes from her bag and set them in front of her niece.

Amber said, "Alex, you didn't have to do that. You're paying for dinner already."

"A birthday means presents," said Jamison firmly, her gaze on Zoe.

Zoe immediately brightened. "Which one should I open first?"

"I think the one on the right. The smaller one."

Zoe very carefully unwrapped the paper. Revealed was a small wooden box. She gripped the lid and glanced up at Jamison, who nodded encouragingly.

Zoe opened the box. Inside was a necklace with a cross on the end.

"Wow." Zoe slowly took it out.

"Want to know something neat about that necklace?" said Jamison. Zoe nodded as her mother helped her put the necklace on.

"It was given to me by my aunt when I turned six, just like you."

"This...this was yours?"

Amber said, "I thought I recognized it."

"But, Aunt Alex, I can't take your necklace."

"Yes you can. Because it's not really my necklace. It's been passed down in our family for seven generations. So now it's your turn to wear it. And when you get older, it'll be your responsibility to pass it on to someone you love too."

Zoe looked up at her aunt with a face full of adoration. "That is so awesome."

"That *is* awesome," interjected Decker as he glanced at his partner.

"Thank you," said Jamison, beaming. "Okay, open the other one."

Zoe unwrapped the other present, revealing a book.

"*Charlotte's Web*," exclaimed Zoe. "Mom read this to me."

"Look inside," said Jamison.

Zoe opened the book and her jaw dropped. "It's...it's signed."

"E. B. White. He signed that for a young friend of his about forty years ago. Do you see what her name was?"

Zoe read off the name. "Zoe!"

"That's right."

"How did you ever find that?" asked Amber.

"I have a friend who works at a rare books dealer in New York.

She's been on the lookout for something like this for me for about a year."

Zoe said slowly, "This must have cost a lot of money."

Jamison leaned over, hugged her niece, and kissed her on the forehead. "What it is, Zoe, is a great book that you can read over and over your whole life."

"And every time I open it I can pretend that he signed it to me!"

"Yes, you absolutely can. That's called using your imagination, which is what Mr. White used to write the story in the first place."

Zoe said, "These are the best presents I've ever gotten."

Amber smiled at her sister and gave her a thumbs-up.

And then the door to the restaurant opened and there stood Detectives Green and Lassiter.

Decker spotted them first, and then Jamison did a few moments later.

Jamison groaned, "Oh no, what do they want?"

Amber and Zoe looked over at the doorway. Zoe said sadly, "Does this mean you have to leave? Before dinner?"

Decker rose and said, "I'll check. If something is up, I'm sure it can wait."

He walked over to the detectives. "Look, we're in the middle of a little girl's birthday party. Can't whatever it is wait?"

Green said, "We're actually not here to see you, Decker."

Decker looked puzzled. "Jamison, then?"

"No, not your partner."

"Who, then?"

Green glanced over his shoulder in the direction of the table. "Amber Mitchell."

Decker froze for a moment. "Her sister? Why? Is it about the murders?"

"That's not why we're here."

Lassiter added, "When the call came in we recognized the name. We thought we'd handle it because we'd already met the family."

"Recognized the name? What name?"

"Frank Mitchell. Amber's husband."

Decker glanced at Jamison and Amber, who were watching him closely, while Zoe was leafing through her book. He turned back to the pair of detectives.

"What about him?"

Green said, "I'm afraid he's dead."

CHAPTER

30

Ten p.m.

Not a good time for introspection.

One was tired. Not ready for deep thought about critical issues. And it was storming hard outside.

Decker sat in his chair, in his bedroom in the stricken house, and looked out at the water bucketing down.

And yet he *was* trying to be introspective, to make some sense of it all.

He set the empty beer can down on the floor and wiped his mouth.

It hadn't tasted like beer, but rather acid. He couldn't imagine anything tasting good ever again.

Streaks of lightning, followed by booms of thunder, seemed to form an uneasy synchronicity with the smacks of his heart.

Though he couldn't possibly hear them over the roar of the storm, he knew that two women in the house, one very young and one only in her thirties, fatherless and widowed, respectively, were probably still bawling their eyes out. In his mind's eye he could see them, hunched over, arms wrapped around their sides, as though struggling mightily to keep what little they had left inside somewhat intact and functional.

He used his finger to trace a circle on the window where condensation had collected.

One of the longest walks Decker had ever made had been from the front door of the restaurant back to the table. He had asked Green and Lassiter for permission to go and get the Mitchells and escort them out. He did not want the news that awaited them to come in a public place.

He didn't know why he had thought of this. His old self would have done so instinctively. To be sensitive and compassionate had been reflexive with the old Amos Decker.

Then the blindside hit on the field had left him pretty much the polar opposite of what he had been. It was, to say the least, unsettling to occupy the same body but be a totally different person.

Yet still, he *had* thought about having them be told of the loss in a private place. And he had acted on that thought.

That's something, isn't it?

He had told them that the detectives wanted to talk to them about something important and that they preferred to do so down at the police station, only a few blocks away. He had told them that it couldn't wait. It had to happen now.

He had seen an alarmed look in Amber's eyes that made him believe she knew that what was happening would be quite personal to her. But she remained outwardly calm and collected. And he thought he knew why.

Zoe had still been looking at her book and smiling. Obviously, the mom was keeping it together for her daughter.

Cassie, Decker's wife, would have done the same thing.

While they were collecting their things, Decker managed to whisper to Jamison, "It's about Frank. It's bad. The worst."

At first, Jamison made no noticeable reaction to this, but then her face visibly paled and her hand trembled a bit as she put it on the table to support herself as she stood.

The detectives drove Amber and Zoe to the police station. Jamison went with her sister and niece in Green's car, while Decker followed them.

At the station they all reunited.

Apparently nothing was said in the police car, because Zoe seemed fine—curious about what was going on, but otherwise all right.

That would not be the case for much longer.

They had gone into a private room. Well, Amber had gone in with the two detectives, while Jamison stayed outside with Zoe.

Surprisingly, Amber had asked Decker to accompany her into the room, where they had her sit, while Lassiter and Green stood facing her. Decker noted that in another corner of the room was a female police officer.

Green had spoken first.

"I'm very sorry to have to bring you this news, Mrs. Mitchell. It's about your husband."

Tears had welled up in Amber's eyes and she had started to shake.

"Oh no, please, oh no," she moaned.

Lassiter glanced at the officer, who came forward with a box of tissues and a bottle of water.

Decker stood back against the wall, watching all of this.

Green said, "There apparently was a terrible accident at the fulfillment center. They did tell us that your husband didn't suffer. It was very quick."

Amber was clearly no longer listening. She was hunched over, her face near the tops of her knees, rocking back and forth. "Oh, God, please. Frank, oh, please. Frank..."

Green looked hopelessly at Lassiter, who pulled up a chair next to Amber and put an arm around her quaking shoulders.

"I'm so sorry, Mrs. Mitchell. So very, very sorry."

Frank Mitchell, gone, just like that.

Amber and Zoe, bereaved, just like that.

Decker could relate. The very same thing had happened to him when, coming home one night, he had found his wife, her brother, and his daughter dead. Murdered. Gone from him for all time. One night. One breath.

If there was anything in life worse than that, he didn't know what it could possibly be.

The mind, breathtakingly special as it was, had never been designed to take in such a crushing event with such little preparation. It took all the air from your body, all the rigidity from your muscles, all the synaptic impulses from your brain.

It left you lessened, hollowed, destroyed.

It had been well over two years now since Cassie and Molly had been taken from him, and Decker was still unable to plumb the total depths of what the loss had done to him.

Amber had composed herself in that police station room, wiped her face clear, walked out on steady legs, embraced her daughter, and escorted her home, her arm never leaving the child's shoulders.

She had asked to see the body, but was told that it would not be a good idea. That there had been…substantial disfigurement. It would most likely be a closed casket unless the mortician could work some wonders.

Jamison had gone with them while Decker had stayed behind to get fuller particulars.

Green and Lassiter provided them.

Green said, "That place is huge. And it's got all sorts of automation. Robots going up and down aisles. These massive metal arm things putting incredibly heavy pallets of stuff way up on shelves. And they each do the work of about fifty people. What jobs are going to be left for humans, tell me that?"

Decker was less interested in the economic challenges of the coming automation revolution than in the exact details of Frank Mitchell's last few moments alive.

"But what happened to Frank Mitchell?" he asked.

Lassiter took up the story.

"They're working on an addition to the fulfillment center. Mitchell had gone there to check on some things. There was a mounted robotic arm that'll be used to lift heavy pallets high up on shelves, like Marty just said. It's in a confined space and wasn't supposed to be operational. But apparently something went wrong. When they went to look for Mitchell they found him crushed against a concrete wall with the robotic arm still holding on to him."

"But if it wasn't operational, how could it have come on?" asked Decker.

Green grimaced. "Now that's the sixty-four-thousand-dollar question. They believe it was a computer glitch. Something in the damn thing's software, or some spike in the power supply. Again, the place is under construction, and I guess all the bugs haven't been worked out yet."

Lassiter added, "I researched it a bit after we got the news. It's not the first death from some robot going nuts. There've been cases up in Michigan and Ohio and other places. It's what you get when you put these super-strong metal beasts in with humans. They've got no shot if things go sideways. That arm can lift ten thousand pounds no problem. You let that loose on a human, well, I saw Frank Mitchell's body. And it was…beyond horrible," she added in a trembling voice.

And that had been that.

Decker had driven back here and met with Jamison.

Jamison had called the rest of her family and Frank's parents, telling them the awful news. His parents and Frank's four siblings were coming in. Two of Jamison's sisters were also planning to attend the funeral. Jamison had given her sister something to help her sleep.

Amber and Zoe were together in Amber's bedroom locked in each other's arms.

Decker and a subdued Jamison had sat up in the kitchen and discussed things. He had filled her in on what had happened.

"This is terrible, Decker. They just moved here. And now this?"

Decker remained silent.

She looked up at him, her face teary. "What are you thinking?"

"That you need to concentrate on your sister and Zoe. Leave the investigation to me. At least for now."

She slowly nodded. "It's not something I want to do, you know that?"

"I know that."

"Zoe's in shock. I'm so worried about her. She loved her dad so much. And on her birthday. I mean, how awful is that?"

"Pretty damn awful."

"We've got to think about funeral arrangements. There aren't many options here. And getting family here for it is a logistical nightmare. And what about burial? Would he want to be buried here? He has no connection to this place. So, cremation? God, I can't believe I'm having to talk about any of this."

She started to sob quietly.

Decker hesitantly rose, went over to her, and patted her shoulder with his hand. His mind had some soothing things he could say to her, but a disconnect did not allow him to actually say them.

Jamison seemed to understand his internal struggle. She gripped his big hand. "Thanks, Amos."

He said nothing. But he kept patting her shoulder, silently cursing his inability to do anything more than that.

Now, in his room, he looked at the spot on the window glass where he had just now wiped away the circle he'd made in the condensation.

Six people were dead.

Indisputably murdered by another with premeditation and malice aforethought.

Now a seventh person, Frank Mitchell, was dead. By an accident, from all accounts.

Jamison had finally gone to bed.

But Decker once again found sleep too elusive.

He decided, despite the rain, to take another walk.

He took the same umbrella from the hall closet, buttoned his coat around him, and set off.

His path took him to the street of the Murder House. The place was dark, but the police tape was still there. The local cop car wasn't there. But one of Kemper's black SUVs was. He could see a man inside it.

Decker looked down the street.

Dan Bond, the blind man.

Mrs. Martin, the Sunday school teacher.

And Fred Ross with his sawed-off shotgun and bitter demeanor.

The only three people who lived on the street and who could have seen anything relevant. And if that was the criterion, then Bond should be struck from the list, though he might have *heard* something.

And Ross too. He said he'd been at the hospital, though Decker would have to check that.

He looked at his watch.

Ten-thirty.

Mrs. Martin lived at number 1640. The lights were on there.

Decker started walking toward it.

31

Yes?" said the voice on the other side of the peephole.

Decker held up his creds to the little circle of glass.

"Mrs. Martin? I'm Amos Decker, I'm with the FBI. I was wondering if you could answer a few questions."

"About what?"

"About what happened down the street."

"It's rather late. And I don't know you."

"I'm sorry for the lateness. But I saw your lights on. I'm working with Detective Lassiter. She told me that you used to teach her Sunday school," he added, hoping that would break the ice.

It worked, because he heard the locks turn, and the door swung open to reveal a tall elderly woman with wispy white hair and a pale complexion. A pair of wire-rimmed spectacles rode low on her long, bumpy nose. She had on a beige cardigan wrapped around a starched white blouse. A baggy pair of dingy gray sweatpants incongruously completed her outfit. A sturdy pair of white orthopedic shoes were on her feet.

"Thank you, Mrs. Martin, I appreciate it."

"Would you like some hot tea? It's so damp out." She shivered. "Gets in my bones."

Decker didn't really feel like tea, but he figured it might buy him some more time with her. "That would be great, if it's not too much trouble."

"No trouble. I've nothing else to do, and I was thinking of having another cup myself. Oh, there's Missy."

This was in reference to a sleek silver and black tabby that glided out from behind the couch in the front living room. It sidled up to Decker and rubbed itself against his leg.

"Nice kitty," said Decker awkwardly to the cat.

"Oh, she's a pain in the butt, but it's just her and me now."

Decker looked at one wall where a deer head was mounted.

"Six-point buck," he said.

"My late husband. He had that mounted, oh, it was almost forty years ago now. But, unlike some hunters, he ate what he killed. That buck gave us enough venison to last a long time."

She turned and put a hand against the wall to steady herself.

Decker spotted a quad cane, so called because it had four sturdy feet for firm support, standing in a corner.

"Do you want me to get your cane?" he asked.

She shook her head. "I need to get the darn thing fixed," she said. "Can't use it inside. It scratches my hardwood floors."

She led Decker into the kitchen, continuing to steady herself with a hand against the wall as she went.

The house, Decker estimated, had been built in the fifties, so the kitchen was small but functional. There were little frilly curtains around the window over the sink and a wooden table with two ladder-back chairs. On the wall was a landline phone, with a long flex cord dangling from it. Next to it were phone numbers written in pencil on the wall, some with names next to them.

Martin glanced at where he was looking and smiled. "I don't have one of those smartphones, and I've no memory for numbers, so I write my important numbers down there. I call it my phone number wall."

"Good system."

"Do you have a memory for numbers?"

"Apparently not as much as I used to."

Martin put the kettle on the stove and lit the gas with a long match. Then she took cups and saucers from a pine cabinet with a sheen of lacquer finish over it.

She opened a plastic storage container and said, "Would you like some cookies? They're oatmeal raisin. I made them myself."

"That sounds great, thanks."

"So you're with the FBI. That is so exciting. But don't FBI agents wear suits? They do on TV." She put a hand to her mouth as she looked over Decker's rumpled appearance. "Or are you undercover? You look like you could be an undercover agent."

Decker took all this in and said, "I did some of that. But now I'm here helping the local police with what happened at the house down the street."

"Yes, it was awful." Martin shivered again. "I mean, I know the town has hit bad times, but we've never had a *murder* on our street before."

She set out the plate of cookies along with paper napkins. "Do you take milk and sugar in your tea, like the British? Not that you're British. Are you British? You don't sound British, but I always like to ask."

"I'm from Ohio. And, no, just tea, thanks."

"It's peppermint. Very good for your throat and sinuses."

"I'm sure."

"I had a friend from Ohio. Toledo. Have you ever been there?"

"Yes."

"I liked my visit. But that was in, oh, 1965. Has it changed much?"

"I expect so, yes."

"Most places change, don't they?"

"Like Baronville?" asked Decker.

She gazed at him, and this time the look was far less like a scatterbrained old lady.

"I've lived here all my life," she said. "Back when times were booming, there were certain elements that were not all that... nice."

"Care to elaborate on that?"

She looked up at him over her cup of tea. "Water under the bridge. Now, what can I do to help you with your case?"

"We're looking for anyone who might have seen something strange at the house in question."

"Have you talked to anyone else on the street?"

"Just one. Fred Ross."

At the sound of the man's name, Martin's face screwed up.

"That man," she said derisively.

"You two don't get along?"

"My husband loathed him until the day he died. Fred is very hard to get along with. Hateful, prejudiced, manipulative."

"The first two I understand, having met the man. But manipulative?"

Martin didn't answer until the water had boiled and she had poured out the tea. She handed him his cup and sat down opposite him.

"Fred's wife died, oh, it's been twenty years ago now or more, about the time my Harry passed. She was a nice lady but he never gave her a moment's peace. If his dinner wasn't ready and to his liking, or she'd gone over her grocery budget, or the house wasn't spick-and-span, he would just abuse that woman no end. It was awful."

"Did she ever call the police?"

Martin took a sip of her tea and set the cup down before answering.

"Now that's where we get to the manipulative part. He would never raise his hand against her. Never scream or threaten."

"What did he do, then?"

"He would just keep picking away at her, little by little. How she looked, how she dressed. How she should be ashamed she couldn't be a good wife and mother like the other ladies on the street. He just played all these mind games with the poor woman, convinced her that everything was her fault. He was quite good at it, the sick bastard. And Fred was cruel to his son too. I think that's why they don't have much of a relationship."

Decker drank some tea and nodded. "I could see how Ross would be like that. Always handy with some reply. Turning things against you. He did that with me."

Martin pointed at him. "Exactly. Exactly right. Turning everything, even your own words, against you."

They fell silent for a few moments.

Martin said, "But you wanted to ask me about that night?"

"Have Detectives Lassiter and Green been by to see you?"

"A Detective Green did come by to talk to me. And then, earlier today, Donna came by. Not in her official capacity, she said. Just to visit and see how I was doing. I hadn't seen her in years. I was surprised she was with the police. I thought she would go on to be a doctor or something. Always very bright and, well, gung-ho. Nothing would stop her."

"Well, you have to be pretty tough to be a cop and homicide detective," noted Decker.

"Oh, of course, and I'm very proud of her. She's come a long way and overcome a lot of obstacles."

"What do you mean?"

"Well, I suppose you know about her father?"

"No, I don't."

"Perhaps I shouldn't say anything."

"I wish you would. It could be helpful."

"Well, that's really why I was surprised Donna went on to become a police officer."

"Why is that?"

"Because her father was convicted of a crime."

"What crime?" asked Decker.

"Of killing someone."

"Who?"

"A banker here in town."

Decker tried to keep his features calm. "When was this?"

"Oh, decades ago. Donna was just a little girl."

"Why did he kill the banker?"

"Because the bank foreclosed on his house. Donna's father worked at the last textile mill in town. It closed down and left Rich Lassiter high and dry along with about a hundred others. He lost his house, he lost everything. He apparently got drunk one night, went to the man's home, and set fire to it. The banker, I forget his name, lived alone. Anyway, he died in the fire. Rich, I guess, was horrified at what happened. But he admitted to setting the fire. He went to prison. And he died there about two years later. Maybe from guilt, I don't know."

"So Lassiter would have still been a little girl?"

"She was a very *sad* little girl after what happened to her father. I think she turned to religion to help her through the tough times. Her mother committed suicide from a drug overdose after Donna came back here when she finished college."

"That's pretty tragic all the way around," said Decker. "Getting back to the present, what did you tell Detective Green about the night the men's bodies were discovered?"

"That I didn't see anything. I had a headache and went to bed early."

"What time was that?"

"*Jeopardy!* had finished up, and I was puttering around for a bit, so it was certainly after eight."

"Did you hear or see anything before you went to bed? Even if it wasn't connected to the house?"

Martin thought about that. "I remember the storm starting to come in."

"Do you remember hearing some sounds right before the rain started?"

"What sort of sounds?"

Decker thought back, pulling the frames up in his head.

Good question, what sort of sounds?

"I'm not sure. Just some unusual sounds. I was staying at the house behind that one. I also saw a plane flying over."

Martin shook her head. "I didn't see or hear a plane. Didn't wake up until around six the next morning."

"The police sirens didn't wake you?"

"I took a sleep aid, so no, they didn't."

"Have you ever seen people coming or going from that house?"

Martin drank some more tea and pushed the cookie plate toward Decker, who took one and bit into it.

"There was one thing," she said suddenly.

"What was that?"

"Well, it didn't have to do with the house where those men were killed. It was the house *next* to it."

"You saw something?"

"It was a couple of weeks ago. I didn't mention it to Detective Green because he just asked me about the night the dead men were found. Anyway, I saw a man enter the house, oh, around eleven at night. Now, I knew the Schaffers, who used to own that house. They died and their children tried and failed to sell it. So it's been sitting empty all that time."

"Go on," prompted Decker.

"Well, this man was walking down the street. I didn't see a car. The only reason I saw him was because Missy wanted to go out, and I opened the door and there he was on the street. It was a full moon and really bright, so I saw him pretty clearly. Well, he walked down the street and into the Schaffers' old house."

"Can you describe him?"

"Tall, over six feet, I think."

"White, black?"

"Oh, definitely white. And he was thin."

"Could you see his face?"

She shook her head. "And then, two nights later, I saw it again."

"The same man?"

"No, this time it was another man. Shorter, under six feet and stockier. He was also white. He went into the house. I kept looking for a while but he never came back out."

"And no car?"

"No, he just came walking down the street and went in. Same time of night. I was up because, well, I'd napped earlier and then woken up around nine. You do that when you're old," she added.

"Did you report this to the police?"

Martin shook her head. "No. I didn't think to. I mean, for all I knew the men had rented the place and had a perfect right to be there. And if they didn't, well, I've seen folks *use* empty houses before. Lots of homeless around here. If they needed a place to stay…"

Decker looked at her curiously because Martin suddenly looked nervous. "Was there any other reason you didn't report it?"

She looked down. "Hard times makes for hard…people. If I called the police and they came and did something and the people found out I'd been the one to call? I'm old and I live alone. I don't want to cause any trouble, for me or anyone else."

"So, a tall, thin white guy and a shorter, stockier white guy?"

"That's right."

A few minutes later, Decker headed toward the house Martin had been talking about.

He could be wrong, but the men Martin had described could very well have been Beatty and Smith, the two dead DEA agents.

32

DECKER STOOD LOOKING at the house where he had found the two dead men. He swiveled his head and stared at the home next to it, where maybe DEA agents Beatty and Smith had been seen going in around two weeks ago.

The black SUV was empty. The DEA agent on watch here was apparently making his rounds.

There were no other cars on the street. Or people.

Decker looked across the street at the house where Dan Bond, the blind man, lived. It was dark. But then again, light and dark wouldn't matter to Bond.

He would deal with Bond later. For now, he had a possible lead to run down.

Decker walked briskly to the rear of the property and looked around. He eyeballed the Mitchells' house, which he couldn't see clearly because, unlike the Murder House, the backyard of this house had bulky, overgrown bushes at the rear fenceline.

He looked to his right and could make out the Murder House, though there was a lot of vegetation growing wild between the two structures. Not surprising considering both of them had been empty for a while.

He eyed the rear of the house. There was a deck tacked on to the back of it too, though it seemed to list to the right a bit, as though the sunken support posts were starting to give way.

Decker could make out the flashlight probes in the darkness from next door, like stabs of lightning in miniature.

The DEA agent making his rounds.

Decker placed his bulk behind a formidable oak tree until the light passed on and the fellow Fed headed back to the front of the house.

He counted off the seconds in his head until he heard the thunk of the SUV door closing.

He stepped up to the back of the house and tried the doorknob. Surprisingly, it turned freely.

Perhaps not so surprisingly, if people had been coming and going from here.

He went inside and used his phone's flashlight feature to look around. The house's interior was similar to the one next door. It had probably been put up by the same builder, perhaps the whole neighborhood had.

He swept through the kitchen and entered the living room and shone his light around. Nothing. No furniture, nothing on the walls. No rugs. Curtains did cover the windows, but they were soiled and falling apart.

He heard a noise and looked around. He passed his hand over a floor register. The heat had just come on, which showed the house had electricity. Yet Decker couldn't risk turning on lights without the agent from next door possibly seeing them and coming to investigate.

The place smelled of damp and mothballs and abandonment.

He checked the upstairs and found the same conditions.

He went to the basement, and, considering what he had found the last time he'd entered a basement, took out his gun.

He reached the bottom and looked around.

Dampness and mildew and dead bugs.

But no dead bodies.

If the two DEA agents had spent time here, there was no sign of it. No discarded takeout meals. No place to sit. No clothes in the closet. At first Decker had thought the two had set up a surveillance nest here, but there was absolutely no sign of that. They could have taken their equipment with them. But why have such a nest here? What was there to see?

And if they were using *this* house, how had they ended up dead in the place next door?

He was about to go back up the stairs when he froze and backed away to a far corner of the basement.

A door had just opened on the main level. Whether it was the front or back he couldn't be sure.

Next, he heard creaks on the floorboards just above him.

It *had* been the back door. The person was now heading to the front of the house.

Decker gripped his pistol.

His dilemma now was obvious. It could very well be that the person above was the agent from next door. He might have seen Decker moving around inside, or maybe had glimpsed his cell phone flashlight and gone to investigate.

Decker did not want to draw down on a fellow Fed.

But if it wasn't the guy from next door?

The footsteps headed up the stairs. Decker waited until they returned to the main level a minute later.

He didn't hear any sirens. He couldn't see outside. Had the guy called in backup?

Then he heard what he knew he eventually would.

The basement door opened.

Keeping to the back corner of the basement, Decker called out, "Amos Decker, with the FBI. Identify yourself."

"DEA Agent Stringer from next door," said the voice immediately.

Decker didn't move. "I'd like to believe you, but I need to see some ID."

"Thinking the same thing. How do you want to do this before I call in reinforcements?"

"Don't you recognize my voice?" said Decker. "I was pretty vocal with Agent Kemper when we were at the morgue."

"I just got to town this morning with a new shift of agents."

"Okay, toss your creds down the stairs and I'll toss mine up."

"Look, I'm supposed to be here and you're not, and I don't know who the hell you are, so toss *your* creds up, right now."

Decker took his time pulling out his creds. He slipped his gun inside his waistband and with his free hand dialed a number on his phone.

"Give me a sec to get them out," he called up the stairs.

Kemper answered after two rings.

"I've got a situation," whispered Decker. "Is an agent named Stringer assigned to the house tonight?"

"No. Jenkins has the night shift. Eight to eight. Never heard of an Agent Stringer."

"Okay, get some guys over here now. I'm in the house to the left of the crime scene when facing it from the street. I'm in the basement, with a guy pretending to be one of yours."

Before she could say anything else he clicked off and looked down at his phone.

"You got two seconds to toss them up or this is going to get ugly," said the man calling himself Stringer.

"Coming right now."

Decker crept forward and approached the staircase from the side.

He put his thumb on the screen of his phone and readied himself, flicking the flashlight on at the same time as he tossed the phone in front of the stairs, with the light shining up them.

Four shots were fired instantly.

Four suppressed shots. The bullets hit the floor and ricocheted off.

Though he hadn't been hit, Decker let out a yell as though he had so the other guy would let down his guard.

A moment later, he fired half his mag up the stairs in an arc wide enough to cover the entire width of the doorway.

He heard an impact, and then another, and then a grunt.

He stepped out of the way as something came rolling down the steps and landed in a heap at the bottom.

Decker retrieved his phone and shone the light on the bundle.

It was a man.

A dead man now, thanks to Decker.

As he stared down at the corpse, Decker felt himself audibly gasp.

Normally, when he was confronted by death, Decker's synesthesia would kick in. The hairs on his neck would rise, as though an electrical current was running through him, he would feel dizzy and nauseous, and, most significantly, he would see the most vivid shade of electric blue. It would assail him from all angles, suffocating him.

Yet he wasn't experiencing any of those things. He just saw a body.

It was as though his synesthesia had simply vanished.

And then he heard the sirens.

And then heavy feet clattering on the front porch.

Agent Jenkins from next door, he was certain.

The cavalry was here.

Decker slumped down on the bottom step and waited.

CHAPTER

33

Okay, you need to stop going out at night, and I damn well mean it!"

These words came from Jamison, who was standing in front of Decker in a long T-shirt and sweatpants. She was barefoot, and her matted hair evidenced that until very recently she had been asleep.

They were in the living room of the Mitchells' home. Amber and Zoe were still asleep upstairs.

Decker had called Jamison from the basement of the house where he'd shot and killed a man.

He had explained matters to the first responders and then to Kemper, and finally to Green and Lassiter when they had shown up, including how he had gotten there in the first place.

The real surprise had come when Kemper had seen the dead man lying on the floor with two of Decker's bullets in his chest.

"That's Brian Collins," she had said.

"And who is he?" Decker had replied.

"He's a drug dealer."

"Do you think he knew Michael Swanson or maybe worked with him?"

"Doubtful. Collins was a heavy hitter. He's wanted in several states for distribution and murder."

Green had asked, "But what was he doing here? And why try to kill you?"

"He must have seen me go into the house," said Decker. "He might have been watching the place."

"Okay, but why take a chance on going after you when a DEA agent is right next door?" asked Green.

"I take that as a good sign," said Decker. "That means they're afraid we're getting closer. Like when they tried to toast me and Jamison inside Toby Babbot's trailer."

"So, *are* you getting closer?" Green had asked.

Decker had looked down at the body. "Maybe too close."

Now Decker looked up at the very pissed-off Jamison. "I didn't know anything like this was going to happen, Alex. I just couldn't sleep and decided to check some things out. I talked to Martin and that led me to the house."

Jamison slumped down next to him. "Decker, I know you may not get this, but my sister and my niece just received horrible news. Frank is dead. This is going to affect them for the rest of their lives."

"I *know* all that, Alex."

"I know you know the *facts*. But sometimes you miss the stuff beyond the facts."

"What exactly is your point?"

"*One* tragedy is enough right now. Please don't add yourself to that tally. I don't think any of us could take that. I know I couldn't. Now, unless you're going to do something else incredibly dangerous and stupid, I'm going to bed before my head explodes. I suggest you do the same."

She trudged off upstairs and Decker slowly followed.

He washed up and undressed.

He glanced down at the hand that had pulled the trigger that had ended Brian Collins's life. He didn't feel bad about that. Collins had tried to murder him, so he got what he deserved.

Which still did not explain why a man he didn't know had tried to kill him tonight.

A heavy-hitter drug dealer. Wanted in several states.

The DEA.

Rogue agents.

Six murders, four of which seemed to involve unrelated parties.

Was it all about drugs? Lots of people had died due to drugs.

And by all accounts, Baronville was in the grips of the same opioid crisis that was terrorizing other areas of the country.

And he and Jamison had apparently run smack into it.

And what about Lassiter's father burning down a banker's house and going to prison for it and then dying there? And her mother later committing suicide? He could see now why Lassiter had a beef against the current John Baron, unreasonable as it might be.

And lastly, what the hell was happening in his head? Why hadn't the electric blue color come? And the nausea and the hairs rising off his neck? It wasn't like he wanted any of those things to happen to him. But at least they were predictable. That they no longer occurred was, in his mind, worse than if they still happened to him.

My brain might be changing again. Who will I be tomorrow?

He sighed. That sort of speculation was not something he wanted to dwell on.

And then a thought occurred to him. Thankfully, it was tied to something about the case.

He took out his phone and called Kemper. She answered on the second ring.

"What would your two agents be doing in that house?" he asked.

"I have no idea."

"Well, they might have been watching something or someone."

"You mean like a surveillance nest?"

"Something like that, though I couldn't find any evidence of that."

"There are only three people who live on that street, Decker, and they're all old and one of them is blind and one of them is a former Sunday school teacher."

"And one of them is an asshole with a sawed-off shotgun."

"Explain that."

He told her about his run-in with Fred Ross.

"I still don't see how a bitter octogenarian in a wheelchair has anything to do with this."

"I don't either."

"Well, I have some news for you."

Decker perked up at this. "What's that?"

"The dead guy, Brian Collins?"

"Yeah."

"I have some more info on him than what I shared at the house tonight."

"And why are you willing to share it with me now?"

"I'm growing to like you."

"Yeah, right."

"We knew his former partner," Kemper said.

"Who was that?"

"Randy Haas, the dead guy who fingered my two agents as rogues."

CHAPTER

34

"SHE WANTS US to do what?"

Decker stared across the breakfast table at Jamison.

She lowered her cup of coffee and said crossly, "Amber wants us to go to the fulfillment center and get Frank's personal effects from his office. And pick up his car."

"But I've got the case—"

She cut him off. "Decker, my sister is having to plan her husband's funeral this morning. The least we can do is help her with this."

"I'm ready, Aunt Alex."

They both turned to see Zoe standing in the doorway, her coat on and her eyes puffy from crying.

"Okay, sweetie, we'll be ready in a minute. Why don't you go wait by the front door?"

Zoe glanced woefully at Decker before trudging off.

Decker looked at Jamison. "Are we dropping her off at school?"

"No, she's coming with us."

"With us? What about school?"

"Decker, her dad just died. She's not going to school today. She's in kindergarten. Her missing a few days is not going to determine if she gets into Harvard."

"Do you think it's a good idea for her to go with us, though? I mean, to see her dad's stuff?"

"There's really no other way. Amber doesn't know anyone here well enough to feel comfortable leaving Zoe with them, especially now. And she'll be running around today dealing with funeral arrangements, picking out a coffin and flowers and a gravesite. Do you think Zoe should be exposed to *that*?"

Decker sat back looking contrite. "No."

"Okay, so finish your coffee and let's get going. I'll drive over and you can drive Frank's car back here."

As they got to the front door Zoe put out her hand, not to her aunt but to Decker. Looking surprised and with a quick glance at Jamison, who nodded at him, he took the little girl's small hand in his enormous one and they set off.

* * *

"Good God, this place is huge."

They had just pulled into the parking lot of the Maxus Fulfillment Center when Jamison made this remark.

The place was truly vast and the parking lot was filled with cars. On the rear side of the building they had seen fleets of semis loading and unloading their trailers at a seemingly endless line of loading docks.

"And they're adding more to it," noted Decker, pointing to the construction on the western side of the building.

Jamison found a parking space a long way away from the entrance and they walked through a sea of vehicles toward the front doors of the building.

Zoe said, "Is this where my dad worked?"

Jamison said, "Yes, it is, honey. We're going to get some of his things."

"Mommy told me that. And his car too."

"That's right."

Zoe peered up at her aunt. "Is my daddy really dead?"

Jamison stiffened and seemed incapable of answering.

Before she could get a reply out, Decker bent down, lifted Zoe up in his arms, and pointed to the building. "You see how big this place is?"

Zoe nodded.

"Well, your dad helped run this whole thing. Look at all these cars and all the people who work here. It was very important what he did. Taking care of this building and all these people. They all counted on your dad. And he did a really good job."

Zoe put her thumb in her mouth and her eyes turned watery.

Decker continued, "So we just need to go in and get his stuff, because his stuff belongs at home with you and your mom, right?"

Zoe nodded vigorously while sucking anxiously on her thumb.

Decker walked on with the little girl in his arms, a stunned-looking Jamison hurrying after the pair.

Inside, they were directed to the office of the person who managed the facility. The nameplate was on the wall next to the office door.

"Ted Ross," read off Decker. "Interesting."

Through the gap in the blinds covering the window looking into the office they could see a middle-aged man in a dress shirt and tie with thinning gray hair sitting behind his desk and on the phone. Three of the walls were white-painted drywall, but the rear wall had been gussied up with wood paneling trimmed with moldings and medallions. A boxed Pittsburgh Steelers jersey with a "terrible towel" suspended inside was hanging on one section of the wall.

"Why is it interesting? Do you know him?" asked Jamison.

"I might have met his old man."

They knocked on the door and they could see Ross glance up, finish his call, and cross the room to open the door.

He looked up at Decker, then Zoe, and his features turned somber.

"I'm Ted Ross. Thanks for coming in. We didn't know what to do with…"

He stopped and glanced uncertainly at Zoe.

Jamison said, "We were glad to come by. Amber is my sister. I'm Alex Jamison and this is Amos Decker."

"You're both with the FBI, I heard."

"That's right," said Jamison. "And this is Zoe, Frank's daughter."

Ross put out his hand for Zoe to shake. "Hello, Zoe, it's very nice to meet you."

Zoe nodded and shook his hand, but said nothing, as her thumb was still firmly planted in her mouth.

"Is your father Fred Ross?" asked Decker.

Ross looked surprised. "Yeah, why?"

"I met him the other night."

"Sorry," said Ross tightly. "He's a real piece of work."

"One way of putting it," replied Decker.

"Anyway, let me show you where the things are."

Ross led them down a long hallway.

"How big is this place?" asked Decker.

"A million two hundred thousand square feet," replied Ross. "And we're adding another six hundred thousand square feet. This is the future of retail, for better or worse. Malls across the country are shutting down and chains are going bankrupt. Consumers are going to the Internet to buy their stuff and these places are how that stuff gets delivered."

Decker said, "I guess that's why these facilities are so big."

"That's right. And it's really a win-win for us and the vendors we serve. It lets them focus on products and services, and *we* handle how the orders get filled. We do order fulfillment for over fifteen thousand vendors and counting. These fulfillment centers are not cheap to build and run. So companies that want to sell online, but can't afford to build a distribution site, outsource that function to companies like Maxus. We charge shelf space to the vendors down to one-twentieth of an inch and we take a cut of every sale, but it's worth it to them for the reasons I just cited. This is our tenth center, and there are plans for ten more to be built pretty much simultaneously in the next five years. Business is booming. We literally can't keep up."

"I guess that's a good problem to have," said Jamison.

"Yeah, but they'll work you to death if you let them."

As soon as Ross said this he paled and glanced at Zoe, but she didn't appear to have heard him. She was busy looking around from her high perch in Decker's arms. He had tried to put her down once, but she had so frantically clung to him that he had kept carrying her.

"Here we are," said Ross.

He unlocked a door and opened it to reveal an office about a third the size of his own. It was neatly organized with a desk and chair, three metal file cabinets against one wall, and on another wall a large whiteboard covered with notations and lists.

A sleek computer rested in the center of the desk.

"Frank was very organized and efficient," noted Ross. He looked at Zoe. "Your dad was *really* good at his job."

She nodded but said nothing.

Ross pointed to a cardboard box on the desk. "We collected his personal items. They're all in there." He fished in his pocket. "And here are his keys. We pulled his car up near the front entrance. It's a blue Kia four-door, but you knew that."

"Thanks," said Jamison, taking the keys and handing them to Decker.

Decker said, "Alex, why don't you take Zoe and head back. I can bring the box in my car."

"My *dad's* car," said Zoe, her thumb out of her mouth now.

"Exactly, your dad's car," said Jamison quickly. "Okay, we'll see you back home."

She took Zoe and they walked off. Zoe looked forlornly back at Decker, before they turned a corner and were out of sight.

Decker turned to Ross. "Hey, you mind doing me a favor?"

"If I can, sure."

"Can I see where it happened?"

Ross looked mildly surprised. "Where Frank was...killed, you mean?"

"Yeah."

"It was an accident. A tragic and stupid one and it never should have happened, but it was still an accident."

"I'm not saying otherwise. And I'm not here investigating. I just want to be able to tell Amber...She might have questions, is all. But she couldn't bring herself to come today. Plus, she has a funeral to arrange."

"Right, I know. It's all so awful. We're paying for the funeral and everything," Ross added quickly.

"That's good of you."

"And look, I know she's going to sue Maxus. Hell, I would if I were her."

"That's a pretty remarkable statement considering you work for Maxus."

"I've only worked for them since they started building this place. And they hired me because I was one of the few people around that had managerial experience running a large facility, and I also advised them during the construction phase. I hope Amber gets all that's legally coming to her."

"What facility did you run?"

"I'm in my early sixties, so I'm old enough to have participated in the salad days of Baronville, or at least the tail end of it. I started out as a finish carpenter, then ran my own construction company. After that I managed the last paper mill in town. It wasn't as big as this place, but we had about two hundred employees, materials coming in, finished product to get out, and trucks coming in and going out at all hours. So running this place was right in my wheel-house."

"So, Frank Mitchell?"

"Follow me."

35

Ross led Decker to a door at the end of the hall. It opened up to a mezzanine with a bird's-eye view of the vast main floor.

"I have that window in my office so I can keep an eye on people coming and going in the management section," said Ross. "But here is where I really focus a lot of my attention. Because this is where the money is made."

Decker looked out over a sea of shelving and miles of conveyor belts, and people and both fixed and mobile robots working in seemingly perfect synchronization.

"Looks like a lot of moving pieces," he noted.

"This place is one big algorithm," said Ross, nodding. "But the general concept is pretty simple. We get product in and we have to get product out as fast and as accurately as possible."

He pointed to the back side of the facility where the loading docks were located. "Product coming off the trucks is opened, scanned, and put in those blue totes. The conveyor belts you're seeing route it to different parts of the FC." He looked at Decker. "Short for 'fulfillment center.' Once it gets to its destination inside here it's unloaded and scanned again, along with a barcode scan of its cubby location on the shelves."

"Cubby location?" asked Decker.

"Right. All the metal shelving you see is divided into small cubbies with barcodes and alphanumeric IDs. It's kind of like the old library catalog card system, only now it's digital. When orders come in, and they do at the rate of hundreds per second, the pickers—they're the ones in the yellow vests—use handheld scanners to find the product to fill the order. They scan the item and place it in the tote. Once the tote is full, it goes to the conveyor belt system."

"How does it get there?"

"Either by humans carrying it or using rolling carts, or robots do the task." He pointed to one device rolling along that looked like a large upright vacuum. "That's an AMR, which stands for autonomous mobile robot. It carries the full tote to the belts using embedded intelligence and application software, its brain if you will."

He pointed to another device that was carrying a large shelving unit. "That's a lifting robot. It looks like one of those robot vacuum cleaners, but it can hoist thousands of pounds on those specially built shelving pods. It moves on a predefined grid system to where it needs to go."

Ross indicated another section of the facility.

"Now, the products arrive there, at the prepackaging stations. The items are sorted into small slots on tall wheeled shelves. Each slot equals one order, because now you're going from bulk to individual orders and the funnel gets really narrow. You deliver the wrong stuff to someone, well, that's not good. The shelves are then rolled to the packaging stations, where they're packed for shipment."

"By people, I see," said Decker.

"Robots can't really pack. At least not yet. An algorithm spits out the right-sized box for each order, rollers kick out the air cushion bags for packing the item in the box as well as the tape to seal it. Then it goes down the belt to the labeling machine where the mailing label is put on. Then it goes to the loading docks where the boxes are put on trucks. Sort of like a jigsaw puzzle because every truck has to be packed as tightly as possible. A couple of wasted inches matters when you're shipping millions of packages."

"And people load the trucks as well?"

"Yeah, robots can't do that either. Yet."

"You keep saying *yet*."

Ross looked at him. "There's one major problem with robots.

They don't have hands like humans. You see those fixed robotic arms over there?"

Decker glanced where he was pointing to see a row of large metal arms lifting huge pallets onto high shelves at the back of the facility.

Ross said, "Now, that's a great application for a robot. Weights that humans can't lift safely. One direction, one spot to place it on. It does not require fine motor skills, only brute strength. Humans can feel things with their hands and work in small spaces in ways that robots can't right now. They can make snap judgments about moving something an inch here or there because it works better. They can also recognize new products they may never have seen before and be able to deal with them on the fly. Right now, robots can't do that reliably. But the industry is working on it. In fact, the Holy Grail in the FC business is something called reliable grasping mechanisms, which is a fancy term for making robots act more human when they're picking up things and putting them in specific places. It'll get solved one day, because people get sick, take bathroom breaks, eat lunch, get tired, and need a vacation and health care insurance. With robots all those things go away."

"So you're saying one day this place will just have *robots*?"

"Businesses don't give a crap about creating jobs. They care about making *money*. With robots, you'll just need some tech guys to maintain and repair them."

"But if people don't have jobs to make money, who's going to buy all the stuff on those shelves?" asked Decker.

Ross grinned. "I don't think the rich guys have thought that one through. Probably leaving it for the government to figure out. God help us if that's the case."

Decker pointed to a set of doors along a far wall. "Are those magnetometers?"

"Yes. That's the employee entrance. We call our employees 'associates.' Anyway, as with any business, you have to deal with theft. They have to go through the magnetometers and also have their bags searched."

"Does everybody have to go through it?" asked Decker.

"Yep, me included."

"I understand the physical demands of working here are pretty tough."

"We have to fill about four hundred orders a second, so it's nonstop movement. A picker's handheld device will receive a ping every time an order is placed. And the system directs the picker to the shelf where that item is. And the process starts. The workers here have to be able to lift about fifty pounds and walk or stand for up to twelve hours a day. And you'll probably end up walking fifteen miles in a shift. But, hey, walking is good exercise, right? I make my rounds every day at the same time, checking on things." He looked at his watch. "In fact, I'll be heading out in about an hour to do just that. I get to hobnob with the workers, and it's good for them to see management out there on the floor. But it's not all fun and games. I have other managers on the floor and their job is to make sure the work gets done. We ride the people pretty hard, because upper level management rides us pretty hard. We don't hit our quotas we're looking for another job. And this place is so big it could hold over twenty football fields, so there's a lot of ground to cover. We sometimes even ride bikes or three-wheelers to get to places faster and cover as much ground as possible. And with the new addition it'll be half again bigger. And we have a climate control system, but it can still get pretty hot."

"Well, obviously people want to work here."

"The pay is good. Pickers start out at ten bucks an hour, plus health care and a 401(k) plan. You're here five years, you're making sixteen an hour. And we give out a decent amount of overtime and during big crunch periods like Christmas we have mandatory overtime, where they'll work fifty-five to seventy hours a week. With the overtime, a lot of people here earn forty grand a year or more. These days that puts you in the middle class, especially if both husband and wife work here, and we have a lot of those. And hell, in this town that could even make you rich."

"But Frank Mitchell told me you had trouble finding workers?"

"And he probably told you why. We have about a thousand

employees but we always need more. And we'll definitely need more with the new addition coming online. Problem is hundreds of the applicants couldn't pass a drug test. Hell, it's like that all over the country. Kids, parents, grandparents, all hooked on crap." He paused. "There you have it, the world of the FCs."

"Now let's go to the world where Frank Mitchell lost his life," said Decker.

Ross led Decker down a set of metal steps to the main floor and then down a long concourse to where the addition was being constructed. He had to unlock a door and they stepped into a cavernous area that largely resembled the space that they had just left. Only there were no people here and no products on the towering shelves.

"Normally there would be lots of construction workers here, but the police have closed that down while they investigate. I hope they let them back in soon. I've already gotten calls from management. They're not happy about the shutdown. We're on a tight time frame to get this piece done."

"Cops don't care about construction schedules."

"I know that. I was on the phone with management when you showed up. I mean, I'm sure they're sad that Frank died. Nobody deserved what happened to him, but it's still a business."

"Right," said Decker, looking around. "So where did it happen?"

"Over here."

Ross led him to an area on one side of the addition.

There was a column of robotic arms located here, although the tall shelves they would be lifting boxes onto were not yet in place. It was only concrete walls.

And on one section of wall Decker could see bloodstains and other human matter. Around the robotic arm at this space was yellow police tape.

"We're not supposed to go inside the tape," said Ross. "I guess you already know that," he added hastily.

"Have the police gone over the area?"

"They were in yesterday and early this morning. Photos and diagrams and measuring stuff and dusting surfaces."

"Pretty routine for something like this," noted Decker. "Has anyone checked that robotic arm to see what happened?"

"The company that installed it is sending a team in to go over it with a fine-toothed comb. We have to get this figured out. I mean, this cannot happen again. No way. When Frank was found the thing still had a hold of him. He was smashed up against that wall. The arm can move in slow motions, or it can do rapid movements with enough force to rip your head off."

"Why was Frank here last night?"

"Part of his job was to oversee things in the addition. He would normally make rounds through here right before he left for the day. The construction workers get in at seven and knock off around five. I wasn't here when it happened, but I got a call telling me about it."

"Who called?"

"Marjorie Linton. She's in operations. She and Frank worked together. She knew that he had gone to check some things out. When he didn't return, she tried his cell phone but he didn't answer. Then she went to look for him. And found his body."

"And then she called you?"

"Yes. She was hysterical. I was the one who called the police after I got her to calm down so I could understand what she was saying."

Decker looked at the murderous robotic arm. "So he would have been here inspecting the robot?"

"Sure, he could have been. Frank knew how the different robots functioned."

"So the thing was operational?"

"Well, it was powered up but it wasn't on. We had tested it, or the company that manufactured it had, on site about a week ago. Everything was good to go."

"So how did it kill him?"

"That's why the robotic company is sending a team in. We won't know until they do their diagnostic."

"But will they be able to tell? To give a definitive answer?"

Ross shrugged. "I don't have the technical expertise to answer that. I hope so, because, like I said, we have to make sure this never happens again."

Decker looked at the bloody wall. "Well, once is one time too many."

They walked past a large table on their way back to the fulfillment center. Decker noted the unrolled sheaf of papers on it.

"What's that?" he asked.

Ross walked over to the table. "Construction drawings for the addition. It's pretty much the existing one just halved in size. Why?"

Decker stared down at the drawings, the mental frames flowing past in his head, until he arrived at one, and then moved on to a second one. When he put the two together in his head, it literally clicked inside his brain.

At least his memory seemed to be working okay now.

"No reason," he said.

36

"Decker, what are you doing?"

Decker had pulled out the construction drawings he'd seen earlier in the Mitchells' front closet.

He had sat down at the kitchen table and was unrolling them as Jamison had come into the room.

He flattened out the drawings and looked up at her. "These are construction plans for the Maxus FC."

Jamison sat down across from him. "So what? And why did you stay behind?"

"I wanted to see where Frank died."

Jamison looked dumbstruck. "Why? It was an accident."

Decker looked over her shoulder at the doorway to the kitchen. "Where are Amber and Zoe?"

"Amber's still out and Zoe's taking a nap. I don't think she slept much last night. She could barely keep her eyes open on the drive back here."

Decker refocused on the drawings, leafing through the pages until he got to the one he wanted.

"Hang on a sec."

He jumped up and ran out of the room.

"De—" Jamison began and then stopped, shaking her head. She glanced over the plans but had no idea what she was supposed to be looking for.

A minute later Decker returned with a folded piece of paper in his hand. He opened it on the table, smoothing it out.

"What is that?" Jamison asked as Decker rummaged in a couple of kitchen drawers until he found a pencil. He didn't answer but sat down at the table and started making lines on the paper.

As Jamison studied him, she said, "That was the piece of graph paper we found in Toby Babbot's trailer."

"Yep."

"What are you doing with the pencil?"

"Filling in the indentations on the paper. Remember, whatever he drew was done on the piece of graph paper above this one in the pad. But his marks were carried onto the paper because of the pressure he was applying."

"Okay, I get that. Probably many a marriage has ended because a cheating spouse didn't know that the bottom page carries impressions made on the top page. But what does that have to do with anything?"

Again, Decker didn't answer. He kept filling in the lines and then sat back when he was finished.

Jamison looked down at the paper.

"Compare it to this page of the construction drawings for the FC," said Decker.

Jamison looked between the two documents and her jaw dropped. "They're the same, just on a smaller scale." She looked at Decker. "Why would Toby Babbot have been recreating the construction drawings for the Maxus Fulfillment Center?"

"I don't know. But I want to find out." Decker picked up the piece of graph paper. "When I saw the plans for the addition, it jogged my memory of the plans I'd seen in the closet here." He held up the paper. "And then it struck me that the marks on this looked very close to the marks on the drawings in that closet."

"Well, I think your memory is as good as ever, then," said Jamison. "But I don't really see why we should waste time on this."

"Because somebody tried to kill us while we were in Babbot's trailer, Alex. Maybe he wanted to kill us, or maybe he wanted to get rid of some sort of evidence." He tapped the graph paper. "Like this."

"But evidence of what?"

Decker sat back. "I don't know."

"He could have just taken it. Why burn the place down?"

"He might have meant to do that, but we interrupted his search. He might have been afraid we'd find it or something else that Babbot might have had. So he torched the place with us in it. Two birds with one stone."

Jamison folded her arms over her chest. "What did you find out about Frank's accident?"

He told her what Ted Ross had said.

She shook her head and scowled. "A renegade robot, great. Makes you want to chuck all this technology and go back to hammers and shovels."

She eyed her partner as he stared at the wall opposite him, obviously lost in thought.

"Decker?" He didn't answer. "Decker, you're not thinking that Frank's death was something other than an accident, are you?"

He finally came out of his reverie. "Just because someone told us it was an accident doesn't mean that it *was* an accident."

"But the alternative would be…Decker, Frank had no enemies here. Why would anyone want to kill him?"

He looked over at her. "How do you know he didn't have any enemies?"

"Why, because…he…They hadn't been here that long. And he was such a sweet guy."

"I didn't know there was a certain time period one needed to create enemies. And even sweet guys can make an enemy of someone not nearly as sweet. What I do know is Toby Babbot had the plans for the FC in his trailer. Someone burned down that trailer. And now Frank dies at that FC because a robot arm that's not supposed to be on suddenly went berserk and killed him."

"How could those two things possibly be connected?"

"I don't know if they are connected. But they *could be.*"

"But we already have six other murders we're investigating."

"I realize that."

"And you have no proof that Frank was murdered." She lowered her voice. "And you cannot go around telling people, especially my sister and Zoe, that Frank might have been murdered, Decker. They're traumatized enough."

"I have no plans to tell anyone that."

"But then how are you going to investigate it?"

"The company that built the robot is sending a team in to see what happened. I'm sure they'll give a copy of that report to the cops and we can get it from them. At the very least they'll have to share it with Amber, so we could get it that way too."

"How quickly will the report be done?"

"No idea. Which is why I'm not waiting. I'll make inquiries." He added hastily when he saw Jamison about to object, "I'll *discreetly* make inquiries about the fulfillment center."

"But you're supposed to be helping Green and Lassiter, and now I guess Agent Kemper, with these murders."

"I'm still going to do that. In fact, I'm going to work on it today."

"So I don't see why you're adding in Frank's death, which may simply be an accident. These sorts of robot accidents involving people have happened before."

"Yeah, they have. I looked it up. The odds, I very roughly calculated, are about the same as dying in a plane crash." He stared at her. "So, do you still think it was *probably* an accident or maybe worth investigating?"

When Jamison didn't answer, he rose and headed for the door.

"Where are you going now?" asked Jamison.

"Back to high school," replied Decker.

37

If this was the current state of education in America, Decker thought, the country was in serious trouble.

Baronville High School looked like it was nearly ready for the wrecking ball to come through. In fact, it wouldn't have taken a demolition team to knock the place down, it appeared one guy with a sledgehammer and a six pack of Red Bull could do the job just fine.

The roof had holes in it, some windows were broken, and the front door stuck so much that Decker nearly wrenched his shoulder out of joint tugging it open.

When he entered the school and headed to the office he could smell mildew and damp everywhere. The linoleum floors looked untouched since they had been installed. The trophy cabinet outside the office had no trophies inside it.

He presented himself at the office and told them who he was and what he wanted. The assistant principal, a petite mousy woman with graying hair, a stiff gait, and a melancholy expression, escorted him to the library.

"Looks like the school has seen better days," commented Decker.

"The whole *town* has seen better days," she replied. "No tax base means no money for this place. And we've only got half the number of students we used to have. The great exodus is on. Actually, it has been for about thirty years now."

"But things might be turning around. There's the fulfillment center. That employs a ton of people."

"And I understand that someone died there."

"Unfortunately, yes."

She led him into the library. The shelves held few books, and there were a couple of antiquated boxy computers on metal tables. There wasn't a single student in the place.

"The yearbooks are over there," she said, pointing to a far corner.

"If I have any other questions, can I just ask the librarian?"

The woman went over to the door and looked back. "You could if we had a librarian. We lost her in the last round of budget cuts. We can spend a billion dollars on a sports arena, but we can't drop a dime on our kids."

Decker just stood there and stared at her awkwardly.

She said quietly, "If you need anything else, Agent Decker, you can come and get me. I'd be glad to help."

"Thanks."

She left and Decker walked over to the yearbooks and scanned the volumes there. He pulled out four of them from the span of time he needed to check, sat at one of the rickety tables, and opened the first one. He found the students he wanted in the freshman year.

John Baron the Fourth looked so young, and he was, barely fourteen at the time. He was still growing into a body that would become long and lean. His Adam's apple stuck out prominently from the photo, along with his toothy grin. Decker ought to have been surprised that the elite Baron would have been sent to a public school, but he had learned that Baron's parents had actually been pretty much broke when their son was growing up. A free public education may have been their only route.

Decker turned the pages until he got to another alphabetical section.

Joyce *Ridge*, who had become Joyce Tanner upon marriage, looked back at him. She was exceptionally pretty, with long blonde hair and soft blue eyes.

Decker had seen her autopsy photo with this same face torn apart by a shotgun blast. He had learned Tanner's maiden name during the course of his investigation.

He flipped through some more pages to find that Tanner and Baron had been members of the school's honor society. He turned to the sports section of the yearbook and saw that Baron, despite being a freshman, was a starter on both the football and baseball teams. His stats as a quarterback and pitcher were listed and would have been impressive for a senior.

Tanner was on the tennis team and was also a cheerleader.

Decker went through their sophomore and junior yearbooks and saw the pair grow up in the photos. Tanner was voted Most Popular as a junior, and Baron's athletic career was on a tear. As a junior, he was all-state in both football and baseball.

Decker next picked up their senior yearbook and slowly went through the pages.

Baron was now at pretty much his full height, and handsome, with strong features, thick dark hair, and a pair of bewitching eyes. An article in the sports section of the yearbook reported that Baron threw for nearly three thousand yards and thirty touchdowns as a quarterback, and as a pitcher on the baseball team, he was undefeated and had tossed the only perfect game in school history. He was one of only two high school athletes named first team all-state in two sports that year, and subsequently had been named athlete of the year for the commonwealth of Pennsylvania.

He had also signed a college baseball scholarship, the yearbook reported, evidencing both his athletic and academic prowess.

Joyce Ridge had grown into a beautiful young woman. She was tall, athletically built, captain of the tennis team, and head cheerleader. Her future seemed limitless, though there was no mention of her going to college or receiving a scholarship.

Decker turned to the prom pages and saw that she also had been voted homecoming queen.

But Baron was not homecoming king. Another young man, named Bruce Mercer, a wrestler and president of the Spanish club, had been chosen to walk the field with Joyce. She didn't look happy about this, Decker concluded as he studied the pair on the field. At the edge of the photo was Baron, his football helmet off.

He was staring at the pair with such a desolate expression that it moved even the normally stoic Decker.

Decker looked back at the sports team photos from all four years.

In each, Baron, though clearly the star of both the football and baseball teams, had been shunted off to the side. Decker knew from experience that your best players, and certainly your seniors, were given prominence in team photos. That was just how it worked.

Yet even in Baron's senior year when he was setting all sorts of records, he was in the back row and off to the right. His being a head taller than anyone else around him was the only reason that he stood out. The same for the baseball team, where the pitcher of a perfect game was relegated to the fringe of the photo.

He should have been captain of both of the squads, Decker felt. But he wasn't.

And Decker certainly knew why, and also why the young scholar-athlete had not been voted homecoming king.

He was a Baron.

For the seniors, there were short biographies on each. With Joyce, Decker learned that her uncle was a pastor at Baronville Baptist Church and that Joyce taught vacation Bible school in the summer, was a lifeguard at the community pool, and volunteered to tutor freshman students in math. She also competed in dance and was quoted as wanting to work with the handicapped. With Baron, Decker found that he had started up a Greek mythology club, could read Latin, and wanted to play major league baseball as well as start his own business one day.

They certainly seemed to be impressive people, Decker thought. Maybe a little *too* perfect. When he'd been in high school all he had pretty much focused on was football and girls.

But then again, Joyce had lost her parents at a young age, and was being raised by her aunt and uncle. And he knew Baron's life wasn't perfect, and maybe Joyce's wasn't either. Perhaps they strove as hard as they did to compensate for negative elements in their personal lives.

Decker next turned to a few other photos that he had found in the yearbooks. Each showed Tanner and Baron together. In the way they looked, or held hands, or rubbed shoulders, Decker could easily see that the young couple were deeply in love.

So, what had happened?

Baron had gone off to college and his girlfriend had stayed here? And done nothing with her life? Ending up fired from a JC Penney. Living in a ratty apartment. Being murdered next to a man with whom she apparently had no connection.

Decker closed the books and replaced them on the shelves.

He sat back down and mulled over what he had discovered.

His coming here had been a hunch based on a few facts, the paramount one being that Tanner and Baron were the same age and probably had attended school here at the same time.

So Joyce Tanner and John Baron had a connection dating back to high school. Baron had lied about that, because he'd said he didn't recall if he had known her or not. Then there was the Bible verse found on the wall behind the bodies of Tanner and Babbot. Was that somehow tied to Tanner's religious background? And was the Thanatos symbol found on Costa's forehead connected to Baron's founding a Greek mythology club?

There were other possible connections.

Michael Swanson may have been living in John Baron's potting shed.

Bradley Costa's bank had been a sponsor of Baron's Little League team, and the murdered man had a photo of the team, and Baron, in his home. And the bank held the mortgage on Baron's property. Decker had made inquiries at the bank about whether Costa had worked on the mortgage, but had received no answer as yet.

But what about Toby Babbot? Did he also have a connection to the man?

If not, three of the four did. That brought it outside the realm of coincidence, at least in Decker's mind.

So what do I do now?

He left the school, trudged down the steps, and headed to his truck.

And stopped.

The pale blue Suburban was parked on the street.

And John Baron the Fourth was leaning against the front fender, his arms folded over his chest, as he watched Decker leaving his old school.

38

Baron said, "Tired of busting bad guys? Looking for a teaching job?"

Decker walked over to him. "No, but the place looks like it could use some TLC."

"The whole town could benefit from that." Baron pushed off the truck and put his hands in his pockets.

Decker noted that he was wearing the same pair of dungarees, though the shirt was different and looked freshly laundered. Sandals were on his feet despite the cool air.

"How'd you know I was here?"

Baron pointed to the truck. "Recognized it from when you came to visit me."

"Right."

"How's the investigation coming?" asked Baron.

"It's coming."

"Read that there was a death at the fulfillment center."

"That's right. It was actually my partner's brother-in-law."

Baron looked genuinely surprised. "Damn, tell her I'm sorry. I like Alex."

"I will." Though Decker was thinking that Baron didn't really know her.

"How did it happen? What I read wasn't really clear on that."

"Accident. Robot met human and the human lost."

Baron nodded. "Sounds like a bad sci-fi movie." He glanced at the school. "So why the interest in Baronville High?"

"Just running down a few things. Joyce Tanner was a student there."

"She was Joyce *Ridge* back then."

"Surprised you knew that, considering you told us you didn't know her."

The two men stared at each other. "Let me guess," said Baron. "You were either checking out anyone still working at the school who knew us, or you were taking a stroll through the yearbook section?"

"The latter."

"Is the fact that I knew her a crime?"

"Lying about it to law enforcement during a murder investigation is. It's called obstruction of justice."

"I guess I didn't see the relevance."

"That's my job to determine, *not* yours," Decker said sharply.

Baron performed a mock bow. "Mea culpa, Agent Decker. I'm in the wrong and you're in the right."

"What happened?"

"To Joyce?"

"To the both of you."

Baron leaned back against the truck fender. "I went to college and she didn't. I don't know why. She was really smart and I kept on her to go. But I think her aunt and uncle laid a guilt trip on her to stay in Baronville, get a job, and help them out because they had taken her in after her parents died. Her uncle was a minister and didn't make a lot of money, and he was really strict with her. But we were still together. I came home as often as I could. We had a plan to have a life together. Then my parents died and I found out I didn't have a dime. I knew we weren't rich, of course. But we still lived at the Baron estate and my father always told me that there would be some money for me, which did not turn out to be the case. Then, I blew out my arm pitching, they revoked my scholarship, and I pretty much went into a tailspin. I didn't have the bandwidth for Joyce or anything else. I could barely keep myself together." He looked down at his clothes and then at the ancient truck. "And some would argue that I failed miserably at that anyway."

"I saw in the yearbook that she taught Bible school. And that you were into Greek mythology."

"I barely remember any of that. It was a long time ago."

"Still into mythology?"

"I have a hard enough time dealing with real life."

"So, what happened with Joyce after she graduated from here?"

"I dropped out of her life because of my own problems. About four years after graduation she married a guy named Rick Tanner and she had a couple of miscarriages. He was a jerk, he drank too much and beat her up. They finally got divorced. By then, she was a totally different person. No confidence, no ambition. She got into drugs. She got a series of lower- and lower-paying jobs, injured herself at one of them, and got hooked on painkillers like a lot of people in this place."

"You seem to know a lot about her. Did you two keep in touch?"

"We were still friends. Neither of our lives turned out as expected. That worked to bring us together, I guess, especially after she was divorced."

"Ever think about getting back together?"

Baron shook his head. "If I married someone, I would like to be able to help support them. I've got nothing. And why would I subject Joyce to all the crap I deal with? Making her a Baron? Worst thing I could do to her. When I thought I would have some money, my plan was to move away and we could have had a life where nobody cared what my last name was. I was going to be a big league pitcher, start my own business. Be successful off my own efforts. That didn't pan out, obviously. But we did keep in touch."

"She was laid off from JC Penney some months before her death."

"I know. Not the future one would have expected for the homecoming queen. But Joyce was also a member of the honor society and also excelled at math. She was no dummy. She could have had a far different life. I wish she had."

"What about you? You weren't the homecoming king. You got

voted best athlete in the entire state and you're not even team captain of your high school squads?"

"We live in a democracy, Agent Decker. One person, one vote. It's inviolate."

"Doesn't mean it's right if people are voting for the wrong reasons."

"Happens every two, four, and six years in this country. And I didn't care about being homecoming king or team captain. I really didn't."

"But you did care about Joyce. Is that why you were supporting her all these years?"

Baron looked at him shrewdly, but said nothing in reply.

Decker continued. "She had no job, but she could pay her rent. She had a car. She put food on the table. And you said she was addicted to painkillers. That's not cheap either."

"Okay, I gave her some money."

"I thought you didn't have any."

"I don't have a lot of money. But I have *some*. I don't actually nap all day. I do work. I do have an income. And I have family heirlooms that I can sell in a pinch. I spend virtually nothing on myself. So I could help her. And I wanted to."

"That was nice of you."

"She deserved it. And for the record, she *used* to be a pain pill addict. She wasn't any longer. She kicked it. It was damn hard, but she did it."

"Did you help with that too?"

"Why does that matter to you?"

"In an investigation, you try your best to get a full picture of what you're seeing. Those sorts of details round things out. Provide motivations on myriad levels."

"Do you mean motivations to murder? I did not kill Joyce."

"There are other kinds of motivations."

"Such as?"

"Such as helping other addicts, even drug dealers. Like Michael Swanson? You said you didn't know him, but I'm pretty sure he was living in your potting shed."

Baron looked unfazed by this revelation. "Was he? Didn't

know. It's a big property. And the Barons haven't had anything to 'pot' for decades."

"So you're saying he was coming and going a hundred yards from your house and you had no idea?"

"You said you were 'pretty sure,' which means you have no proof."

"Are you saying you had no inkling someone was squatting in your potting shed?"

"'Someone' and 'inkling.' Very broad terms. Are you trying to catch me in another lie?"

"It will not end well for you if I do."

Baron cocked his head. "Your tone has become a full degree more serious."

"I just want to impress upon you that a federal penitentiary is not the place you want to be."

Baron thought about this for a few seconds while he stared up at a bird floating along on thermals. "Mike Swanson was...a loser on many levels. I can relate to that. I can understand that. Now, there are losers who are bad people. Really bad people."

"But Swanson wasn't one of them?"

"He was an idiot. But he was a nice idiot. He sold some pot. He sold some pills. He was basically harmless."

"So you gave him a place to stay?"

"I found him in the shed one day sound asleep. He'd been kicked out of so many places, he apparently biked all the way up to my property just to see if there was a place he could land for a while. He ended up staying longer. I voiced no objections. It's not like I lacked for extra space."

"We found his stash in the shed. It wasn't just pot and pills. It was harder stuff than that. And he had a gun and a big roll of cash."

Baron spread his hands. "I didn't condone it. But if I cast out everyone who sold drugs around here, well, I'd be as lonely as I apparently am, if that makes any sense."

"Okay, you knew Swanson and Tanner, after you told me you didn't. And Costa? The banker with the picture of your Little League team in his home?"

"Under penalty of perjury and going to that federal pen you mentioned, I did not know him. What I have, I have in cash and other negotiable instruments, which I keep hidden at my home."

"Is that wise?"

"I don't know. But it's how I do things. The banks did not treat me or my family very well when we needed some help. I had no reason to entrust them with the little I had left."

"So you can think of no reason why Costa would have that photo of you and your team in his home?"

"Other than he was proud we'd won the championship? No."

"What about Toby Babbot?"

Baron shook his head. "Didn't know him."

"He was on disability. Had a metal plate in his head from an industrial accident. Lived in a ratty trailer, because he couldn't afford anything else."

"He's not alone in that in Baronville."

"His place got torched while Jamison and I were inside it."

Baron's eyes widened. "Someone tried to kill you?"

"That's usually the case when you try to burn down a structure with people inside."

"Why would someone do that?"

"Maybe you could tell me."

Baron thought about this. "When did Babbot suffer his industrial accident?"

"Several years ago."

"Here in Baronville?"

"Yeah."

"That's strange."

"Why?"

"What *industry* do we have here where someone could have that kind of an accident?"

Now Decker looked surprised. "That's a fair point. And you've given me something to check out."

"What's that?"

"How broadly someone defines the term *industrial*."

CHAPTER

39

So, my gut was right.

Decker was in the Mitchells' kitchen staring down at a report on Toby Babbot's accident that had required the insertion of a metal plate in his head.

When the "industrial" accident had happened, he'd been working on the construction of the Maxus FC. He'd been driving a forklift that had collided with another piece of heavy equipment. Babbot hadn't been wearing his safety harness and had been thrown clear of the forklift, resulting in the head injury.

A fractured skull.

He had health insurance through his job, so his medical bills had been covered. But apparently alcohol had been found in his bloodstream at the time of the accident. Thus any lawsuit he might have filed against the company was problematic. However, the company might have been hedging its bets, because they had allowed him to stay on for a few months in an office capacity before letting him go.

Decker heard the front door open. A few moments later Amber appeared in the doorway.

She looked so pale and shaky that Decker didn't know how she was able to stay upright.

"Do you know where Zoe is?" she asked.

"Alex took her to run some errands for you."

She nodded. "How are you doing?"

Decker looked embarrassed that she would be worrying about him at a time like this.

"I'm fine. Can I, um, get you anything?"

"No, I…I don't need anything. Thank you for getting Frank's car and personal items."

"It was really nothing, Amber. We were glad to do it."

Her lips trembled. "I got Frank a really nice coffin."

Decker felt his skin turn cold. He wanted to get up and give the woman a supportive hug. But the thing in his head stopped him from doing that.

Tears beginning to slip down her cheeks, Amber said softly, "I'm going to go lie down."

All Decker could do in response was nod.

He listened to her walk down the hall to her bedroom on the main floor.

The door closed behind her.

Next, he heard something hit the floor.

Shoes.

And then the squeak of bedsprings.

Amber flopping on the bed.

And then came the sobs that easily reached all the way to the kitchen.

Unable to endure the cries of the bereaved woman, Decker quickly rose and went out onto the rear porch, where all of this had begun.

He felt himself shaking all over. What Amber was experiencing was what he had experienced. And seeing someone who had lost a loved one to violence had brought all those memories flooding back.

You can't go there, Decker. If you do, you're no good to anybody.

He forced himself to focus on the house behind them.

The spark of electricity. The fire. The discovery of the bodies. All that had followed.

He sat in a deck chair and continued to stare at the place, even as his thoughts wandered to other facets of the investigation. And then he arrived at one particularly disturbing one.

If Babbot had been killed because of something at Maxus, then what about Frank Mitchell?

Was the accident not really an accident?

After all, if you could program a robot to do one thing, you could program it to do another thing.

But why kill Frank Mitchell? What would have been the motivation?

He pulled out his phone and called Todd Milligan, a team member of his at the FBI. He asked Milligan to check out anything he could find on the Maxus Corporation.

Milligan knew Decker well enough to not ask any questions. He simply said, "On it."

Decker put the phone away and continued to stare at the house where the bodies of two DEA agents had been left. They had been killed elsewhere, that was now clear, but Decker had no idea why. Or why that house had been chosen as the location for their bodies.

He closed his eyes and let his memory flash back to the first time he'd met Frank Mitchell.

They had been sitting in the living room after Frank had gotten home from work. Frank had been naturally upset at two murders having taken place almost in his backyard. He'd been curious about the killings, but that was normal too. It would have been unusual if he *hadn't* been curious.

Then Decker moved on to another image.

It was a photo. Of a Little League baseball team.

And maybe something more than that.

* * *

He met Jamison on his way out. She was holding Zoe's hand as they came up the front walk. In her other hand was a bag of groceries.

"Where are you going?" she asked him.

"Just back out to check on a few things."

"How's it going?"

"It's going."

"Don't do anything—" She stopped and glanced at Zoe. "You know."

"I know."

As he hurried away, Zoe called after him, "Mr. Amos, you're going to come back, right?"

Decker stopped and slowly turned. "I'll be back, Zoe. I promise."

He drove over to Bradley Costa's apartment and used the key Lassiter had given him to let himself in.

He walked right over to the photo on the shelf.

A smiling John Baron stared back at him.

The boys all looked happy too. They should have after winning the state championship.

What had been bugging Decker ever since he'd found out about Bradley Costa was one question:

Why would a young and single banker leave New York City and come to this place? Decker had to imagine that especially for a young person with money, the enticements of the Big Apple would trump anything Baronville had to offer.

He stared at the photo and then his gaze slipped to the frame around it.

Why not check the obvious? he thought. In fact, he should have done it before. He picked up the photo, turned it around, and flicked off the little metal tags that held the back of the frame on. He took out the cardboard backing and then the photo itself.

"Damn," he muttered.

There was a name and an address written there.

"Stanley Nottingham," he read off.

Underneath the name was an address in New York City.

Decker slipped the photo into his jacket.

Who was Stanley Nottingham in New York City, and why would Costa have this information written down on the back of the Little League photo?

He thumbed a text to Todd Milligan asking the FBI agent to look into this for him as well. If Decker had to travel to New York to talk to Nottingham, he would. The man might be able to explain why Bradley Costa had come to Baronville. And that information might lead to something else.

And then the case might finally start to make sense.

Criminal investigations usually involved minutiae piled on top of minutiae, until something clicked with something else, or, sometimes, contradicted something else. Either way, it could lead you in the right direction.

And Decker desperately needed something to go right.

He left the apartment, got back into his truck, and set off for his next stop.

Betsy O'Connor, Toby Babbot's last known roommate.

40

I⟨T WAS BEYOND⟩ horrible, what happened to him."

Decker was sitting at a coffee shop. Across the table from him was Betsy O'Connor, who worked as a waitress there. She was about five-five with a blocky build. Her graying hair was cut short and a pair of eyeglasses dangled on a chain around her neck. Decker had gauged her age at closer to fifty than forty.

He spooned some sugar into his coffee and said, "So you lived with him for a few years?"

"Yes. I mean, it was totally platonic," she hastily added. "My husband was an ass who liked to beat me when things went wrong in his life. I dated a couple of guys after my divorce and found them to be much the same. So, I've chucked men, at least for the foreseeable future."

"But Babbot was different?"

"Look, Toby had his issues, but he was basically a good guy who'd had a crappy life. That's why we were living together. We had to. We couldn't make ends meet otherwise."

"How'd you two come to know each other?"

O'Connor looked a bit embarrassed. "At an addiction meeting. We were both coming off *issues* with pain pills and trying to get our lives back on track. We were both working, but the jobs just didn't pay enough. Together, though, we made enough to live in a small house."

"I understand that he'd been in an accident. Had an injury to his head?"

"That's right. At the construction site, when they were building the fulfillment center. That was such a rough time for him. At first the company was helpful, but then they got nasty and cut him off."

"I understand there was an issue with alcohol?" said Decker.

"That was trumped up. Toby hadn't had a drop of alcohol for years. I would know. I lived with him when all that was going on. He worked so hard trying to get back to normal."

"But he never did get back to normal?"

"No. He tried but just couldn't keep a job. And I tried to make things work for us, but in the end my paycheck just wouldn't cover the expenses. So we had to move out. Broke my heart. I really liked that place. It was my first real home after my divorce."

"We found quite a few prescription bottles in his trailer. They were all painkillers."

"Well, he was in a lot of pain because of his injuries."

"I understand that you now live with some other people in an apartment?"

O'Connor dropped her gaze and fingered her coffee. "Yes, like when you're in your twenties. But I'm not a kid anymore. It wasn't the future I had mapped out at this stage of my life, but there you go. This job only pays minimum wage with no benefits. I work another job part time after I leave here, but both don't even add up really to a livable wage."

"Did you ever try getting hired at Maxus?"

"Me and every other person in town. They employ a lot of people and it's really the only thing going here now. But I couldn't pass the physical requirements. Lifting all that weight and walking all that way. Or running, more like it. I'm probably going to have to move. I'm burned out on this place. I need a fresh start."

"Babbot lived in a trailer after he stopped living with you. Did you ever visit him there?"

O'Connor nodded. "Several times. I'd bring him some home-cooked food. Give him a few dollars. I hated that he was living in that trailer. It didn't even have electricity or running water."

"Somebody burned the trailer down."

O'Connor looked alarmed. "What?"

"While my partner and I were in it."

"Dear God!"

Decker pulled out the sheet of graph paper that he had penciled in.

"Did you ever see this while you were at Babbot's trailer?"

She examined the page. "No, what is it?"

"It's basically the construction plans for the fulfillment center."

"Why would Toby have had that?"

"I was hoping you could tell me. Did he ever mention working on the center?"

"Before he was injured he seemed to like the construction work. It paid pretty well, and he didn't have to lift stuff. He drove a forklift and other heavy equipment. Maybe this paper relates to the work he did there."

"But I don't know why he would bother to replicate construction drawings on graph paper. Did he say anything about the center *after* he was injured?"

"Not much until they turned against him. Then he was angry."

"How angry?"

"Well, since he's gone now, I guess it doesn't matter. He said he was going to get back at them."

"How?"

"He never said." She paused. "You don't think he was planning to, oh, I don't know, maybe bomb the place? Would that be why he would have made those drawings?"

"It's possible. Do you think he was capable of that?"

"Before his injury, no. But after, he changed. Head injuries can change you, did you know that?"

"Yeah, I've heard something like that," Decker said drily. "So, you think it was possible for him to be violent?"

"I don't want to think that. He never was with me. But I guess it was possible. They really had screwed him."

"Anyone in particular?"

"It was mostly the company lawyers. Toby didn't have the

money to hire anyone, so he handled all that himself. It was a chore, I can tell you that. Lawyers can be nasty."

"No one wanted to take it on contingency?"

"Toby said there weren't that many lawyers left in town, and none of them wanted to get on the bad side of the biggest employer in town."

Decker nodded. "Did he ever mention Joyce Tanner, Michael Swanson, or Bradley Costa?"

"No, never. But wasn't Joyce Tanner the name of the woman he was found with?"

"Yes."

O'Connor shrugged. "Well, he never mentioned her to me."

"How about John Baron?"

She frowned. "He lives in the mansion on the hill."

"Yeah. Although I've been up there and I wouldn't call it a mansion anymore."

"Well, it's a lot more than I've got."

"But did Babbot ever mention John Baron?" asked Decker.

"Not that I can recall. I'm not from here, but Baron's not very well liked, is he?"

"Not very."

O'Connor said, "I've heard some people say he's really rich. That he has money stashed away up there."

"And he lives like a pauper because why?"

"I know, I could never figure that out either."

"There was a Bible verse written on the wall of the room where Babbot's body was found."

O'Connor looked curious. "The paper said something about that."

"Does that ring any bells for you? Was Babbot religious?"

"Toby never went to church as far as I know."

"So, nothing else you can remember?"

She thought for a few moments. "I really don't think so. Toby was a good man who just got dealt a bad hand. I guess that could describe a lot of us. But then again, our life is what we make it, right? Bad choices. You can't blame others for that."

"I guess not." Decker rose to leave.

"Mr. Decker, do you think you can find who killed Toby, and the others?"

"That's what I'm trying to do."

"He didn't deserve to die like that."

"I can't really think of anyone who does."

CHAPTER

41

BACK IN HIS truck Decker took out the piece of graph paper and studied it more closely. Then he lifted the paper so it was only a few inches from his face.

He had drawn in all the lines, but he had missed some indentations that had appeared at the bottom right-hand corner of the paper.

He took a pencil from the glovebox and ran it over the indentations until something appeared.

As he examined it more closely he concluded it was the scale to which the drawings had been done. An inch per a certain number of feet.

He put the paper in his pocket and drove off. On the way, he called Detective Green and asked for an address for Dr. Freedman, the physician who had prescribed all the pain pills for Toby Babbot.

"He's in prison for being a pill mill doc."

"Overprescribing pain meds to people like Toby Babbot?"

"You got it."

"How long has he been in prison?"

"Nearly a year, so I don't think he has anything to do with what happened."

Decker didn't necessarily agree, but he didn't argue the point.

"Where in prison?"

"It was a federal crime, so he's out of state. Indiana, I think. No rhyme or reason how the Bureau of Prisons allocates prisoners."

"Thanks."

"How's it going with your investigation?"

"It's going."

Decker clicked off and studied the road. If he couldn't talk to Freedman, he'd try someone else on his interview list.

He turned the truck around and headed back toward the Mitchells'. Before he got to their street, he turned and pulled to a stop in front of the residence across from the Murder House.

This place belonged to Dan Bond, the only person who lived on this street with whom Decker had not spoken.

He knocked on the door and immediately heard footsteps.

A voice called out, "Yes, who is it?"

"I'm Amos Decker, Mr. Bond. I'm with the FBI. I just wanted to ask you a few questions about what happened across the street."

"I don't like to open my door to strangers."

"I understand that. But I just need to ask you a few questions."

"Do you have a badge?"

"I do."

"Can you put it through the cat door?"

Decker looked down and saw the small hinged opening. He took out his badge and put it through the slot.

He heard noise on the other side and after about thirty seconds his badge was passed back through the pet door. He picked it up and looked at it. There were fingerprint smears all over it and also what looked to be flour. He rubbed the badge off on his jacket and put it back in his pocket. Then a few moments later he heard three separate locks being undone.

The door opened a few seconds later to reveal a small, shriveled elderly man standing on shaky legs.

"Mr. Bond?"

"Yes?"

Dark glasses covered Bond's sightless eyes.

Over his shoulder, Decker could see the man's white cane hanging on a wall hook.

"Can I come in?"

"I suppose so, yes. I felt your badge. It seemed legitimate."

"That's because it is."

"You can never be too careful."

"I agree with that."

He stepped back and Decker passed through.

Bond closed the door behind him, walked slowly over to a chair in the front room, and sat down.

Decker assumed the man must know intimately where every stick of furniture was in his house.

Decker sat down opposite him. The house smelled strongly of cooked kale and mothballs. But also of freshly baking bread.

"Sorry if I interrupted your baking."

Bond waved this off. "I was already done. The loaf's out of the oven now. It's one of my few pleasures left. I bake at all hours of the day and night. I don't need much sleep. Never did actually."

Bond was completely bald, with a pink, flaky scalp. He was dressed neatly in khaki pants and a short-sleeved blue shirt with a white T-shirt underneath. He had on black orthopedic shoes.

"Do you live alone?" asked Decker.

"Yes, ever since Dolly passed. She was my cat. That's why I have the pet door. I had a wife too. Betty. She died twenty-one years ago last week. Cancer. I'm ninety-one and I look every day of it even if I can't see myself."

Bond cracked a smile at this quip.

"You look fine. Nice house."

"It's old, just like me. I'm not going to get another cat. I won't outlive it, and who would take care of it?"

"Does someone come here and…help you out?"

"Used to, yes. And there used to be a lot more neighbors. But the ones I haven't outlived have moved away for the most part. Sad to see. But just the way it is. Price of sticking around too long."

Decker looked around. "How do you get to the store? And the doctor?"

"I walk with my little cart to the store. It takes most of the day. Sometimes my youngest son comes, but he lives in Pittsburgh. And I don't go to the doctor anymore. I don't see the point. They just give you more pills to take."

"Have you been in Baronville long?"

"All my life."

"What did you do?"

"I was an accountant." He touched his glasses. "I wasn't always this way. Macular degeneration. Started in my sixties. Went totally blind about ten years ago."

"I wanted to ask you a few questions about the night the two men were discovered in the house across the street. Were you home?"

"Oh yes. At night, I'm always home."

"I assume the police have already been by to talk to you?"

"Yes. A Detective Lassiter. She asked me a lot of questions. I don't think I was very helpful."

"Well, I might ask you the same ones. What do you remember about that night?"

"Sirens."

"I mean before that."

"Remember the storm. It was a doozy."

"Anything else?"

Bond sat back in his seat and scratched his chin. "I remember a car starting up and driving off."

Decker said, "I heard that too. And I also saw a plane go over, a few minutes before the storm blew in."

Surprisingly, Bond shook his head. "No, that wasn't a plane."

"No, it was. I saw it in the sky. The blinking lights and all through the clouds and fog. It was pretty damn low. So it was either taking off or more probably landing."

"No, son, that wasn't a plane."

"But I *saw* it, Mr. Bond."

"I know what you're thinking. That I couldn't *see* anything. Thing is, we never have a plane come low over here. No airports of any kind around here that I know about. And Pittsburgh is way to the south of us, and Cleveland way to the west. So even if they were landing or taking off, they'd be far up in the sky by the time they passed over here. But maybe you saw blinking lights and assumed it was a plane. But it was so cloudy, and even foggy, like you said, that you couldn't see the actual plane, could you? You just saw lights?"

Decker blinked and let his memory frames go back to that moment in time.

I saw the lights or the reflection of lights. But that was all. The clouds and fog were too thick. But it had to be a plane.

Seeming to read his thoughts, Bond said, "And if it was that low, did you hear the engines? They're pretty loud at low altitudes, even a prop plane. And I was outside that night, on my rear deck, before the storm started. And I didn't hear anything like that."

Decker broke out of his thoughts and shook his head. "I didn't hear the engines. I just saw the lights."

Bond chuckled. "You just assumed. That's okay. Perfectly natural."

"So, if it wasn't a plane I saw up there, what was it?"

"Well, it does make me think of my grandson Jeremy."

"Your grandson? How so?" asked Decker curiously.

"When he came to visit one time he brought it along to show me. Well, show me relatively speaking. I could *hear* it when he started it up."

"Hear *what*?" exclaimed Decker, because he needed the elderly man to get to the point.

"His *drone*. He's got one of those big ones. He uses it to take aerial photos for his real estate business, and he also shoots amateur movies and uses it to get some neat shots from the sky. A lot cheaper than renting out a chopper. I think that's what you probably saw that night. One of those big drones."

Decker's jaw dropped. *A drone.* "Wait a minute. Can you even fly a drone at night?"

"Oh, sure. Jeremy does it. In fact, he flew his around here last time he came. And that was at night. I'm sure there are rules and regulations about doing it. You have to have lights on the thing and all, I would imagine. And if you're in a flight path or near an airport you probably have to get some sort of permission or waiver. And you have to be careful about what you're taking pictures of. Right to privacy and all. I think you'd have legal problems if you flew over someone's backyard and started taking pictures of them there, or through their windows. At least I think that's what Jeremy told me when I asked him about it."

"Okay, but what would a drone be doing here?"

Bond shrugged. "I don't know, but I know it wasn't Jeremy's. He wasn't here that night. He lives in Maryland. I know it wasn't Alice Martin's because she doesn't have one. I doubt she's ever even seen one. And Fred Ross? Bet if he saw a drone he'd shoot it out of the sky with his damn shotgun. That's it for this street. Nobody else here. But it could have been somebody on another street. Jeremy told me that drones have different ranges. And once they hit the end of that range, they don't go any farther. But Jeremy's is a commercial model and it's got a pretty good range."

Decker had a sudden thought. "Could it have been a chopper and not a drone?"

Bond shook his head. "Choppers are real noisy. I would have definitely heard a chopper, and so would you at that low an altitude."

"Makes sense. And the drone would have a camera attached, right?"

Bond nodded. "Sort of the point. You use a drone to take pictures or video. Though I guess there's talk of using them to deliver stuff too. Anyway, Jeremy's has a fancy camera on his. He told me he slides his phone right into the control box and the drone sends whatever it's seeing right to his phone. Don't really understand how all that works, but then I'm just an old fart. On this street, we're all old farts. Well, I take that back. I never would call Alice a fart. She is a very dignified lady. Taught Sunday school."

Decker said, "So you know Alice Martin?"

"Oh yes. She and my wife were really good friends. She came to the funeral."

"And Fred Ross? You mentioned him and his shotgun. Do you know him well?"

Bond's face wrinkled up. "I've had that displeasure for far too long."

"Yeah, that's what Alice Martin said. You say you were outside that night. Did you hear the drone?"

"No, I didn't. You can hear it when it's on the ground, but not high up in the air. They're pretty quiet. At least Jeremy's is."

"Did you hear any other sound? It's really important."

Bond again scratched his chin. "Well, I did hear a weird sound I've never heard before. Something tapping and scraping. Over and over."

Tapping and scraping. That's actually a good description.

"I heard it too, but I couldn't tell what it was," said Decker. "So, you've never heard it before?"

Bond shook his head.

"But you could hear it from your back porch?"

"The yards here are small, and the houses are even smaller. It's not that far from my back porch to the street."

"And the car starting up and driving along? Did you recognize if it belonged to maybe Alice Martin?"

"Alice doesn't drive and she doesn't have a car."

"I take it Ross doesn't drive anymore, being in a wheelchair."

"No, he does. He's got his big van all rigged out. Chairlift and special controls so he can drive it even though he can't move his legs. Well, at least he used to. When I still had my sight I would watch him driving it."

"How was he disabled?"

"At the textile plant where he worked. Some big piece of equipment fell on him. Paralyzed from the waist down. That was decades ago."

"That's tough."

"Well, it hasn't made him exactly congenial. But, to tell the truth, Fred was an asshole even when he *could* walk."

Decker smiled. "I could definitely see that."

"Back then, I could *see* it too. Sorry I couldn't be of more help."

"No, you were of great help. Thank you."

Decker left and walked back to his truck.

A drone.

So, who was watching what or who that night?

CHAPTER

42

Surely, a stricken place.

Decker was on the rear deck of the Murder House looking at the back of the Mitchells' home.

He had been gone all day. He had covered a lot of ground but didn't feel as though he had made much progress. Unfortunately, that could be the textbook definition of being a homicide detective.

There was still a DEA agent on duty at the Murder House, but the flashing of Decker's credentials had allowed him admittance per Kate Kemper's instructions.

As he watched, the rear door of the Mitchells' house opened and Jamison stepped out. Behind her was another tall young woman who was holding Zoe's hand.

They all sat down around the outdoor table.

While Decker had never met any of Jamison's sisters other than Amber, he assumed the woman was one of them. She had the same long, lithe build and facial features as her sister. She had obviously traveled in for the funeral of her brother-in-law. A moment later the door opened and Amber stepped out. Even from this distance it seemed to Decker that the woman had aged twenty years. She was not so much walking as shuffling along.

He drew back into the shadows so they wouldn't be able to see him. He didn't quite know why he did this. Well, maybe he did.

He didn't want to have to be with them right now because he wouldn't know what to say or do. And he didn't want to blurt out something that would embarrass his partner.

He continued to watch as Zoe curled into her mother's lap and put her thumb in her mouth.

Decker knew that every time Zoe celebrated her birthday the agony of her father's death on the same day would be front and center. Every present she opened, every piece of cake she bit into, every candle she blew out would bring the memory of her father's last day alive. It wasn't fair, it wasn't right, and there was also nothing anyone could do about it.

The guilt at times would be simply overpowering, ripping the smile off your face and the laughter from your throat.

Decker knew this, because almost the very same thing had happened to him. And this thought both enraged and energized him, the twin emotions combining to further fuel his desire to discover whether Frank Mitchell had been murdered or not.

The air was cool and the sisters were wearing jeans and thick sweaters, while Zoe had on a long sweatshirt with purple tights. Decker watched as Jamison went back inside and then came out carrying a tray. She poured out cups of tea. There was also a platter of food, and this sight made Decker's stomach grumble.

It was well past seven and he hadn't eaten since breakfast. Yet watching the group of bereaved women, he felt guilty about his hunger.

He looked to the sky. Bogart had given him the name of a contact at the FAA. Decker had called the person and she had checked on flight arrivals and departures on the night in question in the Baronville airspace. She confirmed that there would have been no planes passing that low over Baronville.

The blind man Dan Bond had been right and Decker wrong. A man who could not see had "seen" far more than Decker had. It was a humbling experience, and one he would never forget.

Now, he wasn't jumping to conclusions and assuming that it *was* a drone, but he couldn't really think what else it might have been.

Decker left the house, got back into his truck, and drove off.

His destination was the Mercury Bar. The last time he'd been there he'd seen that they served a full menu of food as well as drinks.

Before he got there his phone buzzed. It was Milligan.

"How's Alex doing?" he asked.

"As well as can be expected, I guess."

"Give her my condolences." Decker heard some paper rustling on Milligan's end of the line. The FBI agent continued, "Okay, I got some answers for you. Maxus is a publicly traded company. Been in the FC business for about twenty years. Couldn't find anything unusual about them. They're big. They service lots of companies. They're profitable. Their management is all aboveboard. No ties to ISIS or anything like that. They are exactly what they appear to be."

"Okay, what about Stanley Nottingham?"

"He's in his eighties, and while he used to live at the address you gave me, he recently moved to a nursing home in New Jersey."

"What's his background? Ties to Baronville?"

"None that I could find. He grew up in New York and worked in the fashion industry until he retired."

"His parents?"

"From New York too. Dad owned a deli in Brooklyn. Mom was a seamstress. Both deceased."

"Nottingham have any kids?"

"No, never married."

"How'd he get to the nursing home?"

"I couldn't find that out."

"How long had he lived at the address I gave you?"

"Forty years. But here's the other thing we've confirmed. Bradley Costa lived in the same building before moving to Baronville. Which means they *were* neighbors."

"That makes sense."

"But I take it you thought there would be a connection between Baronville and Nottingham?"

"I thought Nottingham was the reason Costa came here."

"Well, I couldn't find anything about that."

"Thanks, Todd. Email me the contact information for the nursing home."

"Will do. And keep me posted. I can come up if things get hairy. Or hairier."

Decker clicked off. All the spots on the street had been taken, so he ended up parking in a vacant lot about two blocks from the bar.

He walked in and the place seemed to be hopping.

A small stage had been set up and a three-person band was playing country tunes. The singer's voice was good and the musicians clearly knew their way around the instruments.

Decker grabbed a two-seater table as far away from the band as he could. He didn't want music. He wanted food, a beer, and the time to think things through.

A waitress came and took his drink order. After she left he scanned the room for the young idiots who had attacked John Baron, but didn't see them. Then he looked for Baron, but didn't see him either. He eyed the bar and saw Cindi Riley juggling about a dozen customers at the same time.

He observed that she mixed, poured, and served myriad drinks with a practiced hand, all the while talking it up with patrons and managing tabs. Decker had basically lived in bars after his family had been murdered. He knew a pro when he saw one.

"You want some company?"

He looked up to see Lassiter standing there with a beer in hand.

Decker didn't really want company and was about to say that when Lassiter, apparently taking his silence for assent, sat down across from him.

She had on a navy blue skirt, a white blouse, and a matching jacket. He saw her holstered service pistol under the open fold of her coat.

"How's Jamison holding up?"

"She's hanging in there. Helping Amber. One of her sisters arrived in town. I think Frank's family will be in tomorrow."

"And are you still investigating?"

"It's what I do."

"Care to share? You did promise to keep us in the loop."

The waitress brought Decker's beer and he ordered some food. He took a few sips before answering Lassiter.

"It's mostly speculation."

"I'll take that. By the way, Marty told me about the trailer. You two were lucky. He also said you thought you might be getting closer."

"Maybe. Have you made any progress?" asked Decker.

"We're both working it, but nothing's shaking loose."

"Same with me," said a voice.

They both looked up to see Agent Kate Kemper standing there with a gin and tonic topped with a lime.

Decker said, "So is this the local watering hole for all cops?"

Kemper sat down. "Not that many choices. So why don't we share info?"

Decker said, "According to both of you, you've got nothing *to* share."

"I tend toward hyperbole," said Kemper.

He looked at Lassiter. "And do you tend toward bullshit too?"

"Depends on the situation."

Decker sat back. "Michael Swanson was staying in John Baron's potting shed and he knew it. Baron also was sweethearts with Joyce Tanner in high school and he was helping her out financially up until she died. He was also into mythology, which might tie into the Thanatos mark on Costa's forehead, and Tanner taught Bible school, which might explain the biblical verse on the wall behind where she was killed."

Lassiter looked surprised. "How do you know all this?"

He gave her a severe look. "I *investigated*."

Kemper said, "I know my jurisdiction doesn't extend to these local murders, but if they're connected to my case I want to know about it. So this Baron guy knows two of the four dead vics. What about the other two?"

"He says he doesn't know them."

"He *says* he doesn't," noted Lassiter.

"Why didn't he come forward when Tanner and Swanson were killed?" asked Kemper.

"If he killed them, the answer to your question is obvious," replied Decker.

"Did he ever mention knowing my guys?" asked Kemper.

"I didn't ask him, because I didn't want to reveal that information," said Decker.

"Since Tanner was found with Babbot and Swanson with Costa, that would mean if Baron was behind it, he killed all four," observed Lassiter.

"And if he didn't kill them?" said Kemper. "Why not come forward?"

Decker said, "The town hates him. I doubt he would want to get scapegoated for something he didn't do."

Lassiter snapped, "That's not how we do things here, Decker."

He looked at her. "I know about your father."

Lassiter's eyes widened.

"What about your dad?" said Kemper.

Decker looked at Lassiter. "You want to do the honors?"

"Why? What does it have to do with anything?"

Decker said, "He was convicted of burning down a home with a banker inside. A banker who'd foreclosed on his house after he lost his job at a company founded by the Barons."

"Again, it's not relevant," said Lassiter.

"It is, because you and this whole town have a grudge against the Barons, so don't try to sugarcoat it and say that no one here might have it in for him."

Kemper was about to say something when Decker's food arrived: a thick steak, rare, fries, and a small salad.

"Why bother with the salad?" noted Kemper wryly.

"Veggies are important, and technically fries are potatoes."

As he ate Kemper said, "So do you have anything else to share?"

"Toby Babbot was injured on the construction site for the Maxus Fulfillment Center. And he had a piece of graph paper in his trailer. It had marks on it from the paper he'd made drawings on."

"Drawings of what?" asked Kemper.

"The fulfillment center construction plans."

"Wait a minute, where did you find that?" asked Lassiter.

"In his trailer."

"And you didn't tell us this why?"

"I didn't know what it was until a short time ago."

Kemper said, "Why construction plans?"

"I don't know. Maybe he was thinking of suing Maxus, although you'd think he would have done it by now. But I talked with Betsy O'Connor, his last roommate. She said Babbot had a beef with Maxus and talked about getting even with them."

Lassiter took a swig of her beer and smacked the glass on the table. "I came to you for answers and now all I have are a ton more questions."

"Anything else?" asked Kemper.

"The plane I saw on the night I found the bodies?"

"You're not going to tell me that was a drug runner's plane landing in western PA," said Kemper.

"No, I'm telling you there was no plane that night."

Both women looked puzzled.

Kemper said, "I don't understand. Are you saying you didn't see a plane?"

"No. I think it was a drone." He explained his conversation with Dan Bond, and that he had confirmed no flights had gone anywhere near Baronville that night.

Lassiter looked chagrined. "When I went to interview him, I didn't ask Bond about the plane you said you saw because I didn't think it was important."

"Neither did I. I just happened to mention it to him. Goes to show that simply assuming something is true is never good enough."

"A drone?" said Kemper. "What would it be doing on that street?"

Decker looked at her. "Remember we were speculating that your two agents had set up a surveillance nest at the house next to the one where their bodies were found?"

"Yeah."

"Well, maybe that drone was doing surveillance too."

"On what?" asked Lassiter.

Decker didn't answer.

"Do you know?" asked Kemper.

Decker had finished his meal while they had been talking. He was looking over Kemper's shoulder at the bar. It had emptied and Cindi was serving only two customers.

Decker dropped a twenty on the table and rose. "I gotta go." He walked toward the bar, leaving Lassiter and Kemper to stare open-mouthed at each other.

Lassiter said, "He's a piece of work."

Kemper stared after him. "Yeah, but I get the feeling we should never, ever underestimate the guy."

CHAPTER

43

Yᴏᴜ'ʀᴇ ʙᴀᴄᴋ?"

Cindi slid a coaster in front of Decker at the bar.

"Like a bad penny."

"What can I get you?" she asked.

"Let me have your best IPA."

She looked dubious. "Beer's in the eye of the beholder."

"I trust your judgment."

She bent down and pulled out a bottle of beer from a small fridge under the bar.

Decker studied her. She was wearing a black shirt with the top button undone, allowing a glimpse of a tan bra and cleavage. Her jeans were snug and her hair bounced over her athletic shoulders.

He assumed the peekaboo shirt and tight pants were all about tips, and he didn't fault her for that. Guys who sat at bars were mostly simple creatures, just dying to be manipulated by a pretty lady.

She poured the beer into a mug and slid it across to him.

"Try that."

He took a sip and nodded appreciatively. "You know your beers."

She smiled and wiped down the bar in front of him.

"So why the Mercury Bar?" he asked. "Into Greek mythology?"

"No, my dad was a big Orson Welles fan. You know, the *Mercury Radio Theatre* I think it was called, or something like that. And Mercury is part of *Roman* mythology, not Greek. Hermes was Mercury's Greek counterpart."

"My mistake," said Decker.

She studied him. "Why do I think you already knew that? You probing for something?"

"Maybe. You seen John lately?"

"Which John? I know lots."

"Baron."

"No, why?"

"Just wondering. You two buds?"

"He comes in for drinks. If that makes us buds, I got lots of buds in this town."

"When I was in here the other night I just thought there was something more there."

Cindi stopped wiping down the bar, pulled out a bottle of water from under the counter, and took a swig. "Why do you care?"

Decker shrugged. "I've gotten to know Baron a little bit. I think he's okay. I'd hate for him to get messed up in any of this."

Cindi put the bottle of water down and picked up her cloth again. When a customer caught her eye and lifted his glass for a re-fill, she said to Decker, "Don't move, I'll be right back."

He held up his beer in answer and took another drink.

A minute later she returned and said, "I've got another bar-tender coming in at ten. You want to talk then?"

"Works for me."

"You're right," she said. "John is a good guy."

"It's nice to be right."

"So, messed up in what?"

"Ten o'clock," he replied.

* * *

At the stroke of ten Cindi handed the bartending over to someone else and motioned to Decker to join her at the back of the bar.

"My car's parked in back."

"Mine's in front."

"I'll drive you back here. It's not that far."

"Where are we going?"

"To my place."

"You sure that's wise?"

"Are you?" she shot back.

They climbed into a midnight black Toyota Land Cruiser.

"Nice ride," he said. "And not cheap."

"I get good tips and good deals on cars."

She drove them to a large brick building on the edge of downtown. As they traveled, Decker could see a number of renovation projects under way.

"Baronville making a comeback?" he asked.

"In parts," she said cryptically.

They arrived at an underground parking garage and she pulled into a numbered space. They took an elevator up to the top floor. Cindi opened the door to her place and motioned Decker in.

She said, "This was an old textile mill. Renovated to luxury condos."

"Yeah, I know, I've been here."

"When?"

He gave her a quick glance. "When I came to check out Bradley Costa's apartment. He lived here too."

"That's right, he did," she said casually.

He looked at the sleek furniture, expensive-looking rugs, and stainless steel kitchen appliances set against exposed brick walls. In a far corner was a well-appointed exercise area with dumbbells, a chin-up bar, a rack of slam and medicine balls, an elliptical, a Peloton bike, and other machines that seemed designed to strengthen as well as torture.

"No wonder you're in such good shape," he said.

"It doesn't just happen," she said. "Gotta work for it."

As Decker looked around at the expensive trappings he said, "Your tips must be *really* good."

"It's not just tips. I actually own the Mercury."

"Yeah, I heard that. Inherited from your old man?"

"That's right."

He watched as she took off the jean jacket she had put on and hung it on a metal coat rack parked next to the front door.

"What are you, twenty-two?"

"I'm flattered. I'm actually almost thirty."

"About the same age as my partner. Still pretty young to own your own bar."

"Well, like you pointed out, I inherited."

"But you've obviously been successful on your own. I take it you're a good businesswoman."

"My dad was a good teacher."

"What happened to him?"

"He died."

"Yeah, that I get. I mean how?"

"Heart attack."

"Sorry to hear that."

"You want a drink?'

"I think I hit my limit. You got a soda?"

She slid open a refrigerated drawer and tossed him a bottle of water. "It's better for you."

She poured out three fingers of Bombay Sapphire, cut it with tonic, and added a slice of lemon, a wedge of lime, and three chunky ice cubes taken from an under-the-counter icemaker.

She tapped her glass against his plastic bottle.

"And is *that* better for you?" he asked, indicating her cocktail.

"I don't drink on the job, bar owner 101. But I do like one drink before I go to bed. And I'm a blue bottle gin lady."

She took off her shoes and curled up on the couch in front of the kitchen area, motioning Decker to sit down in the chair across from her.

He did so and drank some of his water while he eyed her.

"I take it you were born here?"

"You take it wrong. I was born in Philly."

"And yet your father came here and owned a bar? And by the time you came along the bloom was well off Baronville. So why exchange the City of Brotherly Love for this place?"

She shrugged. "I was only one year old and just came along for the ride, apparently." She added, "Okay, full disclosure, my mom *was* from here. They met in college. He always wanted to run a bar. The opportunity came up here, and presto, there you go. Sometimes that's all you need for a major life change: a dream."

"Where's your mom?"

"Good question."

"You mean you don't know?"

"Here today, gone tomorrow. She left when I was little and I haven't seen her since."

"That's tough."

"Not that tough. My dad was great at being a single parent."

"Do you remember your mom?"

"Not really. I was too young. I guess that's a good thing. How can you miss someone you never really knew?"

"I suppose so."

She sipped her drink. "So, what's going on with John? Is he in any sort of trouble?"

"You seem very concerned about a guy who's just a customer among many others."

"He's a very good customer. And a good guy who takes all sorts of crap that he doesn't deserve."

"I sort of got that impression at the bar that night."

"Those guys were morons who don't know any better. But there are many here who do know better. Or at least they should."

"I've met some of them." Decker shifted his bulk in the chair. "You know about the murders?"

"What's that got to do with John?"

"He knew at least two of the four victims. One of them lived on his property."

"Okay, so? Could be a coincidence."

"I'm a cop."

"And that means what?"

"That I don't believe in coincidence."

"Well, what if I told you that I knew all four of the victims?"

"Because they came to your bar?"

"That's right."

"Even Toby Babbot, who I understood was off the sauce?"

"I do serve *food* at the Mercury, as you well know, having eaten there tonight."

"And since you're one of the few places like that in Baronville, it's not surprising that they all went there. But you didn't live with one of them, did you? You weren't high school sweethearts with one of them, were you?"

"I always thought Mike Swanson was kind of cute. And Brad did live in this building."

"Did you ever talk to him apart from when he was at the bar?"

"I actually think he had a thing for me."

"Did he ever act on that?"

"I sort of gave him the vibe that it would be futile if he did. I mean, he was okay, but I'm not into the stiff banker types. Too corporate for my bohemian tastes. I gave out subtle hints and he stopped trying."

"He had a photo of you and him in his office."

She seemed surprised by this. "Did he? From where?"

"Some business event, his secretary said."

"Oh, that's right. I remember now. He had a cocktail party about six months ago. Invited me and a bunch of other local business owners. There was a photographer there."

"That explains it," said Decker.

She sipped her drink. "So, I probably knew all four and I lived in the same building as one of them. Does that mean I'm not a coincidence and that I'm in the same mess John is?"

"You ever been up to the mansion on the hill?"

"Why?"

"Just curious."

"Maybe."

"You don't remember."

"Okay, a few times," she admitted.

"Baron is pretty *bohemian*." He waited to hear her response.

"I admit I find him interesting."

"I think he's *very* interesting. I'm just trying to figure out if he's also a killer."

"I don't think he'd hurt a fly."

"I don't care if he hurts flies."

She smiled at the remark. "John thinks *you're* very interesting."

"He told you that?"

"Yes, he did. We spoke on the phone after you and your partner paid him a visit."

"Has he ever been here?"

"Once or twice. Please don't ask about particulars."

"He's got some years on you."

"He's actually one of the youngest people I know."

"You mean in spirit?" he said.

She nodded. "He's also kept himself in great shape. He was an athlete. You look like you were an athlete."

"I was, about a hundred pounds ago."

"Don't you check for alibis?"

"We do."

"Well, does John have an alibi for when those people were killed?"

"The timelines were pretty broad on the four. But we'll check that. Will you be providing him alibis?"

"Depends on whether I was with him at the time in question, doesn't it?"

"Yes it does."

"You don't believe he did it, do you?"

"It doesn't matter what I believe. It matters what the facts are." He cocked his head at her. "Why do you stay here? You could own a bar in lots of places."

"Town's coming back. You saw that on the drive here."

"Yes, but you said it was only coming back in parts."

"Better than not at all. I've kind of studied the economics of places like this. In any downturn in a small town you always see mom-and-pop operations start up because people lose their jobs, but not their spirit. Local restaurants, fitness centers, tattoo parlors, pawnshops, mani-pedi places, local movie theaters, bakeries, pet shops, stuff like that. People get by, they do what they have to do to survive. You look at Pittsburgh. They turned it around. From steel mill town to a health and financial services kind of place."

"Baronville is not Pittsburgh."

"We don't need to be Pittsburgh. And we have the fulfillment center. It's helped my business, I can tell you that. I'm up about thirty percent year over year for each of the last three years."

"Because after people work their butts off in that place, they need a drink?"

"Bingo. And food because they're too tired to cook for themselves."

"All the development we saw heading over here, that's all mom-and-pop stuff? Looks like it involves more money than that."

She frowned. "I've lost several friends to overdoses. But the one good thing was they had life insurance. Their families got the money after they died, and many of them have opened businesses with it, or used some of the proceeds to invest in the town. The renovation of this building came about because several beneficiaries decided to pool their funds to get it done. And now it's almost all sold."

"That's great, turning a negative into a positive. But six unsolved murders. That's not good for the town."

Her grin faded. "Six?"

"Two more in an empty house. I found those."

"I think I read something about that. No real details, though. Can you enlighten me?"

"No, I really can't."

"Are they related to the other four?"

"No idea."

"You seem to have far more questions than answers," she noted.

"That's usually the case this early on. You ever been to Costa's place here?"

"Once. He had a dinner there to drum up banking relationships."

"You ever ask him why he would leave New York to come here?"

"I did, actually. He was a good-looking guy, obviously smart. He had money and a good career there."

"So, what did he say?"

"Something about following *his* dream."

"What kind of dream?"

"I didn't push it and he didn't elaborate."

"Did he know Baron?"

"I know you believe that he did, but not that I know of. I don't think John has much use for banks."

"But he has a mortgage on his home with that bank."

"Does he?" she said innocently.

"Yeah, he does. But he failed to mention that to me."

Decker pulled the photo of Baron and the Little League team from his pocket and held it up. "You ever see this in Costa's condo?"

She took it and looked at it. "Yeah, it was on a shelf with a bunch of others."

"Baron was the coach."

"I can *see*, Decker," she said sharply. "He led the team to the state championship and then got canned by the powers that be."

"He told us that. Do you know why?"

"I think it made him look too good and they couldn't stand that."

She caught the writing on the back. "Stanley Nottingham. Who's that?"

"I don't know. You ever heard of him?"

She shook her head. "It's funny, though."

"What is?"

She handed the photo back. "I only know this because John mentioned it to me once. Even showed me a picture."

"Of what?"

"No, of whom."

"Stanley Nottingham?" said Decker, looking perplexed.

"No." She took a moment to search her memory. "Not Stanley. Yeah, it was Nigel. Can you believe that? Nigel?"

"You've lost me."

"John showed me a photo of Nigel *Nottingham*. That's why I remembered it. Don't hear those two names much anymore. I mean, can you get any more British than that? But I guess it fit."

"You've still lost me," groused Decker.

"Nigel Nottingham was Baron's butler."

"John's butler?"

"No! John can't afford a butler. I'm talking about the original John Baron. He apparently wanted a full-fledged British butler, and Nigel Nottingham fit the bill."

Decker jumped up from his seat. "I gotta go, thanks."

He was out the front door of the condo before Cindi even got to her feet.

"But, Decker, I drove you over here," she called after him as the door slammed shut.

44

W HAT IN THE world are you doing? Why are you packing?"

Jamison was standing in the doorway of Decker's bedroom as he stuffed some clothes and his toiletry bag into his duffel.

"I gotta go somewhere."

"Go where? Back to D.C.?"

"No, New Jersey."

She gaped. "New Jersey? Why?"

"I've got a lead. A good one. Just happened a bit ago. From Cindi Riley."

She looked at him incredulously. "Decker, Frank's funeral is the day after tomorrow. And you're leaving? There's so much to do."

"I'll be back in time. I'm leaving now. I'll get there early in the morning, do my thing, and be back late tomorrow."

"But my sisters are here now. And Frank's parents and siblings will be here in the morning. I thought you could pick his parents up from the bus station. And one of his sisters too, she's coming in by train. The others are driving directly here."

Decker stopped his packing. "I'm sure your sisters will help out. And just so you know, I have to take the rental."

"Wait a minute, you're *driving* to New Jersey?"

"Only way, really. I looked at flights. First one out of Pittsburgh is ten o'clock tomorrow morning, and it isn't even direct. I have to connect through freaking Charlotte, if you can believe that. And there's no train schedule that works and no bus service that does either. The quickest way is to drive it. I can be there in under seven hours."

"Okay, but you do realize what time it is? When exactly do you plan to sleep?"

"I'm good. The adrenaline is pumping and I'll get some shut-eye when I get there."

"Decker, this is not smart."

"I've got to go, Alex. I found out something tonight that I need to check out."

She sat down on the bed. "You said you had a lead from Cindi Riley. What is it?"

He told her about Stanley and Nigel Nottingham and finding the name and address on the back of the photo in Costa's condo.

He handed the photo to her and she looked it over.

"So let me get this straight—this Nigel Nottingham was Baron the First's *butler*?"

"Yeah. And I'm betting Stanley is his, I don't know, great-grandson or something. That's why Todd didn't find a connection to Baronville. He only went back as far as Stanley Nottingham's parents. He lived in the same building as Bradley Costa in New York. They were neighbors."

She handed back the photo. "So, what exactly is your theory?"

"That Stanley Nottingham told Costa something about Baron *and* this town that made him pull up his roots in Manhattan and come here. Riley told me that Costa told her he came to Baronville to follow his dream, which struck me as really curious. Well, I'm hoping that Nottingham can tell me what that dream was."

Jamison rubbed her forehead, her features exhausted.

"Okay, I can see how that might be important to the investigation. But can't this wait until *after* the funeral?"

"Stanley Nottingham is elderly and just moved to a nursing home. How do I know the guy won't drop dead tomorrow? And if he does, there goes the only lead I have."

She snapped, "It's always about the *case*, isn't it? It always takes priority over everything. No matter what."

Decker stopped packing and looked at her. "It's not like that, Alex."

"It's *always* like that, Decker."

"But this is important."

She rose and walked back over to the door.

"Fine, whatever. I'll just hold down the fort here."

"Alex, I will be back. I promise."

"Yeah," she said absently. "Well, I hope you find what you're looking for."

Decker grabbed his overcoat from a chair. When he turned back she was gone. He heard a door close somewhere in the house.

He zipped his duffel shut and hefted it over his shoulder. He made his way quietly downstairs.

Only sitting on the last riser was Zoe, holding a stuffed cat.

She looked up at him and her gaze fell on his duffel. "Are you going somewhere, Mr. Amos?"

Decker's first impulse was just to rush past the little girl and be on his way to New Jersey without explanation.

But after looking at her disconsolate expression, his second impulse made him set his duffel down and sit next to her.

"I am, Zoe. But I'll be back. See, I have to go check on something in New Jersey. Have you ever been to New Jersey?"

She shook her head. "Is it nice?"

"Yeah, it is."

"What do you have to do there?"

"Talk to someone. An older man."

"What about?"

"He knew somebody here in town. So I just wanted to ask him some questions about the person."

"Is he a nice man?"

"Well, I've never met him, but I'm sure he'll be just fine." He paused and studied her. "How are you doing?"

She clutched her cat tighter. "My daddy's funeral is the day after tomorrow."

"Yeah, I know," he said quietly.

"We're going to bury him in the ground. That's what Mommy said."

"I'll be back in time to go with you."

"You promise?"

"I promise."

Her features turned anxious. "Mr. Amos, do you think he'll be cold? My dad? See, after Mommy told me that he was going to be buried, I got a big spoon from the kitchen and went out in the backyard and dug a hole. And I put my hand in it. And it was cold down there. And my daddy didn't like to be cold. He would snuggle under the blanket with me. I don't like the cold either."

Lending a visual to her words, she shivered.

Decker leaned against the banister even as he felt his chest tighten and his throat constrict.

"I know your blanket doesn't have a name, but does your cat?"

"His name is Felix. Aunt Alex gave him to me when I was five."

"Where'd you come up with that name?"

"It was the name of my daddy's dog when he was little. I thought if I named my cat Felix he wouldn't miss him so much."

"That's really nice, Zoe."

Her face wrinkled up and her eyes filled with tears. "I want my dad to be here."

"I know. And I know he would want to be here too, more than anything. He would never want to leave you."

Zoe leaned against his leg and he gently patted her head.

They sat in silence for a few moments.

"Do you remember I told you about my daughter?"

"Molly."

"That's right, Molly. Well, I didn't really tell you the truth about her."

"You mean you lied?" said Zoe, sitting up, her eyes wide and staring at him.

"No, not exactly. I just didn't tell you...everything. The fact is, my daughter...My daughter...died right before she turned ten."

"Was she sick?"

"No, she...she had an accident."

"Like Daddy did?"

"That's right. Anyway, we had a funeral for her and I had to bury her too. But I go back and visit her, you know, to check on her. And when I go there, I can...I can sense that she's *not* cold.

You can do that with people you love. So, I think that when you and your mom go to visit your dad, you'll be able to sense that too. And by being there, you actually make things warm, because he'll know that you're with him. That people who love him are right there with him. Do you see?"

She nodded slowly, her gaze fixed on him. "Can I talk to him when I visit?"

"You absolutely can. Now, he won't answer you back like he used to. But I can tell you that you'll feel something right here." He touched the center of his chest. "And that's means that your dad is answering you back. And it goes right there, right to your heart. Because…that's where you'll always keep your dad now. Forever. Okay?"

She nodded, leaned over, and gave his thick calf a hug.

"I'll see you when you get back, Mr. Amos."

"You can just call me Amos."

"Okay, Amos."

Decker lifted his duffel and left.

He did not see Jamison standing at the top of the stairs.

She had heard the entire exchange and was quietly sobbing while holding on to the railing to steady herself.

When Zoe started up the stairs, she saw her aunt and ran up to her and flung her arms around her legs. As Jamison continued to shake, Zoe said, "Aunt Alex, are you okay? Are you sad?"

Jamison stroked her niece's hair.

With tears streaming down her face, she managed to say, "I'm okay, Zoe. I'm really okay now."

45

At NINE O'CLOCK in the morning Decker's phone alarm went off.

He sat up in the driver's seat of his rental, yawned, and looked around.

He'd arrived at the nursing home around six in the morning, parked on the street, and settled down to catch a few hours of sleep. He drove to a nearby McDonald's, cleaned up, and changed into fresh clothes in the bathroom. He ate a breakfast sandwich and downed a cup of coffee.

He drove back to the Glenmont Senior Living Center and went inside.

The lobby was large and inviting, with sunlight blazing in through numerous windows. The whole place looked fairly new. It had comfortable seating areas with upholstered chairs, a large reception desk of polished wood, and wallpaper with a soothing flower-and-vine design.

An efficient-looking young woman was seated at the front desk. She looked up as Decker approached.

"Can I help you?"

He pulled out his creds and badge and held them up. "FBI. I need to speak with one of your patients."

"We call them *residents*," she said, eyeing his badge. "Can I ask what this is about?"

"I'm investigating a series of murders in Pennsylvania. It's come to our attention that one of your *residents*, Stanley Nottingham, may have known one of the victims when he lived in New York."

"I think I need to get my supervisor."

"Do what you have to do, but don't keep me waiting long. I'm on a deadline."

She hurried off and came back less than a minute later accompanied by a tall, stout man with thick dark hair. He wore a pinstripe suit along with an important expression.

"I'm Roger Crandall, the executive director. What seems to be the issue?"

Decker explained why he was here.

"Don't you need a warrant or something like that?" asked Crandall.

"No, I don't. Mr. Nottingham isn't a suspect or a person of interest. But he could be a material witness in a murder investigation. And I have every right to talk to him."

"I think I might have to call the company lawyer on this. Can you come back another time?"

In response Decker took out his notebook. "Is that Crandall with two l's? I've seen it spelled with one and just want to make sure."

"It's with two. But why are you asking?"

"My boss at the FBI gets pissed when anyone misspells a name on the arrest warrant."

Crandall took a step back. "Arrest warrant? For me!" he added shrilly. "Why?"

"Well, you're the one obstructing justice, aren't you?"

"I don't believe that I am."

"I already told you that your *resident* is not a suspect or person of interest. He has no criminal liability. But he may be a material witness. And you will find that the FBI has a right at any time to speak to a material witness. But if you won't let me do so, then you are committing a federal crime, which, by the way, has a five-year minimum sentence in a federal penitentiary." He eyed the man's natty attire. "And for what it's worth, you look better in pinstripes than you would in an orange jumpsuit."

Crandall gazed stupidly at Decker for a long moment and then said, "I'll take you to Mr. Nottingham myself."

Decker made a show of tearing the page with Crandall's name

on it out of his notebook, wadding it up, and tossing it into a nearby wastebasket.

"Thank you for your cooperation."

As they walked down the hall, Decker said, "What can you tell me about Nottingham? I understand he came here recently."

Crandall nodded. "That's right. Usually the family will be instrumental in having a loved one come here. We all get old, and when you can't take care of yourself, well, sometimes it's hard to admit it. But Mr. Nottingham was different. He didn't have any close family, but decided he could no longer live by himself. So he came here of his own accord."

"How'd he find out about your place?"

"We get a lot of people from New York. We're just over the state line, so if they do have family it's an easy trip for them to come and visit."

"I understand he was in the fashion business."

"Yes. He worked for several of the big fashion houses. He's very nice. Seems well educated."

"How's his health?"

"We really can't give that sort of information out, but I can tell you that he has the sorts of problems one would typically associate with a person of his age."

"Okay, but I meant is he lucid?"

"Oh, oh yes, there's no problem there. At least not yet."

They stopped at a door. The name STANLEY NOTTINGHAM had been written on a slip of paper and inserted in a brass holder screwed to the door.

"Well, here we are."

Crandall knocked. "Mr. Nottingham? Stanley, can I come in? It's Mr. Crandall."

A deep throaty voice answered in the affirmative and Crandall opened the door. He and Decker stepped in.

Stanley Nottingham was sitting in a chair next to a bed. He was tall and cadaverous, with a fringe of white hair encircling his head. He wore a pair of thick black glasses. He had on what looked to be silk polka-dot pajamas.

A tank of oxygen was parked in one corner.

On the walls were large framed black-and-white photos of a variety of models on the catwalk.

"Stanley, this is—" Crandall paused and said to Decker, "I'm sorry, what was your name again?"

"I'm Amos Decker, Mr. Nottingham. I'm with the FBI."

Nottingham, who had been slouching in his chair and looking immensely bored, immediately righted himself and sat up straighter. He looked positively delighted by this development and clapped his hands together.

"The FBI?" He smiled broadly. "How exciting!"

Decker glanced at Crandall. "I'll handle it from here, thanks."

Crandall looked put off by this, but nodded curtly and left. However, he kept the door open.

Decker went over and closed it and turned back to Nottingham. "Thanks for meeting with me."

"Have we met before?"

"No." He looked at the photos arrayed on the walls. "So, you were in the fashion business?"

"For about fifty years. I worked for all the big houses. Dior, Versace, Valentino, Calvin, Tommy. The list goes on and on."

"What did you do there?"

In answer Nottingham waved his hand at all the photos. "I was a *photographer*. One of the best, if I do say so myself. I flew with Valentino on his personal jet. Giorgio had me on his speed dial. Hubert de Givenchy was a dear friend. Audrey Hepburn. Elizabeth Taylor. Jackie O. I photographed them all. The greatest moments of my life." The man was absolutely beaming even though he had closed his eyes. When he reopened them and gazed around at the small confines of his room, the happy look faded.

He said, "But that's not why you're here, obviously."

Decker drew up the only other chair in the room and said, "Bradley Costa?"

Nottingham screwed up his features. "Oh, Brad, yes, yes, of course." He next looked perplexed. "Is he in some sort of trouble with the FBI?"

"No. Just following up some leads on a case. He was your neighbor back in New York?"

"That's right. He bought an apartment in my building in SoHo. I'd lived there for decades. I sort of took him under my wing. He was a delightful person. Very handsome. He could have been a model, if you ask me. And smart. He was very successful. Worked on Wall Street."

"And then he moved?"

"Yes, yes he did. That was very sudden. I was a little hurt, to tell the truth. He never even said goodbye. Here today, gone tomorrow."

"You have an ancestor, Nigel Nottingham?"

The old man smiled. "Yes. The *butler*. He was my great-grandfather. Worked in a horrible place called, um, well, I can't remember right now, but he labored away for an absolute miser there."

"John Baron. The place is called Baronville."

Nottingham snapped his fingers. "Yes, that's right. In, what was it, Ohio?"

"Pennsylvania."

Nottingham looked sadly at Decker. "In the last year my memory, which used to be razor sharp, seems to be leaving me. That's one reason I came here. I…forget things. And I didn't want to burn my building down by mistake."

"No reason to be sorry. You're doing fine. Was Costa interested in the Barons?"

Nottingham scrunched up his features once more. "Well, come to think, it was at a dinner party I threw a number of years ago. I remember because I had just been given an award by the fashion industry. It was one of those things you get for being around as long as I had," he added with an embarrassed smile.

"What happened at the dinner party?"

"Well, it was after we ate and we were having port in my little room of photos. Brad picked up a picture from off a table and asked me about it. Well, it was Nigel. I told him all about him, or at least what my father and grandfather had told me. Nigel

was born in England, Surrey, long, long ago and then immi-
grated to the United States. I'm not clear on how he made it to
Baronville. But he became Baron's butler. His son, Samuel, my
grandfather, left Baronville as a young man and moved to up-
state New York, where my father was born. My parents moved
to Brooklyn after they were married, and that's where I was
born."

"So no one in your family wanted to stick around Baronville?"

"Oh, God no. From what I remember being told, it was this
dreary piece of dirt where they had coal mines and filthy facto-
ries and people were worked to death. My grandfather actually
told me that he left because he hated the place. Wanted to get
away as soon as he could. And he did. Thank God for that. I
doubt I would have had the same career if I had been born and
raised there."

"What about Nigel?"

Nottingham thought for a few moments, tapping the chair arm
with his long fingers. "That's right. I remember now. He stayed on
with the Barons until he died." He paused. "In fact, I remember
my grandfather telling me that he went back for Nigel's funeral. It
was actually funny."

"What was funny? Not his father dying, surely?"

"Oh, no. It was funny because his father had died on the very
same day that Baron did. The one who started the whole town and
named it after himself."

"They died on the same day? I didn't know that."

"Yes. Apparently they were the same age. Master and servant till
the day they both died. Then who cares about titles and who has
more money, right?"

"Would it surprise you to learn, then, that Brad Costa moved to
Baronville?"

Nottingham slumped down in his chair. "Oh my God, you
must be joking."

"No, I'm not. In fact, he was murdered there."

As soon as he said this Decker realized it had been a mistake.

Nottingham started having trouble breathing. He was gasping, grabbing his chest and pointing at something. Finally, Decker realized what it was.

The oxygen.

He quickly rolled the tank over and helped Nottingham get the nasal cannula inserted correctly. The elderly man drew several deep breaths and slowly calmed down.

Decker sat back, relieved. "I'm sorry, Mr. Nottingham, I shouldn't have just dumped that on you."

Nottingham took another series of deep breaths while he waved off this apology. He said slowly, "I have COPD. Damn cigarettes. Then the anxiety kicks in."

"I take it from your reaction that you had no idea Costa moved to Baronville? Or that he was dead?"

Nottingham shook his head. "None. How did he die? You said *murdered*? How horrible!"

"The details aren't that important, and I don't want to upset you again. But he was murdered and I'm trying to find out why."

"My God, poor Brad."

"Do you have any idea why he would exchange a place in SoHo and a job on Wall Street for Baronville?"

Nottingham slowly took the cannula out of his nose and set it aside.

"About a week after I told Brad about Nigel and the Barons, he came back and asked me some more questions."

"Like what?"

"You first have to understand a bit of family lore that was handed down from one generation to the next."

"What sort of family lore? About the Nottinghams or the Barons?"

"Both, really. My grandfather told me about it when I was just a kid. You see, the original Baron, the one who started the town and everything, as I told you was a miserable old cuss. My grandfather lived in the servants' quarters there growing up. He hated the place. And while he only had a few encounters with the elder Baron, he thought him an awful person."

"If he was that bad, why did Nigel hang around?" asked Decker.

"Good question. However, I got a sense from what I was told that Baron didn't actually treat Nigel badly. On the contrary, he seemed to treat him more as an equal."

"That seems strange, treating a butler as an equal."

"He was Baron's age and Nigel started working for him before he built the big place on the hill. I've only seen pictures of it. What a monstrosity."

"I've been there. It hasn't aged well. But you were talking about family lore?"

"When Baron died, I'm not sure anyone else in his family was interested in actually working for a living."

"They just wanted to sponge off the old man?"

"Yes. And that leads me directly into the family lore. Baron was cheap but he loved money, and was loath to let a penny of it go, if he could help it. He paid his workers next to nothing and never gave a dime to charity. He was rich beyond anyone's wildest dreams and yet apparently it still wasn't enough."

"Sounds like a real peach," commented Decker.

"Well, anyway, he also didn't have a high opinion of his sons, who would be next in line to run the businesses. As I said, they weren't all that interested. From what I was told, they loved spending money far more than making it."

"That's why the family eventually became poor," said Decker.

"Did they? Well, well. And now comes the interesting part. The family lore part is that before he died, Baron hid a fortune somewhere at his home. And I mean an absolute fortune."

"In what?"

"I don't know. Jewels, rare coins. Cash. Negotiable instruments. Stocks. Bonds. But it would have represented a very large part of his fortune. It seems that he didn't want his family to have it."

"And you told Costa this?"

Nottingham nodded. "He was interested, I would say *very* interested, and peppered me with questions. I even showed him some of the old letters my grandfather and father wrote to me. I also had letters that Nigel had written my grandfather."

"In the letters were there any clues as to where he might have hidden it?"

"None, at least that I could see. My grandfather and father speculated about it, but they didn't know. And even if they did, what would it matter? They didn't own the Baron property. They would have had no way to gain access to it to even search."

"But presumably the Baron family would?"

"I suppose. And if they were becoming poor and thought there might be a fortune lying about? Well, I would look for it. I'm sure if my grandfather knew about the possibility of a hidden fortune, the Baron descendants would have as well."

"I think they *did* look for it."

"How do you know that?"

Decker was thinking about all the holes in the walls back at the Baron mansion. "Just something I saw."

Nottingham sat up a bit in his chair. "Do you think Brad went to Baronville to look for the treasure?"

"I can't come up with another reason why he would chuck his life in New York and move there. Do you think he did some investigating on his own before he left New York?"

"It's possible, in fact even probable. Because we had many later conversations about it, and each time we did, Brad seemed to know things about the Barons that I hadn't told him. So he might have been doing research on his own." Nottingham suddenly looked horrified. "So, my telling him about this and his going there. I...I'm the reason he's dead."

"No, you're not," said Decker firmly. "People make their own choices, and they have to live with the consequences."

"I suppose you're right," Nottingham said doubtfully.

"Would you happen to have any of the letters you showed Costa?"

"I would. Not in my room, but there's a storage locker here where I keep my valuables. The letters are in a file in that locker."

"I can make copies and put the originals back in the locker."

"That's fine."

"Thank you for your time, you've been a big help." Decker

handed Nottingham a card. "If you think of anything else, give me a call."

"Of course. And could you let me know how things end up?"

"I will." Decker looked at the photos on the wall. "You were really a great photographer."

Nottingham glanced up from the card and said, "Thank you. What are you going to do now?"

"My job," answered Decker.

CHAPTER

46

WHEN HE RETURNED from New Jersey, arriving back before dinner, Decker was as un-Decker-like as it was possible to be.

He assisted with all tasks, set the table, helped serve the food, talked to Jamison's sisters and to Frank Mitchell's grieving parents and siblings, offering condolences and truly listening.

Afterward, as the others went off to a nearby motel where they were staying, Jamison cornered him in the kitchen, where he was loading the dishwasher after clearing the table.

"Are you feeling okay?" she said, her look a worried one.

He placed the last pot in the dishwasher, dropped in a detergent pod, hit start, and closed the door before turning to her.

"I'm just trying to help out, Alex."

"I know. That's sort of what I meant. It's just not... you know?"

"You mean it's just not like me?"

She looked embarrassed but did not correct him.

"You must be rubbing off on me, Alex."

"Is that a good thing?" she said quietly.

"Must be. People seem to like me better now than when I lived in Ohio." He fell silent for a few moments. "I know I'm awkward in social situations. And I know I have something in my head that makes me unable to say what I want to say in certain situations. Like when people need, I guess, comfort. But just because I don't say it, doesn't mean I'm not thinking it."

She rubbed his arm. "I know that, Amos. I really do."

"But I am trying. It's just... it's just not as easy at it once was."

She smiled. "I think you've come a long way. And it's a two-way street. You've made me a better person. Certainly I'm a far better investigator. When we first teamed up I had no idea what I was doing."

He nodded, leaned against the counter, and studied his feet. "I remember when Cassie and Molly died. Family came in, there was a lot to do. Everybody was crushed and…I couldn't really do anything. I just sat there like a lump."

"But that's understandable. It was such a horrible loss for you."

"Lots of people have horrible losses, every day. And they manage to keep going."

"Well, what you did today was much appreciated. You really helped out a lot. Amber was very grateful."

He didn't respond to this, but simply rubbed the top of his head.

"How does it feel?" she asked.

"Funny," was all he would say.

"Any more memory glitches?"

"Not like before, no."

She nodded, but still looked apprehensive. "What did you find out in Jersey?"

He told her about his conversation with Stanley Nottingham.

"A treasure?" she said. "Do you believe that?"

"I think Bradley Costa believed it. Why else would he come here?"

"But just based on some thirdhand gossip he would pick up and leave New York for this place? It doesn't make sense."

"It *would* make sense if Costa did some digging on his own. Nottingham told me that he seemed very well informed during their later conversations. That means Costa apparently had done some of his own research. Guy was on Wall Street. They're used to doing due diligence. And there's something else."

"What?"

"Remember Costa had joined all the local organizations, Kiwanis, et cetera?"

"Yeah, we saw all those photos. So? Nothing strange there."

"But he had also joined the local *historical* society."

"You think he went there and did more research and maybe found where the treasure might be? Or what it is?"

"It's certainly possible."

"What about John Baron? Do you think he knows about the treasure rumors?"

"I don't know, but I think his predecessors looked for it. That would account for the holes in the walls. And while the grounds are now overgrown, I saw lots of lumpy earth where people might have been digging for it."

"But you don't think Baron knows where it is?" she asked again.

"If he did, would he be living like he is?"

"True. So what are you going to do now?"

"I've got to follow in Costa's footsteps and see what he found."

"But why would someone murder him?"

"If he discovered the location of a treasure, that would be a motive."

"And the three other vics?"

"I don't know."

"Look, once the funeral is over I can start helping you again."

"You don't have to do that. Your family will need you."

"I'm a woman, Decker."

He looked confused. "Yeah, I know. So what?"

"That means I can *multitask*," she replied with a smile.

He nodded. "Okay. But let's keep in mind we've got some violent drug dealer involvement here. I checked out Brian Collins through an FBI database. The guy was a stone-cold killer. If there are more like him out there, this is going to get hairy."

"Hey, it's what we do, right?"

He stared at her so intently that she said, "I know. You don't want anything to happen to me. But I signed up for this. I'm all in. I have your back, you have mine, right?"

He nodded.

"There's one more thing, Decker."

"What's that?"

She said hesitantly, "I...I overheard your talk with Zoe on the stairs, before you left for New Jersey."

Decker glanced away, his brow crinkling.

"It was really nice what you told her. I know that it helped her. And...and I so appreciate your doing it."

Still looking away, Decker said, "She's just a kid. She shouldn't have to go through this."

"But if she does, it's good that she has a friend like you."

"And an aunt like you," he replied.

He rubbed his head again, trying to smooth down the still sticking-up hair.

"You're worried about something, I can tell," she said. "It's not the case, is it?"

He shook his head.

"What is it, then?"

"At the institute in Chicago where I went after my brain injury, they told me a lot of things, but one of them stuck with me."

"What was that?"

"They said that a damaged brain can keep changing. The initial reaction was the perfect recall and the synesthesia. But they said changes could happen again, years down the road."

"But it's been over two decades and nothing has changed, right?"

"Until I got walloped in the head here."

"But you said the memory blip hasn't happened again. And how about the synesthesia?"

He looked at her. "When I shot Brian Collins I didn't see electric blue like I normally do."

"What color did you see?"

"I didn't see any color. And I didn't feel sick or claustrophobic. That's not necessarily a bad thing. But it does mean that something has changed in my head. And that's, well, it's a little unnerving."

"I could see that. So maybe the injury to your head did do something. But your synesthesia might come back."

"Part of me doesn't want it to come back. But—"

"But you're afraid that other things will change about you?"

He looked directly at her now. "I already became somebody else, Alex. I don't want to go through that again. Because I don't know who I might become next." He added with an embarrassed smile, "And let's face it, that person might not be as likable as me."

47

ASHES TO ASHES and dust to dust.

When Decker had buried his wife and child, he had stood at their gravesites as though experiencing a cruel hallucination. He knew what was happening in front of him, but could not believe it actually equated with any sense of reality.

Frank Mitchell's funeral, he understood from this experience, was probably no different for Mitchell's wife and young daughter. They would go through the motions today and go to bed tonight. And then wake up tomorrow and momentarily wonder where their husband and father was.

The weather had turned rainy and cold, with the gloom of clouds adding weight to an already oppressive atmosphere.

Frank's parents, flanked by their grown children, sat looking feeble and dazed.

Directly in front of the coffin, Amber held Zoe in her lap, the girl's head tight against her mother's chest. Her sisters were on either side of her. They were all seated on metal folding chairs set up in front of the coffin. Some people from the fulfillment center, including Ted Ross, were in attendance. There were a few other young women. Decker assumed they might be mothers of kids who went to Zoe's school. Other than them, there was no one. The Mitchells hadn't been here long enough to make many friends.

Decker had had no suit to wear to the funeral, and getting something quickly for a man of his size was out of the question. Thus his khaki pants, sweater, and overcoat had to suffice.

He stood in the very back, almost clear of the tent that had been put up against the inclement weather. Lumpy green turf carpet was under his feet. Rain blew in on him from the rear of the tent, but it didn't bother him, and he didn't try to move in closer. He wasn't part of the family, and he wanted to give the bereaved their space.

His gaze had met Ross's and the men had flicked a hello at each other. He thought it was good of Ross to be here. While he stood there, the man sidled over to him.

"I hope no one minds that I'm here," Ross said quietly.

"You came to pay your respects. Nothing wrong with that."

Ross dug into his pocket, pulled out a card, and handed it to Decker.

"What's this?"

"For what it's worth, he's one of the best lawyers in Pennsylvania. He'll take Maxus for every penny he can." He pointed over to Amber and Zoe. "They deserve it. And then they should just leave this place and find a nicer one to live in."

Decker said, "Thanks. But why are you being so nice? You work for the company that will have to pay out big-time."

"You told me you met my father?"

"I did."

"He's an asshole."

"I wouldn't disagree with that."

"He was terrible to my mother, and to me too, truth be known. I never forgot that. Always being on the receiving end of that crap. Always being the underdog. It leaves its mark on you."

"I can understand that."

Ross said quietly, "So when the little guy can punch back, you gotta take your shot." He pointed to the card. "Have her call him."

"I will."

Ross walked away.

A few minutes later the preacher eulogized a man he didn't know; some hymns were sung and then a final prayer was given. After that the man of the cloth went over and said some private words to the widow and patted Zoe on the head. The little girl recoiled from the stranger's touch, while Jamison put a supportive hand on her niece's shoulder.

And that was that.

A life of roughly three and a half decades ground down to about thirty minutes, that was what constituted Frank Mitchell's exit from this earth.

That's about what most of us will get, thought Decker. *And then we just live on in memories and fading pictures set on tables and hung on walls.*

If that doesn't depress you, nothing will, he concluded.

The funeral party began to disperse as the burly men who had dug the grave came forward to lower the coffin and finish the job of placing the deceased in the ground and shoveling dirt on top.

And Baronville would be Frank Mitchell's final home for eternity.

That thought nearly made Decker sick to his stomach.

He walked back to the rental alone while Jamison joined her two other sisters, who had formed a protective ring around Amber and Zoe.

"Hey, Decker?"

He looked over to see Kate Kemper standing next to a black SUV parked at the rear of the line of cars that had been part of the funeral procession.

She walked over to him.

"Didn't expect to see you here," he said.

"I didn't know them, but a young guy dies and leaves behind a young widow and a kid? I just thought I'd come to pay my respects. At least from a distance. I didn't want to intrude."

"Nice of you."

"I lost my father last year. My mom passed away when I was in college. I'm an only child. So I'm next at the turnstile."

"I think you have a ways to go," noted Decker.

"Tomorrow is guaranteed to no one, especially in our line of work."

"No arguments there."

"Last time I saw you, you were heading out with the bartender from the Mercury Bar."

"I remember," he said.

"So, anything to report?"

Decker leaned against his truck. "How about you enlighten me on one point first."

"What would that be?"

"You never told me what your agents, Beatty and Smith, were doing in the area."

"Yes I did. They had gone rogue."

"According to Randy Haas's dying declaration?"

"Yes. I told you that too."

"But before they went *rogue*, where were they assigned?"

Kemper said, "Why?"

"I'm investigating the case. I need information to do that."

"Okay, there was some work to do in this area. Not in Baronville specifically, but in the general vicinity of northwestern Pennsylvania."

"What sort of work? Feel free to be as specific as possible."

Kemper looked around. "In my truck."

They walked across the road and climbed into her SUV.

Once they were inside, Kemper said, "This part of Pennsylvania, Interstate 80 and some of the state routes are known drug distribution routes. We have a number of heroin and fentanyl drug rings that use it. A lot of it comes from New York and is brought to Middle America through those avenues. There's another pipeline that carries the drugs down from Detroit and over from Columbus."

"So, Beatty and Smith were working on that?"

"Yes. They were trying to identify both suppliers and shippers."

"Had they made any progress?"

"Not really, although we were hoping that Haas would be able to assist. He'd been part of one of the drug crews using those very same pipelines."

"But I don't quite get how, if Beatty and Smith killed Haas, he was able to make a dying declaration."

Kemper said, "He was found in an alleyway in Scranton. He'd been injected with an overdose of morphine. He cried out and some people nearby came to his assistance. The syringe was found in his arm. He told the people who discovered him that it had been Beatty and Smith. Then he died. The onlookers reported his last words to police."

"No prints on the syringe?"

"None. They would have worn gloves. They weren't rookies."

Decker looked out the window at Frank Mitchell's grave. He watched as they lowered the coffin into the ground. He glanced over at Zoe and her mother climbing into the car provided by the funeral home. Zoe was looking back at the coffin going into the ground.

Decker could see her shiver at the sight.

"Did Haas have any family?" asked Decker, his gaze holding on the little girl until the car door closed behind her.

"Family? I suppose so. We really didn't check into that."

Decker turned back to her. "Well, I would if I were you. Did you do a post on him?"

"Of course. The morphine stopped his heart. That was the COD."

"Did the post show anything else?"

"Like what?"

"Like Haas was maybe already dying?"

"What? The ME didn't mention anything like that."

"Because you just wanted to know how he died, probably. Did you actually read the whole report?"

Kemper pursed her lips. "No, I didn't. But I can remedy that right away." She took a moment to thumb in a text. "I'll let you know what they say."

"Okay."

"Why did you even think that a possibility?" asked Kemper.

"Because I don't think your guys went rogue." He glanced at her. "And I'm surprised you were so quickly convinced they had."

"We've had other agents go bad, Decker. Nature of the beast. We chase after guys who literally have billions of dollars to throw at people to make them turn."

"I get that. But that's true of any law enforcement. Was there something else about the pair?"

"We didn't always see eye to eye. They were unorthodox to a fault. I like to do things by the book. Smith and Beatty didn't."

"I'm glad you're not my boss, then."

She smiled. "Maybe I'm glad too." Her smile vanished. "Why would Haas have lied about who killed him?"

"I can think of two reasons. And I hope we'll have answers very soon."

They watched as two more hearses drove past them, headed to other gravesites, the rest of their processions filing in behind them.

"Lot of funerals in this town," noted Decker.

"Dollars to donuts you're looking at ODs there," said Kemper, pointing to some young people getting out of cars and heading to one of the gravesites. "Over eighty thousand people in America this year alone," she added. "More than died in Vietnam and the wars in the Middle East combined. And far more than die in traffic accidents or by guns, and it's only getting worse. Next year we'll probably be looking at over a hundred thousand dead. The opioid crisis is actually responsible for the life expectancy in this country starting to go down. Can you wrap your head around *that*? Nearly a half million dead since 2000. Drug overdoses are the leading cause of death for Americans under age fifty. We had a recent study done at DEA. Life insurance companies value a human life at about five million bucks. Using that number and other factors, our people projected the economic loss to the country each year due to the opioid crisis at about a hundred billion dollars. A third of the population is on medication for pain. And they're not getting addicted on street corners. They're getting addicted at their doctors' offices."

"From prescription painkillers."

"Right. Back in the eighties we had the crack crisis. The government's position was just say no and if you didn't you went to prison. So we locked up millions, mostly men from the inner cities. Then came the nineties and Big Pharma decided that Americans weren't taking enough painkillers. They sort of made *pain* the fifth vital sign. Spent billions on ads, payoffs to doctors, used legit-looking organizations and think tanks to make it all seem aboveboard. 'No possibility of addiction, no long-term negatives' was the mantra everyone was spouting. Turns out all of that was based on either faulty research or no research at all. It's ironic but a lot of opioids were initially given out to combat lower back pain."

"Why was that ironic?" asked Decker.

"Because opioids actually are pretty ineffectual with chronic lower back pain. Last year doctors wrote nearly a quarter billion prescriptions for painkillers. It's a miracle we're not all hooked. And the numbers we see now, bad as they are, are just the tip of the iceberg. It's beyond a national crisis and no one is doing a damn thing about it. Because of our position on crack cocaine in the eighties, we built a lot of prisons but not many treatment centers or addiction protocols. So now this crisis is filling hospitals, prisons, and"—she waved her hand in front of her—"cemeteries all across the country. And to top it off, last year about twenty-five thousand babies were born with what's called neonatal abstinence syndrome because their moms were opioid users while pregnant. What kind of life will they have, do you think?"

Decker stared at the coffin being carried to a gravesite by what looked to be a group of pallbearers who were still in high school. Then he looked at the line of cars parked along the road and was surprised to see some brand-new luxury vehicles along with ancient heaps.

Suddenly they heard a horn begin to blare.

Kemper said, "Where's that coming from?"

"There," said Decker, pointing to a pickup truck parked in the middle of the line of cars.

They jumped out of the SUV and ran across the road. By the time they got to the pickup truck, several people had crowded around it.

In the driver's seat was a young man slumped against the steering wheel. His shoulder was pressed against the horn.

Decker reached through the open window and pushed him back against the seat and the sound stopped.

His breath was coming in gasps.

Decker opened the young man's eyelids. The pupils were pin-pricks.

"He's overdosed," said Kemper, who had also seen this.

"Yeah, he has," said a thin man in a threadbare coat. "Third time this week."

Decker spotted the half-empty syringe on the truck seat. Inside it was a clear sand-colored liquid.

"It looks to be pure heroin," Decker said.

Kemper nodded, punched in 911 on her phone, and requested an ambulance.

Decker said, "Does anybody have any Narcan?"

"I got some," said a woman standing next to the man.

"Give it to me," said Decker as the young man in the truck gasped again.

"He coulda at least waited till after the funeral to pull this crap," said the thin man.

"Give it to me," Decker exclaimed as the young man started to gurgle. "He's going to stop breathing any second."

The woman rummaged in her bag.

The man said again, "Coulda waited. Dumbass."

"Give me the Narcan!" shouted Decker, as the young man slumped against the door, his lips turning blue.

The woman handed Decker a bottle from her purse.

Decker stuck the end in the young man's nose and squeezed.

He waited for a few seconds, but nothing happened.

Kemper looked at the syringe and said, "There must be some fentanyl mixed in with what he took. It's more tightly bound to the brain receptor than morphine."

"That's *heroin*, not morphine, lady," said the thin man. "Don't you know nothin'?"

Kemper whirled on him and flashed her badge. "I know a lot more than you do. When the body breaks down heroin the instant by-product *is morphine*!" She turned back to Decker. "Hit him again with the Narcan. We have to move the drug off the brain re-ceptor."

Decker squirted in another dose.

A few moments passed and then the young man exhaled a long breath, sat up straight, blinked, and looked around, his expression foggy.

"Great," said the man sarcastically. "You brought him back. 'Til the next time."

Decker looked at him. "Who are you?"

"I'm his uncle. And the bastard didn't have the decency to wait till his sister was buried before pulling this shit. Talk about showing no damn respect."

"His sister?" said Kemper. "How'd she die?"

"Damn heroin overdose," said the uncle. "Didn't get her the Narcan in time." He pointed to the young man. "That asshole coulda saved her, but he was in the bathroom doing lines of coke."

A moment later the young man leaned out the window and threw up.

They all jumped back to avoid the vomit.

The young man looked angrily at Decker until he saw the bottle in his hand.

"You almost bit the bullet for good, buddy," said Decker.

"Thanks, man," he said groggily, wiping his mouth.

Decker looked at Kemper and then back at the young man.

He tossed the bottle of Narcan to the woman, walked back to the SUV, and got in.

Kemper turned to the aunt and uncle. "An ambulance will be here shortly. He'll need to go to the hospital."

"Right," said the uncle. "Whatever."

As Kemper walked off, he slapped his nephew on the back of the head. "Dumbass!"

Kemper hurried after Decker and climbed into the truck.

"You okay?" she said once she'd settled in.

Decker didn't say anything for a long moment. "I'm just wondering whether we're ever going to dig ourselves out of this hole."

"I've seen it all at the DEA. Every foul thing a human being can stoop to when they're hooked on drugs. Even that back there didn't surprise me. I've seen worse. Five-year-olds performing

CPR on their parents. A grandmother knocking in her son's head for the cash to feed her addiction. A mother selling her ten-year-old daughter for sex to get her heroin pops. But we'll make it through this, Decker."

He glanced at her. "You really believe that?"

"I have to. Otherwise, I couldn't do my job."

A minute of silence passed before Decker broke it.

"You mentioned insurance companies rating the value of a life," he said.

"Yeah, that's part of their business."

"Cindi Riley told me that she'd lost a number of friends to overdoses here."

"Not surprised. And there are thousands of places just like this one. Where people used to get up every day and go to work with a purpose. And now they don't have a purpose. Or a job. Or any self-worth. That takes its toll, Decker. In a lot of ways. That's why they're calling the opioid epidemic the drugs of despair."

"Riley also said that some of her friends had life insurance policies. And that some of the renovations in town are due to people having received large payouts from life insurance companies." He pointed at the new luxury cars parked along the road. "And maybe those proceeds are also helping to pay for those."

Kemper mulled this over for a few moments before shaking her head. "No insurance company will knowingly write a large life insurance policy on someone in such bad health they're likely to die, or someone addicted to drugs, Decker, if that's what you're thinking."

"Maybe they weren't an addict when the policy was written," he said.

"What are you driving at?"

"It would be interesting to know how many people in Baronville who've died from drug overdoses had large life insurance policies. Can you find that out?"

Kemper stared out at the line of cars parked on the road. "I can try."

"Good." Before she could respond, he said, "I've got to get

back. I promised Jamison I'd help this afternoon. They're having a reception at the Mitchells'."

As he climbed out of the truck Kemper said, "I didn't picture you as much of a domestic."

"Well, these days, I'm even surprising myself."

48

THE RAIN WAS pouring down outside now. It beat on the Mitchells' roof as the combined families and a few others gathered at the house after the funeral.

Decker had arrived in time to help Jamison and her sisters set things up. Food and drinks were laid out and chairs from the kitchen and other rooms distributed around. Decker had also passed on to Amber the lawyer's card that Ted Ross had given him. She said she would call him later in the week.

Zoe was in a chair cuddling with both her blanket and her cat, Felix, while Amber sat with her in-laws quietly talking.

Alice Martin had come over with a boxed pie. She was now holding court in a corner of the room with Jamison and one of the school mothers. Ted Ross and the people with him from Maxus had said their goodbyes at the gravesite and skipped this event. Decker thought that wise, because Frank's father's jaw had tightened back at the cemetery when Ross had come by and offered his condolences to Amber.

The knock on the door caused Decker to flick a gaze at Jamison to let her know that he would answer it. She responded with a smile.

Decker opened the door and gazed dully at the pair standing there.

John Baron and Cindi Riley, both holding umbrellas, stared back at him.

"I take it you're positively stunned at our presence here," commented Baron.

Decker noted that he had on crisply pressed dress slacks, a white button-down shirt, and a faded corduroy sport coat with patches at the elbows.

Under her raincoat, Riley wore a loose-fitting black dress that settled right at her knee and matching pumps. Her hair was done up in a French braid. She held a package in her other hand.

"I am," said Decker.

"We came by to pay our respects," said Baron.

Riley handed Decker the package. "And to bring this. It's a bottle of single malt whisky."

"Okay," said Decker. He just stood there holding it until Jamison appeared at his elbow.

"Hello," she said to the pair.

Baron held out his hand. "We met before. John Baron. This is Cindi Riley."

Jamison shook their hands.

Baron said, "As I told your colleague here, we came by to pay our respects."

Decker said, "And they brought a bottle of single malt scotch." He handed it to her.

Riley said, "I'm Irish. It's what we bring to wakes. I hope it's okay."

"That was very thoughtful of you. Please come in out of the rain," said Jamison.

She led them in and Decker closed the door behind the group.

All eyes in the room turned to the new arrivals.

No one seemed to recognize Baron other than Alice Martin. Decker saw her eyes widen slightly at the sight of the man, and then she returned to her conversation with one of the young mothers from Zoe's school.

Baron and Riley spoke briefly to Amber, offering their condolences.

Then Jamison led the pair over to Zoe and introduced them.

His eyes twinkling, Baron got down on his knees in front of Zoe. "You strike me as a person who doesn't believe in magic."

Zoe had her thumb stuffed in her mouth and didn't answer.

"Do I take that as a yes, that you *don't* believe in magic?" said Baron.

Zoe nodded.

"All right. Now let me see. What did I do with that?"

He tapped his jacket pockets, looked under the chair, and then reached out to the blanket and lightly touched its edges. "No, it's definitely not there."

Zoe removed her thumb and said, "What's not there?"

Baron, pretending not to have heard her, said, "Oh, of course, now I remember. Zoe, could you just reach in your cat's right ear? You'll find it in there, I think."

Zoe looked uncertainly at Decker and then Jamison, who nodded encouragingly at her.

Zoe slowly put her fingers in Felix's right ear and her eyes bulged as she withdrew a small silver coin. She said, "How did it get in Felix's ear?"

Baron clapped his hands together and glanced at Jamison. "Well, I feel sure that Felix is a very special cat, right?"

Zoe nodded.

"Well, special cats can do magical things, like hiding coins in their ears."

He took the coin and examined it. "Now, this is a very rare coin. It will bring whoever possesses it good luck. Okay?"

"Okay," said Zoe, still looking wide-eyed from her cat to the coin.

Baron held it up in front of her. "It's one hundred and forty-seven years old. It once belonged to my ancestor. He had a great many coins and never parted with many, but this one found its way to me and I would be honored if you would accept it as a token of my appreciation for your being such a brave young lady, and the owner of such a special cat. Would you do that, Zoe? Will you take the coin?"

Her fingers closed around the coin as she nodded.

He sat back and looked at her. "And now do you believe in magic? Perhaps just a little? Or at least in very special cats?"

She nodded energetically.

"What do you say, Zoe?" said Jamison, gazing admiringly at Baron.

"Thank you."

"No, thank *you* for doing me the honor of accepting it." Baron glanced over at Amber, who was staring at them from across the room. "I bet your mom could use a hug right about now. And you can show her your brand-new, very old coin."

Zoe smiled, jumped up, and ran over to her mother as Baron stood.

"That was really nice," said Jamison.

"It was," agreed Riley.

Jamison added, "You seem to be a man of many talents."

"No, just a jack of all trades and a master of none, I'm afraid. My lot in life. So, how are things here?"

Jamison said, "I guess what one would expect. I'm just glad the funeral is over."

Baron shook his head. "I don't get the ritual of the funeral and the gravesite service. As if already grieving people need to go through that as well."

"It's a way of paying respects, John," countered Riley.

Baron pointed to the bottle held by Jamison. "I would rather pay my respects by drinking that. And if you point me toward the kitchen, I can get us glasses."

Jamison led him that way, leaving Riley and Decker alone.

"You left my place really abruptly the other night," she said. "You said you had somewhere to go."

"I did."

"Where?"

Decker studied her. "I found Stanley Nottingham."

"Who?"

"The name of the guy on the back of the photo."

"Oh, right."

"He was related to Baron's butler, Nigel."

"Wow, that's a coincidence." She glanced sharply at Decker. "But you said you don't believe in coincidences."

"Even if I did, I wouldn't believe in one *that* big."

"What did you find out?"

"Ever hear any rumors about a treasure being hidden at the Baron estate?"

Riley shook her head. "No, why? Did this Stanley guy say there was?"

"He'd heard stories. And he lived in the same building in New York that Brad Costa did. They were friends, in fact."

"Wait a minute. Are you saying that Brad Costa came to Baronville because he heard about rumors of some treasure?"

"I think it wasn't just based on rumors. I think he did some digging on his own and then came here."

"But he would have had to be pretty sure that it was true to pull up roots and move to this place."

"I agree with you."

"Do you really think there is some sort of treasure up there?"

"I think people have looked for it. But I don't think they ever found it."

"Damn."

"Baron never mentioned that to you?"

"No, never. And if he'd found anything, I doubt he'd be living as he is."

"Agreed. But he had to know about the rumors."

She glanced at him. "Why are you telling me all this? Isn't it part of your investigation?"

"It's a parallel part. And I'm telling you because I'm relying on my gut. And my gut tells me I can trust you. Also, I need some traction on this case, which means I need some local help."

"John would know more than I would. It's his family."

"But can I trust him?"

"I do."

At that moment, Baron and Jamison came back with four glasses. He poured out a portion of whisky in each.

"To Frank," he said, raising his glass.

The others repeated this toast and they all took a sip of the whisky.

Jamison said, "Wow, I'm not used to something this strong, at least not in the afternoon."

Baron eyed her. "If you live here long enough, you'd see the utility in it. But I don't recommend you live here, Alex."

Decker glanced at Riley and then said to Baron, "Nigel Nottingham?"

Baron lowered his glass and glanced at him. "What about him?"

"Baron the First's loyal butler."

"Yes, I'm aware of that."

Riley said quickly, "He talked to a relative of the guy. He lived in the same building as Brad Costa. Decker thinks the relative told Costa about a possible treasure at your house. That's why Costa came here."

"And was murdered," added Decker, still looking at Baron.

Baron said wearily, "Yes, the treasure. The *alleged* treasure."

"You never mentioned that to us," said Decker.

"Why would I? There is no treasure."

"So you've looked for it?" said Jamison.

"No. But my ancestors did, for many, many decades. And it was never found, because our patron would never have left any money for his descendants to find. It wasn't in his DNA."

"Costa must have thought differently," said Decker. "Why else chuck New York for this place. Did he ever ask you about it?"

"As I told you before, I don't know the man. I never met the man, so there would have been no possible way for him to ask me anything."

"And you're certain about that?"

Baron pursed his lips and looked amused. "I'm assuming you're referring to my failure to tell you about Joyce and Michael Swanson?"

"Your credibility is not all that good in my book."

Baron said, "Well, I'm not sure what I can say to convince you otherwise, so perhaps I should take my leave." He turned to Alex. "I am very sorry for what happened. I doubt there's anything I can do, but if you or your sister need anything, please ask and I'll do whatever I can."

Riley said, "Same for me."

"Thank you," said Jamison.

They all walked outside. Fortunately, the rain had nearly stopped. As Baron and Riley were heading to his old Suburban, they heard the sirens.

"Coming this way," noted Decker.

They saw flashing lights turn onto the street where the Murder House was.

All four of them ran over to the next block in time to see the police leap from their cars and run up to a house. The front door was open and an elderly woman was waiting on the porch looking distressed. As they watched, an ambulance slowly drove up to the house, its emergency lights off.

"Who lives there?" asked Riley.

Decker said, "Dan Bond. And from the looks of things, I'm not sure he *lives* there anymore."

49

"WHY WOULD ANYONE want to kill Dan?"

A weepy Alice Martin had asked this same question so many times that Decker thought she might be in shock.

After flashing their badges at the responding officers, Decker and Jamison had been told that the death was not natural or accidental.

"Somebody crushed in his skull," one officer had reported.

Now they were all gathered back at Amber's house after Dan Bond's remains had been removed from his home. The other guests had left and Amber and Zoe were upstairs resting. Jamison's sisters had driven Frank's parents and his siblings back to their motel.

Baron and Riley were still there and were silently studying the floor of the living room. Baron had another glass of whisky in hand.

Jamison put an arm on Alice Martin's shoulder. "I'm sure the police will find out who did it."

The elderly woman wailed to her, "Well, they haven't found out who killed those other people yet."

Jamison glanced at Decker, who was just about to make a comment when someone knocked on the door.

Decker knew who he was going to see when he opened it.

Detectives Green and Lassiter stared back at him.

Green said grimly, "I think we might want to evacuate the other residents from that street, and I'm only half joking."

"One of them is here," said Decker, indicating Martin. "What about Fred Ross?"

Lassiter said, "We woke him up when we knocked on the door. He was in a foul mood."

"You're lucky he didn't have his shotgun with him."

"Yeah, well, he said if anybody tried to bash his head in, they'd get both barrels in their face for the trouble."

"What can you tell me?" asked Decker.

"Care to step outside?" said Lassiter.

They went back out on the porch and Decker turned to face them.

Green said, "He's been dead since around midnight last night."

"Forced entry?"

"No sign of that. An elderly friend came over to check on him when he didn't show up for a church meeting and they couldn't reach him on the phone. She found him in the kitchen."

"How'd she get in?"

Green said, "She had a key. We checked her out, she's what she claims to be."

Decker said. "A uniform told me there was blunt force trauma to the head?"

"Correct," said Lassiter.

"Murder weapon?"

"Didn't find one. Perp probably took it with him."

"And no one saw anything?"

"Well, there were only two other people on the street. Martin and Ross. Both were probably in bed at midnight."

"How about the DEA agent across the street?" asked Decker.

Green said, "Kemper lifted that surveillance yesterday. They finished processing that scene and the one next door where you shot Brian Collins. We don't have the manpower to keep a guy idle like that. So there was no one on patrol duty."

Lassiter said, "The killer must've been watching and knew there was no cop present. Then he goes and does the deed."

Green said, "But why the old blind guy? Why would anyone target him? He couldn't have *seen* anything."

"But he could *hear* things," said Decker. "He knew there wasn't a plane flying over that night. It was his suggestion that it might have been a drone."

Green popped some gum into his mouth. "Donna mentioned your theory about that. You think he might have told someone else what he told you? And that person might have killed him?"

"It's possible. I can't think of another reason why someone would want to murder him. He's not the sort who would have a lot of enemies. Was there any sign of robbery?"

"No. I don't think he had much to steal."

"When I went there to interview him Bond had to open three door locks. I don't think he would have left his door open."

"So someone had a key," said Lassiter.

"Or he knew his killer and let the person in," noted Decker. "And based on my experience with Bond, at that time of night, that would take a lot of trust."

Green snapped, "Are you making *any* sense out of this?"

"Not yet."

Green pulled his badge off his belt and threw it down on the porch.

"Why the hell do I even wear this thing if I can't protect my town?"

Decker bent down, picked up the badge, examined it to make sure it wasn't dented, and handed it back to Green. "We're going to get there, Detective," he said.

"How can you be so sure?" asked Lassiter.

"Because in our line of work, failure is not an option," replied Decker.

CHAPTER

50

Decker was sitting at the table in the Mitchells' kitchen two days after the funeral.

He'd smoothed out the copies he'd made of the letters he'd found in Stanley Nottingham's locker back at the senior living center in New Jersey and placed them on the table. There were several of them, but none seemed to contain any information pertaining to a hidden treasure.

He looked at one of them for the fifth time.

Dear Samuel,

I know that things have been estranged between us and that we have not communicated in a long while. But I'm taking up my pen now because I miss you, son. I wish you had not abandoned Baronville, but I know you have your own life to lead. I realize you were never enamored with Master Baron but he treats me very well. Just last year we went on a long journey that included a months-long trek across Australia. He chartered a private ship for our trip, and though the voyage was long, it was fascinating. Though many of the countries that we visited previously were truly unique and fascinating in many ways, I have never seen such a place as Australia in all my life. We toured through the coastal cities, Sydney, Perth, Adelaide, and the acting capital of Melbourne. I heard they are thinking of a new capital at a place called Canberra. We also visited Geelong, Toowoomba, Kalgoorlie,

Ballarat, Moliagul, and a dozen other places with equally fanciful names. We saw aborigines, as well as kangaroo and emu, wombats and kookaburras and other wildlife I could never imagine even existed. One of our guides killed a serpent three times as tall as I am. There are grand coral reefs and water that is so clear you can see to the bottom. There are vast mountain ranges and dense rain forests along with massive deserts. The interior of the country, called the outback, is beyond description. It makes England seem a bit dull by comparison, though I am proud to say it is still very much part of the British empire. I believe even the mighty Baron, who is mostly focused on business, relaxed and enjoyed himself. However, I am sad to report that upon our return Master Baron began to feel unwell. I believe the arduous journey was too taxing on him. It is now nearly a year after our return and his robustness has failed to return. He attempts to remain strong but I know him better than anyone else, and I can tell that he is failing. Once he goes, I don't know what will happen here. He is not enamored with his children, none of whom have his business acumen. He has done so much for them and yet they really are the most ungrateful lot. And, son, to tell the truth, your father is not feeling all that well either. My bones are creaking and my lungs are heavy. I trust that you and the children are doing well. I hope to see you before I'm gone. If not, come and visit my remains, and though hopefully I will be dwelling in a place far above you, one never knows, does one? I might be lurking below. It's all in God's hands and I bow to his forgiveness.

Yours truly,
Nigel

Decker put the letter aside. If there was a clue in there he wasn't seeing it. It was a bit pathetic how Nigel seemed to worship Baron solely because he was wealthy. But then again, lots of people still did that to this day. And Nigel had not been far off the mark about both men's failing health. The letter was dated only six weeks prior to his and Baron's deaths.

He looked up when Jamison walked into the room.

She sat down across from him and glanced at the letters.

"Find anything relevant?" she asked.

He shook his head and leaned back in his chair. "How are Zoe and your sister?"

"I think it was a good idea to take Zoe back to school today. She needs structure to keep her mind off what happened. I'll pick her up later. Amber is at the bank going over some financial things. And she called that lawyer Ted Ross recommended. He's coming here to meet with her."

"Good. She needs to make Maxus reach into their deep pockets and pay."

"I told her that too, and not to sign anything they might send her. And Frank also had life insurance. A half-million-dollar policy, so that will help too. From what she said, it'll be paid out pretty shortly."

"Did he have that through work?"

"I think so, yes."

Decker nodded and looked down at the letters.

"Any idea why Dan Bond might have been killed?" she asked.

"Because of something he might have known about what happened that night."

"Not something he saw, then, but something he heard?"

Decker nodded. "I did confirm that Fred Ross was at the hospital that night getting checked out. So whatever Bond heard, it had nothing to do with him."

"Do you think Alice Martin might be targeted next? Whoever killed Bond might be afraid she saw or heard something too."

"Which is why I asked Green to have a patrol car make regular rounds down her street for now."

"Good plan," said Jamison.

Decker rose.

"Where are you going?"

"To the Baronville Historical Society."

"Everyone left this morning to go back home. You want company?"

"Good to have you back, partner."

* * *

"Yes, I remember Mr. Costa quite clearly."

Decker and Jamison were at the historical society speaking with the director, Jane Satterwhite, who was apparently the only employee of the place. She was a dowdy gray-haired woman in her late sixties wrapped in a pink shawl and with granny glasses dangling from a chain.

The society was housed in a drab brick building with abandoned structures on either side of it.

"We have a very rich history in Baronville," Satterwhite said. "Only we lack the resources to fully tell it."

She was speaking the truth here, for as Decker and Jamison looked around, the shelves were only half full and the displays looked old and dusty. The entire place had an air of neglect.

"Do you get a lot of visitors?" asked Jamison.

"No, I'm afraid not. People aren't interested in history anymore, it seems."

"Then they're doomed to repeat the mistakes of the past," noted Decker.

"Exactly," said Satterwhite, suddenly animated. "You've hit the nail right on the head. Everyone looks to the future for answers, which ignores the fact that people, despite the passage of years, remain fundamentally the same."

"You were telling us about Bradley Costa?" prompted Jamison.

"Oh, yes. That's right. A very nice young man. Very interested in our town."

"Anything in particular?" prompted Jamison.

"Particularly in John Baron. The First, I'm talking about. The one who founded this town."

"What exactly was he interested in having to do with John Baron?" asked Decker.

Satterwhite led them into another room.

"This is our Baron Room, as I like to call it. Here, we house everything we have about John Baron, from his birth to his death."

"I understand that he died on the same day as his butler, Nigel Nottingham."

"Yes, that's right. Are you an historian too?"

"An amateur one," lied Decker. "Was Costa interested in that fact?"

"Well, he asked me about it. He wanted to know if we had any correspondence from Nigel. He was the first person ever to ask about that."

"And did you?" asked Decker.

"No, we didn't."

"Did he ask about anything else?"

"Any business correspondence that Baron might have had in the time leading up to his death."

"And did you have anything like that?" asked Jamison.

"Just one letter."

She turned to a file cabinet, opened it, and rummaged through its contents. "That's funny."

"You can't find it?" asked Jamison.

"Well, it was right here. Maybe it was put back in the wrong place." She went through the other drawers, without success.

"Well, that is strange," she said more to herself than to them. "It's not here."

"When was the last time the letter was accessed?" asked Jamison.

"Why, when Mr. Costa was here. But I know that I put it back in here."

"Could anyone else have gotten to it?"

"Well, I'm the only one here. We do leave the door unlocked during the day, though, so I guess if I'm in the back and someone comes in but doesn't call out to me, they could come in here without my knowing. But who would do that?"

"Can you tell us what was in the letter?" asked Decker.

"Yes, because I read through it quite thoroughly when I got it out for Mr. Costa. It was nothing special. Baron had written to a company about the construction of another building at his textile mill. It had to do with the purchase of equipment, clay, lots of concrete, brick molds, those sorts of things. I didn't consider it important, really. It was just business."

"When was the letter dated?" asked Decker.

"About a year before his death."

"Was it a local company he was writing to?" asked Jamison.

"No, it was a company from Pittsburgh."

"Do you remember the name?" asked Jamison.

"Oh, let me think. Yes, that's right. O'Reilly and Sons. I remember because my mother-in-law's maiden name was O'Reilly."

"But I presume Costa was interested in the letter?" said Decker. "Since you pulled it out for him?"

"Well, yes. But that letter was really the only thing I could find about any business correspondence. We mostly had to rely on the Baron family for any such materials, and apparently they either didn't have much, or else they didn't want to part with it."

"Well, thank you for your help," said Jamison.

As they were walking back to their truck she said, "Well, that's strange that the letter went missing. Do you think Costa stole it?"

"Maybe. Or maybe someone else did."

"I wish we had learned more."

"Well, we have a new question we need an answer to."

"What?"

"What did Baron the First really use the stuff he ordered for? Because it wasn't for a textile mill expansion."

"How do you know that?"

"Because of what Detective Green already told us."

51

W E'RE EXECUTING A search warrant at John Baron's house if you want to tag along."

Decker stared blankly at Lassiter as she stood on the front porch of the Mitchells' house early the next morning.

"Where's your partner?" he asked.

"Running down some other leads. I'm heading this effort up."

"Why a search warrant for Baron's place?" Decker said sleepily. She had phoned him before coming over, which had allowed him to hastily dress and meet her on the porch.

"We have reason to believe he might be involved in the murders," she said.

"And why is that?" asked Jamison, who had just walked up next to Decker. He had told her about Lassiter's call. Jamison was still tugging down a sweater she had thrown on and brushed her sleep-tousled hair out of her eyes.

"Based on things your friend here told me," said Lassiter, indicating Decker.

"Baron knew at least three of the four vics. We know he knew Joyce Tanner and that Swanson was living in his potting shed. But who's the third?" asked Decker.

"The bank holds the mortgage on Baron's home. And guess who the bank's point person on the loan was?"

Jamison said dully, "Bradley Costa."

"You win the prize."

"So, he has connections to some of the victims," said Decker. "I'm sure other people in town do too."

"And then there's the Toby Babbot connection. That makes it four for four."

"What connection?" said Decker sharply.

"I dug up an old arrest report. Toby Babbot was charged with trespassing on Baron's property."

"What was he doing up there?" asked Jamison.

"He wouldn't say when the cops asked him."

"And Baron knew about this?"

"*He* was the one who caught Babbot up there and reported it to the police. So Baron knew all *four* victims."

"And what's your theory of the case?" asked Jamison.

"Well, the Costa angle is easy enough. The bank holds the mortgage. And as Decker also told me, Baron was into Greek mythology. Thanatos is the *Greek* god of death."

"And Joyce Tanner?"

"He was supporting her financially. He was running out of money. Maybe she had some dirt on him and that was why he was supporting her. So he kills her and writes that biblical crap on the wall about slavery. A financial slave, maybe. And Tanner was into the Bible in high school, something Baron well knew."

"Don't you think all of that is a bit of overkill?" said Decker.

"What do you mean?" asked Lassiter.

"Greek symbols, biblical verses, all things that could be traced back to Baron pretty easily. I did it just by looking in a yearbook. And that mortgage has been on his property for a long time. So why go out and kill a banker over it now?"

"Because I learned he recently tried to get the debt refinanced at a lower rate because of cash flow issues, but the bank refused, meaning *Costa* refused. Consequently, he's in danger of losing the whole property if he can't make payments and the bank forecloses."

Decker looked a little taken aback by these new facts. "That still doesn't prove he killed the guy. And I still think it's way too overdone."

"Killers sometime overthink things, Decker. They make simple complicated. They get too cute."

"Yes, they do. But Baron does not strike me as that kind of a man. What this looks like to me is someone trying to frame the guy and doing a crappy job of it."

"Well, I've arrested people on a lot less, and proved my case."

"And Babbot?"

"He might have found something up on the Baron estate that made Baron nervous. And I think I might know what that is. And you should too since you found the connection before we did."

"What?" asked Decker.

"Swanson was a drug dealer. What if he and Baron were in it together? Baron desperately needed money, and I doubt he would care where it came from. But then Swanson wants a bigger cut or maybe gets cold feet and is going to rat Baron out. So Swanson has to die, and so does Babbot if he knew about it. In fact, Babbot might have been buying drugs from them."

"That's all speculation," observed Decker.

"Which is why we're going to search the property," said Lassiter. "To get the evidence to prove the speculation is actually true. You in or out?"

"We're in," replied Decker, while Jamison looked on worriedly.

* * *

Decker and Jamison followed Lassiter and two police vans up the hill to Baron's property. It was only seven o'clock in the morning and it was clear that Lassiter wanted to take Baron by surprise.

Decker said, "Baron lied to me. Again. He flat-out told me he didn't know Costa."

"Well, maybe they never met. It could have all been through letters or emails."

"That doesn't matter. The guy was going to foreclose. That's a motive for murder and you know it. And he kept that from me."

"Do you really think Baron was selling drugs with Swanson?"

"I don't know. A guy lies to me, that taints everything."

"But you don't think he really is the killer?"

"I don't know that he isn't."

"But he just seems too…"

"Too what? Nice? Eccentric? Good with magic tricks? That doesn't cut it, Alex, and you know it."

Jamison sighed resignedly. "Lassiter looked really happy."

"Considering her father died in prison because of what she believes the Baron family did to him, she would be."

"So, nailing the last surviving Baron would be quite the prize for her?"

"That's what I'm afraid of," said Decker.

52

WELL, THIS IS impressive," Baron said after he opened his front door, looking over the police officers massed behind Lassiter. He was dressed in an old robe and was barefoot.

He glanced at Decker and Jamison, who were off to the side, but didn't say anything to them.

Lassiter held up a piece of paper. "Search warrant for the house, outbuildings, and grounds. I want you to sit down out here while we do it."

"Can I at least have a drink first?" said Baron pleasantly.

Lassiter ignored this and said to an officer standing immediately behind her, "Dawes, I want you to stay here and make sure he doesn't move. I don't want him to have any chance to hide any evidence, or make a run for it."

Baron smiled and said, "Well, I don't run as fast as I used to. And without a drink to bolster me, sitting right here and perhaps falling asleep in the process definitely holds appeal."

Lassiter gave him a look of granite and was about to say something back when Decker moved forward and said, "We'll do the honors, Detective. It's a big place, and you'll need all the manpower you have to search it."

Lassiter gazed at Decker for a longer moment than was probably needed before nodding. "Okay. But when I say I don't want him to move, I mean exactly that."

"Couldn't be clearer," replied Decker.

Lassiter passed out orders to her men; some followed her into the house, while others headed toward the outbuildings and grounds.

Baron sat down on the front porch and stretched. "If any money is found I *will* make a claim. I can use the cash, as you're well aware."

Decker put a foot up on one of the steps and stared down at him.

"You lied to me about Costa. He holds the mortgage on this place and you knew it."

"Well, technically, the *bank* does. He just worked there."

"You know that distinction doesn't pass the smell test. How many times did you talk to him? Exchange correspondence? You wanted to renegotiate the deal but the bank said no. *Costa* said no."

"Banks often say no to people like me. I didn't take it personally."

"But you admit that you knew Costa?"

"It was only business."

"Which means you *did* lie."

"People lie all the time."

"And they get caught in those lies," rejoined Decker. "Just like now. So, Costa stiffs you on your request. Which gives you a prime motive for murdering him."

"Only I didn't. And if I killed everyone who was mean to me, I'd be deemed the world's most prolific serial killer, because I'd have to murder pretty much everybody in this town."

"And Lassiter knows about Swanson being up here. And she also knows about your ties to Tanner. And she dug up an old trespassing charge you made out against Toby Babbot. That means she knows that you have ties to all four victims. That puts you in pretty rarefied company, and also vaults you to the top of the suspect list."

Jamison added, "And Lassiter has theories about how your relationships with all of them could have led to motives for murdering them. It does not look good at all, John."

Baron took all this in and shrugged. "Well, it is what it is, I guess. It's not like I can change any of it."

Decker said, "But why did you lie about Costa? And now Babbot? You didn't think the police would put it all together?"

"Maybe I didn't," conceded Baron. "This town has a police force, but I really thought in name only. They certainly couldn't solve the murders of my parents, so why should I think they could competently solve anything else?"

"Lassiter has a hard-on for you because of her old man. When she was a little girl he lost his job at the textile mill, lost his house to the bank, and burned down the home of a banker while the man was still in it. He went to prison and never came out alive. So how much do you think she loves the Baron family?"

"Excuse me, but why should she be different from anyone else here?" retorted Baron.

Jamison stepped forward. "John, you are in deep trouble. Lassiter is building a case against you for four murders. We're just trying to make you understand the gravity of the situation."

"I've been in deep trouble for most of my life."

"Not this deep," said Decker. "You could get the death penalty."

"I've actually had that ever since I was born here. It's just a matter of time."

"You really need to take this seriously," snapped Jamison.

Baron stood. "And how exactly should I take it seriously?" he said, his eyes flashing dangerously in a way that neither of them had seen before. "If people have a hard-on for me like your friend said, then what does it matter what I do or what I don't do? The result is inevitable. So now maybe you see why I drink so much."

"Did you kill those people?" asked Decker.

Baron held Jamison's gaze for a beat longer and then looked at Decker. "Well, if I had, it's doubtful I would confess my guilt to the FBI." He looked back at Jamison. "Do *you* think I killed them?"

"It doesn't matter what I think. It matters what can be proved."

"That's such a pat response. Frankly, I expected better from you, Alex."

Decker said, "Did you clear Swanson's things out of the potting shed?"

Baron glanced at him.

Decker said, "We told you we found evidence of Swanson staying in the potting shed. And the drug paraphernalia there. Did you get rid of it?"

"I'm not sure I should answer that."

"You're going to have to at some point."

"I think I'll defer for now."

"They're going to search every inch of this place. Odds are very good they're going to find something, including anything that you might have rehidden."

"Do I need a lawyer?"

Lassiter had stepped into the front doorway right at that moment.

"Oh, I think you do, Mr. Baron."

She held up a gun in a plastic evidence bag.

53

"BALLISTICS MATCHED THE gun found at Baron's property to the bullets that killed Costa and Swanson," said Decker.

He was sitting at the Mitchells' kitchen table with Jamison.

"Lassiter just called me. She sounded the happiest I've ever heard her," he added. "And they also found all of the drug stuff in the potting shed. They ran prints and matched it to Swanson. Baron obviously just left it there even after we told him about it."

"So, Lassiter finally nails the Baron family," said Jamison. "But do you believe he did it?"

"Anyone could have planted that gun there," noted Decker. "And Lassiter found it pretty fast."

"She never said where she found it." noted Jamison.

"She told me later. It was in the gun room, in one of the glass cabinets with some of the other pistols."

"So was he counting on the fact that hiding a gun among other guns was a smart idea?"

"Well, it didn't turn out to be."

"With all the grudges people here have against him, I don't see how John gets a fair trial."

"Hopefully he'll lawyer up and they'll probably end up changing venues for the trial."

"What's his story?" asked Jamison.

"That he knows nothing about the gun and doesn't know where it came from."

"Prints?"

"Lassiter said no. But it could have been wiped clean."

"There are too many moving parts to this whole thing, Decker."

His phone buzzed before he could answer. The call lasted a few minutes, with Decker mostly listening and asking brief questions. Finally he said, "Thanks," and hung up.

"What's going on?" Jamison said.

"That was Agent Kemper. I'd asked her about life insurance policies."

"Why?"

Decker explained to her what he had discussed earlier with the DEA agent.

"So what did she find out?"

"Over the last three years or so, nearly three hundred people in Baronville have died from drug overdoses. And about half had life insurance policies of at least half a million bucks. Quite a few had policies of over a million dollars."

"My God, that's almost one person dying every three days."

"And that's also a lot of money cumulatively. Kemper said the insurance companies had investigated a lot of them, but apparently each of the policyholders she could find out about had undergone a medical exam and had no history of drug abuse. So, at least in those cases, the money was paid out to the beneficiaries."

"Damn, so is that the new American dream? Sign a relative up for life insurance and wait for them to OD to cash in?"

"Let's hope not."

They sat in silence for a few moments.

Jamison said, "So what will happen with Baron now that he's been arrested?"

"He'll have a bond hearing. Because of the seriousness of the charges, the judge will probably remand him into custody until trial. But even if bail is set I doubt he could afford it."

Someone knocked at the front door. Jamison rose to answer it and returned a few moments later with Cindi Riley.

She had on faded jeans, a leather jacket, and a flannel shirt, coupled with an exhausted expression and reddened eyes.

Jamison said, "You look like you could use some coffee. I just made a fresh pot."

Riley answered with a nod and then dropped into a seat across from Decker.

"You know what happened?" she said.

"To Baron, yeah."

"He didn't do it. He didn't kill anyone."

"Was it his gun?" asked Decker.

"I don't know. You saw the house. There's crap everywhere. John doesn't know the half of what's there."

"Does he have a lawyer?" asked Jamison, setting a cup of coffee down in front of Riley.

"I got him one. I had to go outside of town to do it. Nobody here apparently wants to defend him. The jerks. I mean what did he ever do to anybody? Somebody killed his parents. Did anybody here do anything about that?"

"Have you talked to him?" asked Decker.

"Yes, at the jail. I'm really worried about him."

"He *should* be worried," said Decker. "They're charging him with multiple murders."

"No, I don't mean just that. I mean that John seems to have finally given up. He's always been so positive. No matter the crap they throw at him here, he just brushes it off, turns it into a joke, and keeps going."

Jamison sat down next to her. "But not now?"

"No. I think he believes this is it. That he's going to die in jail. They set bail because he's not a flight risk. I tried to pay it after his hearing, but he refused to let me."

"If he didn't do it, he won't be in jail long," said Decker.

Riley glared at him. "You're a cop. You should know that innocent people go to jail all the time."

"Not if we can prove that someone else is responsible," said Decker. "Then he's home free."

"How do we do that?"

"It's all we've been doing since we got here," said Jamison. "And we've made some progress."

"Does Baron have alibis for any of the murders?" asked Decker.

"I talked to him about that. And not really, no. Like you said, with some of them it's hard to tell exactly when they died. And John spends most of his time alone at his home, except for a couple hours once a week at the bar."

Decker nodded. "Okay, then we have to approach it from another way to clear him."

"So you don't think he killed anybody then?" said Riley.

Decker ignored this question and said, "You told me before about new businesses popping up around the area."

"Right."

"You also told me about some people using payouts from life insurance policies to do renovations and start these businesses."

"That's right. But so what?"

"Can you remember any of your friends who overdosed and had a policy?"

Jamison interjected, "But, Decker, you said the insurance companies had investigated some of the deaths in Baronville and didn't find anything amiss."

"Answer the question, Cindi," persisted Decker.

"I don't know. Wait a minute." She thought for a few moments. "Keith Drews did. Because his mom opened the new bakery downtown. I remember her telling me it was the only good thing to come out of Keith's death."

"Was he a longtime user?"

"No."

"So what happened? How did he overdose?"

"He got injured, was prescribed Percocet, then Vicodin. Then he got hooked on Oxy. From there it was a downward spiral. He died of a heroin overdose. Whoever he got it from had laced it with fentanyl. Keith probably had no idea what he was taking. It killed him instantly, I heard."

"How old was he when he died?"

"Younger than me."

"His mother was the named beneficiary. How much did she get?"

"Enough to open the bakery. She totally gutted the first floor of an old building and bought all-new equipment. So it was a lot of money."

"Was *she* an addict?" asked Decker.

"Yeah, she was, actually. For many years before she finally kicked it. But what the hell are you getting at?" added Riley angrily.

"A lot of people have died in this town from drug overdoses. And I've found out that a lot of those people had life insurance policies. Now, you have to have an insurable interest in someone to be named a beneficiary. And you can't get much of a policy benefit without taking a medical exam and swearing on an application that the information you're providing is accurate. They may even do a criminal background check on you, access your medical records and make you undergo a physical exam."

"How do they get around HIPAA?" asked Jamison, referring to the law guarding a person's medical history from unauthorized third parties.

"I had a life insurance policy when I was a cop back in Ohio," replied Decker. "On the application, you can waive HIPAA protections. In fact, most insurance companies won't write the policy if you don't waive that so they can dig into your medical background. And evidence of illicit drug addiction would be a red flag for a life insurance company."

Riley looked confused. "I don't understand. You're saying if you're an addict you can't get a life insurance policy."

"I think that's right. At least not one they will pay out for a drug overdose death."

"So—"

"So how did somebody know certain insured people were *going* to become addicts and then overdose and die?" Decker finished for her.

54

IT WAS ONLY four for dinner. It should have been five.

But the fifth was six feet under.

Jamison sat next to Zoe.

Decker sat next to Amber.

They were in the kitchen at the small oval table in the center of the room.

"How was school, Zoe?" asked Jamison.

"Okay," said Zoe, as she pushed food around on her plate without actually ingesting any of it.

Amber had lost weight, and she had been thin to begin with. Her features were strained, her eyes painfully red and her manner as though she had been drugged.

"Mommy, can I go to my room? My tummy hurts."

Amber said absently, "Sure, sweetie. I'll be up to check on you in a bit."

Zoe got up from the table and hurriedly left. They could hear her shoes clattering up the stairs.

"She's not eating," said Amber miserably.

"Neither are you, sis," said Jamison. "You've got to keep your strength up."

Amber waved this off. "I'm fine. Just not hungry right now."

Jamison glanced at Decker and then laid her fork down. "What do you plan to do?"

Amber looked up from her plate. "What do you mean?"

"I mean will you stay here or move?"

Amber looked at her sister incredulously. "I haven't gotten that far. For God's sake, it hasn't even been a week since Frank died, Alex."

"I know. But I don't think there's anything keeping you here. You could move closer to family. They can help out."

"I've thought about that," Amber conceded. "And even with the life insurance, I'll have to go back to work. I'm the breadwinner now."

"You *are* going to bring legal action against Maxus, right?" said Jamison.

"Damn straight I am. But to uproot Zoe again, so soon? I'm just worried how that will affect her."

"A fresh start somewhere else might be best for her and you," replied Jamison.

"How can I be sure of that?"

"Have you talked to Zoe about this?" interjected Decker.

They both looked at him.

"Decker, she's only six," said Jamison.

"That doesn't mean she doesn't have an opinion."

"I'm not sure she can possibly understand the circumstances," retorted Jamison.

"All I'm saying is that her mother should talk to her about it. If it's going to affect her, why not?"

Amber and her sister exchanged a glance.

Amber said, "I actually think he might be right." She rose from the table. "I'll talk to Zoe and then I'm going to bed. I'm just very tired."

Jamison rose too and hugged her sister. "I'm here for you, sweetie. Whatever you need, for as long as you need."

"Alex, you have your own life, and you have a job. You can't babysit us forever. Not that I'd want you to. I'll get my life together. I have to, for Zoe."

She glanced at Decker. "Thanks for the advice, Amos."

Decker nodded.

She left the room and Jamison sat back down.

Decker rose and poured himself another cup of coffee.

He sat down and drank some of it.

"You going soft on me, Decker?"

He looked at her. "How do you mean?"

"You're worrying about *other* people a lot lately."

"I investigate homicides. That means there are always lots of people to worry about."

"Do you think they should stay here or leave Baronville?"

"I don't have a good answer for that, because I'm not them."

"But there's nothing for them here."

"Frank Mitchell is here," replied Decker. "He's always going to be here now."

Jamison changed color and looked down. "Right. I...I guess I wasn't thinking about things that way."

Decker took another sip of coffee and glanced out the small window into the dark. "I didn't want to leave Burlington. And at the same time, I wanted to get the hell out of Burlington. My family was murdered there. They're both buried there. When I left, I felt like I was abandoning them. I used to go to the graves every day when I lived there. I would sit and talk to them. Now I haven't been in months." He set his cup down. "I don't want to end up with my only connection to them being faded pictures on the wall, Alex."

"You of all people should never worry about forgetting them."

"It's not the same. I buried them there. That is my connection to that place. It will always be a part of me whether I want it to be or not."

"So, based on that logic, you think my sister should stay, then?"

"I think...everybody is different."

With that he rose, cleared the table, and he and Jamison loaded the dishwasher. Then he left the kitchen and went to his room.

Decker opened his closet and pulled out two things: the construction drawings he had found in the hall closet, and the piece of graph paper he had uncovered at Toby Babbot's trailer.

After looking over the pages for about a half hour he decided he needed something else in order to make sense of it.

He left his room, walked down the hall, and knocked on the door.

A few moments later, a sleepy-eyed Zoe opened the door. She was in her pajamas and was holding her cat.

"Zoe, I'm working on a very important project and I think you might have something I need."

At this, the little girl perked up. "Sure, Amos, what do you need?"

"A ruler. Do you have one?"

She nodded, hurried over to a small white-painted desk set against one wall, and opened a drawer. She pulled out a green ruler and brought it over to him.

"Thank you very much, Zoe," he said, taking it from her.

"You're welcome."

Decker had turned to go. But then he faced her once more.

"Did your mom talk to you?"

She nodded. "She asked me if I wanted to stay here or move someplace else."

"And what did you tell your mom?"

Zoe shrugged. "Daddy's here. I don't want to leave him all alone."

Decker knelt down so he was eye to eye with the little girl.

"I can understand that."

Zoe stared back at him. "You told me that when I visited Daddy he would know I was there. That he would know here."

She touched the center of her small chest.

"Yes, I did."

"So, I can't leave him or else he'd be sad. He would be sad here." She touched the center of Decker's chest. "Right?"

Now Decker wouldn't meet her gaze. "Right."

She yawned.

"You better go get some sleep, okay?"

"Okay, Amos." Zoe gave him a hug and he quietly returned to his room, his gaze downcast.

Life really is a bitch sometimes.

He sat down on his bed and looked at the plans spread out there.

Then he looked down at the ruler. Written on it in Sharpie was the name "Zoe Mitchell."

He got up and walked over to the window and looked out over a town that was in despair, but that was perhaps slowly coming back.

But at what price?

And how many more people were going to die before it *was* back?

He turned his head in the direction of Zoe's room.

Should they stay or should they go?

It would be very easy to say they should go.

Flee the violence and danger. Go to a safer place.

But where exactly was that anymore?

I guess if I have any purpose in life, it's to help make sure there are safe places left to go to.

With that thought in mind, he sat down and used the ruler to go over every dimension of the construction drawings and Toby Babbot's version of the same.

He used paper and pen to make his calculations, and when he was done he had found only a single discrepancy between the two documents.

But what a discrepancy it was.

CHAPTER

——

55

"CAN I SEE Mr. Ross, please?" said Decker. He showed his credentials to the woman at the front desk of the fulfillment center. "He knows me. I've been here before."

It was the next morning and Decker had driven here at a very specific time.

"I'm sorry, but Mr. Ross is out on the main floor right now, Agent Decker."

"Could I wait in his office? It's really important," he added, because she was the only one working the desk and several people were waiting in line behind him. "I've been to his office before. When Frank Mitchell was killed."

"Oh, right, of course. That was so awful. Um." When she still hesitated, Decker pointed to the bruise on her forearm.

"You bang that on something?"

"Squat rack at the gym."

"You work out, that's good. Keeps you healthy."

"It's not just that. I want to be a picker. I'm building myself up so I can pass the physical requirements."

"You don't like working in the office?"

"Pickers make a lot more money and they get overtime and a better 401(k) match. That's what I'm gunning for."

"Well, good luck on that. So, can I go back and wait for Ross?"

She glanced at the impatient-looking people in line behind him. "That'll be fine. He's doing his usual walk-around. I'm afraid it'll be about forty-five minutes."

"I'm in no rush."

Decker headed off and entered the corridor behind the reception area that housed the offices of the center's management staff.

Ross had told him previously when he did his walk-arounds, which was why Decker was here at this time window. He didn't want the man around.

He made his way swiftly down the hall and reached Ross's office. He tried the door, only it was locked. The blinds were open showing the office to be empty.

He looked around. There was no one in the corridor. He slipped a penknife from his pocket and used it to push back the bolt.

He shut the door behind him and closed the blinds.

The office looked exactly as it had when he'd been in here before. Ross's coat was on a hook on the back of the door and a small duffel bag was on the floor. Decker opened the duffel and looked inside. There were some gym clothes and a pair of sneakers and white socks.

He zipped the duffel back up and took the object he'd brought with him out of his pocket.

It was a measuring tape.

He quickly measured the dimensions of the room.

The depth of the room was two feet shorter than the construction plans had indicated. That meant the entire back wall had been moved forward two feet. And there had to be a reason for that. Decker had seen from the plans that a hallway also bordered the back wall, as it did the front, so there was no wiggle room there.

He walked over to the wall behind Ross's desk and started to examine it.

He had seen before that this wall was paneled wood with elaborate moldings, with a boxed Pittsburgh Steelers jersey hanging on one section. It hadn't made an impact on him before, but now he found it very interesting.

Decker heard a sound that made him jump.

He looked all around the office until he located the source.

Ross's smartphone was on a shelf behind his desk. And it was buzzing.

Someone was calling him. Decker glanced at the number, but

had no way of knowing who it was; there was no name attached to the number on the screen.

He turned back to the wall and used his knuckles to tap against the wood at various spots.

Finally he reached a spot where the sound evidenced a hollow space. This was where the boxed jersey was hanging. He kept knocking against the wall here until he had mapped out a space roughly the size of a large door.

He felt around the edges but without success. The moldings were covering them.

He looked down at the carpet in front of this space.

It looked a bit frayed there, as though something might have been routinely rubbing against it.

He looked back up at the wall and decided to try something simple. Placing his finger against the edge of the hollow space, he pushed in.

Nothing happened. He kept pressing in other spots. Finally, near the ceiling, which he had to stretch to reach, he struck gold. There was a medallion up there and it appeared to be a bit loose. Decker tried turning it clockwise, but it wouldn't move. Then he tried counterclockwise. It moved like a doorknob.

There was a click and the hollow part of the wall swung open. It partially caught on the carpet, which accounted for the wear.

It was a clever mechanism, Decker could see. There were three metal deadbolt shafts on the side of the door, one at the top, one in the middle, and one near the floor. Turning the medallion in the direction that he had caused all three deadbolt locks to recess into the door, allowing it to be opened.

Decker pulled the door all the way open and looked inside the revealed space.

It was about two feet deep and lined with shelves. That accounted for the two-foot-smaller footprint of the office. This space had been used to accommodate this storage closet. Whoever had put it in couldn't simply recess the closet into the original footprint without moving the entire wall back, because of the hallway behind it. And if he had moved only this space forward, leaving the rest of the wall in place, it would have looked suspicious.

On the shelves were rectangular-shaped cardboard boxes.

Decker picked one up. There had once been a label on it, but most of it had been peeled off and there was no information left on it to help him.

He looked over at a shredder set next to the desk and wondered if that had been the fate of the labels.

Probably.

He counted the number of boxes. There were twenty.

He carefully unpeeled the tape from one of the boxes and opened it. Inside was a thin layer of bubble wrap. And under the bubble wrap were a number of plastic bottles. They were all full of a white granular substance.

Thinking quickly, Decker put one bottle in his pocket, closed up the box, carefully retaped it, and put the box back on the shelf. He swung the door closed.

He glanced down at Ross's chair. The seat was scuffed and marked and he knew why.

Decker was six-five. Ross was about five-nine. Unlike Decker, he had to stand on the chair to reach the spot that would open the door.

After checking through the blinds to make certain the hall was clear and then leaving them open, as they had been, Decker made his way out. Passing by the reception area, he spoke to the same woman.

"I actually couldn't wait any longer. You don't have to tell him I was here. I'll catch up with him another time."

"Okay, thanks."

"No, thank *you*. Oh, one more thing."

"Yes?"

"Is there a gym here for the employees?"

"A gym? No. Why?"

"Last time I was here I saw a gym duffel in Ross's office. I thought it might have had workout clothes inside."

"It probably does. He works out at my gym, right after he

leaves here. Like clockwork. I sometimes work out with him. Doesn't hurt to get in good with the boss."

"Right. Does he change here or at the gym?"

She looked puzzled. "At the gym. They have locker rooms and showers."

"Well, good to know he's keeping in shape," said Decker.

Really good to know, he thought as he hurried out.

CHAPTER

56

Decker got into his truck and was about to drive out of the parking lot when he turned in the opposite direction and headed over to where the new construction was under way. He parked his car, got out, and walked as close to the construction site as he could. Workers were racing everywhere and forklifts and trucks and Bobcats were hurtling around carrying materials. Obviously, the police had allowed the work to recommence. Decker studied the activity for a bit and then took a closer look around the area. He spotted something, bent down, and picked it up. Examining it for a moment, he stuck it in his pocket. He got back into his truck and drove off.

On the way, he called Kemper and asked her to meet him in front of the Mercury Bar.

He was waiting for her when she pulled up. He climbed into the SUV, pulled out the bottle, and briefly described to her how he'd found it.

"Can you check to see what it is? I think I know, though."

She looked at the bottle. "It's almost certainly either heroin or fentanyl. They look the same, which is why dealers lace one with the other. Problem is, it takes thirty milligrams of heroin to kill someone, while it only takes three milligrams of fentanyl to do the same. So, you said you got this from a hiding place in Ted Ross's office?"

"Yeah. And there's a ton more in there. I think the shipments are coming in through the fulfillment center."

"Why ship it there? Why not to his home or a PO box?"

"Far easier to search a home or PO box. The fulfillment center gets millions of packages. Like finding a needle in a haystack, if you're the cops."

"But don't they track all those boxes pretty closely? How is he getting them out of the computer system there?"

"He's the manager of the place. If anyone could think of a way, he could."

"How did you even know he had a hiding place in his office?"

"Toby Babbot. He'd drawn plans of the fulfillment center. I found a set of official construction drawings and compared them. Babbot's version showed only one discrepancy from the construction drawings. A two-foot-deep deviation in Ross's office."

"How'd Babbot find out about that?"

"He worked on the construction of the fulfillment center and later worked in the office there. He might've discovered it that way. I used a tape measure. Maybe he did the same."

"Do you think he knew what Ross was going to do with that space?"

"Well, Babbot ended up dead, so chances are he *did* know, or at least suspected."

"I'm surprised that Ross would keep this in his office."

"It's actually pretty secure. You can't accidentally open the closet. He had to stand on a chair and turn a part of the molding to do it. And the panel was seamless. You could look at that wall all day and not know a door was there. And he had a Steelers jersey hanging there to disguise it further."

"How did he have something like that installed and no one know about it?"

"He might have done it himself. He told me he worked construction before he moved on to the fulfillment center. Or maybe one or more of the construction guys is in on this and did it for him. As the manager, he had free run of the space and was overseeing all the construction work."

"But how would a guy like Ted Ross get mixed up in a drug distribution operation?"

"He once described himself to me as the little guy, the underdog. And he said that when the little guy gets a chance to punch back, he needs to go for it. I think that was the reason he gave me the contact information for a lawyer for Amber to sue Maxus. He hates the big guys. And Alice Martin told me that his father, Fred, treated him and his mother really badly. Ted told me the same thing at the funeral. Maybe that screwed him up too. I can vouch for the fact that Fred Ross is a pretty unpleasant guy. That and a boatload of money would be a hell of a motive. Or maybe they approached him because he was the fulfillment center manager and they wanted to use that as their cover."

"Decker, this really is awesome work on your part." Kemper paused. "And now I'll return the favor. I found out what you wanted to know about Randy Haas."

"Our dying declaration guy who fingered your two agents?"

"You asked if he had family and whether he might have been sick. Well, you were right on both counts. He had a wife and two young kids. And he had pancreatic cancer. Advanced. He had maybe two months to live."

"And the family? How are they doing?"

"They apparently had a financial windfall. They're living in Bel-Air, California, in a home that cost three million."

"And their explanation for that?"

"Life insurance. A ten-million-dollar policy."

"That's not cheap."

"No, it's not. But the premiums were fully paid up."

"Okay, but I doubt that Haas listed 'drug dealer' as his occupation on the application. I can't believe a legit insurance outfit would have sold him a policy that large. His odds of dying early were way too high."

"The policy wasn't written by an American company. It was an overseas outfit that we've tried to find out about, but so far we've run into a stone wall. It could have just been a way for his family to be paid off in exchange for his lying about my two agents."

"Life insurance again," said Decker thoughtfully.

"Right. But how'd you know we'd find out Haas was terminal?"

"Because I believed he lied about your guys. He set them up to take the fall. They weren't rogue. I think they had stumbled onto what was happening here in Baronville and they had to be taken out. And Haas, who was already a dead man with a family to take care of, was the one to help do it. He made you think your guys were bad, and the real bad guys killed them. And his family reaped the benefit of his *lying* declaration. For all we know, he injected that fatal dose of morphine himself."

"Okay, we have a major fentanyl ring operating in Baronville. And they're using the fulfillment center to bring it in. What do you think Ross does with it?"

"He must take it from the center and pass it on to others. He's got a duffel bag in his office. I think that's how he's getting it out. I found out he goes to the gym after work. But why carry your gym clothes in with you to work when the gym you're going to has locker rooms and showers? Why not just leave them in the car until you get to the gym?"

"But don't they have security there to check bags and stuff?"

"They have magnetometers, but that wouldn't catch powder like this. Now, they do search bags. But I'm betting the duffel has a false bottom. I opened it up when I was in his office, and it seemed to be shallow for how large the bag was. And it wouldn't take much space to hide bottles like these."

"No, it wouldn't."

Decker indicated the bottle. "So educate me on the economics of this."

"The cost to make a kilo of heroin and a kilo of fentanyl is about the same, about three to four grand. A kilo of heroin will fetch sixty thousand on the streets. But because fentanyl is so much more potent, one kilo of fentanyl can be made into about twenty-four total kilos of drug product, making it far more lucrative than heroin. And a kilo of fentanyl can produce nearly seven hundred thousand pills that sell for about twenty-five bucks each." She looked more closely at the bottle. "This is about five thousand milligrams of powder."

"There were twenty boxes in his office. The one I opened had five bottles inside it. If all the others had the same number of bottles, what would that be worth on the street?"

Kemper mentally calculated this. "If it is fentanyl, you're looking at nearly nine million bucks sitting in the guy's office."

"I wonder how many shipments are coming through there?"

"I wonder too," said Kemper worriedly.

"Why does it strike me that the dollar amounts we're talking about make this seem less like a small-town conspiracy and more like an international one?"

She nodded. "You just read my mind, Decker. I can tell you that the Mexican cartels are all in on fentanyl. They either import it directly from China, where it's manufactured both illegally and by legit pharma corporations, or they buy the stuff they need to make it from the Chinese and do the lab work themselves. They sell it in powder form like in this bottle, or they cut it with heroin. But they're also pressing millions of fentanyl pills. And the thing with fentanyl, when you put it in pills, the dealers usually have no idea it's in there. And the consumers don't either. But people who don't want to snort or smoke something because they're afraid, or it makes them feel like addicts, will take a pill because they think it's safer and it feels more legit. You know, sort of like taking a prescription. The pills will look like an oxycodone pill, or you can cut it with Xanax or other pain pills. They're even stamped with the dosage amount of eighty because that's a typical dose of Oxy. 'Shady eighties,' they're called on the street. As I said, they can cost about twenty-five bucks a pill and a typical addict will take twenty pills a day."

"Five hundred bucks a day. Expensive habit."

"I've arrested dealers who routinely sell a minimum of a thousand pills a day. That much is called a 'boat' on the street. And there are dealers who do a lot more than that."

Decker looked at the powder. "Do you think the plan is to make pills from the powder?"

"That would be my guess. Which means this powder is going to a pill press operation probably somewhere close by. I mean, why else ship the stuff to a place like this?"

"How much space would it need?"

"You can do it in your bedroom, or the back room of a legit business. But they would need to bring in equipment. That would include a pill press, quarter- or half-ton or bigger, depending on your output requirements. A quarter-ton unit can produce three or four thousand pills an hour. And you need people to process and package the stuff. You have to be careful while handling it. I've had local cops go in on drug busts and touch the fentanyl without using gloves. Next thing you know they're on the floor turning blue. It's that dangerous."

"Well, there are a lot of empty buildings around here. In fact, I was thinking about the empty house where your two guys were found. With a whole house, you could probably have a bunch of pill presses going. And that would explain why the power was turned on even though no one was living there."

Kemper's eyes widened. "You think?"

"Like I told you before, they probably had a drone flying over the street that night."

"Yeah, but you never told me why."

"I think maybe they were moving out equipment and then moving in the bodies. And they wanted to make sure no one was watching or coming that way. Best way to check for that was by aerial surveillance. And that's what drones can do really well."

"Then we need to go over the space again, to see if they left behind any trace of a pill press operation."

"I'd check the house next door too, where I shot Brian Collins. That place is empty as well. And has the electricity turned on too."

"And the old man who lived across the street?"

"Dan Bond might have heard something and they needed to get rid of him. They probably picked that street because it was nearly empty. In fact, only three people lived there, including him. And Fred Ross is the father of the guy with all the drugs."

"So what's your suggestion? Do we go in and bust Ted Ross?"

"We bust him, chances are good everybody else gets away. And you can't get a search warrant based on what I told you, because I had no probable cause to do what I did today in his office."

"But when he checks his stash, won't he know a bottle is missing?"

"He might think they just shortchanged him. But we'll need to watch him. If it looks like he's on to it, we'll need to pick him up."

"Okay, I'll get people on that. What are you going to do?"

"We know the endgame here now—drugs. Now I just have to find the rest of the pieces."

"Do you think all the other murders are tied to this?"

"Yes, I do. But there might be something else going on here."

"Like what?"

"As soon as I know, I'll tell you."

57

I TAKE IT you couldn't make bail?"

It was the next day and Decker and Jamison were sitting across from John Baron in the visitors' room at the Baronville jail.

Decker had told Jamison what he had found in Ted Ross's office and about his meeting with Agent Kemper.

Baron was in a white prison jumpsuit. He was unshaven and his hair was in disarray. He looked like he hadn't slept much.

"That's right."

"No, that's not right. Cindi Riley tried to post bail for you after your hearing but you refused."

"It's not her problem. She hired me a lawyer. She shouldn't have to waste more of her money on me."

"Very noble of you," said Decker. "But I don't think nobleness is going to get you out of this. But the truth might."

Baron said sharply, "Meaning I've lied to you? I've admitted that."

"I'm not necessarily talking about you. I'm speaking more generally."

"So why are you here, then, *generally speaking*?"

"It's pretty clear to me that Bradley Costa came to town because he thought he knew where a treasure left behind by your namesake was located."

"And I thought I made it very clear that I don't believe that there is a treasure. It would have been found by now."

"But let's assume there is a treasure, just for argument's sake."

Baron sighed, sat back in the molded plastic chair, and said, "Okay, it's not like I have anything else to do right now."

"If the treasure is located on your property somewhere, it would be difficult for someone to go up there and take it, I would imagine."

"Depends on what it was."

"I don't think we're talking paper. That would degrade over time. And I think your namesake would have wanted something that would be around for the long haul."

"Why would he care? He'd be dead."

"Because he was a son of a bitch," said Decker. "He didn't want his family getting his money. In fact, a letter I read from Nigel Nottingham to his son said that your ancestor considered his children unworthy of his fortune."

Baron mulled over this statement and shrugged. "I didn't learn how desperate things really were until my parents died. It wasn't until then that I found out the house had been mortgaged to the hilt and there was really no cash in the bank. I just assumed that preceding generations had simply squandered it. But I did some digging and learned that there just wasn't a lot of money left by Baron the First to his heirs."

"So if he was so successful, where did all the money go?" asked Jamison.

"My father talked to me about it once. He apparently had looked into it as well. With him being a lawyer he knew where to look, so to speak. After examining the matter, he told me that Baron had largely cashed out from the businesses, meaning he had borrowed heavily against his assets. That was a double whammy for his heirs. The businesses would be heavily indebted and there was little liquidity to support that debt."

"Maybe that's what the treasure is, the missing money," said Jamison.

Baron looked at her. "There's no treasure, Alex."

"Why not?"

"Because lots of my ancestors have looked for it. You saw all the holes in the walls. And the grounds were all dug up too. My father told me it was like someone had been mining on the property. If there was treasure, I'm sure it would have been found by now."

"Why would they have even assumed there was a treasure?" asked Jamison.

Baron said, "I don't know for sure, of course, but I guess because they couldn't believe what they inherited was all there was. And maybe like Decker said, they thought Baron was trying to screw them."

"The businesses were still operating when he died," said Decker.

"Yes, but they all petered out from a combination of a lack of capital and Baron's heirs not being nearly as good at business as he was."

Decker said, "That brings me back to my original question. If there is treasure up there, it would be pretty hard for someone to look for it without you knowing, right?"

"Well, I'm almost always there. And when I'm gone, it's only for a couple hours. And you can't access the grounds without coming right past the front door."

"And you still own the place, right?"

"Of course I do."

"But if you get convicted of murder, what happens?"

"You damn well know what happens. I go to prison."

Jamison interjected, "No, he means what happens to the *property*? The house?"

Baron's brows knitted together. "Oh, I see. Well, I'm barely keeping my head above water. I wouldn't be able to work in prison, so my income, little though it is, dries up."

"You could sell some of your personal assets. Like the old guns you showed us."

"It's not just that."

"What else?"

"Well, although Brad Costa denied my most recent request, I *did* manage to refinance the mortgage a year or so ago. The bank gave me a slightly lower interest rate, but there was language added."

"What sort of language?" asked Jamison.

"A moral turpitude clause. The estate possibly could be designated as a historic site. That gives it value. But any sort of scandal would lessen the worth of the property, and that added value was factored into my refinancing request."

Jamison said, "So are you saying that if you were arrested and convicted of a crime…?"

"The bank would be able to declare an event of default and they could foreclose and sell off the property to the highest bidder. Even if I could continue to make the payments on the mortgage."

"But why would they care, if you could still make the payments?" said Jamison.

"Because the collateral for the loan is the house. If I committed a serious crime, they argued that it would diminish the marketability and value of that collateral. Thus they wanted the right to find me in default so they could try to salvage that asset."

Baron eyed Decker. "You don't seem surprised by this."

"I'm not."

"Why not?"

"If you didn't commit the murders then someone was trying awfully hard to see that you were blamed for them. You knew or had contact with all four victims. This wasn't apparent for all of them. It required some digging on our part. And you didn't help yourself by lying to us."

"Obviously."

"So whoever did kill them didn't want to make it seem too easy."

"Why not?" asked Jamison.

"Because we would have come to the conclusion that someone was *framing* Baron."

"And is that the conclusion you've now reached?" asked Baron.

"I'm getting there. How much is the mortgage on the property?"

"A lot."

"So whoever wanted to buy out the mortgage would have to have deep pockets?"

"Yes. The bank will take less money for it, but not a lot less."

"And Costa knew all this?"

"He was the one who did the new deal, including the moral

turpitude clause. As I said, when I went back to him later for an-other extension at a lower rate and better terms, he refused."

Jamison said, "Do you think Costa was planning to somehow buy the mortgage off and get the property that way? Then he would own the place and be able to look for the treasure at his leisure?"

"I think that was his plan, but I also think he already knew where the treasure was," said Decker.

Baron sat up straighter. "What? Then where is it?"

"I'm not sure. But he nicked a letter from the historical society that I think provided him with the answer."

Jamison said, "But, Decker, Costa couldn't buy the property himself, could he? That would be like self-dealing. There have to be bank regulations prohibiting that."

"I'm sure there are," said Decker. "Which is why he was going to need a straw man."

"Somebody to buy the property in their name and then let him go up there and get the treasure?"

"Yes. He probably offered the person a percentage of the take."

"So now we have to find that person," said Jamison.

"Yes, we do, because that person also murdered Babbot, Tanner, Swanson, and Bradley Costa." He paused and looked at Jamison. "And I think they murdered Frank too."

58

As they were driving back to the Mitchells', Jamison blurted out, "If you thought they had Frank killed, why didn't you tell me?"

"I told you before that I *suspected* his death might not be an accident."

"Yeah, but now you sound a lot more sure."

"That's because I *am* a lot more sure."

"But why would they kill Frank?"

"He saw something he shouldn't have, probably."

"But it was the robot that killed him."

"But people control robots. And what if it did exactly as it was programmed to do, while Frank was standing next to it?"

Before Jamison could answer, Decker's phone rang.

It was Kemper.

"We just did a quick down and dirty on the two houses. Both tested positive for traces of heroin and fentanyl. Decker, I don't know how long I can sit on this."

"We need just a little more time. Have you been keeping Ross under surveillance?"

"Yeah, he left yesterday with his duffel. And I'm betting there wasn't just gym clothes in there. He went into a number of buildings, including the gym. It would have been too conspicuous for us to follow him inside. He came back out each time with the duffel, but there's no guarantee that the pill bottles were still in there. So there's evidence that probably just went poof."

"We'll nail these guys, Agent Kemper."

"We better. Because if we don't my career is over. I just need you to understand that we're running out of time."

She clicked off and Decker looked at Jamison, who had obviously overheard the DEA agent's strident tones.

"She sounds a little panicked," said Jamison.

"Yeah. I guess," Decker said vaguely.

"Don't you ever panic, Decker?"

"Never saw the value."

"We can't tell Amber your theory about Frank. Not until we're sure."

"I know that."

The skies opened up and a fine rain began to fall.

"God, Baronville is dreary enough without the bad weather," observed Jamison as she drove along.

"Dreary with bright spots," amended Decker. "Look over there at that bakery. Cindi Riley told me about it. The owner had a life insurance policy on her son. He overdosed and his policy paid out enough for her to open a business."

"You really think something hinky is going on with that."

"Hinky enough for us to stop there and get some coffee."

Jamison pulled into the parking lot and they entered the Peacock Bakery. There was a neon sign out front in the shape of the colorful bird.

Inside, the place was neat and well laid out with whitewashed wooden tables, multicolored tablecloths, and glass cabinets filled with delicacies. Behind the counter was a large chalkboard mounted on the wall with the bakery's menu written on it.

Jamison sniffed the air and moaned. "God, just the aroma makes me want to eat everything in the place."

A woman appeared from behind a curtain at the back of the counter.

She looked thin and worn and her face was heavily wrinkled, and her hair was shot through with gray. But her smile was pleasant and her eyes twinkled as she looked at them.

"What can I do for y'all?" she asked.

Decker said, "Two large coffees to go."

Jamison pointed to some items in one of the display cases. "Are those carrot cake muffins?"

"Yes, ma'am, they are."

"Awesome. We'll take two."

"That's a right good choice. They're fresh out of the oven. I'm Linda Drews. I own the place."

"Hi, Linda. I'm Alex and this is Amos. So why name the place the Peacock Bakery?"

"When I was just a little thing I always wanted me a peacock as a pet. That ain't never happened. So this was the next best thing. And the sign sure is eye-catching, or so folks tell me."

As Drews prepared their order, Decker said, "This place looks pretty new."

"Open less than a year. I always loved to bake, so why not make money off it? And I like being the boss. And I'm making good money. Have the fulfillment center partly to thank. We get a lot of traffic from there. All the heavy lifting and walking makes people hungry for dang sure."

"I bet," said Decker.

As she poured the coffees Linda Drews said, "How'd you hear about us?"

"Cindi Riley."

"Oh, right. Cindi's real nice. She gets the word out about local businesses. We're all trying to bring the town back."

"She also told us about your son. He was a friend of hers."

Drews had leaned down and was using a pair of tongs to pull out two muffins from the display cabinet. She stiffened at Decker's words.

"Cindi told you about Keith?"

"Yeah. It sounded really sad."

Drews slowly put the muffins in a bag.

"He was my only child. You never get over that."

"I'm sure. It was an overdose, Cindi said," noted Decker.

Drews nodded. "Baronville's got lots of problems. Biggest one is drugs. Now, I admit, I was on 'em for a long time. Started out on Percocet and then became a mixer."

"A mixer?" said Jamison.

"I'd mix the Percocet with Oxy, Xanax, hell, anything I could think of. I'd do a couple hundred pills a week." She put the bag of muffins on the counter. "How old do you think I am?"

Decker shrugged and looked uncomfortable. "I don't like guessing people's ages."

"I just turned fifty."

She smiled sadly at their surprised looks. "Drugs ain't beauty aids. I know I look like I'm sixty-five."

"But you've obviously conquered your addiction," said Jamison.

Drews rapped her knuckles against the wooden counter. "It's a fight every day, but today I'm clean. Tomorrow? Who knows."

"You're remarkably candid about your experience," said Jamison. "I mean, you don't know us."

"I talked about it long enough at the addiction centers. You got to wrap your mind around it. You got to lay your soul bare if you're going to get better. I tried more than one way to do it, because one thing works for some and not for others. But I finally kicked it, thank you God. Hardest thing I ever had to do."

"But not Keith?" said Decker.

Drews started to ring up their order and then stopped. "No." Tears formed in her eyes. "You ain't supposed to outlive your child, but I did Keith. He died sixteen months ago. He would've been twenty-eight next month."

"I'm really sorry," said Jamison.

"But at least you have the bakery," prompted Decker.

"Well, that's due to Keith really."

"How so?" asked Decker.

"Keith had him a life insurance policy for a million dollars, and I was the beneficiary. Never could've afforded this place otherwise. Ovens alone are a damn fortune." She paused as Jamison handed her the credit card for the coffee and muffins. "I'd rather have my son," she said dully.

"Well, it was lucky that he had a policy," said Decker. "I guess he had it through work, maybe."

"No, not through work. He had a job at the fulfillment center.

He was a picker. Running all day long, bending over, lifting stuff. Then he hurt his back real bad and got laid off. He went to the doctor. Got on pain pills. And there you go. He got hooked. Same old story. One day he thought he was taking heroin but it was really that fentanyl crap. He was dead before the EMTs could get to him."

"That's awful," said Jamison.

"Well, in Baronville, we just call that normal and ain't that a damn shame."

Decker said, "Well, it was fortunate that your son got his policy before he became addicted. I doubt he could have passed a medical exam if he'd been addicted."

"I know. Willie said the same thing."

"Willie?"

"Willie Norris is the one who sold Keith the policy. He told me that too when he gave me the check. But Keith was clean when he took out that policy. And then he was dead."

"So he took out the policy *after* he injured himself? And for a million dollars?"

"Yeah. He heard it was a good idea. See, he wanted to get re-hired at the fulfillment center. And that place can be dangerous. What with all them robots and such. Someone just got killed by one of them suckers, did you know that?"

"Yeah, we heard," said Jamison quickly.

"Who suggested your son get life insurance? Was it this Willie Norris?"

"I don't know exactly. But I guess some good came out of Keith's death. I was able to bury him proper with the money and then open this place."

She rubbed her eyes. "I hope you enjoy the muffins. And spread the word."

Jamison said, "Do you have the contact information for Mr. Norris? My sister just lost her husband and I'm thinking she might need some life insurance. She has a young daughter."

"Oh, sure. You got to think about that stuff, 'cause you just never know in this old world."

Linda Drews rummaged around in a drawer and pulled out a business card. "Here's the information. It's about a mile from here. Willie's a good guy. Lived here forever, just like me."

Jamison looked down at the card. "Thanks a lot." She put a five in the tip jar on the counter.

"Thank you," said Drews.

Decker looked the place over. "I hope you make it," he said.

"Me too," Drews replied. "'Cause this is all I got left."

CHAPTER

59

Jamison handed Decker the business card as they climbed into the truck.

"It does make you wonder," he said.

"What?" she asked.

"Keith Drews loses his job and then he buys life insurance. But Linda said he bought the policy *after* he hurt his back. That means he would have been on the painkillers."

"Maybe he wasn't addicted then."

"Maybe not," said Decker doubtfully.

"Do we go see Willie Norris now?"

"No, that'll keep. Right now, let's drive around a bit, have our coffee and muffins, and talk some things through."

"Okay, shoot." Then she bit into her muffin and moaned, "Oh, God, I'm going to need a cigarette."

"Yeah, well, hold that thought."

He took a bite of muffin and a sip of his coffee. He said, "Costa, Tanner, Swanson, and Babbot. Let's take them one by one and see where we stand."

"Okay."

"Bradley Costa figured out where the Baron treasure was and came to town to get it. He got hired by the bank that held the mortgage on the property."

"You think he planned it that way?"

Decker nodded and took a moment to wipe cream off his lips. "I'm sure he did his research and joined the bank because it held the mortgage. He was a hotshot Wall Street type. How many of those do you think come to places like this?"

"Zero."

"So he renegotiated the deal with Baron and put in the moral turpitude clause."

"And then do you think he proceeded to frame Baron for the murders?"

"No. For the simple fact that he ended up *being* murdered. I think he might have had some scheme in mind to nail Baron on the moral turpitude clause. It didn't have to be murder. It could have been drugs. Maybe he knew about Swanson squatting up there and keeping his drug stash in the potting shed. Then Baron goes to jail and the loan is called, the property foreclosed, and the straw man buys the property. Then they get the treasure. But the straw man double-crossed Costa and killed him so he wouldn't have to split the treasure. And then he completed the original plan to frame Baron, by murdering four people. In that way, with Costa, he killed two birds with one stone."

"But that's all speculation."

"I'm going on probabilities."

"Okay. And Swanson died because he was squatting on Baron's property. And he was also a drug dealer, which, like you said, would probably trigger the morals clause if they could tie Baron to drug dealing."

Decker nodded. "And they wouldn't want Swanson around on the property while they looked for the treasure. Again, two birds with one stone. They get him off the property and use his murder to frame Baron."

"That makes sense."

"You remember the nail we found in Tanner's car tire?"

"Yeah."

"Well, when I was at the fulfillment center I drove around to the new section they're building. Guess what I found?" He pulled from his jacket pocket the object he'd found in the parking lot and held it up.

"It looks like the nail you found in Tanner's tire."

"It's exactly the same."

"You think Tanner was at the fulfillment center?"

"I think her *car* was."

"You think she was kidnapped from there?"

"I don't know. But Tanner had a connection to Baron. She was his ex-girlfriend. He was helping her financially. That's why she was killed."

"And Babbot?"

"He'd trespassed on Baron's property, like Lassiter said."

"Why? Maybe looking for the treasure? But how could he have known about that?"

"It's a small town. He might have heard something. And a treasure is a big incentive."

"Do you think Babbot also knew about the drug ring?"

"It's certainly possible," said Decker. "At the very least he might have suspected what was going on at the fulfillment center with Ross. He knew about the secret space in Ross's office, because that discrepancy was on his drawing. I just don't know if he knew what was in it or how to access it. If he did suspect, then when they killed him they also got a double payoff. He was used to help frame Baron, and he would be silenced before he could disclose what he knew about Ross's office having a hollow back wall."

Decker suddenly leaned back in the seat and tightly closed his eyes.

"Decker, are you okay?"

"I'm just trying to remember something but it's not coming."

"Is it because of the hit you took on your head?" she said worriedly.

He rubbed his brow. "It could be."

"What are you trying to remember?"

"Numbers."

"What number?"

"Numbers!" he said testily.

In Decker's mind was a swirl of numbers. They were all different colors. That was his synesthesia talking. Yet it was different, because the colors were different for some numbers than they had been in the past.

Seven, four, three, is that a zero? No, an eight? Red, orange, green, two?

He scrunched up his brow.

Is that a nine or an upside-down six? Come on, dammit, come on.

Finally, the numbers all lined up correctly. And he was able to weigh one set against another. And they tallied perfectly.

He opened his eyes, took out his phone, and hit some keys.

"Who are you calling?"

"No one."

He hit more keys.

"What are you doing?"

"I'm searching for a listing on a phone number I saw."

"Where did you see it?"

"On Ted Ross's phone."

"Why does it matter?"

"Because I saw the same number somewhere else."

He held up his phone for her to see.

She said, "The phone number belongs to Fred Ross, Ted's father?"

"Yes."

"Not unusual for a father to call his son."

"No, but it is unusual that a son doesn't have his father in his contacts list, even if they don't get along all that well. If he had the number in his contacts, Fred Ross's name would have come up on the screen, not his number."

"That *is* odd. Wait a minute. You said you saw that number somewhere else."

"I did."

"Where?"

"On a wall."

"Whose wall?"

"Alice Martin's phone number wall."

"Well, they *are* neighbors."

"She told me that she only kept phone numbers up there that she called frequently, because otherwise she couldn't remember them."

"Okay, but again, they're neighbors."

"Only Martin told me that she despises Ross and has for decades. And after meeting the guy I can see why. Even his own son can't stand him. And he's a criminal!"

Jamison said, "So why have his number up on her wall?"

"Well, I can think of at least one reason."

60

WILLIE NORRIS'S OFFICE was located in what had once been a residence in a neighborhood about a mile from Drews's bakery.

The young woman in the front room immediately rose to greet them when they walked in. She was polite, if a bit shy, though Decker could sense something guarded, almost anxious in her features. She wore faded boots, jeans, and a white cuffed shirt. The computer on her metal desk was at least ten years old. Paper files were scattered over the desk's surface.

They had passed two cars in the driveway, a shiny black new Lexus convertible and a rusted-out ancient Ford pickup truck. Decker thought he knew which vehicle belonged to Norris and which one to his secretary.

A moment later Willie Norris walked into the room. He was short and portly with slicked-back graying hair. His chin was pointed, his nose as narrow and spiny as a mountain ridge, and his eyes were two bits of coal in fleshy sockets. He wore an ill-fitting three-piece gray suit. A cigarette dangled from one hand.

"Come on back, come on back," said Norris, waving a flabby hand.

He shut the door behind them.

Decker looked around the room, which clearly had once been a bedroom. Where the closet had been was a built-in shelf filled with plastic binders. The man's desk was an antique partner's desk with elaborate moldings. A grimy square of rug was set under the furniture. On the wall were a series of framed certificates indicating membership in a variety of insurance organizations.

Norris sat down behind his desk and motioned to them to take seats opposite him. He took one final drag on his smoke and then ground it out in an overstuffed ashtray.

He smiled ruefully. "I wouldn't even insure myself," he said. "Obese, smoker, bad lungs, worse kidneys."

"Never too late to start a new chapter," said Jamison pleasantly.

"Think it's a little late for me. But you folks looking for insurance?"

"For my sister, yes. She just lost her husband."

"Overdose?" said Norris, a little too quickly.

"No, why would you think that?" asked Jamison.

"You must not be from around here. You're young, so I assume your sister is too. And her husband. Young man dies around here, it's either a DUI that went way bad, or it's an overdose."

"He died in an industrial accident."

"Oh, okay."

"Can you give me some information about the process of getting insurance?"

"Sure can."

He pulled open a drawer, riffled through it, and handed Jamison a folder with some loose pages inside. "That will help her start the application process, but I can answer any questions you might have or she can set up an appointment to meet with me."

Decker said, "I assume she'll need to take a medical exam and go through some sort of background check, in addition to filling out the application?"

"Depends on how much coverage she wants. You got companies giving out small policies with no medical exam and no real due diligence. They're just counting on the actuarial tables, but I don't like to do business that way. Especially here."

"Because of all the overdoses?" said Decker.

"That's right. Young man, old man, don't matter. One wrong pill, you're dead."

"How much life insurance can somebody buy?" asked Decker.

"Depends on the individual and what the underwriter will approve. If you want a policy for a ton of money that is out of whack for your personal situation, then that's going to be a problem. Also depends on what you do for a living. If your job is working in a day-care that's one thing. If you're a police officer or a fireman that'll be a factor. An underwriter may not write that policy, or the premiums would be higher. Or the policy might even exclude from coverage your dying from something related to your profession. So if you're a cop and get shot in the line of duty, it won't pay out."

"My sister is thirty-three and in excellent health, and she's a homemaker with a young daughter." She glanced at the overflow-ing ashtray. "And she doesn't smoke."

"Okay, I can't commit to anything based on that, of course, but how much insurance is she looking at?"

"A million, maybe more? I mean, how much is normal?"

"One person's normal is another person's abnormal," said Norris, chuckling. "But there are basic parameters. Now, there are different types of life insurance. You have whole life and universal. They're more like savings plans that actually build up cash value and that you can borrow against and such. Now, universal life insurance policies have some more flexibility than a whole life policy, but I think what you're talking about is good old-fashioned term life insurance. It only pays out upon death. They come with fixed premiums for a cer-tain period of time. Ten, twenty, or thirty years is typical. Now, you got a young kid who'll need support for many years, you'll want a higher policy amount. Or if the insured is a high earner, then you'll want more to continue to support a certain lifestyle in the event they die, that sort of thing. Key man policies are often issued to cover the life of important executives, and the beneficiary is the business. But that's obviously not your sister's situation."

"What would the premiums run for someone like my sister?"

"Don't hold me to it, but for someone her age and healthy, gen-erally speaking, for a twenty-year policy for a million bucks, you're looking at four hundred bucks a year in premium payments. For a thirty-year term, a little over six hundred bucks a year. That's strictly actuarial tables talking. Odds are she'll live another fifty years or so. Of course, after, for example, the thirty-year term is up, she can keep paying the next layer of premiums. But then your sister would be close to her mid-sixties, and the premiums would be a lot higher, so she might just let the policy lapse. That way, the insurance company has collected twenty or thirty years' worth of premiums from the insured and not paid out a dime."

"Nice business, if you can get it," noted Jamison.

"Selling insurance is a *for-profit* business, after all," Norris said, with a laugh tacked on.

Jamison glanced at Decker and then said to Norris, "Thanks, I'll give these materials to my sister and she can follow up with you."

"Sounds good."

Norris rose.

However, Decker remained sitting and said, "We were referred to you by Linda Drews."

Norris slowly sat back down. "Oh, right." He shook his head sadly. "That was tough. Her son dying like that. Broke my heart."

"Yeah. She said he had hurt his back at work and was on painkillers."

"Right."

"That didn't affect his ability to get life insurance?" asked Decker.

Norris eyed him keenly. "I'd love to keep jawing, but the fact is I've got an appointment to get to." He stood. "Jenny can show you out."

As they left the office and headed to their truck Jamison said, "You really spooked him."

Decker nodded. "I think he knows we're FBI."

"Is this some sort of insurance scam?" she asked.

"Could be."

"The premiums he quoted are pretty low. I doubt most people would need help to pay them."

"Maybe not," he said.

"You're obviously thinking about something," she said, staring at him.

"I'm remembering something Fred Ross told me."

"What's that?"

"That nothing in Baronville is really illegal."

61

DECKER SAT UP in bed and listened to the rain pouring down outside.

Does it ever stop raining here?

He looked over at the small table under the window. He'd laid his clothes there. And on top of them was his badge.

He rose, walked over, and picked it up.

It wasn't an FBI special agent badge, because he wasn't one. But it was a federal badge and it did have the authority of the FBI behind it. And Decker had arresting authority as a member of an FBI task force.

Decker had carried a badge for over twenty years now. He'd had it the night he'd discovered that he no longer had a family.

He'd had it with him when Alex Jamison and then Melvin Mars came into his life.

He carried it now in Baronville, PA.

It had provided him comfort when he'd needed it. It had provided him a means to the only ends he had ever cared about.

The truth.

But that was not why he was now looking down at his badge.

He glanced out the window, and though he couldn't see it, he knew exactly where the home of Dan Bond was located.

The old man should have been allowed to live out the remaining years of his life in peace. But someone had not allowed him to do that. And Decker was going to make that person pay.

Decker swiveled his head in the direction of the house where

Alice Martin lived. And just a few doors down from that was Fred Ross and his sawed-off shotgun.

He cast his mind back to that first night, after he'd found the bodies. He and Jamison had driven down the street. There had been no cars parked on it.

However, Fred Ross's van had been parked under his carport.

Ross said he'd been at the hospital. And Decker had confirmed that that was true. And he had been transported by ambulance, meaning his van would have been under the carport that night.

These thoughts were interrupted by a tap on his door.

"Yeah?"

Jamison said, "It's me. Got a minute?"

Decker said, "Give me a sec." He checked his watch. It was after midnight. He pulled on his pants. "Okay."

Jamison, dressed in a robe, came in.

"What's up?" he said.

"I got to thinking about our meeting with Norris and I decided to do some digging."

"Digging on what?"

"Insurance premiums."

"Okay."

"I emailed a friend of mine who's in the insurance business and asked her some questions. Specifically, I gave her Keith Drews's information. The back injury, the fact that he was a prescription drug user, and also where he lived. I just got the reply back."

He glanced at his watch again. "Your friend works late."

"She works in Manhattan at one of the biggest insurance companies in the world, so she's basically chained to her desk. Anyway, she said Baronville is smack in the middle of what the insurance industry has started to call Opioid Alley. Fifty or so years ago insurance companies had different insurance ratings for different communities, but that was outlawed. So even though they call places like Baronville part of Opioid Alley, that's really unofficial because they really can't charge more for a policy simply because of where you live. But insurers *do* file rates based on an entire state and the opioid crisis has grown to such an extent that it's actually affecting longevity, and thus the premiums charged tend to be higher. Like Norris said, it's a for-profit business. My friend said that even though Keith Drews was a young person, the fact that he lived here and had suffered a back injury and was consequently taking painkillers would raise a red flag for them. And the fact that most opioid abusers start with prescription painkillers would also be factored in. And a million-dollar policy for an unmarried and childless person with no job would have also raised questions. The bottom line, she told me, was that because of Drews's circumstances, it's highly doubtful a policy that large would have been approved. But even if an underwriter would okay such a policy, the premiums wouldn't be a couple hundred bucks a year like Norris quoted me for my sister."

"What would they be?"

"She could only give me a ballpark, but she said for a ten-year policy it would be about two thousand a year. For a thirty-year policy about four thousand. So how could Keith Drews have afforded that unless someone was making the payments for him, like you suggested?"

"But your friend said that she didn't think the policy should have been issued in the first place, even though it was."

"That's right."

"Which makes me wonder why an insurer would've taken that risk. And it's not just Drews. As you know, Kemper told me a lot of life insurance policies have been cashed in here over the last few years."

"Either the insurance companies involved have been royally screwing up, or maybe people are lying on their applications."

"They would surely investigate that before paying out," countered Decker. "In fact, Kemper told me that the companies *had* investigated a number of them, but still ended up paying out."

"Well, if they did write the policies and they couldn't find any wrongdoing, they would have to pay out."

"Kemper emailed me a list of the insurers that have paid out money. It's a long list. From all over the place. Some big names, but many I'd never heard of."

"Meaning Norris and whoever else might be doing this are probably spreading it around. My friend also told me that life insurance companies give agents contracts based on the volume of business the agent will throw their way. If the volume isn't there over a few years' time, the contract gets yanked. And with the sort of scam Norris may be running, if you go to very few insurers or even just one, they're going to quickly see something weird is going on and they're going to stop writing policies here and stop doing business with the agent. But maybe Norris doesn't care about that for some reason."

"Which brings up another important question."

"What?"

"I wonder how much of the million bucks Linda Drews got to keep. And who got the rest?"

CHAPTER

62

Decker finally fell asleep a little after one o'clock.

He dozed fitfully for a bit and then woke up coughing. He'd gotten wet yesterday and he was afraid he might have caught a cold.

He drew a long breath and coughed again, this time more violently.

He sat up and gagged, then suddenly lurched to one side of his bed and threw up.

Dizzy, he got to his feet and immediately fell to the floor. He managed to drag himself over to the window, open it, and stick his head out into the rain. He sucked in the chilly, wet air and his fuzzy brain cleared and his nausea passed.

When he brought his head back inside he smelled it.

He lumbered from the room, covering his nose and mouth with his T-shirt.

He pounded on Jamison's door.

"Alex! Alex!"

When she didn't answer, he opened the door and looked frantically around.

All he could see was her foot sticking up from the other side of the bed.

This froze Decker for an instant, because that had been exactly what he had first seen when he had discovered his wife's body at their home back in Burlington.

He raced over to the other side of the bed, bent down, and

checked the pulse at her neck. He detected it and she was breathing, if spasmodically. He lifted Jamison up in his arms and rushed back to his bedroom, where he placed her next to the window and held her head out the opening.

She gasped, came to, and looked up at him.

"Wh—"

"Stay right there, keep breathing in. And don't turn any light switch on. Okay? Any spark could trigger the gas."

She nodded feebly and Decker ran from the room.

He flung open Zoe's bedroom door. She was lying in her bed.

"Zoe? Zoe!"

He sniffed the air. It wasn't that bad in here. Yet.

Zoe slowly sat up in bed. "Amos?" she said sleepily. What's the matter?"

Decker ran over and opened her window. "I want you to put your head out the window, okay. There's a gas leak in the house. I'm making sure everybody's okay."

"Mommy!" Zoe cried out.

"I'm going to get her right now. Put your head out the window and take deep breaths, okay? And don't turn on the lights."

She nodded, jumped up, and ran over to the window.

Decker thundered down the stairs, because Amber's bedroom was on the ground floor, in what had been a den that they had converted into a bedroom. Its bathroom was down the hall.

He opened the door. "Amber?"

Her bed was empty.

He scanned the floor, then he heard a moan from somewhere. His gaze darted to the hall. He ran back out and looked in the direction of the bathroom.

"Amber!"

The moan came again.

Decker ran down the hall and opened the bathroom door.

Amber was lying on the floor in her nightclothes.

As Decker knelt down next to her, she stopped breathing and went limp.

Decker started gagging again because the volume of gas in the bathroom was so high. He lifted her up and took her outside. Laying her on the porch, he started to perform CPR.

A few moments later he felt a presence next to him. It was Jamison.

"I've called 911," she whispered, staring at her sister.

She knelt down and, synchronizing with Decker's pushes on her sister's chest, started blowing air into Amber's mouth.

Finally, after about thirty excruciatingly long seconds, Amber's chest heaved up, air gushed out of her mouth, and she retched.

"Mommy!"

They turned to see Zoe racing out of the house. She dropped to her knees and hugged her mother.

"Mommy!"

Amber slowly put an arm around her daughter's waist. She tried to sit up but Decker gently pushed her back down.

"No, just lie there. The ambulance is on its way."

It arrived a few minutes later and the paramedics put Amber on oxygen and loaded her onto a gurney. Jamison rode in the back with Zoe. Before the ambulance pulled away, a teary Jamison said, "Thank you, Amos."

"Thanks, Amos," said Zoe, still anxiously glancing at her mom.

Decker nodded, closed the ambulance doors, and stepped back as a gas company truck pulled up along with a squad car.

Decker told them about the gas leak in the house and the men hurried around to the back to turn off the gas supply.

Decker recognized the police officer who approached as Officer Curry, the one who had responded when Decker had found the dead bodies.

"You okay?" asked Curry. "You look a little green."

"I'm good."

"Gas leak, huh?"

Decker looked at him. "Yeah."

"That's pretty unusual."

"Yeah."

One of the gas men came back around from the rear of the house and walked over to them looking grim.

"What is it?" asked Curry.

"Somebody tampered with the pressure valve going into the house," said the man, shaking his head. "You're lucky to be alive."

"Yeah," said Decker. "We are."

"I wonder who would've done that?" said Curry.

"It might be a long list," replied Decker.

63

LATER THAT DAY, Decker opened the door to see Alice Martin standing there. Her quad cane was in one hand and she held a pie in the other.

Over her shoulder Decker saw the police cruiser parked at the curb. Lassiter had authorized it after Decker phoned her and told her what had happened.

"I heard," Martin said tersely. "Is everyone all right?"

Decker nodded. "Amber got checked out at the hospital. They're keeping her for a bit longer, but she should be home tonight."

"And Zoe?"

"She's okay. The gas didn't get very far into her room for some reason. They cleared the whole house out and checked for gas levels before they let us back in. She's at the hospital with her mom."

"Do they know how it happened?"

"Still checking on it."

Martin turned and glanced at the police cruiser. "I take it that the presence of the police means that it *wasn't* an accident?"

Instead of answering, Decker glanced at the pie. "Is that for Amber?"

"It's for all of you. Lemon meringue."

She handed it to him.

"Thanks," he said. "I'll be sure to tell Amber."

Martin looked around. "This used to be a very nice neighborhood. Now it's not very nice at all."

"I can see how you would feel that way."

"It might be best for all of you to just leave Baronville."

Decker stared at her without answering.

"Why would you want to stay in a place like this?" she asked.

"I don't live here. But Amber and her daughter do. Her husband came here for a job. It's not like they had a choice. And I have no idea if they'll stay here or move." He paused. "Why do *you* stay, Ms. Martin?"

"Because it's my home and I'm too damn old to move."

"Like your neighbor, Fred Ross?"

She stared at him. "You live long enough, Mr. Decker, you accept things you never thought you otherwise would."

"Is that a good thing or a bad thing?"

"For some it's one or the other."

"And for you?"

"I hope you all enjoy the pie. I'm very good at lemon meringue. At least I'm still good at something."

She turned to leave, but then looked back at him.

"This used to be a nice town way back."

"You mean when the sweatshops were operating and a robber baron was making all the money?"

She smiled. "I guess we all romanticize our pasts, to make them better than they actually were."

"Maybe we do," said Decker. "Nostalgia can be very tempting. And nearly as addictive as opioids."

She said sharply, "You don't seem very appreciative to someone who just brought you a pie."

Decker looked taken aback. "I'm sorry. I...I guess getting nearly killed hasn't put me in the best mood."

"Well, enjoy the pie," she replied in a softer tone.

She walked off while Decker stood there watching. At first, he was feeling guilty about having spoken to her so abrasively. But when she left the gravel walk that led up to the house and reached the sidewalk, Decker stiffened.

Clunk, scrape, clunk.

The sounds he'd heard that night.

Her quad cane was striking the pavement, and the broken foot on the cane she had told him about earlier was making those sounds. It was first scraping against the pavement, and then, when she lifted it and brought it down, it clunked against the pavement.

He closed the door and leaned his head against the wood.

Son of a bitch. Baronville. More like Murderville.

He had some things to do and he didn't have much time to do them.

He went into the kitchen and threw the pie into the trash.

CHAPTER

64

"So what's up, Decker?"

Decker was sitting across from Agent Kemper at the Mercury Bar. Cindi Riley was not working tonight. She might be at the jail with Baron, Decker thought.

Kemper's hair was clipped with a barrette. Her sidearm was on a belt holster and her badge was pinned to her belt.

"Just wanted to check in on a few things."

"Has everyone recovered from the gas attack?"

"News travels fast, I take it?"

"Lassiter phoned me."

"She put a patrol out front."

"Glad to hear that. I take it someone thinks you're getting too close to things. Like when they tried to blow you and Jamison up in that trailer."

"Seems so."

"So, *are* you getting there? Because I see my case slipping away from me by the minute. I don't know how much longer I can sit on this."

"I talked to the hospital where Fred Ross was taken on the day I found the bodies. He called 911 complaining of chest pains."

"Okay."

"The hospital checked him out and found absolutely nothing wrong. They released him the next day."

"Why the interest in Fred Ross?"

"Because the bodies of your two agents were kept on ice before they were transported to the empty house. I think they were taken there in Ross's van. Which means they were probably kept in a freezer shortly before then. And since Fred Ross lived on the street he might have been nervous about us thinking he knew something, or had seen something that night. His being in the emergency room at the time would provide him both an ironclad alibi *and* preclude us from asking him for details about that night."

"How do you know they were taken there in his van?"

"I heard a vehicle start up *after* I saw the lights in the house flickering, which means they had already placed the bodies and poured the blood, which eventually caused the flickering. They must have gone to the house with the bodies before I went out on the deck. And the only car on the street that night was Ross's."

"You can't know that."

"Yeah, I can. It's a dead-end street. While I wouldn't have seen the car, I would've seen the car *lights* if it had gotten to the stop sign at the end of the street. That means the vehicle didn't leave the street. It dropped off the bodies and then it was driven *back* to Ross's house, and the people who dumped the bodies probably left from there on foot."

"An old guy in a wheelchair is in the middle of this?"

"I think he is, because his son is."

"Okay. I guess I can see that, but looping your octogenarian father into a major drug operation can seem pretty unbelievable."

"Well, it's about to get more unbelievable, because Alice Martin, the former Sunday school teacher, is involved too."

"What! How do you figure that?"

"Her damaged walking cane was the sound I heard that night. She was out there, probably checking on the transfer. And she told me she despises Fred Ross, but his phone number is up on her wall along with all her other frequently called numbers. But there's something else."

"What?"

"She was the one who told me that she had seen two men fitting the descriptions of Beatty and Smith enter the house next to where their bodies were found."

"So?"

"So now we know those houses were used as pill press operations. Your guys would not have been going in there, which means Martin was lying."

"But if they were undercover they might have."

"Martin told me she had seen them go in there a couple of weeks before. If they had been in there as undercover agents, they would have reported the pill press operations to their agency contact."

"That's true."

"Martin had to know that I would probably go check that out right after she told me. And I did. Now, why do I think a review of her phone records would show that she immediately phoned Fred Ross or somebody else? And the next thing you know, Brian Collins shows up pretending to be a cop next door and tries to kill me. See, I don't think he was watching the place. Why would he be? There was nothing left there; they'd already cleared out. I think he was called there to kill me, because Martin had basically told me a lie to get me to investigate the place. This was all a setup. And it was prearranged to be initiated if I came to question Martin and seemed to be getting too close."

Kemper looked thoughtful for a few moments, then said, "We obviously know about Ted Ross and the drug ring. But is there something else?"

"I think there're a lot of things, and not all of them are drug-related. So maybe they're of no interest to you."

She smiled. "Before I joined the DEA, I had an ambition to become an FBI agent. It was a last-minute change in my career path."

"Why?"

"On a stupid bet my best friend in the world took a PCP cocktail and it fried her brain. I remember visiting her in the hospital, staring down at a beautiful young woman who no longer had a mind. And from that moment forward, my whole life was going to be about taking down the monsters who sell that poison."

"I can see how that would alter your career path," said Decker.

She leaned forward. "But my interest extends to taking down *all* bad guys."

"Glad to hear that."

She dropped her voice. "As an add-on to what we discussed before, we strongly suspect the presence of a major pill press operation in western Pennsylvania. That's why a big-time operator like Brian Collins would be here too. If he was involved, you can take it to the bank that some heavyweights have descended on Baronville."

"And now we know that Ted Ross is supplying them with all the fentanyl they need."

Kemper straightened. "That's right. But you already know all this. So why did you want to meet?"

In answer, Decker slipped his badge off his belt and laid it on the table.

She stared down at it before glancing back at him with a perplexed look.

"What does your badge have to do with it?"

"Not *my* badge," replied Decker.

"Then whose?"

"You'll see. But I need your help to get there."

65

HE DIDN'T SHOW up this morning. I called his home but no one answered. I drove over there but his car was gone. I peeked in the window, but it was all dark. And a neighbor told me she saw Mr. Norris leaving in the middle of the night with a bunch of luggage. But he never told me he was going anywhere. I'm not sure what to do."

This had all come tumbling out of Jenny, Willie Norris's assistant, as Decker and Jamison stood across from her in the front room of the man's insurance office.

"He had appointments this morning and he missed them all," she added. "Do you think he's all right?"

"I seriously doubt it," said Decker. He looked around. "And if I were you, I'd think about looking for another job."

Her face crumpled. "Hell, I had a hard enough time getting this one."

"And maybe hire a good lawyer," added Decker.

"What!? Why?"

"Because you just never know."

He and Jamison walked out and Decker phoned Kemper.

"We got a runner," he said, filling her in. "I know this isn't exactly your jurisdiction, but for all I know Norris is connected to all the other crap going down in this town. And you might want to have some people start digging through his business records."

"On it."

"And the other thing?" he asked.

"Nearly done." She clicked off.

Decker put his phone away.

"What other thing?" Jamison asked.

"Something I tasked Kemper with. I'll fill you in later."

"You think that asshole was part of the gas sabotage at my sister's that nearly killed us?"

"I would be stunned if he wasn't. It happened pretty quickly after we spooked him. And now he's on the run."

"So what did he get out of all this?"

"Money. His normal commission plus something on the back end. But we can find out for sure."

"How?"

He glanced at her. "You up for another carrot cake muffin?"

* * *

Linda Drews called out to them as they walked into her café.

"Couldn't stay away, could you?" she said, smiling.

"No, we couldn't," replied Decker. "We'll take two more of the carrot cake muffins and some coffee."

"To go or you eating in?"

"Better make it to go. And before you handle any hot coffee, can I ask you some questions?"

She smiled, though her look was perplexed. "Sure."

Her smile vanished when Decker showed her his cred pack.

"FBI? Am I in trouble?"

"That depends. We met with Mr. Norris. He wasn't very forthcoming. I'm hoping you'll be better at that."

Drews put a hand on the counter to support herself.

Decker leaned against the wall. "Your son never should have been able to get that life insurance policy; do you know that?"

Drews lips started to tremble. "Guess I do now, mister."

"But Norris made it happen?" said Jamison.

"It was his idea. I guess I should've told you before, but I didn't know you were with the FBI. He came to me after Keith injured his back. I've known Willie a long time. Got my car insurance through him. And my house insurance, when I had a house. He said in crazy times like these, it'd be a good idea. I wanted to get me a policy too and have Keith the beneficiary, but Willie said with all the drugs I'd done they'd never approve me."

"I think that was a good thing for you," said Decker ominously. "So, Norris filled out all the paperwork?"

"Yeah, and he had a local paramedic do the medical exam."

"A paramedic?"

"Yeah, they can do the exams, Willie said. He said the insurance companies contract out with them, and also with a local lab to do the blood work and such."

"So all local players. Interesting. Did Keith tell the paramedic about being injured and being on painkillers?"

"I don't know, 'cause I wasn't there."

"Did Keith mention anything to you later?" asked Decker.

"Do I need a lawyer, mister?"

"That might depend on your answers."

"Look, Keith wasn't really on them painkillers no more. And his back was a lot better when he got that policy."

"But a million bucks in life insurance? That's a lot. He wasn't even employed."

"Willie said Keith was so young that that would help. He wouldn't die for a long time."

"Uh-huh, well that turned out to be wrong. How was he going to pay the premiums? Even if they weren't that much, your son had no income."

"I was gonna help him, well, if I could. And...and Willie too."

"So Norris was giving Keith money to make the payments on the insurance policy that Norris sold him?"

She nodded, her skin as pale as the napkin she was holding.

"Did you know that was illegal?" said Decker.

She shook her head. "No sir. I just thought Willie was being a good friend."

"And then Keith got hooked on opiates and died?"

"Yeah."

"But you said he was off the painkillers," Decker said in a dubious tone.

"Well, he was *mostly* off 'em."

"You said he overdosed because he mistook fentanyl for heroin?" asked Jamison.

"That's right."

"And where did this happen?" asked Decker.

"At a friend's house."

"And the friend wasn't there to give him Narcan?" said Decker.

"No, he was alone. I didn't find out till later. Cried my eyes out."

"Did the insurance company investigate the death?"

"Yeah, they did. But Willie was on top of that too. He told me he wasn't gonna let them cheat me outta my money. And he came through all right. They paid out a few months later."

"And then you got the million dollars?" said Decker.

Drews didn't answer right away. "Yeah, that's right."

"No, that's *not* right."

"What?"

"You didn't get the full million. How much did Norris get?"

"Well, um, he got his commission."

"Which was how much?"

"Thirty percent."

"So he got three hundred thousand dollars?"

"Yes sir, that's what Willie said was standard with life insurance."

"And how was it paid?"

"Willie took care of that. He just made sure my money got to my account."

"I'm sure he did." Decker paused. "Ms. Drews, did you ever think it was strange that soon after your son took out a million-dollar life insurance policy, which was Norris's idea, he overdosed and Norris got three hundred grand?"

Drews's lips started to tremble and the tears began to slide down her cheeks. "Mister, are you telling me that…"

"Yeah, I am," said Decker. "They set your son up. They got a big policy on him and then rigged it so he overdosed and died."

Drews put a shaky hand to her face and sobbed. "I never wanted my son to die, so help me God."

"But the fact is, he *did* die."

"And…and you really think Willie had something to do with that?"

"I don't think it, I *know* he did."

"Am I in trouble, mister?" she asked again.

"I'd get that lawyer if I were you. And forget about the coffee and muffins. I just lost my appetite."

Decker and Jamison walked out.

Back in their truck, Jamison said, "God, I can't believe that. She *had* to know what was going on."

"Maybe she did and maybe she didn't. If I've learned one thing in this business, it's that people can justify anything they want to."

"So, insurance scams, drug dealers, and framing someone for a treasure. Who would have thought one town could have so much crap going on separately?"

Decker put the truck in gear.

"Only it's not really separate, Alex. It's all tied together with a not-so-neat little bow."

66

A PHONE CALL a while later brought Decker and Jamison to the Baronville police headquarters. They were met at the front door by a solemn Kate Kemper and three of her agents.

When Decker and Jamison walked into the room where the homicide detectives worked, Lassiter was standing next to her desk. She looked up in surprise.

"Hey, what are you guys doing here? I—"

She abruptly stopped when she saw Kemper and her agents file into the room behind them.

Decker said to Lassiter, "Can you have your partner join us?"

"Marty? I think he's around here. I'll text him."

She did so, and about a minute later Detective Green came into the room.

"Hey," he said to Decker and Jamison.

Decker nodded.

Green glanced at Kemper before fixing his gaze on Lassiter. "Did you need me?"

Lassiter pointed to Decker. "No, but he wanted to see you for something." She paused. "You okay, Marty? You look out of sorts."

"Lose something maybe?" asked Decker.

Green looked sheepish as he sat down behind his desk. "My damn badge. I usually put it in my locker at the gym, but I can't find it. I play racquetball next door. It's pissing me off. You lose your badge, that's a ton of paperwork."

He started searching through one of his drawers.

"One question," said Decker. "The night Dan Bond was killed, someone said they saw a squad car parked in front of his house."

"Who said that?" Green asked, quickly looking up.

"It was an anonymous tip," interjected Kemper.

"Any idea who it could have been?" asked Green.

"Well, you've been on that street a lot," said Decker. "Could it have been you there that night?"

Green quickly shook his head. "I don't drive around in a squad car."

Decker nodded. "But you have met Dan Bond before, right?"

Green shook his head. "No. I've never been to the man's house. At least not while he was alive. I did go there after he was found murdered."

"You absolutely sure of that?" said Decker.

Green looked at him curiously. "Yeah, why?"

"What are you getting at, Decker?" interjected Lassiter. "I was the one who interviewed Dan Bond, not Marty."

Decker kept his gaze on Green. He said, "You can stop looking, because Agent Kemper has your badge."

Green shot Kemper a surprised glance. "You? Why?"

Kemper pulled out a plastic evidence bag from her coat. There was a badge inside it.

The blood slowly drained from Green's face. "What is my badge doing in an evidence bag?"

"Because it's *evidence*," said Kemper flatly. "In a murder investigation."

"What are you talking about? What murder?"

"Dan Bond."

"I told you, I never even met the man."

Decker said, "Which raises the question of why Dan Bond's fingerprints were found on your badge."

"What!?"

Decker took out his own badge. "Dan Bond was a careful man. I knocked on his door after dark, and he wouldn't let me in until I put my badge through his cat door. He told me he didn't like to let strangers inside his house. He used his fingers to make sure the badge was legit before he let me in. And, really, who else besides a cop would he let in at that hour of the night?" He held up the badge. "So that was how his prints got on *my* badge. But you just said you never met him, and yet his prints are on *your* badge. So how do you explain that, Detective Green, unless you were the one who visited Bond that night and killed him?"

"That's bullcrap!"

Green looked at Lassiter, who was staring at him openmouthed. "Those can't be his prints on my badge. It's impossible."

Decker said, "The day you threw your badge down and I picked it up? I saw it was smudged with prints, and something else that I realized later was...flour. Bond told me he liked to bake at all hours. He got flour on my badge too when he was checking it out. Agent Kemper also informed me that traces of flour were found on your badge. Now, I don't know if we can match it to the flour in Bond's kitchen but we really don't have to since we have your prints."

Green said nothing. He just glared at Decker.

"The thing is, Detective, if you're going to the trouble of killing someone, you really need to sweat the details," added Decker.

Green turned on Kemper. "You bitch! You took my badge without a warrant. That makes it inadmissible."

Kemper held up a piece of paper.

"I got a warrant, signed, sealed, and delivered."

"Based on what?"

"Based on the fact that we checked Alice Martin's phone records. Dan Bond called her the night he was killed. Then she immediately called Fred Ross's number. Shortly after that, *you* received a call from Fred Ross. And an hour after that, Dan Bond was killed. So our theory is that Bond called Martin and told her something that alarmed her, and she phoned Fred Ross to have it taken care of. And he dialed you up to do it."

"But what could have alarmed Alice?" said Lassiter. "She's just an old lady who used to teach Sunday school."

Decker said, "She's actually a lot more than that. I believe Bond was killed because he recognized that the sound he'd heard the night the two DEA agents' bodies were discovered was Alice Martin's recently broken quad cane hitting the pavement. Maybe she walked past his house the day he was killed, said hello to him, and so he knew the sound was being made by Martin's cane. He might have later called and asked her what she was doing out that night. That was not good, because Bond might tell somebody else, like me."

Green barked, "I want a lawyer."

"Yeah, well, maybe your lawyer will convince you to talk so you get life instead of the needle," said Decker.

Kemper looked at her men. "Cuff him, read him his rights, and take this scum to to the holding cell downstairs."

The men moved forward and handcuffed Green.

"You don't know who the hell you're messing with, Decker!" the detective shouted as he struggled helplessly.

"Funny, I was going to say the same thing to you."

67

Y OU HAVE NO reason to protect anyone," said Decker.

He was sitting in an interrogation room at police headquarters with Lassiter on one side of him and Kemper and Jamison on the other.

Across from them was Alice Martin sitting very primly in her seat. She didn't answer.

"We checked the big game freezer in your basement," said Decker. "The one presumably your husband used to store his venison in. But you didn't just keep deer meat in there. Whoever put Beatty and Smith in there wasn't all that careful. Their DNA has been recovered by the DEA." He glanced meaningfully at Kemper. "And that particular federal agency is out for blood. So, I say again, you have no reason to protect anyone."

She lifted her gaze to his. "How can you possibly know that?"

"Convince me otherwise."

She smoothed out her long skirt and rested her hands in her lap.

"I have children and grandchildren, and soon I'll have great-grandchildren. I have to think of them."

"How did you even get mixed up with something like this?" asked Lassiter.

"I outlived what little money I had a long time ago. I'm eighty-eight and in reasonably good health. Once you've reached this age, your odds of living another ten years or so are pretty good. I did not wish to do so in abject poverty. I'm tired of never going any-where. Of never having anything."

"Your kids couldn't help?"

"My children are barely making ends meet themselves. I have Social Security and that's it. And even here that does not go a long way."

"Lots of people have only Social Security, and they don't join a drug cartel to earn more money," pointed out Kemper.

"I did not join a drug cartel!" she said sharply.

"Then why don't you tell us what you *did* do," said Lassiter.

"I merely looked the other way," she said, her gaze perhaps symbolically averted from them. "When things began to happen on our street."

"What sorts of things?" asked Decker.

"When certain equipment was brought into the house where those men were found and in the one next to it. When unsavory types started coming and going at all hours."

"They were pill presses," said Decker. "And they picked this street because it only had three people living on it and one of them was blind."

"And one of them was also in on it," added Lassiter. "Fred Ross. Was he the one who approached you and asked you to look the other way?"

Martin nodded. "That's why they picked this street. Like you said, Dan was blind. Fred was just a horrible person. And I..." Her voice trailed off. "If I hadn't gone along they would have just killed me. What was I supposed to do?"

"Call the cops?" said Jamison.

"The cops?" she scoffed. "Fred told me that half the force is in on it."

"That's bullshit!" exclaimed Lassiter. "You could have come to me, Alice. I would have done something about it."

"What did they offer you?" Decker asked.

"Compensation."

"How much?"

"Two thousand dollars a week. In cash. And I really had to do nothing. Just...look the other way."

Jamison said, "No, you let them put bodies in your freezer."

Martin shivered at this comment but said nothing in reply.

Decker said, "That's a lot of money. What did you do with it?"

"I...bought things. I started eating food other than ramen noodles and mac and cheese. I fixed items in my house. I sent some money to my children. I bought my grandkids presents for the first time in years. I put the rest away in a trunk in my house to leave to them."

"So you were outside the night the bodies were transported?" said Lassiter.

Martin nodded. "They...they took the bodies from my freezer and put them in Fred's van. Then they drove it to the house and unloaded them there. They'd cleared out their equipment earlier. I went outside because...well, I didn't want to be inside when they brought the bodies out. And I wanted to make sure that no one was around, even though they had this drone thing flying over to do that. They usually did that when they were moving people or things in and out of there, just to make sure the coast was clear. Fred told me they had wanted to wait until it was very late at night to do it, but they figured with the storm coming in that no one would be out and about, and they wanted to get it done sooner rather than later. Anyway, they pulled the van into the carport and brought the bodies in through the side door. Afterward, they drove the van back to Fred's and left on foot. I walked back to my house before the rain started."

"That's when I heard your cane clunking and scraping against the pavement," said Decker. "I'm glad I never really described the sounds I heard to you when we spoke before. You would have been tipped off. But Dan Bond heard it too. He confronted you about it, didn't he?"

For the first time, tears glimmered in Martin's eyes.

"He was out on his front porch the other day when I passed by. I called out to him and he said, 'Good morning.' But then he looked kind of funny-like. I went home. And later he called me and wanted to know why I was outside that night. He wasn't accusing me, really. But he said that you had asked him about the sound, that you considered it important. And he was trying to remember where he'd heard it before. I never even thought about my cane making those noises. I just used it outside to walk without falling. I should have gotten it repaired."

"So how did he end up dead?" asked Decker.

"I was afraid he would tell you it had been me out that night. So I phoned Fred and told him about it."

"From the number on your phone wall," said Decker.

Martin locked gazes with him. "Yes."

"And what did Fred say he was going to do?" asked Lassiter.

"He said he would take care of it." She started to tremble. "I never thought he was going to kill him! I never, ever wanted Dan to die. He was a good man. A good friend all these years."

"What the hell did you think he was going to do?" said Decker. "A guy who'd stored the bodies of two federal agents in your *freezer*?"

Martin shook her head. "I..." She fell silent.

"And you called Fred again, after I met with you that night, didn't you?"

She glanced at him but said nothing.

"And he or someone else called Brian Collins and told him to kill me. Did you know that was going to happen when you lied to me about seeing Beatty and Smith going into that house?"

"I...I just did as I was told if you showed up at my door. That was all."

A long silence followed, during which all that could be heard was Martin's rapid breathing.

"You know, you should thank us for bringing you in," said Decker.

She looked up at him. "Why is that?"

"How long do you think they were going to let you live? I'm surprised they haven't already killed you."

"Maybe they took mercy on me."

"I highly doubt these guys have any mercy inside them."

"I have to look for the good in people," she said.

"And I have to look for the bad. It's not hard to find."

Martin's eyes fluttered. "It didn't use to be this way here."

"Back in the good old days?" said Decker.

"They *were* the good old days," she snapped.

"To some people. To others, they were as bad as today is for you."

"What will happen to me?" asked Martin, regaining her composure.

"Well, for starters, you won't have to worry about housing for the rest of your life," said Decker. "Or food. The government will be providing both."

She held her chin high and stared pointedly at him. "I just wanted to live in peace and dignity. I didn't mean for any of this to happen. Doesn't that matter?"

Decker eyed her back. "I've heard a lot of people say that over the years. Even the ones who put a gun against a guy's head and pulled the trigger. So, no, it doesn't matter at all."

Lassiter said, "But if you testify against the others and help us build a case against them, that *will* help you. You might get some leniency."

Martin looked at her. "Throwing a bone to your old Sunday school teacher, Donna?"

Lassiter shook her head. "You helped a drug ring pretty much slaughter this town, in exchange for money. So I just want to nail every one of these bastards. And if you can help us do that, great. If you can't you can rot in prison for all I care."

"I've really screwed everything up, haven't I?"

Decker glanced at Jamison and then looked back at Martin.

"Well, maybe you can teach Bible classes in prison to redeem yourself."

"Now you're mocking me," said Martin bitterly.

"No, I'm actually serious. And if you can help turn one life around?"

"Do you think that's really possible?"

"After what I've seen in life, anything is possible."

68

"DECKER, WE HAVE a big problem."

Decker was in the truck driving away from the police building with Jamison when Kemper had called.

"What?"

"I just got a call. We lost track of Ted Ross."

Decker swore under his breath. "How the hell did that happen?"

"I honestly don't know. He must have found out we arrested Green and Martin and now he's disappeared down a rabbit hole."

"How about his old man?"

"Now that's one card we might be able to play."

"How so?"

"Fred Ross is sitting in a holding cell at the Baronville jail. I had him arrested based on the phone call from Alice Martin after Bond had phoned her. Now we have Martin's evidence of the guy's involvement in the murders of my two agents and the drug ring. We'll arrange to have him transferred to a federal lockup shortly. But in the meantime, we're going to grill him until he screams he wants a lawyer."

"Then I suggest you wear earplugs." He clicked off and threw his phone down on the front seat of their truck.

"Bad news?" Jamison asked.

He told her.

"Okay, really bad news. What do you think Ted Ross is going to do?"

"For starters, he's going to try to avoid the death penalty."

"What do we do?"

"We go home and get Zoe and Amber and get them the hell out of Baronville."

"Right." Jamison stomped on the gas so hard, Decker's head snapped back.

* * *

When they pulled into the driveway of the house, Decker noted that the cop was still stationed out front in his cruiser.

"Tell your sister to pack up and we'll drive them someplace safe. I'm going to call Bogart and have him put some agents around them both."

Jamison jumped out of the truck and ran into the house while Decker phoned Bogart and filled him in. They made arrangements to meet a team of FBI agents in Pittsburgh. It was dark now and would be darker still by the time they got there.

Decker put his phone away and studied the house. It was almost impossible to believe that just a short time ago he and Jamison had traveled here for some rest and relaxation.

If I survive this, I'm never taking another vacation in my life.

He checked his watch. They needed to get going, and he hoped that Jamison had told her sister and niece to just grab the essentials. They could get whatever else they needed in Pittsburgh.

"Decker!"

He looked at the front porch and saw Jamison waving her hands at him.

He jumped out of the truck and raced up to the house.

"What is it?"

"They're gone. There's no one here."

Decker looked at the two cars parked in the driveway.

"Could they have gone somewhere on foot?"

Jamison looked over his shoulder and said slowly, "Why didn't the cop get out when I yelled for you?"

They hustled over to the car.

Decker knocked on the window. And when he didn't receive a response, he pulled his gun and slowly opened the car door.

The dead officer slumped sideways, held in only by his seat belt. Jamison said, "Oh my God! Decker!"

Decker looked up at the house. "You sure it's empty?"

"I called out to them. Nothing. I looked around the first floor."

"Were there signs of a struggle?"

"No, nothing that I could see."

"We have to search the rest of the house. But hang on."

He called Lassiter for backup but got no answer.

He next called Kemper.

Again, nothing.

They both went to voicemail.

He put his phone away. "Okay, it's just us. Get your gun out and follow me."

They entered the house and searched the first floor thoroughly, including the closets.

The place looked normal. There was an empty bowl and glass in the sink. No overturned furniture.

They headed upstairs and went bedroom by bedroom until they got to Decker's.

He opened the door and looked around. His gaze fell on the folded piece of paper lying in the center of the bed. Next to it was a cell phone.

He picked up the paper and slowly unfolded it.

You will wait to hear from us on this phone. Any mistakes, they are dead.

Jamison held out her hand for the note and he passed it across. She read it and plopped down on the bed and buried her face in her hands.

Decker walked over to the window that looked out over the rear of the house.

That was how they must have taken them. Through the backyard, over the fence, and onto the next street.

Where it all began.

He said, "They're going to call, Alex. We just have to be ready when they do."

Jamison said nothing.

He sat down on the bed next to her, picked up the phone the kidnappers had left, and stared at it.

* * *

About the time that Decker and Jamison discovered the dead cop outside the Mitchells' home, Donna Lassiter, three uniformed officers, and two DEA agents led Alice Martin and Detective Green out of the police station after they had been booked, photographed, and fingerprinted. The next stop would be jail, where each would be kept in an isolation cell until their arraignment.

The alleyway here had been closed off and Lassiter had men all around looking for threats.

Lassiter spoke into her phone as they exited the building from the rear and the transport vehicle immediately pulled up.

As they moved toward the vehicle Martin looked at her.

"I'm sorry for all the trouble I've caused."

"Well, that really doesn't matter. But what will matter is for you to make amends by testifying."

"I understand. But I was wondering something."

"What?"

"Can the prison where I'm sent be close to my children?"

"Look, you're hardly in a position to be making demands."

"I know. And I don't expect that it will happen, but I was only asking for your help. For your old Sunday school teacher?"

Lassiter sighed. "I have nothing to do with where you'll be sent, but I can speak to someone about it. But it might not do any good. In fact, it probably won't. But I will make a call."

"Thank you for trying."

"But my help is contingent on you testifying truthfully about all that you know."

"I understand. I'm looking forward to it, actually. It'll give me the opportunity to make penance. They said no one would get hurt. But they lied about that."

"Where did you think it was going to end?"

"I... I guess I never really thought about that."

"Well, it's a little late now."

"Is it too late for me, Donna?"

Lassiter turned to look at her former partner.

"There's nothing I can do for you."

"I was just trying to get what was mine."

"Nobody's entitled to shit, Marty."

"Been pounding the pavement for next to nothing all my life. Protecting the public. Hell, the public's not worth putting my ass on the line for."

"Well, you won't have to worry about that anymore."

The next instant, the long-range shot hit Martin directly in the chest, blowing a chunk of the woman out through her back. Blood and splintered bone smacked against the window of the transport truck.

Green screamed, but it died in his throat as the next round went through his head, taking a large piece of his brain with it.

"Shooter!" screamed Lassiter, pointing her gun in the direction from where the bullets had come. She managed to fire several shots.

The next bullets slammed into Lassiter and two others, dropping them all to the ground.

69

THE PHONE RANG.

But it was Decker's phone, not the one left by the kidnappers.

He looked down at the number on the screen and swore.

He put the phone in speaker mode and barked, "I tried calling you."

Kemper said, "I'm sorry, Decker. I was tied up. And this is turning into a real catastrophe."

"Look, I can't talk right now, I've—"

"Decker, haven't you heard?"

"Heard what?" Decker thought she was referring to Amber and Zoe being taken, but he didn't see how that was possible.

"We've got two dead that we know of."

Decker tensed. *Amber and Zoe? It can't be.*

"Who are you talking about?" he said between clenched teeth.

"An ambush while Martin and Green were being transported to jail."

"They're dead?"

"Yes. And Lassiter and two others were wounded and are in the hospital."

"So, an inside job?"

"Appears to be. They knew where and when they were coming out of the building."

"We've got other problems too."

"Come again?"

Decker explained what had happened to the cop out front and the disappearance of Jamison's family.

"Damn!" exclaimed Kemper. "I want these bastards so bad I can taste it."

"All I care about is getting Amber and Zoe back safe."

"Are there any clues to who might have taken them? Or where they might have gone?"

"No. I was waiting for them to call me when you phoned."

"You think they were taken as a bargaining chip?"

"Yes. Otherwise they would have just killed them like they did the cop out front."

"So what do you think they'll ask for?"

"I'm sure they'll tell me," he said grimly.

"I'm going to get a BOLO out on them."

"Okay," said Decker absently.

"You don't think it'll do any good?"

"I think they're too smart to be tripped up by that."

"It was a big risk killing a cop and then kidnapping two people."

"If they had unfinished business and needed the leverage that hostages give them they'd take that risk."

"But they cleared out the drug stash, and they killed the only witnesses we had. We have no case against them."

"That may not matter to them."

"What else *would* matter to them?" retorted Kemper.

"Like I said, unfinished business."

"Such as?"

"If I knew that I wouldn't be sitting here waiting for them to call," snapped Decker.

"Okay, okay, but we need to come up with a plan."

"That's hard to do, since we don't know what they're going to throw at us."

"But once they make contact, you have to loop me in. Then we can go after them in a coordinated effort."

"You need to let me play it out the best way I see fit."

"What precisely does that mean?" said Kemper warily.

"That means I'm going to do all I can to make sure this doesn't go sideways and two innocent people end up dead."

Jamison shuddered next to him and looked down at the floor.

"Decker, I don't know if I can do that," said Kemper. "I have people to answer to."

"So do I. Their names are Amber and Zoe. And if you don't want to do it my way, I'll just have to do this solo."

"You are putting me in an impossible situation," complained Kemper.

"This *is* an impossible situation."

Kemper calmed and said, "I guess I don't have much choice. But I hope you know what you're doing."

Decker clicked off and stared down at his phone.

Jamison said, "Do you?"

"Do I what?" he asked quietly.

"Know what you're doing?"

"I'll be able to answer that after they call me."

"We can't lose Amber and Zoe."

"We won't."

"You can't be sure of that," she exclaimed.

"No, I can't," he conceded.

"Then what are you telling me?" she demanded.

"I promised Zoe that I wouldn't let the bad guys get you. And now I'm promising you that I'm not going to let them hurt Zoe, or your sister."

Jamison pulled out her gun and looked at it. "Oh, we're going to get them back safe, Decker. And then we're going to nail every one of these assholes right to the wall."

70

THE CALL CAME at midnight.

Before Decker could answer it, Jamison had snatched the phone away.

"I want to hear Amber and Zoe's voice, right now," she said into the phone.

"Who is this?"

"Alex Jamison with the FBI, and the seriously pissed-off sister and aunt of the people you kidnapped. Put them on the phone. Now!"

"You're making demands?" the person said.

"No, I'm making *one* demand. Put them on the phone."

There were a few moments of silence.

"Alex?"

It was Amber. She sounded exactly as she should: terrified.

"Are you okay, Am? Have they hurt you?"

"No, they haven't."

"And Zoe?"

"She's right here with me. She's okay too, just scared."

Jamison turned to Decker and mouthed, "They're okay."

Amber continued, "Only I don't know what they—"

The other person came back on. "Okay, you've heard them. Now hear me. You want them back, you will do exactly as I say."

Jamison handed the phone to Decker.

"I'm listening," said Decker. "What do you want in exchange for them?"

"We want Fred Ross."

"I don't know if I can make that happen."

"You better hope you can. Or else the next time you see the woman and the kid, they'll be corpses."

"Where and when?"

The man gave Decker the location and time. "You bring anybody with you, they're dead."

"And you're just going to let us walk out with Amber and Zoe?"

"You bring us Ross, we have no reason to harm any of you. We just want the old man."

"I didn't think Ted was that fond of his father."

"Just bring him! One minute late, they're dead."

Decker put down the phone.

"What do they want?" Jamison asked.

"They want an exchange."

"An exchange? What does that mean?"

"Fred Ross for Amber and Zoe."

"Why would they want Fred Ross?"

"Probably because he can testify against them."

"But he's in jail!"

"Then we need to get him out of jail."

"How?"

Decker was already on his phone.

Kemper answered on the first ring.

"They want Fred Ross in exchange for Amber and Zoe."

"Okay."

"You'll need to arrange for Ross to be released into our custody."

"I can make that happen. Where and when do they want to meet?"

Decker told her and added, "The guy said if we bring anybody, Amber and Zoe are dead."

"Decker, you're not that naïve. You go there without any backup, you're all dead."

"Which is why you're going to get there before us. You got a chopper available?"

"Yes."

"Then I suggest you fill it up with agents and get in position. When the crap hits the fan, it's going to get hairy for everyone."

"This is what we do for a living, Decker. See you on the other side."

Decker clicked off and looked at Jamison.

She said, "They said not to bring anyone."

"I know what they said. But they're not going to let me just walk away with Amber and Zoe."

Jamison looked up at him angrily. "You?! Do you really think I'd let you march in there alone? Where you go, *I* go."

Decker's ringing phone interrupted this discussion.

He recognized the number and answered it.

Cindi Riley barked, "What the hell is going on?"

"With what?" he said. "And why are you calling so late?"

"Because you're my last chance for John."

Decker said, "What about him?"

"He finally let me pay his bail. But they still wouldn't release him."

"Why not?"

"Because they said Detective Lassiter had to sign off on it," she said.

"That doesn't make sense. But she's in the hospital. She was shot."

"No, she's not in the hospital."

Decker tensed. "What do you mean?"

"I mean they told me at the police station that she was in the hospital, so I called over there to talk to her. I was going to bring the paperwork there."

"And what did they tell you?"

"That she checked herself out," she said.

"Checked herself out?" said an incredulous Decker. "She was shot, how could she check herself out?"

"I don't know. But that's what they said."

"Have you tried calling her cell?"

"About a dozen times. No answer. What does this mean, Decker?"

He didn't answer her right away. "It means that we'll meet you at the jail in about ten minutes."

FRED ROSS LOOKED up at Decker with a malicious grin.

"Figured I might see you again, fat boy."

An officer had wheeled Ross down the hall and into the lobby of the police station, where Decker, Jamison, and Riley met him.

Decker ignored this and looked at the duty officer. "We also need to pick up John Baron. His bail's been paid."

The duty officer said, "We can't release him until Detective Lassiter signs off."

"Detective Lassiter has gone AWOL."

"That doesn't matter—" began the officer.

Decker slammed his fist down on the counter. "I'll tell you what matters." He pointed to Riley. "She paid the bail set by the judge. You have the paperwork in hand. Lassiter doesn't have to sign off on shit. So unless you want a big-ass lawsuit against this town that'll drain the little money it has left, you better go get John Baron right now." He held up his phone. "And if you don't, a team of FBI agents will be here in about ten minutes and they're going to arrest you and everybody else in this fucking place."

The duty officer stiffened like Decker had just clocked him.

Someone behind them said, "Hey, Agent Decker."

Decker turned to see Officer Curry standing there.

"I take it you've got a problem?" said Curry.

"My problem is bail has been paid, the paperwork has been filed, and this guy won't release the prisoner because Detective Lassiter won't sign off on it. But Detective Lassiter, who was supposedly shot today, has checked herself out of the hospital and *conveniently* disappeared."

Curry glanced at the duty officer and then back at Decker.

"I'll go get Baron for you right now."

"But Detective Lassiter—" the duty officer began.

"Shut the hell up, Bobby," said Curry. He turned and walked off.

A minute later he was back with Baron.

Decker said, "I appreciate the assist."

"No problem. I'm getting sick of all the crap happening in this place," said Curry. He put his hand on his gun and glared over at the duty officer before returning his gaze to Decker.

"How about I stay here and make sure that no one gets a heads-up about anything you might be planning?"

"I would appreciate that even more," said Decker. He looked at the rack of shotguns behind the duty counter. "And while you're doling out favors, you mind if I borrow one of those shotguns? It might come in handy."

"No problem." Curry looked at Bobby, the duty officer. "Give it to him."

"I can't—"

Curry drew his pistol. "Now!"

Bobby unlocked the rack, took out a shotgun and a box of shells, and handed them to Decker.

"Good luck, Decker," said Curry.

"Thanks."

Decker handed the gun and shells to Jamison and wheeled Ross out to their SUV. He and Baron lifted the old man into the backseat and Decker stowed the wheelchair in the rear cargo area.

They climbed into the truck, with Decker in the driver's seat.

"What in the hell is going on?" said Baron.

"A lot," replied Decker. He pulled out his phone.

"Who are you calling?" asked Jamison.

"Nobody. I'm doing some fast research."

"On what?"

"Australia."

He scrolled through screen pages for a few minutes.

"Decker, we're going to be late for the exchange!" snapped Jamison.

"No we're not."

He read through the screens for another few minutes and then he sent off a lengthy text. Only then did he put the phone away and start the truck.

"Find what you needed?" asked Jamison.

He nodded. "Yeah, I found pretty much everything."

* * *

They drove fast and were soon out of the downtown area.

From the backseat Fred Ross said, "Wait a minute. This isn't—"

He clamped his mouth shut.

"This isn't the way to the exchange?" said Decker. "I thought you might have known about that since this conspiracy reaches all the way into the police department. But you're right, it's not the way to the exchange. I'd rather go where the real action is."

"What are you talking about?" said Jamison in a worried tone.

"Trust me, Alex, I know what I'm doing."

"Well, *I* don't trust easily," interjected Baron.

Decker said, "If I were you, I wouldn't either. In fact, I'm not sure I'd trust anybody in this damn town."

They began the climb up the winding road leading to the top of the hill where the Baron mansion was located.

Baron looked around, puzzled, and said, "Why are we going to my house?"

"Because I want you to meet the people who tried their best to send you to death row."

72

Decker stopped the truck before they got to the front drive leading to the mansion. He cut the engine and looked around.

"What are we going to do now?" Jamison said.

His phone dinged and Decker took a few moments to read it. It was the answer to the text he had sent previously.

"Finish this, I hope," he said to Jamison.

"But what about the exchange for Amber and Zoe?" she exclaimed. "We've got to get them back."

"We will, because they're *here*, Alex."

"Here! But the exchange spot is over four hours away."

"Which is what they wanted us to think." He looked at Fred Ross. "Right?"

Ross eyed Decker darkly. "You got no idea who you're dealing with, fatso."

"Yeah, so everybody keeps telling me."

They climbed out of the truck. Decker went to the rear cargo area and took out the collapsible wheelchair and set it up.

Baron said, "Decker, we can just leave this creep here. He can't go anywhere."

"No, we need him. But we have to take an obvious precaution." He took out a roll of duct tape from a toolkit in the back and, despite the old man trying to stop him, taped Ross's mouth shut. Next, he put the struggling Ross in the wheelchair, and then bound his forearms to the arms of the wheelchair.

He took out the shotgun and shells from the front seat and handed them to Baron. "I assume you know how to use it?" he said.

Baron expertly loaded in five shells and looked up. "Lord-of-the-Manor 101 stuff."

Decker took control of the wheelchair. As they reached the asphalt in the front court of the house he picked up his speed but then stopped.

They had reached the potting shed. On one side of it was a huge mound of dirt and the door to the shed was open.

"What the hell is going on?" exclaimed Baron. "Who dug that up? And why is the door open?"

"They were obviously looking for the treasure here," said Decker. "Hold on." He left them and crossed over to the potting shed. Using his cell phone flashlight, he climbed down into the hole. They saw his light flashing around for about a minute before he emerged. Next, he went into the shed. Less than a minute later he came back out and rejoined them.

"What did you find?" asked Jamison.

"Exactly what I thought I would: nothing."

"And inside?"

"They broke through the floor, but it was just set on a thin concrete slab with dirt under it."

"So what does that mean?" said Riley.

"That means we keep going to where the treasure really is."

They took the paved road that led off to the right. As they approached the end of the road, Decker stopped and wheeled Ross off to the side.

He took out his gun and Jamison did the same, while Baron brandished the shotgun. They all followed Decker down the road. They cleared the curve and looked up ahead.

There was a lot of activity going on.

They noted a large dump truck parked in front of the gates of the family cemetery. Attached to it was an empty flatbed trailer. They watched as a Bobcat sped past the truck and entered the burial ground. Two SUVs were parked next to the dump truck, and through the open gate they could see people moving around inside the burial ground.

Decker skittered forward with the others close behind him. The sounds of the Bobcat covered any noise they made. Decker opened the back door of one of the SUVs and looked inside one of the duffels piled there. It was filled with the same bottles he had found in Ross's secret closet.

He quietly closed the door and they edged up to the gate and peered inside. A group of people were gathered around the mausoleum. Portable work lights had been set up, illuminating the area around the crypt.

"There's Ross," hissed Jamison.

"And Lassiter," whispered Riley. "But I thought she'd been shot?"

One of the detective's arms was in a sling and she was moving slowly.

Decker said, "She was, but not nearly as bad as everyone probably thought."

A large hole had been dug next to the mausoleum and they could hear what sounded like a powerful drill being operated. After a few minutes, Ross took a light and disappeared into the hole, with Lassiter right behind him.

Decker counted ten other men with guns standing around.

A few minutes later, Ross and Lassiter came out of the hole. Neither looked pleased.

"Decker," said Jamison, pointing to her left.

Off to the side, seated on the ground, their backs against a large gravestone, were Amber and Zoe. They were tied up and gagged.

Decker slipped away and returned a minute later pushing Fred Ross in his wheelchair.

He rolled him past the dump truck and edged the wheelchair into the open gateway of the graveyard. He traded his pistol for the shotgun Baron was holding, and then pressed the barrel against Ross's neck.

He looked at the others and nodded. Baron and Jamison took up positions on either side of the brick wall, their guns pointed at Lassiter and the others. Cindi Riley peered anxiously over Baron's shoulder.

Decker called out, "Okay, we're here for the exchange."

Everyone next to the mausoleum froze. Then Lassiter and Ted Ross slowly turned and saw the elder Ross with Decker holding a shotgun against the old man's head.

Ross shook his head, put his hands on his hips, and smiled. He glanced at Lassiter. "How many damn times did I tell you we had to get rid of this guy, Donna!"

Lassiter called out to Decker, "This was not smart coming here."

Decker used his free hand to point to Amber and Zoe. "It's the only place we *could* go. The exchange, remember? You set it up, not me."

"This is not going to end well for you," said Lassiter.

Decker said, "You really should have posted some lookouts, Ross."

"I guess I underestimated you, Decker."

"I like it when people do that. I assume you have an escape plan. You give us Amber and Zoe. And we give you this piece of scum, and you make your run for it."

"It's not that simple," said Ross.

Decker glanced at the mausoleum. "Because you haven't found it?"

Ross's smile faded. "Found what?"

"The treasure that Baron the First left behind."

"How do you know anything about it?" snapped Lassiter.

"I know all about it. But why do you need the treasure? You haven't made enough off the fentanyl?"

Ross glanced at Baron. "It has nothing to do with that. It's about the fact that I can take it from *him*!"

Fred Ross was wriggling in his wheelchair.

"You want to throw in your two cents?" asked Decker. He reached down and ripped the tape from the man's mouth.

Fred Ross screamed, "Shoot the son of a bitch, Teddy. Kill his ass!"

"Shut up, Pop," said his son derisively. He looked back at Decker. "Well?"

"Like I said, I think we can work something out."

Ross looked at the mausoleum. "Okay, you tell us where it is and you can have mom and the daughter." He pointed his gun at his father. "And you can keep him too, because I've had enough of his crap to last the rest of my life."

Fred Ross screamed, "You little piece of worthless shit! I was the one that told you about it. You ungrateful bastard!" A long flow of obscenities followed, all directed at the man's son.

"See what I mean?" said Ted Ross as he raised his pistol. "Shut up, Pop, or I swear to God, I'll shoot you myself."

Decker said, "Fred, you're not that smart, are you?"

"What the hell is that supposed to mean, fatso?"

"You knew about the exchange. But when we got there, nobody would be around to exchange for you. So your son was going to leave your butt high and dry. You go to prison while he jets off to a new life."

The elder Ross said nothing, but he now glared at his son.

Decker said to Ted Ross, "That was the other reason I knew your exchange request was probably a sham and that you were up here trying to get the treasure." He glanced at the malignant Fred Ross. "Why would you want him back? The guy who was so cruel to you and your mother? Just so he couldn't testify against you? Hell, if it were me, I'd take my chances over having to listen to this asshole and I think you would too."

A fresh burst of obscenities from Fred Ross was only halted when Decker put the duct tape back on.

Decker looked at the hole next to the mausoleum. "You thought it was either under the potting shed or under the crypt? Because of the letter to the O'Reilly company?"

"Not nearly enough concrete for a textile mill addition," said Ross. "Besides that, old man Baron would not have built one at that point, because the business was going south. But he used it for the foundation under his crypt. We know that now."

Decker nodded. "Green told me about the textile business petering out when he was giving us a little tutorial on Baronville. Although he couldn't have known that later I would see a letter that would put that knowledge to good use. So what do you think the treasure is?"

"Precious jewels, maybe. Coins. Cash would have rotted."

Decker nodded. "Did you find anything down there?"

"A big hollow space inside the foundation they laid with all that concrete."

"With something other than treasure?" said Decker. "Like some skeletons maybe?"

Ross said, "There *are* some bones down there. But how did you figure that?"

"Baron was an old man. He didn't hide the stuff personally. So how could he leave behind the guys who *did* hide it? They'd just come here and try to steal it after he died, or else they'd tell somebody. And that space would make a convenient burial spot."

"But where is the treasure?" snapped Ross impatiently.

"The O'Reilly order told you, but you focused on the *wrong* parts of the letter."

"Then enlighten me," growled Ross.

"I read a letter from Baron's butler, Nigel, to his son. Costa read it too. That was a clue to the treasure."

"Costa never told me about any letter like that."

"But he obviously thought it was under the mausoleum."

"Costa had done a ton of research. He'd read a lot about the history of the estate and he thought he had narrowed down the location, but he wanted to be sure. We needed somebody to come up here. So I called Toby Babbot."

"Why Babbot?"

"He'd gotten hurt working on the FC. I was throwing him a bone. Anyway, he did some poking around. See, Costa had determined that there were only *two* new structures put up after Baron wrote the letter to O'Reilly ordering those supplies: the potting shed and this place. So Toby came up here and took precise measurements of both. He figured the footprint of either one pretty much aligned with a concrete foundation built with the materials that Baron bought from O'Reilly's."

"And Baron caught him trespassing and filed a police report?"

"Well, actually Mike Swanson was also up here when Toby was poking around. He and Baron chased him off the property. Swanson knew Toby and apparently identified him to Baron, and Baron filed the police report. But that was no big deal," Ross added offhandedly.

"Actually, it was a *very* big deal for Babbot *and* Swanson. Because that signed both their death warrants, in your eyes," added Decker. "Baron now had a beef and a possible motive against Babbot, so you could include him with the others you killed in order to incriminate Baron. And because of Babbot, you knew Swanson was up here, probably with drugs. You could also use that to frame Baron, and you needed to get Swanson out of the picture." He paused. "And I think you had another reason to get rid of Babbot."

Ross stared darkly at Decker but remained silent.

"He found out about the space in your office, where you kept the fentanyl shipments. He was obviously good at measuring: the mausoleum *and* your office footprint."

"I thought there was a bottle missing from one of the boxes. That was you?"

"That was me."

"Donna told me about your finding out Toby had the construction plans for the FC. But I never thought you would put two and two together. You made it sound to her like Toby just had a beef with Maxus because of how they treated him."

"I got lucky there because I didn't know at the time that Lassiter was a bad cop."

Lassiter barked, "You know nothing about me."

"I know enough," said Decker.

Ross said, "So getting back to business, what was in the letter from this Nigel guy?"

"It told about a trip that Baron and Nigel took to Australia."

"Australia? What about it?"

"They visited the typical places. But then there were a number listed that I'd never heard of. I googled them before I came here. Only one of them interested me: Kalgoorlie."

"What's so special about this Kalgoorlie place?" asked Ross.

"I'll show you. You got a sledgehammer?"

Ross glanced at the mausoleum. "Why? The treasure's not here."

"I think it *is* here. It's what I meant when I said you'd focused on the *wrong* parts of the O'Reilly letter. Have one of your guys take a sledgehammer to the *wall* of the mausoleum." Decker pointed at the wall right behind Ross. "*That* wall."

Ross jerked his head around. "Why?"

"Just do it, you got nothing to lose if I'm wrong," said Decker.

Ross ordered one of his men to grab a sledgehammer and attack the mausoleum. The man hefted the tool and slung it against the wall. The marble cracked. He did it again, and then again. A chunk of the marble fell off. The man kept hitting it until revealed behind the marble was a large section of mortared bricks framed by the marble.

Ross looked over at Decker. "What the hell is going on? They're just damn bricks!"

"Loosen one up and take it out."

The man did as Decker said, using a crowbar. When he finally pulled out a brick, he stumbled under its weight and nearly dropped it on the ground.

"It's heavy as hell," said the man as he set it down in the dirt.

"Gold usually is," said Decker.

Ross exclaimed, "*Gold!* You're saying the whole mausoleum is made of gold?"

"No, I think just that wall." Decker pointed to the ground. "That's why the crypt is only sunken on this side. That was the reason for the concrete foundation—to keep it stable because of the added weight of the gold. Only over the years it didn't work out so well. The gold's under the brick veneer."

"Check it," Ross ordered another of his men.

The man grabbed a chisel and hammer and worked away at the brick until he had chipped off part. He gasped and looked up. Ross held a work light over the brick. The veneer of brick was gone and underneath was a lustrous gold color.

Decker said, "Now you can see the connection to Australia."

Ross glanced at him. "But what is this Kalgoorlie place?"

"Kalgoorlie is the site of the Golden Mile, perhaps the greatest concentration of gold deposits on earth."

Lassiter said, "But how did you figure that out?"

"I couldn't think of another reason why Baron would have gone there. From all accounts, he just cared about making money, not taking vacations. He engaged a private ship, and brought back a fortune, probably in gold dust and nuggets. And then he turned it into gold bars covered by a brick overlay, using the molds he ordered from O'Reilly's."

Ross looked at the large wall of bricks and did a swift calculation. "There must be hundreds and hundreds of gold bars in there."

"Must be," agreed Decker.

"But Decker, how did you work out it was in the wall of the mausoleum?" asked Lassiter. "Not just from the thing being partially sunk in the dirt."

"I knew something that you didn't, and neither did Costa." He pointed to Baron. "He let me in the mausoleum when we first came up here. Inside, I saw that a couple of walls were fouled with the stains that you would expect to see in an old burial vault. But on the interior *that* wall was all covered with white streaks just like it is on the outside. Over time brick and mortar will leach out white alkaline. You've probably seen it on brick chimneys and walls. It actually happened to my house back in Ohio, and the guy who repaired it told me about it. Now, marble is a porous material, so what's underneath it will eventually end up on the outside of it. Knowing from the O'Reilly letter that Baron had purchased molds and clay, I knew he was going to make bricks. I also figured the brick was probably under the marble and that the white alkaline had eventually leached through. Coupled with the trip to Kalgoorlie, it made me think that concealed in the brick were the gold bars. And on the inside of the mausoleum I noticed that the interior was about a foot narrower on that side of the wall." He rubbed his leg. "I smacked my leg on a crypt because it was jutting out farther than the ones on the other side." He glanced at Ross. "Sort of like in your office. The extra space was to accommodate the brick. The other walls didn't need that additional space. They were just solid marble."

"But why bother covering the gold with brick veneer if the bars were going to be inside a wall?" asked Ross.

"Well, even though they were heavy, it would at least hide the gold bars from the workers who built the mausoleum, and if the marble ever got damaged it would just reveal bricks underneath and nothing more, just like you thought when your guy opened up the wall."

"But who killed the men and put them under the crypt?" asked Baron.

Decker shrugged. "For all I know, Baron the First and his butler did. They could have put the bodies inside that chamber and then had somebody come in and close it up. In fact, in the letter to his son, Nigel said it was possible that he might end up in hell and he was sort of asking for God's forgiveness. That might have been his guilt as a murderer coming out."

"What would a wall of gold be worth, do you think?" Ross asked.

Decker quickly tallied the number of bricks on the wall. "Gold's over thirteen hundred bucks an ounce now. A gold bar like that weighs over twelve kilos or about twenty-six pounds. So that one bar would be worth nearly six hundred thousand dollars."

Lassiter exclaimed, "Oh my God. Each bar?"

"Yeah," said Decker as he ran his gaze over the crypt wall. "I'd say you're looking at maybe nine hundred bricks or so. Maybe more."

"So that means..." said Ross, obviously trying to do the math in his head.

But John Baron answered. "That comes to over half a billion dollars in gold."

"And despite the old saying, Baron the First apparently wanted to take it *all* with him when he died," quipped Decker. "That's why I knew the gold wouldn't be in the potting shed."

Lassiter said, "God, I knew old man Baron was rich, but damn."

Decker said, "Well, gold was a lot cheaper back then. Turned out to be a good investment."

Ross lifted his gaze from the gold bar to Decker. "So, do we have a deal?"

"Actually, I don't really see how that could happen," said Decker. "You've killed at least ten people that I know of, including my partner's brother-in-law, not to mention thousands more who've overdosed on the crap you've been selling. So I'm actually here to arrest you."

Ross looked at Decker like he was insane. "Okay. But you're outgunned and in no position to negotiate. And I've got hostages you want back. All you've got is my old man, who I could give a damn about."

"No, you've got it all wrong, because you made a big mistake."

"What's that?" said Ross warily.

In answer, Decker used his free hand to take out his phone. It was on, and in speaker mode. "Assuming I'd be stupid enough to come here without any backup."

73

The lights hit them from all directions.

Long guns slid over the brick walls of the burial ground as the men there stood on breach ladders.

A voice on a PA called out, "Federal agents! Guns down! On the ground, hands behind your heads! Now!"

A chopper emblazoned with DEA on the side suddenly roared over the tree line and cast its spotlight down on them. Assault rifles were trained from the bird on Ross and his group down below.

In the cemetery, some of Ross's men fired up at the chopper and at the armed men who had suddenly appeared at the top of the brick wall.

Shots rang out all over. The burial ground was quickly shrouded in smoke from all the discharging weapons.

Flash-bangs went off and people screamed. The smoke grew denser. The screams grew louder.

Decker quickly pushed Fred Ross's wheelchair over next to one of the SUVs.

"Keep your head down," he told the old man before rejoining the others.

Jamison shouted to Decker, "I'll get Amber and Zoe."

She sprinted forward, with John Baron joining her.

Ross and one of his men had also raced toward the hostages.

The two groups clashed right in front of Amber and Zoe.

Ross started to point his weapon at Jamison.

"You piece of shit!" screamed Jamison.

She kicked the gun out of his hand and drove her fist into his nose, and when he staggered back in pain, she nailed him with her knee directly in his crotch. He went down and stayed there. Just to be sure, she jerked his hands behind his back and cuffed him.

Meanwhile, Baron gripped the gun hand of the other man, stripped him of the weapon, bent his arm behind his back, and launched him headfirst into a granite tombstone. The man slumped to the ground and didn't move.

Jamison lifted Zoe up into her arms and Baron helped Amber to her feet. They took cover behind a crypt as the firefight continued.

Jamison slipped off Zoe's gag and the little girl looked up in amazement at her aunt.

"Aunt Alex, what you did, that…that was so cool."

At the gate of the cemetery, something came out of the smoky darkness and struck Decker. He stumbled to the side, slammed into the wrought iron gate, lost his balance, and fell down.

Cindi Riley helped him up as shots continued to ring out and people screamed inside the grounds.

Decker could hear feet running away into the darkness. It had to be the person who had struck him.

He looked into the graveyard and as the smoke cleared he saw several of Ross's men down on the ground. Others were on their knees, their hands over their heads.

Body-armored DEA agents with assault weapons were swiftly moving in and taking control of the situation. The short battle was over.

The chopper had landed next to the cemetery and Agent Kemper jumped out and hurried over to them.

She said, "I have to tell you, that text you sent telling me to come here blew me away. But I trusted you and it damn sure paid off."

Decker nodded and looked over at where Baron and Jamison were escorting Amber and Zoe to a group of DEA agents.

"Did you use rubber bullets?" asked Decker.

She nodded. "Like you suggested. We figure we can get these guys to turn on whoever they're working for higher up the food chain."

As the smoke cleared further, Riley said, "Decker, I see Ted Ross, but not Lassiter."

They all looked over to see Ross, his face bloodied from Jamison's blow, being hauled to his feet by two agents.

Decker said. "Someone ran off back toward the house. It was probably Lassiter."

"We'll get her," said Kemper confidently. "This place is surrounded. I have agents barricading the road up. There's no way out."

Decker glanced over at the SUVs. Ross and his wheelchair were gone.

He rushed over there only to find pieces of duct tape on the ground. The old man must have managed to free himself somehow.

Kemper joined him a moment later.

"What is it?" she said.

"Fred Ross is out there in his wheelchair somewhere," added Decker.

Kemper smiled. "Again, not a problem. Thanks for the assist, Decker."

She left to confer with some of her men and to confront Ted Ross.

Decker watched her go for a few moments and then looked at Riley.

"Go help the others. I'll be back."

Before Riley could say anything, he had already hustled off.

A few minutes later he emerged from the road to the cemetery and looked up toward the house. He stopped and gazed around, listening for someone running. He heard nothing and started moving again. He was listening for the sound of Ross's wheelchair, but again he heard nothing.

Where could the old man have gone?

He picked up his pace. And where was Lassiter? She couldn't leave on foot. She would easily be caught. But with a *vehicle* she might have a shot at running Kemper's barricade. Decker had the keys to the truck they'd driven up in. But he knew there was *another* vehicle available.

He hustled toward the garage.

Right as he got there, the truck started up. He heard gears gnashing and the old Suburban hurtled backward out of the garage bay.

He had to throw himself sideways to avoid being run over.

He rolled and sat up as Lassiter spun the wheel and the Suburban cut a one-eighty, its hood pointed toward the road.

From a kneeling position, Decker settled the shotgun's stock against his shoulder and took aim.

"Get out of the truck, Lassiter! Or I open fire."

Her answer was five pistol shots fired at him through the open driver's side window.

Fortunately, she couldn't really aim and drive at the same time, so her rounds sailed wide.

Decker fired several shotgun blasts at the side of the truck.

The pellets slammed into the old Suburban, blowing out both tires, shattering a window, and pockmarking the doors.

Lassiter screamed and a few moments later the passenger door flew open. He heard feet hit the dirt and then she was running away.

Lassiter came into his sightline and he watched as she ran to the front door of the mansion and disappeared inside.

He slowly walked up to the truck and peered inside.

He saw the blood inside the cab, so he knew he'd hit her.

He followed the trail of blood to the front door and poked his head inside.

He heard it before he could see her.

Moaning.

He made his way slowly down the grand hall, peering cautiously into each room he passed. The sounds of moaning were growing louder, but in this cavernous place they seemed to echo everywhere.

He stopped and listened intently.

"Decker?"

He took a few steps forward and peered into the gun room.

Lassiter was sitting on the floor with her back against the wall.

The arm that had been in the sling was bloody and hanging limply by her side.

Decker fixed his gaze on the pistol in her right hand.

"Yeah?" he said.

"Go to hell!"

"It's over, Donna. So put the gun down and I can get you some medical attention."

She laughed, grimaced, turned to the side, and threw up.

She wiped her mouth with her gun hand and looked over at Decker standing in the doorway. "You got me good, Decker." She touched the muzzle of the gun against the side of her bloody face. "Not so pretty anymore, am I?" She laughed and then doubled up in pain.

"Why, Donna? You're a cop."

She sat up straighter. "Too much money, Decker. Too damn much."

Lassiter groaned and slumped back against the wall.

"You also wanted to stick it to Baron, because of your dad. And your mom."

She pointed to the bloody sling on the floor. "The plan was to take out Marty and Alice when we were transporting them. Then they were going to shoot at me and a couple others to make it look legit. Only the damn round glanced off my body armor and knocked out my left arm. Had to down some serious painkillers just to function. Then you really messed it up with your shotgun. Feels like it's going to fall off. And I think my lung's filling up with blood."

"You made a mistake in checking yourself out of the hospital. That's what led me here."

She waggled her head. "Had to. I couldn't trust Ted not to screw me."

"Right, honor among thieves. Why all the crap with Beatty and Smith? Freezing their bodies and dumping them in that house?"

"I knew our ME was incompetent. But we knew the DEA might swoop in after they were identified, so Ross thought the freezing would help us there." She coughed up some blood. "But if

I'd known you were in the house behind it, believe me, we'd have dumped them miles away."

"Put down the gun, Donna, and let me get you some help. You're not going to make it otherwise."

"Who gives a shit!" She paused and took in a long, ragged breath, no doubt drawing more blood into her damaged lung. "Baronville! This place sucks all the life out of you. Every time I saw that name on every damn street or building, it made me want to blow my frigging brains out. My dad was a good guy. This place ruined him. It ruined everything!"

Decker said, "You went to Philly for college. You could've stayed there."

She shook her head. "Had to move back here, take care of my mom. Then she killed herself anyway. By then, I'm stuck."

"Right, your crappy life, it's somebody else's problem."

"You're damn right it is." She waggled her head again. "All that gold. What did he say, half a billion?"

"Something like that. But it's just money, Donna."

She laughed bitterly. "Easy to say unless you don't have any." She groaned and clutched her side. "Shit, it hurts so bad."

"Put down the gun, Donna. I can get you some help for the pain, but you have to put the gun down first."

She sat up straighter and her features calmed a bit. "I'm gonna get the death penalty, Decker," she said quietly. "All the stuff I've done."

"Even if you do, it never happens fast."

Decker could tell that her blood loss was nearing the critical stage. She started to stammer. "I'm n-not going to prison. Ex-cop. Not going to p-prison. No way. N-no way."

"You don't want to do that," said Decker, seeing where this was going.

"I was a g-good cop. I really was. And…and then it all w-went t-to h-hell."

Decker could see that her face was growing pale as her blood pressure dropped with each pump of her heart. There was clearly only one outcome now.

"How'd you get hooked up with Ross?" he asked, trying to distract her.

She seemed to perk up with his query and said clearly, "Known him forever. He needed some help on the inside. He knew about my dad, and my mom. He knew I was kind of desperate. He made me an offer I couldn't refuse."

"Alice Martin didn't know about you, did she?"

She shook her head. "T-to her, I was the nice, good c-cop."

"What about Green?"

She shook her head again. "Nobody knew about me other than Ross. He had Marty and a bunch of other cops on the payroll. But I was the f-fail-safe. Otherwise, Marty c-could've fingered me when you nailed him on Bond's m-murder."

"Put the gun down, Donna."

"Not gonna do that." She looked up at him with pleading eyes. "Shoot me, Decker." She pointed to her forehead with her gun muzzle. "Right here. Please. Fellow cop asking a favor. Just do it."

"I'm sorry, I can't do that."

"Okay, I just thought I'd ask," she said grimly.

She stuck the pistol in her mouth, closed her eyes, and pulled the trigger.

Decker didn't react to this. In fact, he knew it was the logical outcome. And maybe it was better that way. He stepped over to the body, which had slumped sideways. The wall behind Lassiter was smeared with her blood and brains.

As Decker looked down at the body he closed his eyes as the electric blue color that he normally associated with death flashed across his mind. The hairs on the back of his neck stood up, and he felt slightly nauseous and claustrophobic.

He almost had to smile, and would have if he hadn't been standing over Lassiter's corpse. She was a bad cop, for sure. But she was still a cop. And he wasn't going to celebrate her death.

Yet maybe tomorrow he would be the same old Decker after all, at least the one the blindside hit had created. And in a world that seemed to be nothing except unpredictable, maybe that was as good as it got.

74

"WHAT WAS THAT?"

Baron, Jamison, and Riley were leading Amber and Zoe back up the road toward the house when Baron had stopped and stiffened. His gaze was pointed down the path that cut through the woods.

"What was what?" asked Jamison.

"I heard a sound down that way."

"You think it might be Decker?"

"It's not me," said Decker.

He had appeared in the road leading from the house.

"Decker, where were you?" asked Jamison.

"At the house, with Lassiter."

"What happened?" asked Jamison.

Decker glanced at Zoe. The little girl looked exhausted and scared.

"I'll tell you later. I just got a text from Kemper. She called an ambulance for Amber and Zoe. It'll meet you in front of the house. Alex, can you and Cindi take them up there and wait with them?"

"Why, where are you going?"

"I think John and I have someplace to check out."

Baron was still staring down the path.

Jamison glanced at Baron and then back at Decker. "I think I'll come with you."

"No, you need to go with your sister and niece. You have a gun and I don't know who else might be out there. Kemper's sending some agents to you. Until they get here, you need to stay with them."

Jamison looked torn.

"Okay, but can you at least tell me where you're going?"

Decker, his gaze on Baron, said, "Maybe into the past."

* * *

As Baron and Decker headed down the path, Baron looked at him. "You know where this leads, right?"

"I do."

"And do you hear what I'm hearing?"

"I do," Decker said again.

"But he would have no way of knowing about this. He would never have been here."

"He would have *one* way of knowing about it," replied Decker.

They cleared the trees and in front of them the large pond appeared.

They stopped walking as they both saw it at the same time.

Fred Ross was in his wheelchair at the edge of the water.

"Mr. Ross?" said Decker. "Going somewhere?"

Ross swiveled around in his chair and saw them. His mouth freed from the duct tape, he hurled one curse after another at them.

Baron started marching down toward the old man and Decker followed.

Before they reached him, Ross lurched sideways and turned over his wheelchair. He started clawing his way to the water, his useless legs dragging in the mud.

Baron stepped in front of him and looked down.

Ross looked up at him. "If I had my damn shotgun," he snarled.

"Only you don't," said Decker. "How'd you manage to get loose?"

"You didn't tape my arms that tight. Had some wiggle room. All I needed. Probably thought because I'm old I'm weak. Well, I'm stronger than I look, fat boy, from working hard all my life and pushing myself around in that metal cage all this time."

Baron said, "How did you know this pond was even here?"

Ross laughed. "How do you think I know?"

Decker knelt down next to Ross. "Why did you kill his parents?"

Baron shot Decker a stunned look and then stared back at Ross.

"They were Barons. Ain't that reason enough?"

"Why in the pond?"

"Because I didn't want to get caught, that's why, you dumb son of a bitch."

"Why were you up here in the first place?" asked Decker.

"Looking for it, wasn't I?"

"The treasure?"

Ross eyed him shrewdly and nodded.

"How'd you even hear about it?" asked Baron.

"When she was younger, my grandmother worked up at your damn *mansion* as a maid. That fancy-ass butler was an old man then, and he would get drunk and run his mouth in the kitchen. Right before he died, he bragged to my grandmother that he was going to be buried with Baron. He was so giddy about it. Like that made him somebody. And he said that Baron wasn't going to leave much of anything to his kids. He was just going to hide his money from those spoiled brats because they were nothing to him. Somewhere up on the estate, he said. Well, she told my mom and my mom told me. One night years later, I went up there to look for it, but couldn't find it. Figured I'd get the damn Barons to tell me."

"They didn't know either, you idiot!" roared Baron. "Do you think if they did they wouldn't have already gotten it?"

Ross ignored him and kept his gaze on Decker. "Only they wouldn't tell me. I got even more pissed and knocked 'em in the head, put 'em in their fancy car, and drove it over here and rolled it right into the water."

"But how did you know about the path or the pond?" asked Decker.

"My grandma told my mom." He looked at Baron. "She said the high-and-mighty Barons used to come here for picnics and shit. I figured I'd give 'em a *picnic*, all right. Twenty feet under." Ross eyed the water. "And then I went back to work at the damn textile mill and got paralyzed." He glared at the wheelchair. "Been trapped in that piece of shit ever since."

"Well, they say God works in mysterious ways," said Decker disdainfully. "But what are you doing here now?"

"Hell, I ain't going to prison. Rather drown my ass."

Baron pulled his gun and pointed it at Ross. "How about I do the honors?"

The old man grinned maliciously up at him. "Yeah, you go ahead, prick. Pull that trigger."

Baron cocked the hammer.

"Do it, rich boy, do it. I dare you," squealed Ross.

Decker said, "He wants you to do it, John, because then he knows I'll have to arrest you. It would be like he'd be killing you too, just like he did your parents. You gonna let him sucker you like that?"

Baron pressed the barrel against Ross's forehead and held it there until the old man started to shake with fear and tears spilled out of his eyes.

Then he uncocked the hammer and handed it to Decker with a smile. "You can't be serious. I'm far too *high-and-mighty* to fall for that."

Ross cursed and spit at him, even as Baron righted the wheelchair, lifted the old man up, and placed him back in it.

"Come on, Mr. Ross, I'll even push you right up to the paddy wagon. You can ride to jail with your son. Two peas in a thoroughly rotten pod."

Decker leaned down to stare at Ross.

"You were wrong."

"About what?" snapped Ross.

"There *are* some things illegal in Baronville."

As they headed back up through the woods Baron looked over at Decker.

"The only friend I have is Cindi Riley."

"I know."

"Until now, that is." He paused and stopped pushing the wheelchair. "I count you and Alex as friends. It's very clear where I would be without both of you caring enough to figure out the truth to all this."

Decker glanced over at him. "I believe in second chances, John, because I got one, right when I really needed it. How about you? Do you believe in them?"

Baron looked around at the grounds that were once part of his family's elegant estate.

"I didn't, until a few minutes ago."

"Well, that's all that really counts."

75

I⊤ CAME TO well over six hundred million dollars in gold. Even after various taxes are paid, it'll be a huge sum."

Baron was sitting in his study with Riley, Jamison, and Decker.

Decker and Jamison had returned to Washington for a few weeks, but had traveled back to Baronville for a visit.

"I'd call that quite the turnaround in prospects," said Decker.

"What are you going to do with all the money?" asked Jamison.

"Well, knock this place down for starters, and put up something a little more minimalist and a lot more tasteful. And then I thought I'd invest in Baronville."

"How so?" asked Jamison.

"Put money into local education, retraining centers, and a new opioid addiction facility. Try to get new businesses to come here and employ people. Have an incubation place for start-ups. Whatever I can do to help turn this place around."

"Pretty nice of you to help a town that's been spitting in your face all your life," said Riley.

Baron's features changed from light to somber. "I really wanted people to believe that none of their vitriol affected me, and so I returned their anger with witticisms and quips." He paused as they all stared at him. "But behind the façade was a man filled with nothing but anger." He let out a sigh. "That's no way to live." He smiled. "Especially after life drops that much money in my lap. It's funny, I've never been rich, though everyone seemed to think I was. Now that I am actually rich, I certainly know first-hand that it's a short path from being rich to being poor. And I should use it to help others. Hell, it's not like I did anything to earn it. It's only because I happened to be born into a certain family. But the truth is, the first John Baron *was* an awful man, and both the town and I have suffered at his hands through no fault of our own. And it really is the sweetest sort of irony that I can use his money to try to fix both injustices." He glanced at Jamison. "Beginning with your family. Even though I know your sister's going to sue Maxus, her case is complicated by the fact that Ross was really behind what happened, and Maxus may use that as a defense. So I'm setting up a trust for your sister and niece. They won't have to worry about money again."

Jamison said, "She told me, John. That is really very generous of you."

He glanced at Decker. "I can't afford to waste a second chance."

"Where are they thinking of moving?" asked Riley.

"Well, as of right now, they might stay in Baronville," replied Jamison.

Baron said, "I have to say I'm surprised."

"Me too," echoed Riley.

"I'm not," said Decker.

They all looked at him, but he didn't elaborate.

"How do things stand with Ted Ross?" Baron asked Decker.

"He's cooperating, and for that he'll get life without parole. Ross's operation was a major conduit for the drugs being distributed across the country. Based on his information the DEA has already broken up rings in four other states. Kemper told me that the Mexican government has arrested two cartel chiefs. And the head of a large Chinese pharma company committed suicide before he was about to be taken into custody."

"How did Ross get hooked up with such heavy hitters in the drug business?" asked Riley.

"The guy has always lived on the edge. Whether he was doing construction or running a paper mill he was either committing fraud or embezzling funds. He told us that when the opioid crisis took off he sensed an opportunity and started some small-scale distribution in the Baronville area. Through that he told us he met

Brian Collins and they did some deals together. After he was hired
to run the fulfillment center Ross went back to Collins with the
idea of using the place to run the fentanyl through. The authorities
have been cracking down on smuggling and the distribution of the
drugs through the mail, but the FC business is enormous and with
its volume it provided a really clever way to run the drugs without
anyone catching on. Through Collins's connections they were able
to set up a truly massive drug ring. When Ross went to collect the
packages on his rounds, he only went to areas where he had people working for him. The tracking system had been rigged to make
sure the drug packages went only to those sectors of the facility.
And he had someone in the IT department cover his electronic
tracks when the packages were taken out of the system. They all
did it for far more money than they could make anywhere else.
Hell, they were paying Alice Martin six figures a year for basically
looking the other way. That shows how much cash this thing was
throwing off."

Jamison added, "And smaller towns like this with not nearly as
many cops and oversight resources as the bigger cities have made
it ripe for infiltration by these criminal organizations. Couple that
with the fact the unemployment rate is so high and you have people desperately looking for any way to make money, and it's a
recipe for disaster."

Riley said, "I wonder how many other places like this one have
the very same thing going on?"

Decker said, "I think it's a safe bet that Baronville is not the only
one."

Baron said, "Okay, but if Lassiter and Green were both in on it,
why did they work with you on the case?"

"Green didn't know about Lassiter's involvement, although
Lassiter was aware of Green being part of it. As she told me, she
was Ross's fail-safe. Green didn't tell us that there had been other
murders in town. Amber told us that. But when we directly asked
him about it, Green probably made a snap decision to bring us
in so he could watch us closely and take necessary action if we
seemed to be getting on the right track. And it would throw sus-

picion off them too. At first, Lassiter didn't want us on the case, but then I guess she came around to the idea so she could keep close tabs on us too. But it's not like they helped us solve the case. They were just hovering and checking in from time to time to see how we were progressing. Lassiter knew the ME here was a dud. And experienced homicide detectives should know about things like livor mortis and blowflies, but both of them played stupid on that. I didn't really suspect anything because I have run across people in law enforcement who actually didn't know much about those things. And I've certainly encountered part-time MEs who don't know what they're doing. But my bet is Green and Lassiter were playing ignorant to confuse the matter and slow down the progress on the investigation. And they neglected to tell us that Toby Babbot's injury happened at the FC, because they didn't want our attention to be drawn there. But later it was anyway, for a terrible reason."

He looked at Jamison, who said quietly, "Ross told us why they killed Frank."

"But I thought he died from some robot going nuts," said Riley.

Jamison said, "No, Ross said that Frank had seen him going through his daily 'rounds.' He was actually collecting the latest shipment of fentanyl powder. He had a special vest made up with interior pockets that matched the drug shipment boxes exactly. Then he'd hide them in his secret closet before periodically taking them out of the facility and delivering them to the pill presses they'd set up in town mostly in empty houses."

Decker picked up the story. "Frank apparently started asking questions about Ross's daily rounds. Like I said, Ross had people at the fulfillment center in his back pocket, and Frank had the bad luck of asking one of them about what he called Ross's *suspicious* behavior. That guy told Ross. So after the construction crew had gone for the day, Ross had Frank go 'check' on the addition. But he had a couple of guys there who knocked him unconscious. Then they carried him over to the robotic arm, and the rest we know."

"I'm surprised that Frank didn't mention something to us about his suspicions," said Jamison.

Decker shrugged. "The last thing Frank would want was to make trouble for his new boss when there might be a perfectly sensible explanation for what Ross was doing. And Ross used that to his full advantage."

"What a bastard!" exclaimed Riley angrily.

Decker nodded. "Ross also told us that it was Marty Green who almost fried us at Babbot's trailer. Ross said Babbot started getting weird and talking about knowing things that Ross was up to, outside of the treasure. That was the reason he had to die."

"So did Lassiter plant the gun at my house?" asked Baron.

Decker nodded. "That was all part of the plan to get you out of the property. When everything was ready, Ross had Lassiter pull the trigger and search your place. She had the gun with her and did the deed. Your butt ended up in jail. Later, they used the subterfuge of the hostage exchange to try to get us out of the way. They made the exchange spot far away to give them time to search for the treasure at the two possible locations, the potting shed and the mausoleum. That way they could look for it without worrying about us showing up." He glanced at Riley. "If Cindi hadn't called and told me that Lassiter had checked herself out of the hospital, things would not have ended the way they did."

Baron gripped Riley's hand. "Well, Cindi has always been smarter than me."

Jamison shook her head. "I thought Lassiter was a good cop."

Decker said, "She *was* a good cop, and then she was a bad cop. Ross didn't entirely trust Green, and he wanted another cop on the payroll that he alone knew about. Lassiter already hated Baron and she wanted money. It was easy for Ross to persuade her. And she ultimately paid the price for it."

"And the pig's blood and the cop uniform?" asked Jamison.

"The pig's blood was Fred Ross's idea of a sick joke. And Fred Ross wanted the guy hung because he said that's what you were supposed to do to *spies*. Ted Ross told me later that he thought the blood and hanging were stupid, but his old man just wouldn't leave it alone. Ross especially regretted doing it because it was the blood that led to the electrical short, which was the only reason

Alex and I became involved. The idea of using the police uniform was Green's. There were a number of officers paid off to look the other way. Green didn't want any of the bad cops having a change of heart. Now all those people have been arrested. The police force has really had to clean house, and it was about time."

"But how did Ted Ross hook up with Costa?" asked Riley.

Decker said, "Pretty simple. The bank handled the fulfillment center payroll. It was the biggest account they had. So Costa and Ross became friends. Ross said that Costa started talking to him about a possible treasure at the Barons'. It helped that Ross had heard the stories from his father too. Together with Costa's research, they narrowed it down. It was Ross's idea to frame John and get him off the property so they could look for the treasure. You saw how involved it was and how long it would take with all the equipment. They couldn't very well do all that with you there, John."

"But they could have just killed me and then looked for the treasure, or gone and gotten it while I was in jail awaiting trial."

"I asked Ross about that. He couldn't be sure that while you were in jail Alex and I or someone else wouldn't come poking around. That would be disastrous. He also said it was too risky if you went missing or your body was discovered. Costa was going to try to get you on a drug charge, especially after they found out Swanson was living in the potting shed, and use that to foreclose on the mortgage. Ross told me that Costa had no interest in murdering anyone, and he didn't know Ross also ran a fentanyl ring. But Ross had a different idea. He wanted to get rid of Costa and Babbot for his own reasons. So the moral turpitude clause Ross envisioned being invoked by the bank was your being a murderer. He couldn't accomplish that by simply killing you. The thing is, you have to understand that he didn't just want the treasure. He wanted to see you rot in jail or else be given the death penalty. So did his old man. In their warped minds, it was personal with them. You were a Baron, which meant you were everything they despised."

"And then the bank could sell the property and Ross could buy it through a straw man using his drug profits," said Jamison.

Decker added, "But when they had to kill the DEA agents and things started going sideways, they changed their plans and kidnapped Amber and Zoe to use as bait to get us out of the way. They had to kill the DEA agents because they had uncovered the fentanyl ring. Ross knew that he had to close things down quickly because once the agents were identified, the DEA would be swooping in, which they did. He wanted to take the treasure and his drug profits and disappear before that happened. Only he never expected us to be involved in the investigation. He was counting on Green and Lassiter slow-walking it. If it had been left up to them, the DEA agents would have remained John Does for a long time. It was only when I suggested that their prints be run through law enforcement databases that the truth of their identities came out."

"And they almost succeeded with all that," noted Riley.

Decker said, "And just as I did, Ross got a copy of the senior yearbook and looked through it. They did all the weird stuff at the crime scenes, the Bible verse and the death mark on Costa, based on their learning that John was into mythology and Tanner was his girlfriend and had taught Bible school."

Riley said, "Which is why you were interested in the genesis of the Mercury Bar. What, did you think I was involved in the murders?"

"Just covering all the bases," said Decker diplomatically.

"But what about the life insurance thing?" asked Riley. "You said my friend Linda Drews might be in trouble."

Decker said, "I don't think anyone is interested in going after Drews. She lost her son and there's no evidence she knew what was going on. Now, the cops did find and arrest Willie Norris. Turns out he had paid off paramedics and a local lab to fudge the health exams. He also used a lot of different insurance companies so no single one would catch on. When they investigated any of the deaths he used a variety of tactics to throw mud on everything, so most of them ended up paying out on the policies. It seems about two dozen policies are suspect. But if the guy was getting three hundred grand or more per policy, he wouldn't need more than that. And he used various means to slip pain pills laced with fentanyl to people who'd bought policies. Not all of them died, but many did. Ironically, Norris bought those pills from dealers working for Ross. He'd collect the payout on the policy and take his cut. It was all about the money." He paused and glanced at Jamison. "And it was also Norris who sabotaged the gas line going into Amber's house. He apparently got desperate to silence us before going on the run."

"And Fred Ross?" asked Baron, eyeing Decker.

"He confessed to your parents' murder. He's never going to breathe life as a free man. And I don't see him lasting long in prison."

Riley said, "You have closure, John, finally." She gripped his shoulder.

Decker stood and held out his hand. "Good luck with the second chance."

Baron rose and shook his hand. "There wouldn't have been one without you and Alex."

"We all need a little help every now and then," said Jamison graciously.

Baron took Riley's hand. "Cindi is going to help me with all this. She's been a great friend." He smiled. "Maybe she sees me as a father figure."

Riley kissed him on the cheek. "Maybe I see you as something else."

Jamison said, "You guys up for some lunch before we say our goodbyes?"

"Sounds great and I'm buying," said Baron quickly.

"No you're not, because it's on *me* at the Mercury," said Riley.

"Sorry, I have to get going," said Decker. "You guys go ahead."

Jamison glanced quizzically at him. "You have a date or something?"

"Actually, I do."

76

DECKER STOPPED THE truck, got out and hurried around to the other side, and helped Zoe Mitchell out.

He closed the door.

She reached up for his large hand, which he took.

In her other hand, she held a small arrangement of flowers.

In his other hand was a folded blanket.

They walked along to where they were going.

The sky was clear with not a single cloud intruding upon it. The wind was light but crisp. It was the most perfect day Decker could recall while he'd been in Baronville.

"Thanks for coming with me, Amos," said Zoe.

"No place I'd rather be," replied Decker.

"It's really pretty today," she observed.

"I think somebody's watching out for you."

Zoe glanced at the sky and then at Decker.

"You really think so?"

"Yeah, I really do."

They reached the spot and Zoe looked at the raised mound of dirt. There was no headstone there yet, but her mother had told her that it was coming soon. It would attest to Frank Mitchell's being a good husband and father. Decker knew that it would be a place that Zoe would be drawn to for the rest of her life, even if she ended up moving far away.

For her, Baronville would always be a touchstone, a place she would want to forget, and also a place from which she could never separate herself.

Decker knew this from experience.

With Zoe's assistance, he carefully laid out the blanket on the ground next to the grave.

He helped her position the flowers at the head of the mound, and then they sat on the blanket.

Zoe was in her best dress and her hair was done in the pigtails that she had told him her father had loved.

Decker was dressed in the best clothes he had brought with him. They weren't fancy, but they were freshly laundered and ironed.

Zoe looked at him anxiously. "Now what do I do?"

"You can talk to your dad."

"What do I say?"

"What did you used to say to him?"

"I told him what I did at school and what Mom and I would do while he was at work. And about a book that I really liked."

"Well, go ahead and do that. I'm sure he wants to hear all about it. You can catch him up on things."

Zoe dropped her voice and looked anxiously around at the other graves. "Do I whisper? I don't think you're supposed to talk loud here."

"That's fine, Zoe. Your dad will be able to hear you no matter what."

"And he'll talk back to me?"

"Yes, just not in the way he used to. But just think about him in your head, and you'll hear your dad. You just have to let it all come out. Okay?"

"Okay."

She leaned close to the mound and started to quietly speak.

Decker patiently sat there while she did so. He looked around at some other people visiting the graves of loved ones.

Baronville had a lot of problems, just like other places, rural, suburban, and urban. But problems could be solved. And lives could be changed for the better.

It wasn't impossible. If anything, Decker believed in the resilience of the human spirit.

I'm actually a living example of that.

Yet as he continued to look around, a bit of trepidation crept into Decker's thoughts. Would he wake up tomorrow with his perfect memory gone? Would he no longer see colors where he used to? Even more troubling was the possibility that his mind, instead of increasing its abilities in certain ways, might begin to go the other way, leaving him with a diminished capacity.

He had spoken in an indifferent manner to Jamison about his football career and all the head shots he had taken over the years. But he knew his chances for having some brain damage were heightened because of it.

He was beginning to sense his anxiety levels edging up when he felt a hand on his arm.

He turned to see Zoe staring up at him.

He smiled at her innocent and trusting features, and the wave of panic that had been about to overwhelm him immediately receded.

"Did you tell him everything you wanted to?" he asked.

She nodded. "I think so. For now, anyway. But I'll have more to tell Daddy on my next visit."

Decker touched his chest. "Did you feel it here? All warm?"

Zoe nodded vigorously. "I *did*. Just like you said. And he did talk back to me. In my head."

"I know it means a lot to him that you're here. And he'll always be with you, Zoe, your whole life. No matter where you go."

"Because he's really in here?" she said, touching her chest.

"Yes."

"I wish he were here with me, like you are," she said, her eyes suddenly becoming wide and watery.

"I wish Molly was with me right now too. But since they can't be, we have to keep on living our lives for them. Do good things. Things they would be proud of, okay?"

Zoe nodded.

"Can we stay here for a little while, Amos? With my dad?"

"We can stay here for as long as you want, Zoe."

When Zoe reached out and took his hand, Decker gripped it back.

In a way, he was holding on for dear life to the hand of a child.

Yet Decker had not felt such calm, such inner peace, for a very long time.

His time was consumed with hunting down those who committed bad acts, but Decker knew that evil would always be outweighed by the good.

Actually, he *had* to believe that, otherwise he wasn't sure, like Kate Kemper, that he could continue to do his job.

Sometimes you just had to believe.

He let out a deep breath, and kept hold of Zoe's hand.

And the little girl and the giant man sat there, while both life and death revolved around them.

ACKNOWLEDGMENTS

To Michelle, because every day with you is a reminder that I fortunately married way above my pay grade!

To Michael Pietsch, for being a great and caring publisher.

To Lindsey Rose, for being so wonderful at your job.

To Andy Dodds, Nidhi Pugalia, Ben Sevier, Brian McLendon, Karen Kosztolnyik, Beth deGuzman, Brigid Pearson, Bob Castillo, Anthony Goff, Michele McGonigle, Cheryl Smith, Andrew Duncan, Joseph Benincase, Tiffany Sanchez, Stephanie Sirabian, Matthew Ballast, Jordan Rubinstein, Dave Epstein, Rachel Hairston, Karen Torres, Christopher Murphy, Ali Cutrone, Tracy Dowd, Martha Bucci, Lukas Fauset, Thomas Louie, Laura Eisenhard, Anne Twomey, Mary Urban, Barbara Slavin, Sean Ford, and Genevieve Kim, and everyone at Grand Central Publishing, for working so hard on my behalf for over twenty years.

To Aaron and Arleen Priest, Lucy Childs, Lisa Erbach Vance, Mitch Hoffman (and thanks for another fine editing job), Frances Jalet-Miller, John Richmond, and Rachael Burlette, for being the absolute best at what you do.

To Anthony Forbes Watson, Jeremy Trevathan, Trisha Jackson, Katie James, Alex Saunders, Sara Lloyd, Claire Evans, Rob Cox, Stuart Dwyer, Geoff Duffield, Jonathan Atkins, Anna Bond, Leanne Williams, Natalie McCourt, Sarah McLean, Charlotte Williams, and Neil Lang at Pan Macmillan, for being a world-class publisher. I'm lucky to be part of the family.

To Praveen Naidoo and the team at Pan Macmillan in Australia, for continuing to outdo yourselves with each book.

To Caspian Dennis and Sandy Violette, for being so fun and delightful to work with, and even more fun to party with!

To Kyf Brewer and Orlagh Cassidy, for your incredible audio performances. We get a ton of fan mail about the audio books, all well-deserved.

To Steven Maat and the entire Bruna team, for continuing to build the brand.

To Bob Schule, for once more taking up his "consultant" hat on the manuscript.

To Terry Williams of Langford Insurance, for educating me on the finer points of insurance!

To Roland Ottewell, for superb copyediting.

And to Kristen White and Michelle Butler, for keeping Columbus Rose on a terrific roll!

ABOUT THE AUTHOR

David Baldacci is a global #1 bestselling author, and one of the world's favorite storytellers. His books are published in over 45 languages and in more than 80 countries, with over 130 million worldwide sales. His works have been adapted for both feature film and television. David Baldacci is also the co-founder, along with his wife, of the Wish You Well Foundation, a nonprofit organization dedicated to supporting literacy efforts across America. Still a resident of his native Virginia, he invites you to visit him at DavidBaldacci.com and his foundation at WishYouWellFoundation.org.